❦ MARION ZIMMER BRADLEY ❦

"ONE OF THE BEST WRITERS IN THE FIELD."
Analog

❦ ANDRE NORTON ❦

"A SUPERB STORYTELLER"
The New York Times Book Review

❦ MERCEDES LACKEY ❦

"HAS A GIFT FOR CREATING COMPELLING CHARACTERS. SHE COMBINES A LIVELY STORY AND FASCINATING MAGIC WITH A POWERFUL CONCERN FOR ITS ETHICAL IMPLICATIONS."
Diana L. Paxson, author of *The Lord of Horses*

Three acclaimed bestselling authors . . .
Three extraordinary fantasists unite in

❦ TIGER BURNING BRIGHT ❦

TIGER BURNING BRIGHT

MARION ZIMMER BRADLEY
ANDRE NORTON
MERCEDES LACKEY

AVON BOOKS • NEW YORK

TIGER BURNING BRIGHT is an original publication of Avon Books. This work is a novel. Any similarity to actual persons or events is purely coincidental.

AVON BOOKS
A division of
The Hearst Corporation
1350 Avenue of the Americas
New York, New York 10019

TIGER BURNING BRIGHT

ADELE

Gemen Elfrida knelt on the cold stone floor in her place
in the Temple, surrounded by her fellow Grey Robes,
chanting the praises of the Goddess and contemplating
the Heart of Power, the physical representation of the
Bright Goddess, and the powerful core of all worship in
the Temple. The Great Temple of Merina was as much
home to her as any place on earth, and she found no
difficulty in losing herself to prayer-trance when she knelt
here.

The Heart, which hung suspended from the ceiling in
the middle of the Temple, was said to have been a piece
of the Sun, the body of the Goddess, fallen from heaven,
still burning when it landed on this spot. The Temple had
been built specifically to house it, and over the years Temple craftsmen had adorned it lavishly. According to legend,
it had originally been a strange glowing rock, but since the
time it had come to earth it had been coated in gold and
set with so many massed rubies that the gold was entirely
invisible. This was not the only Temple in the world with
a relic of the One Who Dwells Beyond the Stars in it, but
it was one of the holiest. Others might be larger, more
beautifully adorned, or known for more miracles, but Gemen Elfrida would rather have been here than anywhere
else.

The Heart hung from the very center of the vaulted ceiling, with no other decoration than the ribs of the vaulting, which led the eye inexorably to the Heart no matter which direction one looked to begin with. It sparkled in any available light, even the faint candlelight of the first of the night rituals, and thus drew the attention of the worshipers toward heaven, where the Goddess dwelt. That was as it should be, since most of those worshiping here rather than in their parish Temples were of the Four Orders, either vowed Gemen or Novices, rather than ordinary citizens of Merina. The Great Temple of Merina was not a place for romantic assignations, gossip, or other intrusions from the mundane world—intrusions that occurred all too often in other Temples.

Since most of the Temple community, whatever the color of their robes, knew the chants to the Goddess without having to read them, there were frequently more people looking at the Heart than at their chant-books, anyway. It was always possible to tell who was truly pious by the degree to which they buried their noses in their chant-books.

Gemen Elfrida suddenly came out of the half-trance which the chanting always put her into and realized that something was looking at her, by the faint feeling of *presence* and a sense that someone wanted her.

Who could it be at this hour? Or—perhaps I should ask, what could it be—

Focusing her weary eyes closer to where she knelt—not without difficulty for, like the rest of her, her eyes were not as young and flexible as they once had been—she saw that it was an angel, one of the smaller ones who served as messengers for the Goddess. For a moment, she felt the flutter of excitement and exaltation that always came when she was privileged to see a heavenly visitant, a flutter than never failed to stir her with elation, no matter how many angels she saw—and by now, over the years, she had quite lost count.

Of course, that could simply be due to my failing and too-frail mortal memory!

It stood to one side of the altar, nearer to the rows of kneeling figures than to the altar itself. It might have been taken for one of the acolytes, except that it was in no way *ordinary* in appearance. Like all of its kind, its face was sexless and inhumanly lovely, and the power contained within it gave the illusion that it was glowing with its own light. The power it held carried out beyond its head and shoulders, giving the feeling of a vast pair of wings rising from the shoulders, and a halo of brightness about its head furthered the impression of Light. There could be no mistaking it for anything other than what it was, and Elfrida spared a moment of pity for her daughter and granddaughter, who could not see such messengers in all their terrible beauty.

As soon as it saw that it had her attention, it lifted an arm from its side, a gesture as graceful as its face was beautiful, and pointed in the direction of the royal palace.

Gemen Elfrida stifled a sigh of weariness and bowed her head, signifying assent to the angel and either exhaustion or piety to anyone else watching. She was quite sure that no one else could see this particular angel, even though several members of the Temple were able to see most angels. This one was sent to her alone, to tell her that now, instead of returning to her room at the Temple and sleeping between the end of this ritual and the beginning of the next one, she would need to resume her worldly identity and be in her suite at the palace. Someone would be looking for her there tonight.

One does not normally have angels trailing one about like eager young pages with messages to be heard. Something else must have gone badly wrong. She knew what it had to be, of course; Emperor Balthasar and his Imperial Army had been threatening in the direction of Merina for some time now, but within recent weeks, the threat had turned much more immediate. There had been some faint hope even a few days ago that he might be lured by another, richer plum—the Sarcen lands with their pearls and silks, perhaps. There had even been a hope that he might be bribed or bought away from Merina. Tonight, in all probability, all other plans and hopes must have failed, and that threat must have become a reality.

Which meant that Balthasar, leading the largest conquering army this world had ever seen, was marching to take their tiny haven.

And we are in no case to withstand an army.

Fortunately, at night the Gemen did not speak to each other, and she would not be missed here unless she did not return for the next ritual. And even if she were not in her place then, no one would search for her until morning. It was not unknown for a Gemen to sleep through some of the rituals of the hours of darkness; everyone did it occasionally. One could not take full vows until one was at least thirty-five, which meant that a large proportion of the Gemen were quite old, indeed, and as Elfrida could readily testify, the elderly were in need of more rest than the youthful and vigorous.

And I feel my years more with every passing day. A heavy, though invisible, cloak of exhaustion dropped on her shoulders. This double life she was leading did not help. She would have been mortally glad to take her aching knees and creaking ankles back to her own tiny cell for her well-earned rest—but it did not appear that she was going to get that chance. So, once the services were over, instead of returning to her room, Gemen Elfrida stepped quietly into a side hallway, followed it to the lowest level of the Temple, and entered a secret passage known only to her and to the Archpriestess Verit.

The passage ran between Temple and palace, with carefully hidden branches to several other places in the city and kingdom of Merina. The stone hallway was dark, cool, perhaps a bit damp. A trick of construction deadened all footfalls so that one could not hear them more than a few feet away.

Near the entrance to the palace there was an alcove containing a chest, a stool, a small table with a mirror on it, and a lamp hanging from a spike in the stone wall. Gemen Elfrida lit the lamp, opened the chest, removed an ornate brocade bedrobe and a box of cosmetics, changed out of her shapeless grey habit and into the robe, and carefully began to make up her face. The bedrobe was a bit warmer than the habit, but correspondingly heavier— and the duties it represented weighed more heavily on her than any weight of cloth.

When she was done, no one would have recognized Gemen Elfrida, who had spent the last two years under vows in the Temple. But anyone in the city would have recognized Adele, the Dowager Queen of Merina, the Reverend One, who was the secular head of the Temple, just as the Archpriestess Verit was its spiritual head.

Adele blew out the lamp, checked through a spyhole in the wall to be sure her bedchamber was empty, and opened the secret panel beside her bed. The panel was heavier than it looked, though easier to move than one might have thought. Whoever had made this particular entrance had taken thought to the fact that those who were to use it would probably not be in the prime years of their lives. It was wood-faced on the side of the chamber, carved wood that hid the seams, but backed with stone so that there would be no betraying "hollow" sound should anyone test for such things. Most of the doors into the hidden passageways were built to deceive in that way. It pivoted on a clever center-point, making it easy for an old woman with stiff joints and tired muscles to swing open and closed again. There were no servants here, although with her rank she should have had at least a body-servant—under the guise of piety she had dismissed them all soon after she began this double existence, knowing that a servant would notice if her bed had not been slept in.

After closing the hidden door behind her and locking it in place, she got wearily into bed, determined to catch what little sleep she could before she was looked for. She had a feeling that she was going to need all the rest she could get in the days to come.

Sleep eluded her for a moment, though. She quelled

the urge to go hunting a servant to find out what had happened. Patience *was* a virtue, and impatience likely to bring little reward in this case. It was quite likely that no one, not even Princess Shelyra, who was now in charge of the corps of spies and information-gatherers, knew what "was going wrong" yet. The angel had been sent to tell her that she *would* be needed, not that she was needed at that particular moment. Once she had signified she understood, it had, of course, vanished.

That was the problem with these otherworldly visitants. They never bothered to explain themselves.

The chill sheets warmed to her body, and she began to relax. This one worldly comfort she *would* miss when her time came to become Elfrida in truth. The beds in the Temple cloisters were not particularly comfortable, since the thoughts of the Gemen were supposed to be on the Goddess and not on their bodies. . . .

Though it might be easier to concentrate on the Goddess if one's bones weren't aching. I understand the need to forget the comforts and indulgences of the world, but if we put in benches for those who cannot kneel, should we not make allowances for those whose joints ache at night?

Perhaps when the time came for her to replace Verit, she could see about that one tiny reform.

Provided they all survived what the emperor had planned for Merina, of course.

And with that cheerful thought, the sleep she had sought finally relented and came to her.

§ 2 §

LYDANA

The woman in the great curtained bed awoke, but she neither moved nor opened her eyes, though she was as alert as one of the emperor's well-trained scouts. Over the years her five senses had been honed deliberately to the sharpness of a well-kept dagger's edge—and with them was that slowly awakening sixth sense which was the private gift of her house and breed. She used that now—questing forth as a spider would loose a thread.

Yes, the room had been invaded. Under the heavy cover her hand moved cautiously. She dared to raise her eyelids a fraction. There was no light; still she sought a shadow within the dark.

Her hand was above her head now, her fingers under the edge of the wide pillow, to close on what she sought—the hilt of a slender but deadly skirt-knife, one forged to be hidden in dress folds by day, make no betraying ridge in a sleeping place by night. A weapon whose worth she had proven twice in years past and was ready to put to the test again, here and now.

Her left hand slipped as silently as a watersnake toward the other side of the bed until she touched firm, warm flesh. Her finger tapped twice before she spoke. Her sense of smell had come to her aid now—there was the faintest whiff of moltanleaf soap.

"Well, Shelyra, so you have again been exploring the inner ways and found a new path to astound us?"

There was an exclamation in the dark, half chagrin, half irritation.

"And you have gained full night sight, dear aunt?" The voice was soft, but low for a woman.

"I have the eyes I was born with, but you are less accomplished in lurking than you think, my dear niece. Someday you may play such a trick and find Skita awaiting you with attention for some part of your body you have no wish to have harmed—a most regretful happening for us all."

Lydana, of the House of the Tiger, ruler of the great port of Merina, both state and city, sat up in bed. She had given no order, but a lamp flared to a revealing glow.

The one who held it was only a child in height. However, her slender, finely boned body, with its ivory-hued skin, was that of a well-developed woman, and her narrowed eyes were not to be found in any youngling's face.

The invader strode into that same circle of light. This, too, was a woman, or rather a girl not so far into the womanhood she craved. She had the same slightly imperious features as the queen, still softened by youth. Her dark hair had been plaited and anchored to her head, with a small metal circlet locking it in place. Beside the lamp-bearer she seemed to tower, her body covered with a tight-fitting, one-piece black garment, broken only by the belt from which swung the sheathed blades of both a skirt-knife and a hunter's longer blade.

What skin she showed was weather-browned, and save for the small jut of her breasts, she might have been a lad. She made a face directly at the lamp-holder and without invitation moved to seat herself on the foot of the bed.

Once in position, she slewed around to face the queen directly and held out one hand. On the palm lay an oval box no larger than an amble nut, fully coated by black enamel, making it seem as dull as any stone one might pick up from one of the out-wall roads.

Lydana stared at it for a moment. There was no change in her usual carefully maintained impassivity of face, but this, here and now, was a shock.

"Who?" she asked shortly.

"I think—" Shelyra hesitated, and her mouth twisted as if she had bitten into something bitter. "Rosthen."

"You think—"

The girl shifted and there was a shadow of fear mixed with disgust on her young face. "The under-ones had been at him. He lay just within the fourth entrance. There—there was a quarrel between his shoulders—and a blood trail. He was not struck down where he last fell." She kept her voice steady, Lydana noted, despite the fact that she must surely be shaken. Yes, this brother's daughter was of the true blood.

Swiftly, the queen leaned forward and took the small box. The nail of her forefinger touched the hidden clasp and the box opened with some force, the reason plain, for it had been so tightly stuffed that there must have been a good strain on its tiny hinges.

Without any order, the small woman moved her lamp closer so that its light fell clearly across the page Lydana smoothed out. Lydana read the beginning lines and for the first time her voice cracked.

"To the Reverend One," she said, holding the message closer to her as she slid out of bed.

Skita trotted ahead, lamp in hand, Lydana and Shelyra close behind. It was the younger woman who swept aside a panel of brilliant embroidery allowing Lydana room to press the small locks. Within this ancient pile of a palace there were many underways, and those of the House of the Tiger learned to make use of them from childhood on, carefully schooled in strange locks, presses, and twists and turns of narrow, hidden ways and stairs.

They did not have far to go. Skita stood aside and allowed the queen to tap four times on a smooth panel set in the wall. There was a pause, then it opened.

Facing them was Lydana's mother, Shelyra's grandmother, the Dowager Queen Adele, who was in the process of making the change from the full life of the court of Merina to the dimmer outer life, brighter inner life, of the Temple of the Heart of Power.

"There is trouble?" Adele's voice held a note of breathlessness and Lydana wondered if she had been right in late suspicions. Adele's years were many and the last two of transition seemed to exhaust her. Lydana knew that Adele spent a great deal of time at the Temple and frequently wondered why her mother was still at court at all. In looking at the small figure using the door frame to hold herself upright, her face shadowed by the dim light in the room behind her, Lydana could foresee her own fate. People who did not know called them blessed, but she sometimes felt rather that they had been burdened by a curse. Though Adele had appeared to welcome the transition with a quiet joy, she still clung to life at court as well, and her divided life was draining her.

Until menopause, all the true daughters of the Tiger were as other women. Oh, they had small skills which, if they were wise, they exercised. But when menopause befell them there began the great change—certain talents long lying dormant arose and forced their owner to exercise them. It was then that she who ruled the House and Merina herself must surrender temporal power for spiritual and yet, it was rumored, take on a heavier burden of marshaling out-world forces for the protection of all.

They would well need such forces, Lydana thought grimly, seeing the full might of the worst menace of their world and time was now turned against them. Which brought back her mind to the message.

"Shelyra found—Rosthen—"

She saw her mother's thin hands rise to make the Blessing-for-the-Dead sign.

"He had managed in spite of his wound to reach the fourth way. He was carrying this." She held out the paper.

"Rosthen was the first of our Ears and Eyes," Adele said. "Read what message he gave his life for us to have."

"Balthasar moves—there is no defense against his

forces. Behind him stands one Apolon—a high servant of the Dark. Apolon wants the Heart and all it holds."

Adele drew a deep breath, close to a sigh. She raised her hands again in a gesture they well knew, and they stood silent as the old woman's eyes closed. She was seeking a prayer-trance, striving to expand her opening powers to their aid.

The minute seemed very long before Adele's eyes opened and she sighed again. "So be it," she said quietly. "Merina lives or dies by our decision. Let us think on what must be done and gather again at the third hour."

Lydana bowed her head, noting her mother's absent-minded use of the Temple's schedule. The Temple broke the day into hours, beginning at dawn. Meeting again at the third hour would allow all of them to breakfast before making what would doubtless be a difficult decision. Shelyra seemed about to speak, but her aunt frowned and she remained silent. They trailed back through the passage to the queen's chamber.

"We must rouse the guard—the guilds—" the girl burst out even as the panel closed behind them. Lydana shook her head.

"This Emperor Balthasar is pitiless. And now he holds near all our world within his iron-gloved fist. Child, you have never seen a city put to plunder—blood of all, even children, running in the street gutters, torture, death by the thousands. Do you wish that for Merina? I have seen—overseas—the taking of a town—" The queen's eyes closed for a moment and her mouth tightened. "It was such a sight as might greet one thrust into hell. Do you think our small levies who mainly police our streets, our untrained guildsmen, can stand against an army which has nothing but victories in its wake?"

"But—" Shelyra protested. Lydana continued mercilessly. As well that the girl hear the full truth, with no sugar-coating.

"Balthasar covets Merina and her rich trade—this we have known for years. He cannot be bought off, for he must be supreme wherever his shadow falls—that is his nature. Now Rosthen—may the Angels of Warriors bear him swiftly to the Place of Peace—has brought us worse news. I have heard something of this Apolon, but very little. He keeps to the shadows behind the emperor's throne and perhaps because of that he is even more deadly. If he possesses dark powers, then he can indeed bring unchancy influences to bear on the man who believes he is his master. Apolon wants the Heart—I believe that Rosthen brought us the blackest of warnings."

"But"—the girl was fingering the hilt of her longer knife—"the Heart is above all sorceries—"

"The Heart is earth-rooted now in the Archpriestess Verit. She is powerful—and she has those of the cloister for her guard. But it may be that a single life can stand between this Apolon and what he wants."

"Then what do we do? Go—load ourselves with slave chains to greet Balthasar lying on our face in the dust?"

"We do as the Reverend One has suggested: we think. Go now and rest, child. Morning's problems will come soon enough."

Shelyra went—with visible reluctance. But Lydana did not return to her bed. Skita had set the lamp on a small table and had gone to a tall wardrobe, where she pulled out a suit much like that Shelyra wore. She tossed it on the bed, added cape and a pair of boot-shoes. Lydana smiled.

"You are right, my war-sprite, we must seek council of our own. If one seeks to learn of weapons, one goes to him who knows them best. So be it."

She changed quickly into the black clothing, pulling the cowl of the cape well over her head. Skita had assembled similar clothing from a box near the door. She did not pick up the lamp, not needing the light for a way they both knew well and had used often before. A narrow hall, steps, a low door from which moisture rose in beads. Then they were at the small landing and into a dull brown craft, lacking all insignia, like any other which might be in common use.

The canals laced Merina. Though the city was not directly on the seacoast, it was a prime port because of those same canals. On the other hand, they made the city difficult to patrol as one would a land-bound town. Lydana was well aware that smugglers and others of even darker occupations knew well their ways through the waterways. But she also knew of the probity of her police and the fact that they were loyal to the Tiger. Balthasar had never striven to hold a waterlogged city before. He might find it more difficult than he expected. She put that thought carefully to the back of her mind, hoping it would ripen well and bear usable fruit.

⸙ 3 ⸙

SHELYRA

*"G*o to bed, child," she says. *As if I have not been commanding all of our spies for the past three years and more! As if Grandmother had not put their command directly into my hand! As if I had not been accepted by the Horse Lords as a chief among them! They* don't *call me "child" and send me to bed!* Shelyra seethed with resentment, taking shelter in that emotion from other feelings—

Fear, for one: a soul-chilling, profoundly depressed fear. Her aunt thought she did not understand the situation— and perhaps, up until a few hours ago, she had not. But now the Emperor Balthasar and his all-conquering armies were no longer a distant threat but a reality. *Now* he had struck down, not some stranger in another land, but someone she knew, someone she had worked with, someone who trusted her—and he had done so on the very threshold of *her* city.

If he could do that so easily, what else could he do? More to the point, what *couldn't* he do?

She stepped softly along the ancient hallway, as the few candles left burning at this time of night made dim, honey-colored puddles of light on the polished wood of the floors and walls. Out of habit, she traced a path that wound back and forth along the hall in a most peculiar manner. Had anyone been watching, they might have thought her drunk with strong spirit, had her steps not been so steady.

She was neither drunk nor weary; she was avoiding the boards that creaked. This entire hallway was a trap for the thief, the assassin, the stranger; no one who was not intimately familiar with the "singing hall" could avoid the randomly placed boards. She knew every one of those boards in the halls of this palace, and in the Summer Palace across the river. There wasn't a great deal that she *didn't* know about those two buildings, actually. Certainly she had long ago ferreted out every secret of those most secretive and ancient structures.

Not even Grandmother or Aunt Lydana know all of the secrets, the passages, the spy holes, the hidden doors— As a tiny child she had stumbled on the first of the passageways, discovering a way out of her nursery that no one else seemed to know about. As a means of escape when she was supposed to be asleep or otherwise incarcerated away from the fascinating activities of grownups, the discovery had meant more to her than sweets or toys—and she had set about discovering more.

Eventually, her grandmother Adele had shown her all the secret ways that *she* knew, but Shelyra's own explorations had more than doubled that knowledge.

She made use of one of her secrets when she was halfway down the hall, stepping aside into a deep pool of shadow, slipping into it like a moving shadow herself. Setting three of the fingers of her right hand into the centers of three carved flowers, she pushed, lightly, as she pulled on another section of the carved panel with her left. The whole panel rotated silently about a center-post, allowing her to slip inside the hollow wall.

With the faintest of *clicks* the panel closed again, leaving her in the thick, velvety darkness of the hidden passageway. She relaxed, marginally, once she was safely inside. Even if the emperor had inserted spies in the House of the Tiger, those spies would never trace her movements in here.

I am a mouse in the walls. Or, perhaps, a serpent—with a very sharp tooth. Her right hand caressed the hilt of her longer knife, the gift of the Horse Lords, and she reached out for the wall of the passageway with her left, before stepping out confidently into the darkness. The floorboards in *here* did not squeak, needless to say.

There were no spy holes along this passage, which led ultimately to her own bedroom, twisting and turning as it wound its way around the rooms that lay in her path. She smiled to herself, though without humor. Neither her aunt nor that odd little manikin she kept as her servant had yet discovered *how* she could come and go from her aunt's rooms at will and without discovery. *Not a mouse, nor a serpent. A spirit of darkness, a dream, a vision that haunts the palace, I go where I will, shrouded and protected by the shadows.*

A charming conceit; but now was not the time for conceits or fancies. Her hand slipped along the polished surface of the inner wall, warning her of the turnings, even if she had lost track of the number of steps to each one. Occasionally the passage seemed to come to a dead end; that was deceptive, and would certainly have fooled anyone unfamiliar with the hidden ways. Those dead ends were the only times when the wall was pierced by a door; her hands felt for the clever, shallow hand- and footholds before her, and she climbed, then crawled along the top of the door frame, and descended again, all without thinking about it.

Inside she seethed with frustration and anxiety. She had been prepared, mentally, for a battle; it seemed her aunt was going to hand the entire kingdom over tamely. *We must fight. Surely we must fight! But how?* As her aunt had pointed out, Merina had no army, and never had possessed one. The kings and queens of the past had relied on clever alliances, bribery, blackmail, and the occasional purchase of a mercenary company to keep them safe from the wiles of others. When the rulers of Merina could not buy the safety of their city, they could ensure that safety through judicious use of the information gathered by a network of spies that monarchs of greater lands might well envy.

But as her Aunt Lydana had rightly pointed out tonight, nothing and no one could prevail against the juggernaut that Emperor Balthasar currently had bearing down upon them. Misdirection had not worked, nor had blackmail, and Shelyra had instructed her agents to try both. Not that Balthasar had led a blameless life—but his power over his land and people was so absolute that he simply could not be blackmailed, for he did not *care* what information was revealed about him. In fact, the worse it was, the more he seemed to find it—amusing.

That left bribery and alliances. But the allies had already fallen, or were quaking in fear, awaiting their own turn—and as for bribery, well, why should the emperor accept the pittances of a bribe when he could so easily take everything that he wanted?

The queen had done everything she could to avoid this moment, everything both overt and covert. Only assassination had not been tried, and *that* was not to be thought of. No matter how much blood the emperor had on his hands, to murder him or to plan to murder him would put his death on their souls. Murder was a terrible sin and not to be contemplated seriously. On that, all three of them had agreed.

Though Aunt and I agree on little else, it seems. Lydana persisted in thinking of Shelyra as a hotheaded child, wild and impulsive. Well, she *had* been those things, but a season with the Horse Lords had taught her better. Her temper was still hot, but although she might give tongue to her anger in private, she no longer acted on it, nor did she show it in public. She could plan as calculatedly as Adele, and as craftily as Lydana—yes, and carry those plans out, too!

But the queen still did not see how she had changed; she saw only the child whose antics had made chaos of the palace time and time again.

And she did not see how her unvarying attitude exasperated her niece and brought that famous temper to the boiling point, over and over.

Strange how people can care so much about each other and be so incapable of understanding each other! Shelyra knew that she certainly did not understand her aunt—her grandmother's mysticism was easy to grasp, although she did not share it, but the queen's attitude towards the Heart and all it stood for was baffling. At times she acted as if she believed—and yet did not want to admit that she believed. As if the very ideas embarrassed her.

As for Shelyra herself—well, she had never seen an angel, and she didn't expect to now. There were perfectly practical explanations for much of what went on in the cloister, and as for the rest—it didn't concern her. *Practical* things, now—those concerned her. Things like—how to defend this city of theirs! And how to ensure her own safety in the process. Let Grandmother call upon angels and Ministers of Grace to defend her—Shelyra would rely on Horse Lord steel and Gypsy lore.

Shelyra's questing hands touched what *was* a dead end: the end of this passage, the hidden door into her own rooms. But she paused before fingering the catch that opened the door in the headboard of her bed.

There must be something I can do now. It was going to be a long night, and a sleepless one. *I wouldn't be able to sleep, anyway. Everytime I closed my eyes, I'd see—the body—*

Convulsive shudders shook her for a moment, and nausea made her gorge rise, choking off her breath. She swallowed with difficulty and leaned weakly against the wall as her knees threatened to give out beneath her.

This is not the first time I have seen a dead man, she reminded herself again. *There was poor Taz, who was trampled by the stampeding herd—that maid who just dropped over dead in the hallway—* Finally she got a grip on herself, straightened, and took thought for the hours ahead.

Take thought for the future: how *could* one fight in a city that had surrendered?

Fight from the shadows? Use strike-and-run tactics?

Any war waged in Merina would have to be fought covertly. Between the guards and those guildsmen who could be persuaded to show some spine, a steady war of attrition *might* be waged successfully along the streets and the canals. Shelyra had to assume that the Great Palace would be lost, of course—but the Summer Palace was not as attractive a structure for conquest and lay across the river. Once the bridges were taken, the Summer Palace would be out of reach, theoretically, of the city.

She smiled mirthlessly. Little they knew!

Little even her aunt knew—although she suspected that Adele was aware of the under-river passage between a certain stone bridge support and the Summer Palace. *Certainly Grandmother knows of the twin to it that leads from the palace to the temple.* How and why it had been made through the solid rock of the riverbed, Shelyra had no notion—it was older than the bridge, and certainly as old as the Summer Palace.

Assume, then, covert warfare between the invaders and the natives. There were things that she would want—no, *need*—that lay here and in the Summer Palace, and she needed to get those things to safe concealment—just in case the invaders *did* take the Summer Palace.

And the safest place of concealment? In the Summer

Palace itself! Even if the palace was taken, there was the palace within the palace. . . .

Or rather, there existed a certain set of hidden chambers, chambers reached only by more of those secret passages, chambers that had not been disturbed in at least a dozen generations until Shelyra stumbled on them. Why would anyone look for her, or for her secrets, within the Summer Palace once it was captured?

Very well. She had a goal, for this night at least, and probably for the next few nights, until the emperor's army finally arrived. She would set up hiding places and escape routes for herself, stock them with money and stores, plant disguises there. And she would have to work quickly.

Fortunately, most of what she wanted already lay in her armory in the Summer Palace. The things she needed from here, she could carry in a single pack.

She tripped the catch, and the center panel of the headboard of her bed slid aside, allowing her to crawl out over her pillows and onto the mattress. The soft featherbed tempted her not at all; she was too tense, every nerve afire, to want even to lie down for a moment.

There was a night-lamp burning beside the bed, lending light as bright as day to someone who had just spent as much time as she had in the pitchy blackness of the hidden passageways. She scrambled out of the bed and went straight to her massive closet, a closet that took up one entire wall. She opened the door nearest the wall, taking up a leather pack from among her hunting gear and opening a single cabinet within the closet, ignoring the chest of jewelry and the selection of sumptuous gowns next to it.

I will take some of the jewels, later—but only such as can be easily disposed of. The gowns glowed softly in the warm candlelight, luxury enough to tempt even the hardest female heart under ordinary circumstances. Shelyra let her hand caress the sapphire velvet sleeve of one, briefly, in a moment of regret. It was likely to be a long time before she had a chance to wear such gowns again—if ever.

Then she turned her full attention to the walnut cabinet. *This* cabinet must be quite, quite empty if the invaders took possession of the palace, for it held secrets she doubted anyone knew she possessed, other than the ones who had entrusted them to her.

The secrets the shaman of the Horse Lords and the Gypsies of the city had taught her ranged along the inside of the cabinet, each in its own little, stoppered vial or leather sheathe. The vials resembled perfumes; innocuous—and deadly. Some of them, at least.

And with them, the means of their delivery and other strange weapons—and the rest of the gear her stalking-by-night required. She moved quickly and surely, filling the pack until it bulged, and finally lacing the top shut with an effort. She stepped back and surveyed the closet with satisfaction.

There was no longer any sign that Princess Shelyra, Designated Daughter of the House of the Tiger, was anything other than a perfectly ordinary young noblewoman with an occasional interest in hunting.

Good. But they may wonder at the empty cabinet.... She took every vial and jar from her dressing-table and ranged them along the shelves. *There. That's better. No reason why I shouldn't have kept precious cosmetics and perfumes out of reach of the servants. They are very expensive, after all, and I wouldn't want the servants to have access to them.* She cast one more look around the room to make certain she had left nothing of her "real" self behind.

But she had been both swift and thorough. There was nothing here, not even in the many hiding places the room and the furniture in it afforded, that would give any clue to Shelyra's true nature. Let Balthasar and his agents look for a pampered princess when she disappeared; they would look in vain.

Time to go. She slung the pack over her back and moved

to another section of the wall, this time beside her fireplace. A section of the vast, tiled facade swung aside, and she stooped and vanished within.

There was much to do—and too little time until dawn.

§ 4 §

ADELE

Adele went back to bed after the others departed, slipping back into the warmth of blankets and smooth sheets with decidedly mixed feelings.

There was the sourness of fear for herself; the sharp stab of anxiety for her daughter and granddaughter—but there was a certain underlying sense of relief, and not just because the waiting was at an end.

She had wished any number of times to be able to leave court and devote her entire life to the Temple, and now she would get her wish. In a few short days, a week at most, she would be able to become Gemen Elfrida in truth. Adele would be gone forever, and with her all the trouble and exhaustion of her dual identity. But the cost was horrible.

Nothing is ever going to be the same again.

She turned over on her side and cradled her head against her arm. She wanted to weep, to weep for her city as well as for herself and her kin. No matter what happened, something would be lost. Lives, property—Balthasar's people, balked of a fight, would cause trouble. The only surety was that it would be less costly than a fight, in terms of lives and pain.

But there was one problem, now relatively minor in the light of the threat descending on them, that had been solved for her, and that was the cause of her leavening feeling of relief. She knew that Lydana had been wondering why her mother was leading a double life, why she had not simply entered the Temple two years ago. Lydana did not realize, and Adele did not wish to tell her, that the ruling queen was unfit to be even the secular head of the Temple. And as if that was not bad enough, Shelyra was even worse as far as spiritual matters went.

My dear family—how could they ever understand? But how could I ever have let them take control of something they could not handle? The pair of them are as suited to dealing with spiritual matters as sheep are suited to flying.

As ever, acknowledging this made a lump rise in her throat, and a sense of having been cheated in some way overcame her for a moment before she shunted it away. She had not been cheated; Lydana and Shelyra were their own persons, and no one had the right to assume that they would be younger copies of Adele herself. Yet—the women of the Tiger had carried that inner *something* that made them true daughters of the Goddess for as far back as the records went, and it hardly seemed fair that this unbroken tradition should break *now*.

Yet, it had. Neither the princess nor the queen were suited to take the chair beside the altar. This had been made unmistakably plain to Adele about five years earlier, when the three of them had ridden out of the city together on a hunt. They had been a bit ahead of the rest of their entourage when an angel had appeared before them. Adele saw and heard it quite plainly, but Shelyra had remarked that the white deer was too beautiful to kill and tried to frighten it away before the rest of the hunt caught up with them. The angel had departed, looking amused, and Adele had wondered if the fact that Shelyra was her son's daughter instead of her daughter's was what made her unable to see it for what it was. But when she questioned Lydana, she discovered that all that her daughter had seen was a bright light! It had been most upsetting to Adele to discover that both her heirs were blind and deaf to messages from the Goddess. How could either of them sit in the high chair before the altar next to the archpriestess when they hadn't the sight to know what was happening before their eyes?

She tossed, wincing as her back warned her that her movement had been too abrupt. *If I were a carriage driver, how could I turn the reins over to someone who could not see the horses, did not understand the horses, and was not certain they even existed?*

Lydana had reluctantly accepted the secular rulership of Merina when her brother died, but her unease whenever the subject was mentioned had made it clear that sheep would be flying in flocks above the Temple spire before she felt any joy about taking on the nonsecular tasks. So Adele, although she turned the kingdom over to Lydana, had retained her position as secular head of the Temple. She had hoped that time would improve things for Lydana, or that her daughter would suddenly discover her vocation. Neither had occurred. When the time came for any Temple ceremony, Lydana acted like a young boy forced to play at house with his younger sisters: stiff, resentful, and wishing profoundly to be elsewhere.

Now none of them would hold either position; Balthasar's coming had seen to that.

A stab of sorrow as deep as pain pierced her, and her eyes stung with unshed tears. Loss, loss, and more loss. Things were about to change drastically, and she could not foresee how and where they would change, nor what the outcome would be.

For a moment, she felt a cold hand of fear clutching at her throat. Her certain life, which had been progressing exactly as she had planned, was being swept from beneath her. The Emperor Balthasar was like the tide: nothing would stop him—at least at the present. She was no stranger to change, but it had always been change that she herself had orchestrated. Now it was all out of her hands. She could neither control nor predict the outcome.

She suffered that chill of fear for a moment longer, then resolutely drove it away.

Surely Lydana was planning a way to escape in disguise even now—and as for Shelyra, her forays among the Gypsy clans gave her any number of allies she could turn to. Probably both of them had slipped out of the palace already, planning their means of escape and setting up places to hide. That was what she would have done if she were younger. In fact, now her dual identity would serve a greater purpose than she had anticipated. When *she* vanished, the emperor might well look for a new Gemen among the rest, and if he found one, he might well assume it was her. But Gemen Elfrida had been serving in the Temple for two years; she was not new, she was familiar to all the rest. Even if the emperor had spies planted around the Temple, he would have no reason to think that Gemen Elfrida and Adele were one and the same. She could even stage her own death—in fact, that was not a bad idea. The emperor would have no reason to go looking for a woman he supposed was dead.

She hoped that Lydana and Shelyra had plans that were as sound. Certainly Shelyra had established an identity among the Gypsy clans a long time ago—an identity that Lydana was quite unaware of. If the queen had known, she might well have been horrified at the very thought.

But if Shelyra and Lydana had guises as complete as Adele's—and ways to escape the palace that were as clever as a feigned death—perhaps all was not dark yet.

And probably neither of them think for a moment that I might guess what they are doing. What was it about younger people that made them certain they could hide what they were doing from their elders? She knew the look she had seen in Shelyra's eyes, the look that bespoke a sleepless night. And she knew its mate in Lydana's eyes, the sudden opaqueness that told her that her daughter was planning something she thought her mother might not approve of. *I have known them all their lives, they have known me less than half that time; does it not occur to either of them that I have more practice in reading their intentions, since I knew them when they were unable to cloak those intentions?*

Well, doubtless, her own mother had thought the same about her.

We will plan, and we will plot, and we women of the Tiger will find a way to beat this emperor from within his conquest.

They were not defeated yet. This was—how did one of the mercenary captains put it?—a "strategic withdrawal." There were more ways to defeat an army than by facing it head-on. A war fought in tiny skirmishes, from within territory that was thought to be conquered, was always more wearing than a straight-on confrontation. If they gave Balthasar enough trouble here, perhaps word would spread to his other conquests, and they would resist him in the same way. It was impossible to fight a war on a hundred tiny fronts; even she knew that.

Her legs twitched once, then settled as she persuaded tight muscles to relax. As long as there was life in any of them, there was hope that something could be done. She must remember and believe that.

Yes, Balthasar was as inexorable as the tide. But tides ebbed as often as they flowed. The women of the Tiger would disappear, and when Balthasar's tide ebbed, they would be ready. And, for the minute, Adele would sleep.

§ 5 §

LYDANA

They had kept from the better-lighted ways, but were forced to approach into the light as they neared their goal—the Inn of the Sea Dragon. There was a guard on the landing platform there. As Lydana raised oars skillfully and allowed her craft to slide in, Skita tossed him a rope. He caught it mechanically with one hand, but his other was near his sword hilt.

Lydana's hand was white against the darkness of her cloak and her fingers crossed in a pattern. He nodded and helped them to disembark, standing aside as they went up to the door of the inn. There was a cresset blazing there, but they kept their disguises well about them as Lydana pushed open the door.

Though the hour was late, there were still patrons at the tables, drinking horns to hand. And a chorus of a most bawdy song offered up by voices far from musical assaulted the ear. The newcomers made no effort to enter the larger room but slipped along to the stair leading to the upper quarters. The hall above had a single lamp, and that halfway down, but Lydana had no difficulty in finding the door she wanted. Her knock was soft and it followed a pattern. The walls were stout enough that she heard no movement from within, but the door opened and an up-held lamp revealed the man who stood on the other side.

With a single glance at them, he made a beckoning gesture, and they came into a decently furnished room of one of the best of Merina's inns.

"Your Grace—" He bowed. "Mistress Skita—" The wave of his hand further indicated a chair by the fireplace and a stool near it. Apparently they had not caught him in righteous slumber for, though his shirt was well open, it was still tucked smoothly into his breeches. He had, however, kicked off his boots for softer room slippers.

He was a tall man, narrow of waist but wide of shoulder, quick and neat in all his movements. His ruffed hair was short by city standards and was a shade between light brown and dull blond—being gold in the sun as Lydana knew.

A scar formed a faded white seam from eyebrow to hairline on the left side of his face, but that did nothing to detract from the rugged strength of jaw, the firm set of mouth, and the steadiness of his sea-green eyes. In all he was a handsome man of early middle years and bore himself with the assurance of one well used to giving orders—and having them quickly obeyed.

Lydana unfastened her cloak and let it droop across the chair-back behind her. When he made a motion to fill a horn from the jug sitting on a small table, she shook her head in dissent.

"There is trouble." He made that a statement rather than a question.

Lydana's answering lift of lip was hardly a smile. "When in these late years is there not?" she countered. "But now—no, Captain Saxon, it would seem that we are faced with a bitter choice—Merina goes to Balthasar without a blow, or else will be given over to his troops for their pleasure."

The man nodded. "It is a choice which has always lain before us in these past years. To fight for a cause lost from the beginning will avail us nothing. But—is there not a third way, Your Grace? I can get you and those you trust out of the city and cross seas to where you can perhaps summon aid—"

Now her smile was wide and sour. "What aid? Even overseas they quake a little when they think they hear Balthasar's battle horns. Also for near one hundred generations we of the House of the Tiger have been sworn to hold our posts through any matter of good or ill. You yourself brought down the Rapparian pirates who preyed upon our sea lanes to the south—but Balthasar leads no unruly collection of gallows-ripe captains greedy enough to give oath together to get at us. I do not belittle the Battle of Ourse, Captain—it is one of the bright and shining triumphs of our past few years. But—"

He had leaned back against the edge of the table, his arms folded across his chest. There was a shadow of deep thought on his face.

"But—" he prompted her. "No, I will not urge any flight on you, Queen Lydana, for it does not lie within those of your breed to take to heel at the signs of danger. If you cannot fight, and will not flee—then what lies in your mind?"

She no longer looked at him eye to eye, but rather fastened her attention on the heavy seal-ring which burdened the forefinger of her right hand, raising the fingers of the other to turn it around.

"In the morning we shall take council. However, this night we have learned of something else—this mage Apolon who whispers ever in Balthasar's ear—he has also a goal which lies here in Merina. The High Seat of the Heart, no less. And his allegiance is to the Dark. The Reverend One is on the eve of her retirement. Her powers are growing, but that comes slowly. There remain the Designated Daughter and me."

"At whom Balthasar will aim!" His jaw was outthrust now as if he were a hound ready to defend his mistress.

"If—if he can find us. Now," she leaned forward a little, still caressing the ring, "as you know I am craft-mistress— I have proved my art with the Gem Guild. There is thus a trade in which I can conceal myself—"

"Conceal yourself!" He came close to a snort. "You

would be picked up as soon as you showed your face at any gem dealer's bargain table."

Now she laughed in earnest. "Women's wiles, women's arts, Captain. I have my ways to so deal. There is She-lyra—she must be out of the city—she is young, hot of head and heart, and she has not yet proven herself in any trade."

"You would have me take her—" he began.

Lydana shook her head. "We both well know that Balthasar is not stupid. He will have his sea-watchers to take any ship leaving port for the next few weeks. No, I have another thought for her. Now"—she raised her eyes once again and looked him up and down—"we come to you, Captain Saxon.

"The guilds rightly made you harbor master after Ourse—they could certainly do no less. My father's seal—near the last time he used it—is on the patent giving you the title you would not accept. But you know the water-ways in the city, on the river, and to the sea. Balthasar moves with an army. An army must eat, be clothed, armed. Thus supplies will be in constant flow. He may think that such would come more swiftly by water—the more so when he has seized our fleet. But there can be many perils at sea—as you well know, Captain Saxon."

Now his smile was also broad. "Just so, Your Grace."

"One who has dealt with pirates must know pirate tricks or he could not have brought them down."

"True, Your Grace."

"Now, our time is very short, Captain. I must leave you—with the best of my wishes—" She held out her hand and, with the grace of any courtier, he kissed the hand she had nursed during their conversation.

"If there is need for any message," she had picked up her cloak but held it for a moment before drawing it on again, "why, there are confessionals in the Great Temple, and—" She hesitated. "He or she who would confess might well seek out the third to the right of the High Heart."

He nodded. "Well enough." But when she would have moved toward the door, he held out his hand as a light barrier.

"My Queen, those who play devious games tread on the edge of a sword blade over a maelstrom. Take what care you can—I know the temper of your house, and the depth of your breed. Take care—"

Once more their eyes met and then she gave that smile which was from good will. "Be very sure, Captain, that I shall. And for yourself, take care also—we cannot lose one such as you to mischance."

They were back in their skiff and heading out into the canal again before Skita broke the silence.

"Lady, if you remain in Merina, this hog-born emperor will turn the city upside down and shake it to get you."

"That he will perhaps, but he seeks Lydana the Queen. Her he shall not find. Skita—do I remember rightly, in the Water Tower Thom Talesmith lies tonight?"

"What would you have with such as he, lady? He is as devious and slippery as a kockworm."

"Just so. But even kockworms have their place in the world. He is the most cunning of thieves, the most sly of spies, and—he is accepted by the Horse Lords. I have even heard he has sworn blood oath with one of their minor chiefs. It is near time for them to come to Merina for trading. They may well hold off if they learn of Balthasar's plans. On the other hand, armies need fresh mounts to a great degree and so they may think otherwise. Tonight, Skita, you will carry a message for me to the Water Tower."

Lydana had already begun to feel within her the excitement which she knew when planning a goodly bargaining with the craftiest of her guild peers. Her half-thought plans deepened and began to fit together in an intricate design. She sent the skiff skimming at a faster rate.

§ 6 §

SHELYRA

Two days had passed since the evil news had reached them, and Shelyra had not had a moment of leisure in all that time. It was just a good thing as far as Shelyra was concerned that the office of Designated Daughter was largely a title and had very few duties attached, all of them largely ceremonial in nature. She needed every moment she could get for her own preparations. When Balthasar came, he would not find her unready.

She had cached clothing, supplies, and small amounts of money at the end of each of her own special exits from the palace. Her aunt had a few favored exit routes of her own, and those she left alone. She did not want the queen to know how well-prepared for escape her niece was. She had no doubt that Lydana was making her own preparations to escape and hide—Lydana was not so foolish as to be standing in the throne room of the palace when Balthasar came to take possession! No, her aunt knew what—in the best of cases—would lie in store even for a ruler who had willingly abdicated. If Balthasar was feeling generous, she would *only* go into a kind of house arrest, become a hanger-on at his court, always watched with suspicion, and kept one step away from total impoverishment.

Aunt could never tolerate that. She'd go mad first.

As for Shelyra—well, she was not going to let anyone

31

else, not even the queen, decide *her* fate. There was always the chance that Lydana would try to bundle her away into the Temple. If that happened, Shelyra might go under duress, but she didn't plan to stay there very long. She had enough escape routes prepared now that, unless they chained her in a cell in the Temple, she would be off as soon as they left her unwatched for a single moment.

Her hideaway in the Summer Palace was also well-stocked now, with water and food as well as clothing, weapons, and her "special supplies." She could hide out there for a week or more if she needed to.

But now she had one last task to accomplish—and by all reports, Balthasar's envoy would reach the gates of Merina tomorrow with his ultimatum. There was no time to lose in making her final arrangements. She *could* live entirely in the hidden passageways—but she didn't want to. She wanted to fight Balthasar, and to do that, she had to be out in the city.

This time she went openly to the stables, clothed in a handsome riding habit of dark green velvet; but once there, she took to a tiny room hidden beneath the floor of the tackroom, changing out of her riding costume to that of a middle-level servant. She had chosen her costume carefully, picking someone who would not be questioned or detained as she left. It was the servant who departed the palace grounds, riding on a shaggy little pony, presumably on some errand since the pony bore a pair of panniers behind the saddle.

Her "errand" took her, quite openly, to the Gypsy Quarter, and the walled compound of a horse-trader, Gordo Kaldash. The walls about his place were tall palisades of peeled and sharpened logs, liberally whitewashed. The compound looked very like a fortress, and the comparison was not far off. Gordo could hold off a siege here, if he had to. That alone was a good reason to cultivate him and gain his help.

She rode in through the open gates, ignoring the shouts and bustle all about her, noting only what the shouts and bustle meant. Gordo was taking no chances; his best stock was going out today, presumably to his breeding herds on the plains where the horses and herders would be difficult to find.

He probably thinks that the emperor is likely to confiscate as many horses suited for warfare as he can. The ponies and lady's palfreys are safe enough, but he's getting rid of all the heavy draft horses, the horses that might be used for cavalry, and the mules. Her eyes, sharpened by work with the Horse Lords, picked out every beast likely to be useful to Balthasar, and her guesses were confirmed as each one of those beasts was added to the outbound strings.

She noted also that the walls and gates were in fine repair—and that someone had added reinforcements to them within the past few days.

So, Gordo knew what was coming—possibly before even their own spy had brought the word. Interesting.

"Girl!" That hail, in the common tongue, brought her to a halt. The one who accosted her was a likely-looking Gypsy lad, about twenty or thereabouts; he led a horse with each hand, both stallions, and both on their best behavior, since they weren't trying to nip or kick each other or their handler. They weren't happy about their situation, though, and she made haste to offer her right to be there.

"I'm looking for Gordo Kaldash," she said, reaching under her collar and flashing a particular bronze medallion at him. He peered at it, raised an eyebrow in surprise, and then nodded.

"In the stable," he said shortly, and went on his way to add his two stallions to the string being readied. Two more such strings were on their way out the gate with their drovers even as they spoke.

She dismounted and led the pony to the huge stable, which took up most of the center of the compound. And there was Gordo, right at the entrance, bawling orders in a voice like a drill master. A big man, he was as hairy as one of the bears he used to befriend, with a huge barrel of a chest that the colorful scarlet shirt of a gypsy strained to cover. The slight bow to his legs proclaimed him a life-long horseman, and Shelyra knew that those enormous hands he was waving about were equally adept at delicate surgery on an ailing colt and holding down a terrified stallion.

"Not *that* one, you fool, that one stays. The mare, the gray mare! Can't you tell a mare from a gelding?" He turned to face her as she approached him, clearly with words of dismissal on his lips. Then he caught sight of her face, and the words died unspoken.

A false, affable smile spread across his mouth. "Ah— Buttercup!" he said heartily, and she winced at the name he had chosen on the spur of the moment. "Does your mistress need a new pony? I'm a bit busy at the moment—"

"My mistress needs a special horse for tiger hunts," Shelyra said flatly. "I need to discuss it with you."

Gordo paled, just a trifle, then turned and issued a barrage of orders at the dozen handlers still sorting through the horses in their stalls. "See to it!" he finished. "I'll come back and check on you all in a moment! Don't let that string leave until I've double-checked it!"

Then he quickly turned back to Shelyra, took the reins of her pony from her with one hand, and grasped her elbow with the other. "Are you mad, coming here?" he hissed in the Gypsy tongue as he handed her pony to a stableboy to take. "Do you have any idea what is coming upon us? Do you think this is a time for foolish games?"

"I have a precise idea of what is coming upon us," she replied briskly. "That is *why* I am here."

Quickly she outlined her aunt's position: that it would be suicidal for Merina to resist, that the queen intended to abdicate and turn the city over to the emperor. Gordo listened and nodded, but with a frown on his face, as he took her to the small office in his stable.

He shut the door behind her and leaned against it with his arms crossed. "That is both wise and stupid," he said at last, "but I cannot think of any other course for the city that has a chance of saving it. What of the Tiger? Do you run? Are you looking for fast horses and an escort to the Horse Lords? I can provide that."

"My aunt thinks we should run—or rather, I believe she thinks I should run." She let that statement hang in the air between them.

Slowly, Gordo's frown changed to a smile. "Ah. And you do not. In fact, you are thinking upon—what? That soon or late, the fat traders of Merina will tire of the kind of ruler Balthasar is said to be? That they will endure, and endure, until the emperor milks them all dry and leaves nothing for them? That soon or late, they will gather their now threadbare robes about them and do something to throw his yoke from their shoulders?"

"Something like that," she admitted. "That is why I am here. My aunt might think to send me out of the city, but I have other ideas. And *you* have a distant cousin who once came here out of the north to learn the ways of horse-healing."

"I remember little Raymonda, yes, and more to the point, others of the clans here will remember her as well. And there are very few of us who knew that Raymonda's parents were not Gypsy by blood but by blood-oathing." Gordo's head bobbed slowly, twice, and his stance relaxed just a trifle. "Fewer still know that her father was the King of Merina. But—"

"But I do not wish the Kaldash Clan to suffer from the loss of trade they *will* have when the emperor takes the city," she continued smoothly. "That is the other reason I am here. So before we speak more, go have my panniers fetched from the pony."

Gordo's expression was bland as he opened the door a crack and shouted an order to that effect. In a moment, the two panniers were on the floor of the office between them, and the door was shut tightly once again.

Shelyra rummaged through the rolls of clothing until her hands touched the heavy bundles in the center of each. She hauled them out and dropped them on the floor, where they made quite a heavy *thud*.

"Look," she said, gesturing. "The emperor will confiscate as much of your stock as he can, and make it hard for you to sell the rest. The House of the Tiger wishes to protect its allies and friends from such financial ruin."

Gordo bent to pick up one of the two bundles, the one she had laid nearest to him, which was about as large as Shelyra's two hands could hold. He teased open the knot holding it shut, and heavy quilted fabric fell away to reveal gold and gems, shining in the lantern-light.

They shone no less brightly than Gordo's eyes at that moment.

"That bundle in particular is entirely for Kaldash Clan," Shelyra said. "I should break up the jewelry and melt down the gold, if I were you. Those were all gifts from would-be suitors, and are not likely to be missed if Balthasar takes an inventory. I must leave enough of my jewels to seem reasonable for a young maid, but I have no intention of leaving him more to plunder than I have to."

"And the other?" Gordo asked, nodding at the bundle still on the floor.

"More such," she replied. "A little less valuable. I would have you convert that to a useful form and hold it for me—if the Kaldash Clan is willing to take in Raymonda again."

It was not exactly bribery—and it was entirely possible that Gordo and his people would have taken her in and kept her identity secret without the extra incentive. But Shelyra knew that the payment—or rather, the "gift"— would put them in her debt, making it more likely that they would do so without a grudge or a backward glance. And once the gift was accepted, nothing and no one would get her secret away from them. As her father had once said, "The thing I like about a Gypsy is that once you buy him, he stays bought."

"Raymonda would be welcome, as always," Gordo said quickly, stooping to scoop up the second bundle, and stowing both in the capacious pockets of his vest. "Is she not of the blood?"

"Then let me leave the pony and the rest here with you,"
Shelyra replied with relief. There had always been the
chance Gordo would refuse. But he had named her "of
the blood," giving her the full clan-rights of any Gypsy.
He would as soon betray or turn away his own child as
her, now that he had done that. "The panniers hold the
rest of my Gypsy clothing and horse-healing paraphernalia."

"And you will take a hired skiff back?" At her nod, he
made an approving grunt. "Wise. If there was anyone
watching, he will not believe you could have left a valuable
beast here, among us thieving Gypsies. He will watch in
vain for the servant and the pony."

He opened the door of the office and gestured for her
to take her exit. "I may not come here," she cautioned
him. "Taking shelter with you is not my only plan, it is
just the one I prefer. It will depend on many things. If I
do not come immediately, you must wait as long as seems
reasonable, then the second bundle is for the clan also."

He grunted. "Or I wait until this emperor drives us out
or tries to kill us. The Gypsies are no friends of his, and
he only tolerates us because if he offended us, our cousins, the Horse Lords, would not sell him horses."

She made a sour face. "If that happens, no one will be
safe in Merina." She did not elaborate, but she wondered
if at that point she would have to consider the option of
fleeing and saving at least her life.

*No. While I live, I will fight for this city, whether or not
it wants me to!*

She took her leave of Gordo, turned her shawl inside
out, which changed its color from brown to green, and left
with a basket over her arm. Once at the edge of the Gypsy
Quarter she hailed a boatman, and handed him the fare
that would take her to the Temple square. She stepped
into the tiny skiff, pulled her shawl over her head, and
pretended to doze. There was no sign on the water yet
that anyone knew anything was amiss. In fact, there were
even people selling flowers and produce from their boats,

just as always. The boatman left her at the steps leading up to the Great Temple; she stepped out of the boat and onto firm ground with the nonchalance of someone who has used small boats all her life, not even needing his hand to steady her.

The Temple and palace actually shared the same grounds, with gardens tended by both Gemens and palace gardeners stretching between them. She paused within the Temple, taking a seat on a bench just inside until her eyes adjusted. It was almost time for one of the services, and as usual, the Temple held enough people that her presence was not noteworthy. It was no great effort to slip through the Temple into the gardens—losing her shawl and basket on the seat she had taken—then, walking briskly as if she had an important errand, she cut across the gardens to the palace stable. As she had expected, no one stopped her. She wore the correct clothing to be there, and she looked as if she was going someplace in particular.

Which only showed how easy it would be for the emperor to have any number of spies among the palace staff.

Once inside the stables, she changed her clothing back. She considered the palace for a moment—considered her duties. Her only "duties" at the moment consisted of a set of language lessons.

And I am not going to learn enough of Olar Islander in one day to make any difference whatsoever. Her aunt and grandmother persisted in pretending that this was a day like any other, but there was no reason she had to.

Turning on her heel, she went back into the darkness of the stable, in search of a stableboy. This would be a very good time to cross to the Summer Palace and make certain of her arrangements there. Perhaps some additions would occur to her on the way.

⚘ 7 ⚘

ADELE

The past three days had been more of a strain than usual, for Adele had been forced to shuttle from Temple to palace and back again so many times she was afraid that she was wearing out her shoes at an alarming rate. She *had* to spend every night in the palace, lest another emergency arise and she be found out of her bed. One couldn't depend complacently on angelic messengers coming to wake one, as if they were one's body servants, after all!

But that left her with very little time for sleep and was exhausting her thin resources quickly.

Well, at least I shall look the part when I "collapse."

She had warned Verit of as much as she dared, and they had been in consultation for almost as many hours as they spent in prayer. They had attempted to work out some kind of plan for protecting the Temple and the Heart, but until they actually saw the face of the enemy and knew what his weapons were, there wasn't much they really could do that was concrete.

The general air in the Temple itself, with the exception of the Flames, was increasingly unreal to her. The ordinary Gemen acted as if these days were no different from any others. Couldn't they at least sense the tension in the city? Did no news ever penetrate from outside? Or were they so secure in their presumed safety and the safe harborage the presence of the Heart offered that they were under the illusion nothing would ever change here?

Such an attitude was incomprehensible to her, although Verit seemed to understand it well enough.

So she continued to ferry back and forth between the palace and the Temple, and felt her strength fading with each journey.

She already had planned how she would disappear into the Temple. It would be logical, for the closest healers were within the Brown Robes. Adele would enter the Temple in a state of terrible health, and would never walk out again.

Last night had been no exception to her pattern—except that her dreams had been so full of warnings and portents, so thick with images of marching armies and threatening weapons, that she knew their fate was going to descend upon them as soon as she woke. From long habit, Adele woke an hour before dawn. Making sure that the door to her room was locked, she entered the tunnel to the Temple, removed her makeup, put on her grey robes, and hurried back to the Temple.

She was in her place for the first service of the morning, as if nothing was going to happen, and chanted along with the other Gemen. The service ended with the joyous salutation to the dawn, although this morning the salutation seemed to fall rather flat. That *could* have been her imagination, although she didn't think so.

So, finally the others had noticed that something was amiss.

Dread portents were in the air, and at last all of the Gemen of the Temple were aware of them as a threatening atmosphere even if they were not aware of what the real threat actually was.

The Flames, of course, had already guessed that there was something dreadfully wrong. Even those Flames who were not privy to Verit's secrets knew something was in the air. But now the alarm had spread to the general populace, and it remained to be seen if Verit could control them if they began to panic.

Elfrida had more than once sensed someone faltering in the chant and looking up to the Heart for strength and solace. As the Gemen filed out of the Temple to the common room for the first meal of the day, there were many who glanced about, as if seeking someone who might know a reason for the general air of foreboding.

Silence officially ended after that, even though it was not the custom to talk at meals, so she was able to speak to the Archpriestess Verit immediately after breakfast and get permission to spend the day in private meditation in her room. This was not unusual; each of the Gemen would spend a day alone in fasting and silence every few months, so Verit granted Gemen Elfrida's request without question. From the look in her eyes, however, it was plain that she knew something was about to happen and was prepared to make certain that Gemen Elfrida's part in it was not noticed. They parted at the door to the chapter room, the archpriestess entering to announce that Gemen Elfrida would be spending the day in retreat, and Gemen Elfrida disappearing into the shadows to return to the palace and her other life—for just a little bit longer.

For today would be the last time that Adele, the dowager queen, ever appeared in public. She had seen the image of herself laid out in state and surrounded by mourners. Whether this was a portent of her "death" to the outer world, or her death in truth—or even another death that she held in reserve, just in case—she was not certain. All that she knew for certain was that Adele was about to die—and Gemen Elfrida be born into the full life of a Flame.

๖ 8 ๖

LYDANA

The past three days had been hard ones, the past three nights full of secret works. Once again at the palace, Lydana set out three lamps on the table in her room to throw maximum light around a piece of polished wood, and from her craft table brought out her kit of tools as well as a small box. Then she swiftly wrote a note, sealed it with the royal ring, and gave it to Skita, who had been waiting impatiently.

Once the child-woman had gone, Lydana laid the ring down on the piece of wood and opened the small casket. Her hand moved quickly in an averting sign as her fingers hovered over the unset gems, which were cradled, each in its own hollow, within. Lydana knew stones—perhaps in some ways better than any of her guild. What lay here were the jewels she would not willingly use for any purpose save such a one as now moved her. For these were truly gems of ill-omen—stones which were cursed and bore with them ill fortune, even the summons of death. This collection had been the result of years of discovery. She sighed and then shook her head at her own regretful thoughts. This was no time for squeamishness.

Out of its pocket she picked a gleaming red gem, like in color and in the engraving upon it, to that which was set in the royal ring. The seal of Tartus of evil memory, this stone had been symbolically washed in blood from the death warrants it had sealed until the half-mad king who had worn it had been butchered by his own guard.

Lydana worked quickly, with long-trained skill, freeing the gem she knew, inserting in its setting the stone of Tartus. When she was done at last, she rubbed her hands together and then rose and washed them at the chest basin as if to rid her fingers of some vileness.

The stone she had freed she set in a brooch, a fastening which lay with her tools, and then pinned it to the underside of her garment. Though she did not want to take it up, she pushed the ring back on her forefinger.

Her work was well done, she could admit that herself. Again in her heart she thanked her father for his wisdom. He had realized her skills early and had also wanted to make sure that she would be provided for. Her brother was heir. But in spite of that he was far-roving and had already fathered a daughter, though she was of the younger generation and could not inherit directly. At that time Lydana had not foreseen her own rulership—how could any of them?

Then when Shelyra was but a baby, her brother and his wife had died of a strange wasting fever brought back to Merina by a floating plague ship. It was in those days that her father had summoned her. She had been very young, even younger than Shelyra now, and all she had really cared for was her art.

She remembered now her father's careful questioning and then that of her mother, who could already see deeper into the soul than most. No, there was then no wish for a mate, a family in her. But by law she must be wed. So her father had selected one of his own close friends, a captain much like Saxon, old enough to be her sire and often at sea.

They had been wed with great pomp to please the city and that had been the end of it. She understood now that her father had deliberately chosen a husband he was certain she would outlive—and thus she would be free to hold both guild and throne without question. So it had been. She remembered Captain Lord Gorganius with calm affection, and had been sad at the news of his death at sea, but he had not really been a part of her life.

Although, it had been he who first turned her attention to those cursed stones and had speculated as to whether they could indeed influence the lives of men.

There came a knock at her door which set her snapping shut the case of evil gems in a hurry before she gave the call to enter. She was surprised to see her maid with the morning tray of rusk rolls and steaming spiced wine. The night must be already gone.

"Your Grace, the Reverend One requires your attention when you have eaten—and—"

Lydana followed the girl's glance downward. No, she must go more respectably dressed for a council. But Esma must have read her thought as she was already, throwing back the window draperies, going to the wardrobe. Lydana ate hungrily to the last crumb, and then dressed as befitted a formal occasion.

She did not hurry so that her haste was marked, but she reached her goal in good time, though Adele was already in her cushioned chair, looking, Lydana thought with a pinch of concern, even more wraithlike. Shelyra stood by the table, the flush of what must be temper on her smooth cheeks.

"I won't—" she was saying when her aunt entered, but the rest of her words were drowned out by the brazen boom of the great gong. Subdued, the girl dropped into her own place on Lydana's left when the great doors were flung open for the guildsmen.

They did not come with their customary ceremony today, but rather crowded forward together, and hurried to take their seats after their bows to the three women.

"There is a herald at the gate, Your Grace." That was Totas, guild master of the silk merchants, his small gray chin-beard wobbling up and down as he spoke.

So—so little time! Lydana did not look at Adele, but she felt the flow of energy in the other, released in her direction.

"He is to be received, given guest rights—and he is to wait," Lydana said calmly.

She was watching the company before her as one of the officers hurried from the chamber to obey her orders. In some of the younger ones she could sense anger, but it was overlaid by despair. No man in his right senses would suggest that Merina attempt to stand against the might of the emperor's army. And with some of the elders—well, she wondered if there might not be even a touch of sly satisfaction, a belief that under the emperor they might even prosper the more—fools that they were!

"Listen," Lydana raised her voice with the crack of an order. "We all know well what our enemy covets—we are rich, we are ripe for his plucking, and there are two choices. Balthasar might well be reluctant to storm Merina—he wants what we have, not the dregs of a bespoiled city. If we open our gates to him freely, that means no killing. We shall speak with this herald and this we shall say: This is the city of the Heart, here is the innermost shrine of the Temple. Balthasar is still of the Temple—at least he follows the forms when it suits him.

"Thus let him, through his herald, swear at the high altar that he will offer no harm where there is no opposition and Merina will be his."

That raised their voices. Lydana let fall her hand once more upon the table, with force enough to rise above the jangle of their speech.

"You are the people of Merina, it will be your decision. We shall leave you now to make it."

She was on her feet, her arm out to give Adele support and Shelyra beside her. Together they went through the curtains to the small ruler's closet. Once there, the girl raised her voice again.

"You give away all. We are of the Tiger—where are your fangs, your claws now, Aunt?"

"Listen—" it was Adele who held up her hand "—I bade you all think, plan, and what have you to offer?"

"This," Lydana said quickly. "You, Reverend One, will

enter the cloister, though earlier than we planned. Since we have learned that part of the forces turned against us are of the Dark, you can best judge what can be done there. Also, listen: though we may all disappear, yet we can keep word with one another—"

Adele was before her. "The confessionals!" Her eyes were bright, perhaps too much so. "We can pass word through the confessionals to each other."

"The third confessional from the Heart," Lydana responded.

Adele nodded. "I shall arrange to have someone trustworthy there during the hours of confession, if I myself cannot be there."

"What of me?" Shelyra's flush grew stronger. "I do not go into the Temple—I will not!" She lifted a fist in the air and shook it.

"No," agreed Lydana, "you have a place, and one which will help us fight the battle we are forced to—one of hidden ways and unseen attacks. Shelyra, in other years you have visited with the Horse People—it is near time for them to come again. Remember, no army moves without supplies. Perhaps the chiefs will deal with Balthasar, perhaps not. But they will not be his liegemen. You know them, you can talk to their war chiefs—suggest mischief—" She was trying to find the right words.

Shelyra's flush was fading. Her hand was on the hilt of her long belt knife. She slid that out, and then thrust it back into its sheath with force.

"Yes—" She was like a child facing some treat.

"And you, daughter?" asked Adele.

"Balthasar will seek a queen. He will find none. If there is a small trader in gems and the like in the poorer marketplace, I do not think they will note her very much."

Adele shook her head. "Do not be too sure, daughter. But I understand that you must play your own game."

"Shelyra, as soon as this council is over, go to my chamber. You will find Skita and another. No one goes into battle without a skilled man for one's back. I am now giving you one who is strange but who has those qualities which are needed. This I must order you, be guided by him—he knows what is to be done and he is blood-bound to a horse chief."

Just as the girl nodded there came a voice from beyond the curtains.

Lydana looked from her niece to her mother. "We are agreed?" she asked softly.

Once more they stood behind the council table. Slowly Lydana slipped the ring of state from her finger, laying it before her. It was plain the guildsmen had also agreed, for the symbolic gold key already lay there. Adele suddenly leaned forward and looked at the ring; she might have been bidding farewell to an office she, too, had once held.

Her whisper was the thinnest trace of sound. "Be careful, my daughter, as to what games you would play."

The herald, in all his stiff robes of presence, was ushered in and came to stand facing the queen. He was not smiling, but there was a smugness about him, as if he had been very sure what he would find.

"You have been told what Merina requires?" Lydana asked.

The man nodded his head so the plumes of his hat fluttered.

"His Imperial Majesty is always thoughtful of the people. He wishes no warring when there is no cause. As a chosen herald, I shall swear and it will be as if his Imperial Majesty spoke the words."

"Do you hear this, men of Merina?" Lydana asked. "Will you stand witness before the Heart to this promise and oath?"

There was an assenting murmur. Lydana indicated the ring and the key. "Here is the seal and there is the key. Take them to your ruler once the oath is given—"

She had no time to say any more, for suddenly Adele slumped forward, gasping for breath. She would have struck the table had not Lydana and Shelyra jumped to aid her.

"My mother ails, herald—" Lydana nearly hissed the words. "You do your duty and I shall do mine."

§ 9 §

LYDANA

Though Adele kept her feet, she leaned heavily against Lydana; but her faint whisper was also meant to reach Shelyra.

"Let them believe me far spent. This will work the best now."

However, Lydana could not be sure whether her mother was playing some role of her own devising, or wished to lift from those with her a part of their burden of concern.

They were met on the way to her mother's chambers by several of the Brown Robes, members of the Temple's healing order.

"The archpriestess knows," one of them explained as they took Adele's slight form and placed her in the litter they had brought with them. "She has sent us to take the Reverend One to the Temple. Content your minds, those of the Heart guard well their own. Look now you to yourself—and to this future hope." She nodded toward Shelyra.

But Adele was not yet ready to dismiss them; her head turned toward them and she said, her voice now having much of its old vigor, "Be not sure of any death until you see the grave. If you show remorse that I have entered the

Inner Gate, it will be cover for this time. Since we know of this Apolon's ambitions but not of the extent of his strengths, take double care. You, son's daughter," she spoke directly to Shelyra, "must learn the armor of being less than the lowest and put a guard upon your temper. This shall be such a testing as few have known, for it will call upon the spirit and the will more than on strength of body."

Shelyra nodded, her lips compressed into a thin line.

"While you, daughter—" Now she regarded Lydana. "You have your own training. This, however, I will speak of again—those sources of evil which you have so guarded—perhaps you are not immune in turn to what they bring. Take great care when you use them. The law of the Heart is true—send evil, even for a hoped purpose of good, and it will grow double and return! Now, the both of you, get you gone. If we must speak to each other in the future, it will be through the confessional in the Great Temple. And may the Heart enclose you around until the day when these ill-rooted shadows are torn away."

She did not look back at either of them again as the Brown Robes carried the litter away. Adele was right: they had their own roads to travel and to do so— Lydana caught Shelyra by the arm.

"Come!"

There were no guards in the hallways—Merina's rulers had kept such only for ceremonial occasions, and Lydana was sure that they had been summoned by their commander to escort the herald to the Great Temple. However, she could not be sure their going would not be marked, and what they must do must be done quickly.

With Shelyra in tow she entered her own chamber. They were awaiting her. She had no doubts that they would not be. The message Skita had carried at dawn was not one to be questioned. She did not even glance at the small maid sitting on her low chair, swinging one foot back and forth; Lydana's attention was all for the other.

So this was the hero of so many ballads, sly stories

which set chuckling those who had not suffered from his tricks of mind and tongue. He stood there as if he had already cataloged all within the chamber, sorted out the best and most easily transported bits of treasure to be collected as soon as his chance came. And his attitude was that chance was indeed close at hand.

"Thom Talesmith." Lydana looked him up and down. He had about him the guileless look of a youngster new to the wide world, a little overawed by the richness it had to offer. Nothing could be further from his reputation.

"The same, Your Grace." He swept a bow which was as finished as any courtier's best effort.

"Thief, rogue, under the sentence of death," she answered with the practical tone of one summing up a problem.

"Yet I am here—" He was still grinning that boy's grin, innocent as the first rays of early day. But the eyes above—he could not so well control those eyes. He was as wary as a trapped beast and had all the beast's intention to either win free or collect blood-tribute from his captors.

"The High Judge gave you sentence," she pointed out.

"Then why do I stand here by royal command?" he countered. His grin had faded and his chin was a little outthrust.

"Because thief, rogue, and all else they claim of you, there are several other things man can say truly of Thom Talesmith. He has courage which does not depend upon familiarity with steel, or club, or the dagger of a shadow-killer."

He bowed again as she continued:

"Yes, courage, and wit—also this I have heard of Thom Talesmith. If he gives full oath for any venture, he will hold to it, no matter what may seem to prevail."

Shelyra had gone to sit on the foot of the bed, watching him with a hawk's eyes. At her aunt's new statement, she caught her lower lip between her teeth and frowned.

"Merina falls," Lydana continued.

He shrugged. "How else? One cannot stand against the

full force of the emperor. And to die uselessly is the choice of a stupid man."

It was Lydana's turn to smile. "Which Thom Talesmith is not! Merina may fall, but she is not dead, nor can she be safely buried while our illustrious new overlord moves on to further conquest." She reached out to the nearest table. There lay a slender poniard, meant for slitting open documents.

He was eyeing her sharply, but there was certainly no touch of fear in the survey, only curiosity and excitement.

"What does our gracious queen desire?" There was a light trace of mockery in that, but Lydana continued to smile.

"Your services—as blood liege man—" She brought the poniard into the full light.

He had lost his smile; Lydana saw his hand move toward the sash belt at his waist as if hunting for a weapon he no longer wore.

"I give you a chance, Thom Talesmith, who has tricked and thieved and made himself the hero of those in the alleys; a chance to become a hero, indeed."

His eyes dropped to the poniard.

"Assassination? Who—His Mightiness Balthasar himself?"

"We do not ask the impossible. No, this is what we do want of you. This—the next heir to Merina." With a nod of her head she indicated the girl. "She will be one Balthasar wants within his hold—or perhaps dead."

Thom glanced away from the knife for the first time to look directly at the girl. They eyed each other with the unwinking stare of two cats about to contest territory.

"They say that you are blood-oathed to one of the Horse Lords—"

Without breaking the locked stare with Shelyra, he nodded.

"Thus you can find your way to cover for Shelyra until those come, and perhaps even speak for us with them. I would lay blood oath on you to be sure that she is served, and through her the future of this city."

He frowned. "She is a princess, a lady of consequence. She would be known for what she is in a moment in the hidey-holes I know."

"Then make sure she is not." Before he could move, Lydana's right hand shot out and caught him by the wrist, where there were still traces of prisoner's irons to be seen. He gave a little cry and then stood looking down at the growing drop of blood on his grimed skin.

Lydana held the blade steady so that a twin drop of blood on its point could not fall. With a quick jerk of her other hand she summoned Shelyra to her and, luckily without any protest, the girl obeyed. Again Lydana held a hand, this time palm up, and into the hollow of that palm she let slide that drop.

"By the Heart, by the greater Powers, by all which dwells above and slays the Dark below, be it witnessed that this Thom is now liege man—but also is she of the House of the Tiger to remember that he will strive for her and she will not break liege ties with him."

Slowly they both mouthed the age-old words of liege-taking. Lydana tossed the poniard to Thom, who caught it skillfully out of the air and thrust it sheathless into his belt sash. "Skita will see you away. There is a skiff—take it and find your bolt hole. Also," suddenly she laughed, "if you can discover any deeds which will embarrass our new ruler—you have my permission to act, as long as Shelyra is safe."

He was grinning again. Then he raised his lightly blooded hand in salute, as an armsman to his officer. "So be it, My Queen."

She watched the three of them disappear behind one of the hangings. This palace was indeed a warren of unseen ways. Perhaps if Balthasar thought to enthrone himself here, that also could be to their advantage.

She had done her best for Shelyra—now she must prepare for her own disappearance. And, luckily enough, through the years she *had* prepared, not knowing why, for that very project.

So far as she knew, Skita was the only person who shared the full of their secret. It had begun some six seasons ago, soon after Ourse, when she had been restless and eager to know more of Merina than the one who was always surrounded by the Might of the House of the Tiger, and a woman who might carry the precious talent with her, could learn. Skita had, in fact, been a part of it.

When Captain Saxon had destroyed the pirate fleet, there had been a great scouring out of their filthy nests along the shores and islands to the south. Some strange things had been discovered. If the pirates had taken slaves, they did not live for long, that was well known. But in a cage—as if she were some kind of oversized bird—Skita had been found.

Saxon himself had freed her, but she had refused to talk to any man and he realized that she was indeed alien to any race he knew. He had brought her back to Merina when it was plain there was nothing else he could do for her protection, and presented her to the king—but at that time of presentation in open court, Skita simply walked across the floor to the lower dais stool where Lydana had been seated that day, and held out her hands to the king's daughter.

Startled at first, Lydana had simply stared. Then within her there was awakened something—some emotion she could not define. It had nothing to do with any feeling she had ever known, but at that moment some empty place within her had been filled. Skita was not quite the daughter she had never had, but she was close as any blood-kin and, though Lydana had never learned more of the history of her small companion than that she had lived on an island which had been attacked by a pirate vessel driven off course, Skita had never expressed any desire either to be returned to her people, nor had she been able—or perhaps wished—to give any of the map scribes Lydana had consulted directions or a name to her homeland.

She was quick-witted and had certain talents of her own. She often seemed able to pick up thoughts when Lydana was in serious contemplation on some matter, and she had a strong ability to gauge nearby danger. Lydana had taught her something of jewel-craft, and she had the ability to remember word by exact word anything she had heard or read. Also—and this Lydana never tried to put into words—her very companionship somehow was soothing and encouraging. One might almost imagine—if one was very fanciful—that she was one of the guardian angels so often spoken of in the missals of the cloister and the library of the Great Temple.

It was after Skita's melding into her household that Lydana had at last summoned up the determination for a course of action she had been considering ever since the news had come of the death of her husband. The freedom she required to work out her plans would not have been hers had he technically remained the head of her own household.

Again, as she had many times before, Lydana made use of the secret ways of the palace. She had found a small chamber well suited to her only half-imagined purpose, and there began to establish what she needed to experiment in becoming, not a lady of rank, but a common tradeswoman of Merina.

There was a chest, laboriously transplanted there by Skita and her, a mirror for the wall, and something which had never openly appeared on the sparsely furnished resting table of her official quarters: a box of mixed cosmetics.

Thus Matild had been born. The plain, dark-colored clothing which was Lydana's by choice was here laid aside for brilliant colors she would have shrunk from wearing in her rightful person. Her mouse-brown hair was shaken out of its tight tiara of braids and carefully smoothed over and over again with a comb such as was sold in the markets for one past her prime who would not surrender to any gray strands, darkening it in shade and giving it odd reddish lights. Nor was it then returned to its braids.

Rather it was twisted and rolled—it had taken Lydana some impatient tries to achieve what she wanted—into two coils over her ears. Over these there went pockets of tarnished silver nets, the fastenings of which met on the crown of her head and dangled tassels of glittering glass beads down over her forehead.

She had learned to tightly lace a belt which brought into prominence both the curve of her hips and pushed up, in a near-unseemly fashion, her breasts. Over this went a kirtle of silk frayed about the hem, and then a tightly fitting bodice, displaying neck and shoulders to a questionable degree.

Before she laced the latter into place, she now swiftly selected from the wide chest of cosmetics a bottle from which came a liquid the hue of cinnamon-thickened punch. A soft brush and a square of stained silk were put to use, and her ivory skin was gone, leaving the roughish look of a woman much in the open who had used cosmetics for too many years and far too lavishly. Then came the darkening and shaping of her brows, and a slapping of red rouge on each cheek. From a small box she took a black spot, which adhered to the end of her forefinger, and planted it on her upper lip above a smearing of thick lipstick.

After surveying herself critically in the mirror, Lydana added a number of necklaces, semiprecious stones and crystals interwoven with dingy, unpolished silver and copper beads. Then a thick cluster of dangling bracelets for each wrist.

While Lydana had so busied herself, Skita, newly returned, had also been assuming her other persona—one which knew well some very dubious centers of city life. She had used a lotion similar to Lydana's, not only on her neck, face, and arms, but, shedding all clothing, she made sure her small body was now a shade which suggested that she needed a bath—or a series of such—before she would again be fit for good company. Her hair she dipped into a bowl into which she had poured the last of the liquid, and then she had dug her fingers in a jar of greasy unguent and combed them through those locks until they hung in ugly strings.

Her body now being dry, she picked up a width of very coarse grayish cloth and bound it tightly over the curves of her breasts. Now she could well be a boy—one of the very youthful gangs who hung about the canals. And the too-loose breeches she put on and secured with a twist of thin rope, surmounting them with a smocklike shirt confined by a very worn and mended belt, completed the disguise. There was no more Skita, even as there was no more Lydana.

Rather, as they closed their boxes and gave one last critical survey to each other's person, there was Matild, who dealt in beads and small gauds and had a blind hole of a shop down by the far south canal, and Eel, her imp of a nephew whose ability to separate a citizen from his purse was a matter of admiring comment among his street companions.

Matild had already built up the character of a wanderer in such a fashion that those few decent goodwives along the street would whisper behind their hands. Rumor had it that she had a quick eye for a seaman, though none had ever seen her entertain such. But when she disappeared for days, it was thought that she was busied with some free-handed mariner back from a profitable voyage. On the other hand, though they might smirk and roll their tongues about her supposed goings-on, the women of Stingray's Court also had a grudging respect and some awe for their neighbor. She had been well proven several times over to have second sight, able to gain news of missing men—or daughters—and she had given advice which had gotten their kin out of the hands of the police.

Though what she sold were only flashy gauds, yet they were pretty enough to catch any woman's eyes, and she did a brisk business with young apprentices wanting to make an impression on some serving wench.

It was still day. Matild yawned and realized that she was

hungry. When had she eaten? In the early morning, and then only a roll and a glass of wine. But it would seem that Skita had thought ahead, for she produced a basket and shared out cheese, bread, and some dried meat, as well as two juice-leaking pastries.

They must wait until the city was well aware of the invaders. Now that she had made her change, Matild settled herself cross-legged on the floor and began to consider in detail all that Lydana, the queen, had done this day, seeking to discover if there were any weak points in their hasty preparations.

"Thom will hold to his given word." Skita had turned down their lamp to the faintest of glimmers. "He is a man of many parts."

Matild sighed. "One can hear much, but all which is said is distorted in the telling by the very thoughts and feelings of the ones who have passed it along. Yes, I have heard Thom can be held to a trust. I only hope he is wily enough to deal with Shelyra. At the moment she does as she is told because she has no time to think or imagine her own way of dealing with things. But"—Matild raised her hands in a slightly helpless gesture—"what else could we do, having so little time?

"We did have the time." Now her mouth twisted and the red of her lips stained her teeth as she corrected herself. "But it was as if we were blinded—until this past half year. We saw Balthasar and his armies busy in the north— one city state—we were not worth his trouble until he had contained the lord barons of the Shlad. Though even had we set in to defend ourselves, what could we have done? Townsmen will fight for their homes and families, yes, but they are not trained veterans. We have no walls which could stand against the siege equipment such as brought down Hardclaw. No, we can only burrow and wait—and use the patience of those wood ants who by their labor can tumble a century-old house."

She picked up the nearly empty food basket and began to pack it with precision. Strange weapons, but the best she had. Into the bottom went the box of ill-fated gems. Over that heap upon heap of beads, some strung, some in packets. It was difficult for her to curb her impatience— she wanted to be out and on her way, but they needed a curtain for their movements.

"Shall the Eel go sniffing?" Skita edged her body closer. Perhaps she, too, could not take the pressure set on them by the need for caution. Matild thought, and then gave a nod, and the small gamin moved with an eager speed, to be lost to sight beyond the walls.

Matild had kept one of the strings of beads in her fingers—jade, yes, but flawed and of a poor color. Deliberately she set her mind on another, Adele, as she began to pass those beads through her fingers one by one, following the pattern of inner prayer. She believed in the Temple, she had been raised to do so, and she knew that such as the Reverend One had abilities which seemed miraculous to the ordinary person. Yet, in her heart she dealt better with action and held to a small belief that the Heart and all it stood for favored those who battled for themselves— if their cause was just.

Adele was safe. She did not believe that even Balthasar—or this Dark-endowed mage of his—would dare enter the cloister. The Temple was too deeply a part of their life, and even his own lords would turn against any such action. But there were more ways of entering the cloister than by battering down an unprotected door with armed men. Unprotected? She slipped another bead between her dirty fingers. There were more subtle—and more powerful—protections than any man-fashioned gates.

Archpriestess Verit was old. She had held the High Seat now for some forty seasons, though she seemed no less keen of wit or lacking in power because of that. Did Apolon have some way of wreaking harm unknown even to those bound to the Heart itself? There was no use in frightening oneself with such musings. Better to think about what she would have immediately before herself.

Saxon—yes, the harbor master was very much a part of any plans she would lay. But Saxon was as much in the public eye as Lydana had been when she sat at the council table. He could be counted on to make sure of his own safety. For the present, she must hold to that.

֍ 10 ֎

SHELYRA

The three of them emerged from the hidden passage into one of the corridors of the third story. Skita set off down the corridor ahead of them—quite openly. Thom Talesmith started to follow the tiny woman, but stopped when Shelyra did not move. Skita turned to look behind her as soon as he paused.

Shelyra frowned at both of them, but graced Thom with the more reproving expression, one that said, without words, "*You* at least should know better."

"Go back to the queen," she told Skita, with a wave of her hand. "She has more need of you than we do."

"But the skiff—" Skita protested.

Shelyra shook her head. "I might take the skiff, or I might not. The fewer who know what means out of here we take, the better. Even *you* can be caught and caged for questioning, Skita."

She had chosen those words shrewdly, knowing Skita's history as she did, and saw the tiny creature wince slightly.

Without further objection, Skita turned on her heel and hurried back toward the queen's chambers. Shelyra waited until she was out of sight and hearing, then waved to

Thom to follow her. She could tell by the tightening of his lips that he did not care for being in the position of the one taking orders, and suppressed a smile of grim satisfaction.

She had not asked to be saddled with this particular galled steed, and she was not going to put up with any nonsense from him. *I do not care for this man's reputation, and his attitude just confirms that reputation. He takes stupid risks for the sake of notoriety; given a choice between an effective act with no attendant public admiration and an ineffective one that would enlarge his legend, he will take the latter.* She knew from the moment he had set eyes on her that he was counting on his charm and good looks and her presumed susceptibility to both to win his way with her. He expected her to be nothing more than a pampered and adored princess, easily flattered, easily led—and had said as much. Well, that was his mistake, thinking that because she had been raised in a palace, she had no experience with the real world.

He had not counted on the fact that she had grown up in a situation where she was constantly surrounded by handsome young men with ambition and very little brain, and nothing to do with their time but be charming to her on the chance that she might advance their ambition. Truth to be told, many of those young men had been better-looking than Thom, and she had never failed to see past their blandishments.

Aunt Lydana never knew the half of what I did among the Horse Lords—and nothing at all of my Gypsy friends. I suppose it is just as well. Just as Skita could be caught and questioned, so could my aunt. The thought sent chills running down her arms. *Best I stick to my own plans. Hers may not be safe for long. I won't turn tail and run, anyway, not while there is a chance I can do some good.*

She stepped aside into the office of the palace housekeeper, who would not be in until the afternoon. Thom followed, still scowling.

"What—" he began as soon as the door closed behind them.

"Hush," she interrupted, before he could even complete his question. "There may be ears anywhere."

She went to the back of the office as he sighed melodramatically and cast his eyes upward, as if imploring the angels above for patience. Clearly, he thought she was being ridiculously overcautious.

Her scorn for him only increased. *Fool. How has he survived this long?*

The release for this secret door was so well hidden that even the housekeeper, who used the books in the bookcase at the rear of her office daily, had never found it. Like the door Shelyra had used in the hallway last night, this one pivoted on a center pillar. She took care that her body hid her hands from Thom as she manipulated the catch. She intended to win this conflict with the emperor, which meant that the House of the Tiger *would* regain possession of this place, and she did not intend to make Thom privy to any more of its secrets than she absolutely had to.

She did not see his expression as the bookcase pivoted, but when she turned to gesture him inside, his face had lost that look of faint mockery.

Once they were safely inside the passageway, here, in this passage where the walls were thick enough to stifle even the sounds of someone screaming, and where there were no chinks to betray a light to the outside, she felt for the match and lantern that were always kept waiting on a ledge beside the door. She struck a light and lit the lamp, locked the secret door behind her so that it could only be opened from this side, and only then turned toward her supposed liege man.

She surveyed him with a critical eye, as she had not had the opportunity to do before. At first, he grinned and posed, but as her expression did not vary nor her demeanor soften, his smug smile faded, and he began to look uncomfortable beneath her unwavering gaze.

He was a comely enough fellow—if he would just wash a little more often and more thoroughly. Taller than her by a head and a half, his brownish-blond hair was cut just below his ears and was held out of his startlingly blue eyes with a headband made from a red silk scarf. His face was beardless, boyish, seemingly innocent, and made him look much younger than the true tally of his years. He wore a much-abused, loose, brown leather vest over a threadbare silk shirt, faded from whatever color it once had been to an indeterminate beige. This was tucked into brown linen trousers, which were in turn tucked into the tops of knee-high, brown leather boots that laced up the side—boots of the sort that the Horse Lords wore. She had a pair of them herself, safely spirited away into hiding. A faded scarlet silk sash completed the whole outfit, all of which could have done with a good laundering.

He shifted from foot to foot, uneasy under her continued scrutiny, as she took in the measure of the man beneath the clothing. He was fit, obviously; well-muscled, but not overly so—and not of her own "type," wiry and thin, but with tough, whipcord muscles.

She let out her breath in a sigh. "Let us have no illusions between us," she said, regarding him with a gaze that was both aloof and challenging. "No matter what the queen told you, *I* am in charge, and you will follow my orders. Or you may take your leave of me as soon as we reach the streets, and trouble me with your unwelcome and unasked-for presence no longer."

With that, she took up the lantern and turned about abruptly, striding off down the passage, leaving him to catch up to her.

"Now, wait a moment, Your Mightiness," he said sarcastically as she continued to set a pace that forced him to walk as fast as he could. "I am—"

"You are a thief with an overblown reputation," she replied crisply. "You have no resources beyond that knife in your belt and whatever you might have cached out in the city, which your dear friends and colleagues may already have looted. Merina will shortly be swarming with the emperor's men, if it is not already. If you wish to share in the resources that *I* have hidden away—I who have entrusted those secrets to no one—you will follow my orders. If you do not, you may take your chances with the emperor's men."

The passage made an abrupt turn; she knew it was there, but he did not. He didn't run into the wall, but the sudden change in direction made him stumble and lose his bearings for a moment, and he had to run to catch up with her again.

"What resources?" he asked, when he was again a few paces behind her.

She didn't answer him. He might be useful, if only as an errand runner, but not unless he could bend his overweening pride beneath her hand.

"We were supposed to take a skiff—" he said, then suspicion crept into his voice. "We are supposed to go to the Horse Lords. *You* don't intend to leave the city, do you?"

"Your decision," she reminded him. "I want it before I tell you anything. I entrust my secrets to no one, let along a rogue who only just escaped the gallows, and who might choose to find his own way out of the city. *And* get caught for his pains."

I have him, and he knows it. He gave his word and oath to be my liege man. My orders supersede my aunt's. I wonder if she thought of that? I know he didn't; I have the feeling that most of his daring and "cunning" escapes have been accomplished through luck rather than planning.

He groaned in an exaggerated manner. "What choice do I have?" he exclaimed. "The queen has my oath in blood!"

"And I have the power to release you from it," she reminded him coolly, maintaining her brisk pace. "Save only the condition that you leave Merina at once and never return again."

She knew by his silence, broken only by his breathing, that he was torn in his decision. Cynically, she thought she knew why.

With the emperor's men taking over the city, there will be confusion, and where there is confusion, there is a chance to loot and steal. Neither his face nor his name are known to the emperor's men, and if he stays with me, he has a chance at some choice pillaging. But if he goes—he escapes with his life, which he did not have any hope of doing this time yesterday. It is a difficult choice to make.

Something else occurred to her, a reason why he might be hesitant about following through on his promise to take her to refuge with the Horse Lords. The rumor that he was blood-brother to one of their chiefs might only be that—a rumor, one that he himself had started to enhance his stature and myth. He was not called "Talesmith" for naught.

At this point, she was ready to dismiss just about everything that was said of the man as a lie or at least a great stretch of truth. Let him *prove* himself to her; she would believe none of the stories. Storytellers and balladeers often lied.

As witness all those foolish songs lauding my gentle manners and lily white skin!

If there was no more truth in the tale of blood-brotherhood than a pair of boots he might have picked up secondhand in the clothing market, she had every reason to doubt him.

Likely he never expected anyone to catch him in his fabrication, and he is trying to think of a way out of the situation. The Horse Lords give short shrift and little welcome to penniless and troublesome strangers. He can't know that I enjoy some status among them in my own right, and he fears what will happen if he rides into their land with me in tow, expecting hospitality!

She was not particularly minded to tell him of her own

ventures, either. Let him squirm his own way out of the trap of his own spinning. It would have been entertaining to watch, had she not far more pressing concerns.

She, too, was torn, between wanting to be rid of him and wanting to have him available. Where she planned to go, a man at her side would be useful, if only as a foil to avoid the unpleasant confrontations anyone female was bound to encounter. At the moment, her plans took her only as far as the Gypsy Quarter and a certain horse trader, where the talismanic pendant she wore under the high collar of her gown would serve to gain her entry and a position among the breakers and trainers. From there, she would wait to see what the emperor did—

—and what steps her grandmother took.

She seethed inwardly with impatience to *do* something, but for the moment, there was nothing she could do, and she knew it.

"I'll stay with you." She started; she had been so deep in her own thoughts that she had almost forgotten Thom. "I gave my oath; I won't have it said that Thom Talesmith went back on his word the moment things turned black."

"Fine," she replied. Let him put whatever face on it he chose, so long as he made up his mind and stuck to it. "We're going to the Gypsy Quarter, for now."

He laughed, a single, short bark of a laugh. "Oh, truly? And you will blend in so *well* there, Your Imperiousness!"

She ignored the snide retort, gathering up the velvet skirts of her gown to break out of her walk into a run, forcing him to do the same.

The passage descended abruptly: a long flight of perilously narrow stairs. At the bottom of the staircase was a stone box of a room at the level of the ground floor—although this room was not properly in the palace at all. Shelyra put the lantern up on the tiny shelf waiting for it and opened the bag she had left here last night.

Ordinarily, she would have needed a tiring-woman to unlace the back of the tight-fitting gown—but she did not plan to wear this dress ever again, so there was no real need to waste time unlacing it. She lifted her heavy skirts and removed a tiny knife from a sheath strapped to her ankle, then slit the left side of the dress from armpit to below the hip with brisk efficiency along the seamline. As Thom stared at her with his mouth agape, she cut the tight-fitting left sleeve loose and pulled it off, dropping it to the floor, then slit the shoulder and the high collar and squirmed out of the remains of the gown.

"Don't you—want me to turn my back or something?" he stammered.

She turned a cool gaze on him as she pulled off the elaborate corset (cutting the strings to do so) and removed the heavy silk petticoat, leaving her standing in only her shoes and a mere slip of an undergown. The shoes were a great deal plainer and more practical than the gown; she had taken a chance on the herald not getting a good look at her feet. "No," she replied flatly. "Why? I have no interest in you, and if *you* were to try anything, you would lose the hand you touched me with."

With that, she turned to the contents of her bag.

The Gypsies, who shared blood and blood-ties with the Horse Lords, recognized four castes—Tinkers, Entertainers, Healers, and Horse-breakers—in their tongue, Caldesh, Getan, Dukke, and Romer. Some added, "Horsethieves," but these were only partly right. Each caste had a form of dress peculiar to it.

The costume she removed was not that of a Horsebreaker, for someone might recall that she had ties to the Horse Lords and look for her among those who worked with horses, or rather, with those who trained and tamed them. That was a pity, since the costume of leather vest, trousers, and dark linen shirt was well-suited to someone who might need to run in a hurry. Nor did she don the sober brown cowled tunic and skirts of the Healers, for her healing-knowledge was mostly limited to the dressing of wounds and those ailments that struck horses, not humans. No, she had deliberately chosen the one caste she was unlikely to be associated with—the Entertainers.

First, as Thom Talesmith watched in shock, she donned a faded scarlet blouse with tight sleeves ending just above the elbow in wide flounces; over this went three circle skirts, of black, yellow, and red, the last with a high, fitted waistband that reached to the bottom of her ribcage. She reached up into her hair and released it from its confining pins and circlet of silver, shaking it down until it fell loosely about her shoulders, reaching to her waist. No well-born maiden wore her hair loose, of course, and she knew from past experience that having it so changed the look of her face entirely.

Out of the bag came a belt hung with tiny bells and copper coins that she fastened about her waist. A red scarf emerged next, to be tied about her head, surmounted with a brow-band of more copper coins and bronze chains. Slender copper bangles bedecked her arms, and enormous bronze disk-earrings replaced the precious sapphires in her ears—which she threw to Thom. He was not so stunned that he failed to catch and pocket them.

"A surety," she said, and went on with her transformation.

Last out of the bag were a shawl, which she draped over her arms, a set of castanets, and her weapons.

A bodice-knife slipped into a hidden sheath between her breasts. Another knife in a leg sheath joined the first. Her Horse Lord fighting knife hung openly and properly from the belt of chains and coins, at her side; two more dainty stilletos went into her hair, as fasteners for the scarf and brow band at the rear of her head.

The castanets went on the belt, on the side opposite her knife. The pouch containing her valuables went under the first skirt, and could be reached through a slit in the side.

Lastly, she wiped her face free of every trace of cosmetics. No gypsy could afford such things. Her face, paled from its usual weathered bronze by many layers of pearl-powder, took on its proper color.

Her talismanic pendant, a bronze disk with the Horse

of the Sun on one side, and the Hand of the Healers on the other, now hung openly at her throat from a leather thong.

She turned to face him, schooling her expression into amused irony. "I believe," she said, into a silence so thick that her words dropped like stones into water, "that I shall not cause too great a stir in the Gypsy Quarter."

He only shook his head with disbelief. "Your shoes are wrong for southern dancing," was all he could say. "There's no heel for the percussive steps—"

"I am no trained dancer," she replied. "I shall, if forced to perform, muddle my way through the northern style. Soft slippers are adequate for that."

He lifted his hands in defeat and acknowledgment. "And likely no one among the emperor's men has been to the plains to see the northern style and know if you are a dancer or an amateur. Good enough."

She swept him an ironic bow, as a dancer would, exaggerated and full of impudence. She felt freer in this clothing; no longer the Designated Daughter, but someone with more options and fewer restrictions.

"This door will lead us into a forgotten corner of the garden and a gate to which I have the only key," she said, laying her hand on the blank wall. "That will let us in turn out into the street. We shall see about this skiff; it might be useful after all. Are you ready?"

He nodded, his innocent-seeming face blank of all expression as he tried to assimilate everything that had just happened to him. She had him off balance.

She intended to keep him there.

Without another word, she fingered the hidden catch on the door into the garden, and they slipped out together.

§ 11 §

LEOPOLD

Outside the four canvas walls surrounding Prince Leopold droned a soporific hum comprised of the voices of many men. There was no sign in that monotonous sound that this was the front-line come off a long, long warcampaign; the steady murmur was actually soothing.

Leopold slumped in a canvas and wood camp chair at the rear of his father's spartan war tent, waiting for Emperor Balthasar to think of something useful for him to do. He had worked his nerves up for an impending battle as soon as the herald returned, and now—now, he was caught in the lassitude that invariably followed if he did not get an opportunity to discharge his nervous energy. He was grateful that he had at least not donned his full plate armor this morning, although he normally did so in anticipation of a siege or a pitched battle at the gates of any city they came to conquer. Something had made him wave the squire away just as the boy brought the breastplate up, and he had called for his black chain mail and the tunic of black leather with metal plates riveted to the inside instead. Over it he wore the surcoat of his father's empire, a Sun-in-Glory in brilliant gold, emblazoned on stark black, surrounded by golden stars.

Now he was glad he had waved off the heavy armor; the plate-and-chain was barely tolerable to wear all day; the full battle-plate impossible.

The capitulation of Merina had caught Balthasar completely off guard; the emperor had been expecting a long siege, for even Apolon had declared that nothing would make the rulers of the city of the Heart surrender without a fight. All the signs pointed to Queen Lydana, female though she was, stubbornly gathering up her people to defend the rich prize of Merina to the bitterest end.

But the emperor's herald had returned with the keys of the palace and the signet of the House of the Tiger in his hands, and the capitulation and abdication in a document tube at his belt. He had given oath in Balthasar's name that the people and the city would remain unharmed, which Apolon had not much liked, but the emperor himself had been pleased enough to send the herald away with a gold chain around his neck. Balthasar had taken the ring and placed it on his own finger immediately, though Apolon made an abortive motion, as if he would like to have examined it first.

Apolon. That sly serpent; what was it he wanted to do? Somehow pocket the signet himself? I wouldn't put it past him.

Apolon was furious that the victory had been so easy. *That* made Leopold very curious, indeed. . . .

"And what of the queen?" the sorcerer spat as the herald finished his recitation of the oaths he had sworn in the emperor's stead. "What of the Dowager Queen, Adele? What of the Princess Shelyra? *Her,* at least, you should have insisted on obtaining as hostage for her city's good behavior!"

That had also seemed very curious to Leopold. *Why? Why would the people of Merina care what happened to the princess? Only her own family would be held from action by the fact that we had a hostage, and they have abdicated! There is nothing more they can do against us, even if they wanted to—* Curious, indeed. Apolon should have been rejoicing in this bloodless victory; Leopold certainly was. *I have seen too much blood, these past years. How long have I been fighting?* Since he was a bare fourteen, surely, and he was twenty-six now. *A bloodless victory is preferable to one bought with death.*

Apolon, who professed to have the best interests of emperor and empire always before him, should have been even happier at the herald's word than Leopold. Instead, he seemed angry, as if he had been denied something choice that he had been promised.

"I would not wager on the dowager living past midnight," the herald said, with a callous shrug of his shoulders. "She collapsed as I left, and was taken up by the healers to the Temple for tending. Surely she cannot live out the week. The word in the Temple was that she is dying. They blamed us for it, of course, but that hardly matters."

"And as for the other two, where could they go? Use some sense, Apolon," the emperor said quellingly. "They are two highborn women alone—perhaps with a few loyal retainers, but no more than that. It is most likely that they are shivering in their palace, waiting for us to march in and take the city. Even if they have the spine to attempt an escape, where could they go, and how could they possibly escape us? We hold the roads and the river, we own the sea; they cannot slip past us, and if they hide themselves in the city, their natures will betray them. We will have them soon enough."

Apolon subsided, but he was still furious; the clenched jaw, the set of his shoulders and the tense line of his back told Leopold as much. It was strange enough to see the emperor's sorcerer worked up over anything; normally he was the most colorless and emotionless man Leopold had ever seen.

Colorless—in the way that a scorpion is colorless, in the way that a viper is colorless, so that it can hide among the weeds until it is ready to strike. Leopold did not like Apolon, nor did he trust the man, although his father scarcely made a move without the sorcerer-scholar's advice. *If I had my way, I'd have him chucked out of this tent and whipped out of the empire as a charlatan. I only wish he* were *a charlatan. Unfortunately, he's quite genuine.* Apolon could—and did—work wonders and perform genuine magics. His powers had turned the day in battle more than once—and when he performed an actual divination, rather than simply acting on information his spies had brought him, he was never wrong about what the immediate future held.

Needless to say, people feared him and avoided his company at all cost. Apolon did not seem to mind; in fact, Leopold had the suspicion he enjoyed his sinister notoriety.

Apolon had never done anything to Leopold directly; he had never even spoken a single disrespectful word to him. But Leopold listened to the whispers in the camp, whispers that spoke of Apolon doing unspeakable things in the dark of the night, of Apolon sending his servants out to the surgeons' tents and taking away wounded men from among the defeated foes—men who were never seen again. Nothing could be proved, but Leopold had been a soldier long enough to tell when there was truth behind the camp tales. The wilder the rumor, the more it was told with relish, the less likely it was to be true. But when a story was retold reluctantly, with a glance over the shoulder to make sure the speaker was not being eavesdropped on—

"I—*we* need those women in custody, Your Majesty," Apolon said tightly. "As soon as possible. If they are allowed to slip through our fingers, they could easily organize a rebellion against you. You would be fighting a war of attrition in the very streets and alleys of this place."

Balthasar waved a hand at him. "Be at peace, I will have them soon enough. If they summon up the courage to attempt escape, which I gravely doubt, their descriptions and habits will be circulated, their acquaintances and allies watched. Apolon, they are *highborn*. How could they ever disguise what they are? If they do not leave the palace—once my men have secured the city, I shall take them into custody. Protective, of course. For their own good. They are only two weak women alone; they will need a strong male hand to guide and protect them from their own hysterical natures."

"Naturally." Apolon mouthed the word, but his grey eyes were colder than ice, and Leopold suppressed a shiver. Everything about the man revolted him, from the grey of his velvet tunic and breeches—too like the color of a shroud—to the precise and fussy trimming of his neat little gray beard, to the very shape of his face, sharp and too angular. The thin lips were somehow greedy instead of ascetic; the broad brow suggestive of cunning, rather than scholasticism. There was nothing to show that Apolon was not the Temple-trained scholar he professed to be—and Leopold was as certain as he was of his own name that Apolon had never set foot in the Temple schools.

Leopold shivered again, and this time he must have moved, for his father's eyes were suddenly upon him, measuring, watching, waiting.

For what?

Leopold had a guess. For the past six years, Balthasar had watched his son for signs of rebellion or ambition, probably assuming that Leopold would happily take any opportunity to seize the imperial crown. Balthasar did not trust anyone, not even his own son.

He trusted me once, but that was before Apolon came.

Apolon's cold gray eyes joined Balthasar's sable ones, both sets of eyes regarding him with cool calculation.

"It seems we will not need you today, Prince," the emperor said with no inflection whatsoever. "Perhaps you should find employment elsewhere for now. We will see to this oath-taking, then leave the city alone to think upon obedience for a day while we send in men to secure it. There may be need for your services later."

A clear dismissal, and Leopold was not loathe to act on it. He rose from the chair with what grace the weight of armor permitted him, and bowed deeply from the waist. "Thank you, Your Highness," he said formally. "I shall inspect the camp, with your permission."

Balthasar nodded, acknowledgment and dismissal in one, and Leopold left the tent, taking advantage of his position and status only in that he did not back out of the tent but walked out with his back to his father. As the tent flap fell down behind him, he felt a palpable relief as those two pairs of eyes left him.

"Inspecting the camp" was a mere excuse for wandering; with no battle in the offing, the men were standing down, relaxing, taking advantage of the easy victory to break out celebratory rations. As he traversed the camp on the way to his own tent, commanders and sub-commanders approached him, asking permission for the men to indulge themselves in this way. Leopold gave it, knowing that the only troops Balthasar would permit in the city today would be his own Elite Guard and his Specials.

Let the men have their wine; there are enough of them who didn't expect to live to drink it. Balthasar would secure the city, but not by flooding it with armed men and frightening the common folk, who, being the most numerous, were the most dangerous. No, he would secure it by sending his Elite Guards in to strike at the top. This was not the first city that had capitulated without a fight, although such easy conquest was the exception, rather than the rule.

Balthasar knew how to place such a city under his complete control in the shortest possible time—by attacking the real heart of such a place, putting the leaders in custody and robbing them of the only weapon they had for resistance: gold. Fat, complacent merchants would never anticipate that. Once the chief citizens were under guard and under control, and any potential leaders neutralized, the city would lie down tamely and show its belly.

Among those secured would be the queen, the princess, and—assuming she was still alive—the dowager queen.

Somehow that left a bitter taste in Leopold's mouth. *One does not make war on women. . . .*

Leopold clasped his hands behind his back and ambled through the camp, noting that there was no sign of laxness or disorder anywhere—which was just as it should be. The tiny two-man tents shared by the common soldiers were laid out in proper, neat rows, gear that was waterproof stacked in an orderly manner at the mouth of each. Each unit had a fire beside the tent of its sergeant; each company had a cook tent and a larger fire about which they were now gathering, as word of "permission to celebrate" spread.

All was as it should be. Which meant that, as usual when there was no actual fighting going on, Leopold had nothing to do.

Balthasar at fifty looked and acted as healthy and vigorous as any warrior of half his age. It was entirely possible that he would live to be a hundred, and remain alert and in complete control to the last.

And where did that leave Leopold?

As usual. With nothing to do. Running the emperor's errands, but given no real authority. At one point there had been talk of a marriage for the sake of alliance, but no longer. Balthasar did not want to risk the birth of yet another claimant to his throne, so Leopold was denied even the faint comfort of a wife, children, a home life. Balthasar would not risk having his son out of his sight, lest he begin plotting.

Leopold clasped his hands tightly across the small of his back to avoid showing any sign of his frustration. He *must* maintain his passive facade at all costs. He was no fool; he knew he was constantly being watched. He must appear as he always appeared: a simple man, a warrior with no ambition to rule, a fighter with no interests off the battlefield.

That was the only way to survive, for although he was his father's only heir, Balthasar did not need him *here*. Balthasar could have him sent away under genteel, but obdurate, guard, to spend his life in idle captivity. That was the only possible alternative to having Leopold under his own supervision.

If I thought that I was bored now. . . .

But Leopold was wiser than that. And for all of that, he admired his father and wished for Balthasar's approval with a desperation that at times seemed absurd even to himself. Before Apolon—

Father was a true father to me. I believe—I believe he cared for me, loved me, in his own way. He was a stern taskmaster—but not the way he is now.

The times that Balthasar smiled upon his son, or even praised him, made all the rest of it worthwhile. Somewhere inside the emperor was the man who had taken time from important state dinners to tell his son bedtime stories, and see to it that the demons lurking under the bed and in the wardrobe knew they would face the emperor's sword if they so much as troubled the dreams of his son.

Someday, he may remember that. Someday, he may realize that I have not changed.

Leopold longed for that day as he longed for little else.

And in the meantime, Leopold tried to prove he was worthy of trust by being steadfast and trustworthy, hoping for the day when his father would finally realize how much his son cared. . . .

§ 12 §

LYDANA

A slight sound brought her to look over her shoulder, her hand going to the one weapon she had allowed herself, her skirt-knife.

The small shadow of Skirta—Eel (she *must* think of her companion by the name the streets had given him—her) tumbled through.

"The herald comes—he goes to the Heart. Those of the town are crowding in—"

Matild bit her lip and let the string of prayer beads slip into the basket. Then as swiftly as she drew breath, she made her decision. It might be a chancy one, but she felt this was something she must do. She snapped shut the basket.

"We, too, shall watch this oathing." She moved toward the hidden door, basket on one arm. Eel gave a swift nod. They found their way through the inner passages until again they came to that hidden entrance which let out upon the canal. The skiff was gone, so Thom and Shelyra had followed her orders.

However, there was a narrow, slippery footpath which they followed with care until they came to a set of water-worn steps leading upward. Matild had been aware ever since they had come into the open of the pulsing roar of the city. It would seem that all those who lived within

Merina's walls and canals were pressing on toward the Great Temple. The crowd was so dense she did not believe they could even push into it.

There was anger in those raised voices, and the sharp scent of fear hung over the throng. She could see women holding their children close, and some were weeping as they stumbled along.

Already there were those ready to marshal them, but not the soldiers pictured so often in representations she had seen of the emperor's forces. These were men dressed all in black, so they stood out against the motley-colored crowd. And they had staffs which they used to prod and guide the townspeople as a drover would move his kine.

"In with you—" Matild felt the push of one of those staffs and looked around in anger. Catching the cold eyes of the drover, she dropped her own and started on, holding close her basket lest the pressure of those about her tear it out of her clasp. Eel had disappeared, and she must leave—*him*—to his own chances now.

Large as the Great Temple was, it could not begin to contain a fraction of the crowd which had been pressed toward it by the time Matild arrived. There was no hope of seeing what was going on beyond those doors. But the crowd was not stilled. Instead, words, bits of sentences, flew from mouth to ear and then from mouth again.

"She must be dead—the Reverend One!"

A stout guildsman before her roared that into the ear of what was plainly his wife.

"They killed her—" the woman's voice shrilled up, and Matild saw how viciously tight her husband's hold on her arm became.

"Shut your mouth, fool." He was looking fervidly over his shoulder at the nearest of those black staff men. Apparently the fellow had taken no notice, but was looking in the opposite direction.

The crowds behind Matild were forced apart, not by staff-holders now, but by armed troopers, their horses nervous and hard to handle due to the packed people.

Between this escort rode another man. He was, by his

clothing, no officer, perhaps not even a noble; rather he had the loose robe of a Temple man, save that this bore no holy symbol on back or breast and was of a dull, dead, earth-gray velvet. The robe was cowled, and he had pulled that up over his head in a manner to mask his face.

Apolon! As if that name had been shouted aloud, Matild knew it was so. She wanted to see more of him than just an untidy bundle of somewhat anonymous robe, perched unhandedly on the back of a wild-eyed horse, but there was no chance. Already the small procession had pushed by her, heading to the Great Temple.

The passing of the man and his small escort seemed to silence the crowd. They pushed back of their own accord now, leaving as much room free as they might. Then the small group of riders had reached the foot of the Great Temple steps. To Matild's surprise, the man made no move to dismount. The cowled head raised and turned a fraction back and forth as if he were taking in every detail of the building and impressing it firmly on his memory. He was still engrossed in that study when there came a great blast of sound from the interior of the building.

Those about Matild found their voices. "The oath is given," they told one another. There was something of relief in their faces, but it did not banish the underlying fear. However, the crowd began to break apart, and the staff-men were falling back to form a company of their own.

Matild hitched her basket higher on her hip. So, at least for now, Merina was safe from the sacking given a conquered country. Adele—had her mother been wrong in her diagnosis of her own condition? Was she indeed dead? No, Matild drew a deep breath—in this much she would hold to hope—when one of the women of the Tiger entered the Great Gate all those of the blood knew it. Adele was alive, doubtless playing her own role. As Matild must begin hers.

Pushing her way through the crowd at what seemed its weakest point, Matild headed for her own bolt hole.

❧ 13 ❧

ADELE

The Dowager Queen Adele lay in the Temple infirmary, listening to the healers report on her condition to a hastily summoned Archpriestess Verit. Although they tried to keep their voices low, a few words were audible to the old woman.

"—her heart gives out and her lungs fill with fluid. Perhaps if we were to bleed her—"

"No!" Adele interrupted sharply. *Damn. I must remember that I am supposed to be dying. That sounded far too lively.* She continued, remembering to gasp for breath at appropriate intervals, "If my time has come, I will not struggle against the Goddess' will."

Ignoring the horrified looks of the healers, she fixed her eyes on Verit. "Reverend One, will you hear my confession?"

That was a clear signal to Verit that she wanted to talk, and the archpriestess took it as such.

The archpriestess nodded and sent everyone else from the room, including the infirmarian, who was ordered to guard their privacy from the end of the hallway. Adele gave silent thanks for the custom of absolute secrecy of the confessional. It might save lives in the days to come, as well as souls.

When they were alone, Verit pulled a stool to the side

of the bed, sat down, and looked at her sharply. "All right, enough of this mummery. I assume that you are not dying. How sick are you really?"

"Not very," Adele admitted, feeling a little like a naughty child who was feigning illness to avoid the schoolmaster. "I ate some berries this morning that I usually avoid because they make me ill this way. All I have to do is rest and I'll be well enough by the first of the night rituals. And I'm supposed to be in retreat in my room until then anyway."

"Gemen Elfrida is," Verit agreed. "And the Dowager Queen Adele?"

"Will be dead of heart failure within a few hours, if necessary," Adele said calmly. "Can you organize the effigy for the lying-in-state?"

"Easily," Verit replied. "You are not the only one the angels speak to, my daughter. The effigy has been ready for over a week. And I shall see to it that everyone involved thinks someone else took care of disposing of the body." Then she frowned. "But I think we should wait for a day or two at the very least."

"Why?" Adele asked more sharply than she intended. She did not *want* to be anyone other than Gemen Elfrida anymore! She wanted the double life to be at an end!

Verit shrugged. "Just a feeling. Or rather, something of a premonition, though nothing as concrete as a Seeing or a Visitation. Once we've killed you, we can hardly bring you back to life, so let's wait until we are certain that you are no longer needed."

Adele frowned, still not certain she wanted to stay "alive" and possibly within the emperor's reach. What if he decided to send soldiers into the Temple after her, under the guise of "taking her to his own healers"? She wasn't in sanctuary, technically—he could do that if he chose. "I can't think of anything I've left undone, but I suppose it can do no harm to drag out my last illness. . . ."

"Good." Verit stood up, crossed to a cupboard against the wall, and took out a spare set of grey robes. "Let's get about our business. Can you stand?"

Adele sat up, swung her legs over the side of the bed, waited for the ensuing coughing fit to subside, and stood. With Verit's help she changed into the robes, then sat on the stool while Verit quickly tucked additional extra clothing and bedding into Adele's discarded robes, and rolled one into a ball to resemble a head. As if she had done this any number of times before, Verit arranged the "body" on its side on the bed, facing the wall, and covered most of it with a blanket.

Adele watched her with complete astonishment. *My, my. One wonders about Verit's misspent youth! And why she learned this particular skill! Was she inclined to go roaming out in the evening without her parents' permission?*

Both women surveyed the results critically. In the flickering light from a single candle, it looked quite genuine. The moving light gave it the illusion of breathing.

"It will do," Verit decided. "The infirmarian will make certain that no one gets a close look. What else must we do now?"

"The emperor has a dark mage with him, a man called Apolon," Gemen Elfrida informed her. "We believe that he wants the Heart, or at least some access to the power within it." Even as she said it, she felt the same chill of fear she had experienced the first time she understood Apolon's threat.

Verit's crossed hands moved quickly to her own heart, and Elfrida automatically echoed the gesture.

"Indeed," Elfrida agreed, seconding the archpriestess' horror at that suggestion. "I do not think that Balthasar will move openly against the Temple—his herald did take the oath, did he not?"

Verit nodded. "I witnessed it just before I came to you."

"Good," Elfrida replied. "I expect both Balthasar and Apolon to search for Lydana and Shelyra, but I don't expect them to find what they seek. The women of our house have skills that the emperor does not expect from the highborn."

"What can we do to help them?" Verit asked hesitantly,

as if she was now out of her element entirely. "Can we do anything at all?"

"First, pray for them," Gemen Elfrida said firmly. For all of Verit's ability as archpriestess, she sometimes seemed a bit lost when it came to dealing with those of the common world. "They have chosen paths much more difficult than mine."

"Don't be too certain of that," Verit advised her. "*You* start work as a Flame in three days."

Elfrida raised her eyebrows, startled, then smiled with a certain sense of anticipation. "It's certainly time for that," she agreed, feeling a touch of cheer amid the heavy thoughts that this entire, horrible day had brought.

The Flames were small groups of both men and woman drawn from the Gemen of the four orders: Grey Robes, Brown Robes, Red Robes, and Yellow Robes. They were the ones with high levels of magical ability, the ones who performed the more difficult and secret rituals of the Temple. Elfrida would have been one a year ago had she not been leading her double life. Now her life would be a single one—and the one she would have chosen in the first place, had her duties and heart not been so divided.

"There are two other things we must do for them, and two things we must do for us and for the protection of the Heart," she continued.

"And these are?" Verit asked, as if their positions had been reversed.

Well, in a way, they have been. Verit knows everything there is to know about the Inner Paths—but I am the one who has been walking in the mundane world. I think she entered the Temple as a Novice the very day she was permitted to, and has not looked back since.

"Lydana wishes to use the third confessional to the right of the Heart to pass messages, so we will need to have someone absolutely trustworthy there during the hours of confession." She thought for a moment. "I'll do it myself as much as I can, but I can't be there all the time. I'll need someone else to take my place if I have to be elsewhere. The meditation chapel at the end of the middle passage will also have to have trustworthy people in it at all times, day and night. I think Lydana might know about the middle passage, and I *know* that Shelyra does. They might need to use it. I would suggest at least two people, and three would be even better."

"We'll need to stock extra robes in the colors of each order in the passage, so that if one of your kin comes through, we can disguise them to blend in with the Gemen," Verit added with a nod. "It shall be done. What do you recommend we do for the protection of the Heart?"

She had thought about the possibility that Apolon had infiltrated spies among the Novices. "Divide the orders into four groups and stagger the hours of our rituals, so that they go on day and night, so that the Heart is never less than well-guarded."

Verit nodded, and Elfrida continued, "If Apolon is going to plant spies—and I'm sure he is—they will have to be among our newer members. I wouldn't be certain of anyone in the Novitiate. . . ."

"Lady Bright!" Verit exclaimed with shock. "But some of them have been here almost a year!"

"And how long do you think the emperor's spies have been in Merina?" Elfrida countered. "My guess is, at least that long. I doubt that he could have gotten anyone into the orders, but the Novices?" She shrugged. "We always have a few whose vocations seem less than firm. They *could* be his."

Verit nodded unhappily. "We can use the vigil, and then the funeral and period of mourning for the Dowager Queen Adele as an excuse to delay final vows—at least for a time. Then—well, we'll have to see what events arise and make use of them. But I feel sorry for the Novices who are genuine. It seems a pity to punish them along with the false ones."

"Good." Gemen Elfrida nodded briskly. "If I might make a suggestion, Reverend Mother, the members of the Novitiate should be kept together and well supervised."

"Quite," the archpriestess agreed. "What about the

ones in the Houses of the Healers? They are scattered all over the city."

She'd considered that as well. "Bring all the Novices to the Temple for safety."

"Theirs," Verit asked dryly, "or ours?"

"Both," Elfrida replied as her earlier cheer faded. She was beginning to feel very like a general marshaling his forces for a long and costly battle—and it was a sobering feeling. "Apolon—and any other servants of the Dark with him—will seek out the youngest and weakest among us as their first prey. We do not want them to draw any additional power from our people. And we don't want him to take any of them for his own perversions."

Verit shuddered as she considered this. "I will order the Novices to the Temple at once," she said. "And I will send a letter to all of the houses, reminding them of the need to be especially vigilant in prayer during these times of change."

"Tactfully expressed." Gemen Elfrida smiled wryly. "I believe that covers everything we need to do at this moment. I'd best get back to my room before I'm seen out of it."

"Can you make it on your own?" Verit asked in concern.

Elfrida stood slowly and smoothed her veil. "Yes. I'm feeling much better now. And these robes were designed to make each Grey Robe look like every other Grey Robe."

"True," Verit agreed, "which is why we all look at faces, not clothing."

"I'll make certain that no one sees my face," Elfrida promised.

ৡ 14 ৡ

LYDANA

The crowd was a barrier through which it was hard to push her way, but she made good use of the basket for protection. However, as she approached the meaner quarters of the town, the mass of people thinned. Those who would prey upon the crowds, the cutpurses and the like, were ably busied, she thought, near the Great Temple. But what did disturb her was the fact that nowhere had she seen a law-keeper in his distinctive grey-and-green surcoat. Those meant for the protection of Merina and its citizens appeared to have vanished during the last few hours into which she herself had packed so much.

It was late afternoon when she made her way over the last of the canal bridges and came into the section of town Matild knew. Now and again she was hailed by people the beadswoman recognized—a woman from her doorstep, a small shopkeeper fastening up, hours early, the street shutters of his workplace.

There was poverty in Merina, as in all cities, though there was also work—if hard and demanding—for any able-bodied man or woman. And the number of beggars was, she had always believed, less than in some of the greater cities—say Arkanade, the emperor's own famed capital.

She answered questions with no more than a repetition

of such rumors as had been quickly born in the crowd. But there was a strange feeling in this crooked street leading to the tiny court in which her own shop was set. As she went, there was suddenly a quick closing of doors, a disappearance of those who had been well in sight ahead. She felt a shiver between her shoulder blades. It was plain that there was something or someone behind who was better not faced. All of the shops were closed, even those selling lamp oil and the few things which might be needed in the coming night hours, and which usually stood open beyond moonrise.

She listened. It was quiet enough that she could hear the scuff of her own boots, but now she could hear something else—a more resolute tread, the trained rhythm of an armsman. However, she held to her cloak of innocence and did not look behind, though her faint worry concerning Eel was becoming stronger.

Matild reached the darkened niche of the small court which was her goal, and brought out from her girdle the long-shanked key which she fitted into the door now well shadowed as twilight began to draw in.

This part of Merina was very old. Though the guilds strove to keep the city in good order, passing resolutions that required of every householder his or her dwelling be kept in repair, the shabbiness of years hung heavy here.

As she turned her key and set a shoulder to the stubborn door (which always resisted the first opening push) Matild dared at last to look behind. She could no longer hear the cadence of those footsteps, but there were indeed two men in the street, and they were standing at the very entrance to her court, their eyes upon her.

Even if they had not worn their dull black there was no mistaking their breed. They were law-keepers—of a sort— though whose laws they kept might be questioned. Balthasar had not sent squads of soldiers to patrol his newly acquired city. These men were not of the army. Yet he had held them ready—pushed them into action even as Merina surrendered. And Matild did not care for the look of them at all.

"Dame—" One of them had raised his voice as he walked toward her. "Is this your household?" His glance at the door and the single, narrow shuttered window flanking it held little approval.

"I be Matild Rankisdaughter, licensed beadseller." Matild allowed herself a sniff. It was not in her to cower, and she had long since learned that to meet insolence with a strong tongue was often the best defense.

He was close enough now to strike at her, as she half-thought he might, thus proving his importance to all now peering through shutter cracks who might need to be impressed by his dominance.

"And where have you been, dame?" His voice was even, and he was watching her intently. She felt that gaze as if his hands were searching her body, somehow reaching into her very head to grip her thoughts.

"With all the city—a-seein' what the emperor's man did at the oathin'."

"How many in your household?" He switched to another subject.

Matild set down her basket and put her hands on her hips, facing him squarely.

"Them as asks questions have some need for the knowin'. What be yours, black man?"

"Watch your tongue, dame. We are the new ward watchmen and you will not find us easy to cozen. Each and every household is to be listed and there will be rules posted. Not to abide by them will bring you such trouble as you cannot think on. Now—who abides herein?" He gestured toward the now partly open door.

"Me an' my poor dear sister's son, the lad Eel. Look for yourself, if you will, you shall find no other—" She nearly held her breath—what if this prying fellow was to get inside? There was evidence that the cramped quarters had not been in use of late, and that would give her away at once.

However, it seemed that fortune was going to favor her. He gave a slight shrug and turned away. But she was well aware that, after the fashion of law-keepers, he had marked her well and she would have to be very careful in her comings and goings.

Now she caught up her basket and swirled wide her petticoats as she went within, closing the door carefully, though, not with a slam. It was very dark, but her hand went to the shelf on which stood the dusty candle and she clicked the snapfire against its wick.

The room ahead of her was long and narrow. To her right by the shuttered window was the folded down half-table which she could use to display wares when the shop was open. There were two stools nearby.

However, it was toward the far end she made her way now. There was her cookplace, a cupboard, a table, and three more stools. And a waiting lamp which she lit from the candle. Matild sniffed. Mice, certainly mice—and the fust of a room kept closed. It needed a good sweeping out.

Against the wall was what seemed to be another long cupboard. Matild pulled this open with a jerk hard enough to loosen the swollen wood and surveyed the pile of cov-erlets within. Those must be warmed before the fire, and dusting of herbs made, before anyone intended to sleep there.

Food would be important, also. She had planned to go to Berta the Baker and Goodwife Lanny, who dealt in cheese. But if that black bird of ill omen was still watching in the street, she could not do so. He would well wonder why a housewife's shelves were not better supplied.

The bead coils and box she dumped into the long drawer beside the sales table and then returned to the basket. They had eaten heartily of the supplies before they had left the palace. She set out, with a sigh, what was left. It would have to do for the night.

More important than food for the moment was her com-panion in disguise. She trusted Eel/Skita with a good sup-ply of prudence, but if those black coats had already worked their way this far into the corners of the old city, it might take more than all of the girl's skill to pass un-noted. There was, of course, the other route.

Matild pushed back the table and dragged one of the stools into its place. Balanced on that, she reached above her into the shadows, which hung as thick as curtains, sweeping spread fingers back and forth until she found a length of dangling chain. Taking a good grip on that, she pulled down as if she were ringing a bell.

As with the door, the ancient wood resisted. Then came a shifting of dust, which made Matild spit out a rude word or two, and a dim square of light opened overhead. She had been right, and just in time, for now she could hear a scrabbling above and then a slim young body squeezed through. Matild caught it about the hips and lowered it to the floor before she attacked the chain again; this time with a different, sidewise, pull, which creakingly closed the aperture over their heads.

Eel crouched where he/she had hit the floor, breathing heavily. From the begrimed face round eyes stared up at the woman.

"Watchers." The word was hoarse.

Matild had stepped from the stool. Now she stiffened. "Here?" she demanded.

Eel made a quick gesture, signifying what might lie beyond all the walls about them.

Matild poured a portion of their watered wine into a small horn cup. The other drank and then choked before sipping more cautiously a second time.

"They came—out of nowhere—the ground maybe." He grimaced over the rim of the cup. "They—they must have been within the walls even before the herald."

Matild caught her lower lip between her teeth. Yes, they had known that the emperor had had his spies in Merina. That only made common sense. But they had expected an inroad of troops to be quartered at strategic places as was the custom—not these black coats. They must have been here long enough to know the city. She sank down on the stool on which she had lately stood. How long—how well? The plans, half-plans, various devices she had held in mind when she had left the palace—were they all endangered before she could even start?

Eel felt within the folds of the tattered oversmock he wore and held out to Matild what might have been a nut left from last season's gathering. The woman caught it quickly, using her thumbnail to pry apart an invisible seam. What lay within was a button earring, the head of a groshwak finely wrought, with a fierce blue eye of fine sapphire. Shelyra's!

Then at least Thom had done his duty; the girl was safe for the present. Though with these black ones about . . . She would have to trust Thom. His famous feats of thievery had always hinted that he had near-invincible powers. If that would only work for the two of them until matters settled a bit, she could perhaps understand this new problem and perhaps find a counter to it!

She was still thinking as she motioned to Eel to eat, allowing her companion to finish before she began questioning all that the other had observed since they had been separated by the crowd.

The black men were not only to be seen on the city streets but in skiffs on the canals. Eel had watched them being stationed at the doors of the principle guild masters, but none of Balthasar's soldiers had entered the city. The rumors were that the new ruler of Merina remain encamped with his army beyond.

Now—Matild drew a deep breath which was close to a sigh—it was wait and see until they could learn more, though she felt her nerves grow ragged as she refused herself action. In the meantime, she would carry on her life here as she had long ago designed it.

She had thought that she was too overwrought, her thoughts too pressing, to find sleep. However, once she and Eel were stowed away in the cupboard bed sleep did come, deep and dreamless.

❧ 15 ❧

SHELYRA

If Thom had expected her to sit in the stern of the skiff and be punted along the canal like a wealthy woman in her private boat, he was probably very much surprised when Shelyra did nothing of the sort. She hopped into the tethered skiff as nimbly as he and took the second pole only a fraction of a second after he picked up the first. *She* was the one who cast off, as well, and she was the one who poled them away from the bank of the canal and out of the sheltered and hidden little mooring where the skiff had been concealed. It was just as well that this part of the canals was in shadow all the day long and had no street running beside it; there was no one to be startled by their sudden appearance.

"Where are we going?" he asked finally, and with visible reluctance.

"As I said before, the Gypsy Quarter," she replied promptly, then with heavy irony, "I trust you know how to get there?"

His only reply was a snort as he dug in his pole. She did the same, but wished she had been able to take the time to kilt her skirts up above her knees; it would have made poling much easier.

But then, suddenly, as they eased into another canal with a footpath beside it, she felt a coldness on the back of her neck, as if something or someone was watching her with ill intent.

She did not turn to look immediately. Instead, she put her back into the poling, concentrating on the feel of the smooth pole in her hands, matching Thom stroke for stroke, until the motion of poling brought her eyes around naturally to study the banks of the canal on either side and behind them.

There were many folk hurrying along the footpath, which was unusual, since people normally sauntered down the canals, taking their time, enjoying the sun on the water, even if the water was not the cleanest. There was an air of fear about them that made the hair stand up on the back of Shelyra's neck. But there was one man who was not moving at all, and that was the one who made her bite her lip and turn deliberately away from him before she could meet his eyes.

He stood beside a mooring pole and wore a livery of sorts, all black, with no crest or badge, and he carried a staff. Somehow she *knew* he was one of Balthasar's men—and she knew he had noted her and her companion, although he had not confronted them. Now she was glad she had gone to some extreme with her appearance, for there was nothing in Raymonda the Gypsy dancer to suggest Shelyra, Designated Daughter of the House of the Tiger.

But it was something of a shock to see the emperor's men out on the streets even before the ink was dry upon the documents of surrender.

"Pole," she muttered to Thom. "And look purposeful, as if you're on an errand. We're being watched."

Again there came a snort. "Tell me something I don't know," Thom retorted. "I hope you've got your bolt hole well prepared. I do not like these strange birds with their black feathers. I feel like a worm being watched by hungry crows. I want to crawl into your hiding place and pull the entrance in after me."

After feeling those eyes on her, Shelyra—*Raymonda*—felt the same. She changed the subject hastily to avoid revealing her fear to him. "We must have our tale straight before we get there. I am Raymonda, and you are my— what? What is Thom to Raymonda?"

"Your lover?" The saucy and confident tone of his voice implied that she would leap at that suggestion, and the assumption made her bristle.

"My cousin; near enough relation that you could not be my lover, but less suspect than a brother, since we look nothing alike." She made her own tone firm as she punctuated her sentence with thrusts of the pole. "And you would still have reason to want to protect my—ah—virtue."

A grunt suggested that Thom was less than pleased with that scenario, but he would accept it for now. And that he honestly expected her to fling herself into his arms— once she came to her senses.

You haven't the morals of a he-cat, Thom Talesmith, and I would not let you near my bed if you were the only unwedded man in all of Merina. Among the many legends of her companion was the litany of his many lovers. She did not intend to give him the slightest opportunity to add her name to that litany.

They were poling in the opposite direction from the Great Temple; most people seemed to be streaming away from there. The emperor's herald must have made his oath, then; most of those afoot kept their heads down and faces hidden, but the expressions Shelyra caught were not happy ones. She wished she knew what rumors were running about the streets.

There were more of the black-clad staff-wielders along the canals, and she was mortally glad when there were more boats on the water to keep them company, from tiny skiffs to larger cargo vessels. They were no longer so conspicuous in such company.

Poling the skiff was hard work, even for someone accustomed to controlling a restive stallion and sharing out the work of poling similar vessels along the streams of the land surrounding the Summer Palace. But Thom was less used to this sort of hard labor than she, and she felt a smile of amusement cross her lips for a fleeting moment as she realized that *he* was slowing the pace, resting more often than he poled. Out of pity for him, she slackened her own pace and let the sluggish current of the canal take over some of the work.

Not so bold now, Thom Talesmith? Of course not, there's no notoriety to be had in honest labor.

What traffic moved on the canals now seemed to be heading quickly into safety, which was indeed odd for so early in the day. This was not a good sign; people's instincts were urging them to shelter, and she trusted those instincts. *We should have fought!* she thought rebelliously. *Nothing will hold the emperor to his promise but his own honor—and what kind of honor does a butcher have? He will loot us at his leisure, instead of all at once, and kill the city by inches. Better that Merina went to her death in flames!*

For every moment they were out in the open, she felt exposed. Horribly, terribly exposed, and very vulnerable. The time it took to reach the quarter stretched into an eternity of nerves, and she was quite certain that not all of the sweat drenching Thom's shirt was due to the work. The canals were as wide as two ordinary streets set side by side, so that swifter-moving craft could pass slower ones. Beyond the banks and mooring posts were paved footpaths, and beyond them, shops and homes, two and three stories tall and crowded so closely together that you could not send a cat between them. Bridges arched at intervals above the canal, and on every bridge there seemed to be a black-clad watcher.

I must think of myself as Raymonda, act and react as Raymonda, she reminded herself. *Shelyra is a royal lady; I am only a dancer, of no importance to anyone, insignificant. I cannot, dare not, challenge the authorities; I am the kind of woman who could easily "disappear" without anyone noticing, and Raymonda would know that with her bones.*

Finally, at long last, they reached the Gypsy Quarter; the street beside the canal was much broader here, and there were horses everywhere—horses being led, driven, ridden, horses of every size, shape, and color. There were many women dressed as Raymonda was dressed, and she began to feel less conspicuous, though no less vulnerable.

Unfortunately, there were staff-men here, too. And there was only a single common mooring place for tiny skiffs like their own. Predictably, there was a staff-man waiting there, watching all people who brought a boat in to moor, and stopping them for questioning before allowing them to go on.

Raymonda felt sweat breaking out along her brow and under her arms. They bumped the nose of the skiff up to the stone of the mooring, and Thom got out to tie it up beneath the black-clad watcher's suspicious gaze. She stowed the two poles carefully in the skiff itself, doing her best not to meet the man's eyes.

"You, there! You—you and the wench!" The man took three belligerent steps toward them as she stepped out of the boat and barred their way with his staff. "What business have you here? Where are you going? What are you planning to do here? Do you live in this quarter?"

She was glad now that she had left the remains of her dress in the secret room, and gladder that she had already brought everything that she thought she would need to her several caches. There was nothing more incriminating on her person than a few coins in her belt pouch—although she wished she'd had some way to color her hair before she left her shelter. There *were* light-haired Gypsies, but not many. Were the emperor's agents already looking for her? Had she been missed?

Thom stuck his hands in his pockets and looked up at the man with a mildly bemused expression. "That's a fair passle of questions, lad," he drawled. "A man hardly knows where to start." Thom scratched his brow and looked amiably perplexed. "In fact, all those questions have just jumbled themselves up together in my head! I can't remember a one of them!"

"Start with where you're going and what business you

have there." The man's hard, cold eyes showed no trace of amusement at Thom's casual manner, nor at his convincing imitation of a slow-witted fool.

"Horse trader by the name of Gordo Kaldash is where we're going," Thom told him, still wearing that beguiling and cheerful smile. "We live there, me an' my cousin."

"Cousin, is it?" The man's eyes raked Raymonda head to heel, and she suppressed the urge to box his ears for his insolence. "You don't look anything alike."

"Same could be said of some brothers and sisters, lad," came Thom's ready answer. Then his voice hardened. "She's kin enough to me that I don't let anyone mess with her."

The man's cruel chuckle made shivers run up Raymonda's spine, and she felt through her skirts for one of her knives, no longer wanting to box the questioner's ears. Was he going to start something? How many more of his kind could he call up, if he decided they were lowly and helpless enough that their disappearance wouldn't cause awkward questions?

But Thom whistled shrilly through his teeth, a call that Raymonda recognized with a start—and in the blink of an eye, there were thirty men, all of the lean, saturnine breed of the Horse Lords, clustered behind the man with the staff.

"Eh, jo, something wrong?" asked one loudly. "This *gajo* fellow think you don't belong here or something?"

The man with the staff started—clearly he had not heard the Horse clansmen materializing out of the streets and alleys behind him. His expression froze, and he turned quickly. His eyes widened for a moment as he realized he was outnumbered. People of the Horse Lords generally bore no arms other than their long knives—but they generally didn't *need* to. Those long knives, combined with the special training that Horse Lord clansfolk had in close fighting, made a knife as formidable as a sword. The Horse Lords were distinguished from the Gypsies with whom they shared this quarter by their dress: leather, every bit of it, from side-laced boots, to tight-fitting trews, to long-sleeved leather tunics laced at the neck and the wrists. The lacings at the neck were usually left open to display their clan medallions. The women of the Horse Lords dressed in the same clothing as the men, occasionally varying the trews with knee-length split skirts.

The Horse clansmen surrounded the black-clad stranger, hands resting lightly on the hilts of their knives. Still, the staff-man stood his ground. "You know these people?" he demanded. "Are they registered here?"

Raymonda scanned the crowd and, with a leap of her heart, saw a familiar face. "Laika!" she called. "Tell this—*man*—that we live here! He seems to think Horse People and Gypsies couldn't pole a boat without falling into the canal!"

A hearty, and taunting, laugh rose from the throats of those gathered here, and Laika stepped forward from the rest of his fellows. "*I* know these two, they live back of Gordo's stables," he said arrogantly, staring down his nose at the staff-man and daring him to contradict him. "Girl does a bit of horse-doctoring, a bit of dancing; her cousin does as little as he can get away with."

Another guffaw arose from the group as Thom's head came up indignantly. But the man in black reluctantly raised his staff to let them past. Raymonda shot past him, Thom proceeding at a more leisurely pace.

"You tell this Gordo he had better get the names of everyone living on his property to the authorities!" the man shouted after them in frustration as the crowd closed protectively about them. "That's the law! From now on, the only people let into this quarter after sunset will be the ones registered to live here!"

"And we're the Horse People, and we move where the wind blows!" someone shouted back. "Why don't you go get the name of the wind and all the little breezes while you're at it?"

Leaving the disgruntled guard quickly behind them, the crowd hustled Thom and Raymonda into the maze of streets that was the Gypsy Quarter and out of the man's sight. Once there, most of their saviors melted into the streets as quickly as they had assembled, leaving behind only Laika and a man Raymonda did not recognize.

But Thom did. That much was plain as the two of them eyed each other and grins spread across their faces. The stranger spoke first.

"I told the girls not to rub ashes in their hair until we'd seen the body, you son of a dog!" the man crowed. "Thom, you slippery snake, you dog-fox, you got away from the queen's own lockup!"

He flung himself at Thom, who met his back-pounding embrace without even a touch of embarrassment. "Didn't I tell you I have more lives than a cat, and more luck than Evan the Quick?" Thom retorted, with some back-pounding of his own. "Don't any of you believe me, even yet?"

"Oh, *I* do, but—" The stranger pulled away. "So, who's the dancer? Another one of your—"

"Not likely, Pouli," Laika said quietly. "I know this one, and I think maybe it wasn't Thom Talesmith's cleverness or his luck that got his neck out of the noose this time." He glanced around at the seemingly empty street and frowned. "But this isn't the place. Let's get to Gordo's, then we'll talk." He looked for confirmation to Raymonda, who nodded. "We'll leave our brothers to watch the docks for more strays from the herd while we get these two into safe stabling, eh?"

"Good enough," Pouli replied agreeably.

The four of them hurried along the dark, narrow, twisting streets as quickly as they could without breaking into a run. On the whole Raymonda was pleased to see Laika, even though he was one of the three people in the city who knew that Raymonda the horse-healer and dancer and Shelyra the princess were the same person. The other two were Gordo and his clan lord, who had stood sponsor to Shelyra when the clans adopted her. This wasn't the same as swearing a blood-oath, as Thom apparently had done, despite her doubts as to the truth of his tale.

She was now Horse-blood, as her children and children's children would be. He was still an outsider, though an ally. *She* was a full member of the clan, entitled to the protection and help of anyone in the clans. And if the queen had known about *that*, she would have had a litter of kittens on the spot. Thom could claim help only from those he had directly sworn oath to.

Gordo Kaldash had further fortified this compound of his own, surrounded by the high wall that contained his horse yard and all of the buildings therein. There were four strong men of the Horse clans standing watch outside the front gate, which for the first time in Raymonda's memory was closed.

Somehow I don't think the Horse Lords plan to have much commerce with the emperor. He must have done something to offend them. Good. That just makes my job easier. One of the men, recognizing their escorts, knocked on the closed gate as they hurried toward him across the cobblestones. Raymonda heard the banging and thudding that indicated a bar was being lifted out of its supports across the gate, then the gate itself opened the merest crack, just enough to let the four of them through.

Raymonda slipped inside first, followed by the rest. As soon as they were all inside, the two women on the other side of the gate lifted the bar back into place, sealing the gate shut.

"All right," Laika said as soon as they were inside, standing in the courtyard where, in better days, Gordo had his stock paraded in front of prospective buyers. "We know that the queen abdicated. Balthasar's herald swore oaths binding the emperor to leave the city in peace, but nothing prevents him from squeezing it dry and putting his heel on the head of every man, woman, and child here, and that's what he's doing. He's putting a tax of half the value on every horse Gordo has, and he *tried* to send more of those black-liveried flunkies to carry Gordo off."

Raymonda felt her lips curving in the first real smile

she'd had this day. "I take it that since he's still here, Gordo's wee black doggies objected to having their master taken away?" she said lightly.

"The little pups might have nibbled at one or two, and they might have growled a bit," Laika admitted.

Raymonda laughed. Gordo's "wee black doggies" were a pack of black wolfhounds, each the size of a smallish pony. It would take killing those dogs to extract the Gypsy horse dealer from his home without his consent, and apparently the emperor's men weren't prepared to do that yet.

But she stopped laughing abruptly as she considered the rest of her friend's words. "Does Gordo have that kind of tax money? Would the emperor confiscate stock to make up for it?"

Laika shrugged. "No—but we're about to have an outbreak of spavins, thrush, and foundering. By the time the doctors in the stable are through, those horses won't be worth the time it takes to kill them. That will lower the value of the ones he has left to nothing, which means the tax will be a few coppers at most, now that he's sent the good stock out of the city." He eyed her speculatively. "They could use you back there, if you know any of the tricks of the trade."

She met his eyes. "I know them," she replied stoutly. "And maybe a few more. But what's the rest of the word from the city? You're holding something back from me."

Laika's mouth twitched. "Rumor is the dowager queen is dead—and that they killed her."

"She's like a twisty alley-cat—don't rub the ashes of mourning into your hair until you've seen the coffin and I've sworn she's in it," Raymonda said steadily, although her heart skipped a few beats. "But meanwhile—put black ribbons on the ponies for show and withered branches on the front gate. The dowager queen was your ally, remember. It will look odd if you don't mourn her, even if it's only a rumor."

Laika nodded briskly. "I'll do that," he said. "And mean-

while—you go back of the stables with your 'cousin' while
I tell Gordo you're here."

Before she had a chance to respond, he was off. She
shrugged philosophically and turned toward Thom and his
own friend, both of whom had been listening to the conversation with interest.

"So, who's *your* friend, brother?" Pouli asked. "Since
Laika didn't bother to introduce us."

"Her name's Raymonda," Thom replied easily, and Raymonda breathed a sigh of relief, since she hadn't been
certain that he wouldn't slip and give out her real name.
"And what we need is a place to stay until we all see what
the emperor is going to do, and then we need—"

"A reason to keep staying here," she interrupted him,
before he could say they were looking for a way out of the
city and the lands that were in Balthasar's hands. "Although if we're going to keep the horses 'sick,' there's
plenty of reason for a horse-healer to be here."

Pouli nodded. "That should cover both of you—any fool
can shovel horse dung, even a piece of damaged goods
like Thom, and sick horses make more messes than
healthy ones."

Thom glared at him, but said nothing. Once again, despite the deadly seriousness of the situation, Raymonda
was tempted to laugh. Maybe now Thom was regretting
his end of the bargain—he certainly hadn't reckoned on
being forced into hard, physical labor when he'd agreed to
Lydana's conditions!

*Poor thing, first it's poling the boat, now it's shoveling
manure! And he thought all he'd have to do would be to
slip us both out a gate when no one was looking!*

Laika came back, then, with a bundle in his hands and
a look of extreme concern on his face. "Here," he said,
thrusting the familiar, heavy package at her. "Gordo says
you left this with him. He wants to know, is anyone going
to miss you? If so, maybe you ought to turn 'Raymonda'
into 'Raymond.' "

She shook her head. "Not yet, I don't think—and anyway, we got out into the street from where we were hiding without anyone seeing where we came from." She cradled the bundle in both her hands, feeling a bit of confidence coming back to her now that she had more resources at her beck and call. Fitting enough, really. Any trader in this city knew that, with enough gold, you could buy everything but a reprieve from the Angel of Death. She had in this bundle enough—possibly—to do even that. It was certainly enough to buy a great deal of unpleasantness for the emperor. Gold was power, as any scion of the Tiger knew, and she held enough power now to do a great deal, for good or ill.

This, in fact, was why she had brought the last of her personal and state jewelry, and all of the loose money she could get hold of here last night, with instructions to Gordo to break it all down into its component parts. None of it was recognizable anymore, for Gordo should have broken the larger coins into smaller ones, and all of it was now in a form she could use. As Shelyra, she had turned a blind eye to the fact that Gordo was a known fence of stolen goods; as Raymonda, she had been proud of the fact.

And no one from the emperor is going to be able to recognize any of the jewelry now, even if they somehow got hold of a complete inventory of my jewel chest.

"There's a stall for you in the stable if you want it, or there's plenty would give you tent space," Laika continued.

"I'll take the stall," she said firmly. "I need to give your other people a hand with those horses before Balthasar's men manage to get in here to look them over. If at least one of your horse-healers is sleeping in the stable, it will look more like you really do have a problem. Just lead the way."

If I have something to do, something to keep my mind off all this until I'm so tired I'm likely to drop . . . She didn't finish the thought. There was always the chance that Adele had *not* feigned her own death—and that Lydana had not made her own escape in time.

There was always the chance that none of this would work. If she had a chance to think, she might lose her tight grip on herself. She dared not break down, not now.

Laika nodded sympathetically, as if he had heard her unspoken thoughts. "Come along, then," he said, and took them all to the stables.

Once there, Raymonda was immersed in a whirlwind of activity, as she and Gordo's two trainers set about making every horse in the complex look as if it was mere hours away from collapse. Some were dosed with the medicines to make them shiver and sweat as if with fever; others were poulticed behind the knee or given oddly shaped shoes on one hoof in such a way as to lame them temporarily. All of them were given skin treatments that left their coats harsh and staring, their manes and tails brittle and stiff, and left seeming sores and scars. By the time the small hours of the morning came around, Raymonda was ready to sleep standing up, and there wasn't a horse on the property that anyone would have accepted as a gift.

She stood up and swayed for a moment with fatigue; Thom was right at her elbow to catch her, and she favored him with a smile of thanks. She hadn't even known he was there.

"Your aunt's little friend dropped in just after you started on the horses," he said as he guided her to her appointed stall. "She couldn't say much, but I'd guess your aunt is safe enough for now. I gave her one of your earrings to take back with her, so she would know you were all right."

Raymonda nodded weary approval. "That will do, but from now on—no more contact. We can't know—" She broke off to yawn hugely.

"—We can't know if we're talking to someone who's been subverted," Thom finished for her. "That's just what I told her."

He steered Raymonda into the stall, where clean blankets had been laid out over a thick padding of straw. And right at the moment, it looked as inviting as a featherbed.

Raymonda dropped down onto it as Thom let go of her arm, her entire body crying out with the need for sleep.

She thought he said something more—a question, perhaps—but it was too late. She was fast asleep.

§ 16 §

ADELE

"Oh Thou that dwellest in the heavens, have mercy upon us," the archpriestess chanted. Gemen Elfrida knelt in her place for the second ritual since her return from her "retreat." It was now the middle of the night, and after the regular ritual for that hour, the archpriestess had added the litany for the dying. So now Elfrida prayed, along with all the rest of the Gemen, for Adele, who supposedly lay dying in the infirmary. And if her prayers were more for the living, the soon-to-be-deceased's daughter and granddaughter, well, the Goddess knew and understood.

Perhaps we ought to be chanting for the city as well, she thought somberly. *I begin to regret our decision already.*

Elfrida looked around her, using her chant-book as a shield to disguise her inspection. The choir section of the Temple was more crowded than it had been in many years. Elfrida had not realized how many Novices the various orders had, but now they filled the front rows of each order's section, subject to the scrutiny of all their elders.

She searched for guilty faces, although she was not entirely certain how a spy *would* look. Some of them seemed nervous, but more seemed to wish themselves back in bed; except for the Brown Robes, most of whom seemed shaken by what they had seen this day and glad to be in the main Temple.

The healers . . . already there are rumors that the emperor's men are causing trouble in the streets, and the healers would be the first to see the results of that trouble.

Elfrida hoped that the Novices would be safe here. It wasn't as if they were young children; the Temple did not take novices under the age of thirty, and forty to fifty was a much more common age at which to enter the Temple. The Goddess did not accept servants who saw her service as an escape from life; She required that they live a useful life outside her precincts before they were allowed inside. But to Elfrida, they looked childlike and unprepared for what she feared would come. She prayed for them also, and for all the Gemen, that they might have the strength and purity of the Heart in the times to come.

But we are all mortals, with mortal failings . . . when the testing comes, some will fail it, some strive to avoid it, and some deny that there is any testing.

When the litany ended, Verit issued the orders they had discussed the previous afternoon in the infirmary, the ones which would provide constant prayer around the Heart.

Clever of her, Elfrida thought. *By issuing the orders at night, during the Great Silence, she isn't going to get any arguments about them—at least not before chapter meeting tomorrow after breakfast. And we won't be having full attendance at chapter while we're split up to attend on the Heart.* Elfrida was glad to find that she was not in the group which would be required to remain here now; she would have time for a few hours sleep before she had to be back here for her next ritual. She intended to make the most of them.

Odd, how in the midst of crisis, at the beginning of what she suspected would become terrible danger, the body insisted on having its way.

She stifled a yawn as she hurried back to her room; at the minute, that hard, unforgiving pallet seemed as luxurious and desirable as her bed in the palace—

The bed in the palace!

She stopped dead in her tracks for a moment. What if Apolon were to get in there and take the bed linen from her bed? He was a mage, surely he knew ways to use it to trace her whereabouts! And the past three days had not only forced her to *use* that bed, the strain had given her dreams and nightmares that had soaked the linen with sweat before she woke!

The servants have surely changed the linens, she told herself sternly, forcing herself to walk quietly and normally back to her cell. *Even if they have not—why should he bother to trace my whereabouts? He knows where I am. And once Adele is dead—why try to trace a dead woman?*

But that left Shelyra's bed, and Lydana's—

For that matter, had either of them taken thought to the fact that Apolon could use personal objects to find them? Had anyone?

They are not children, they know the laws of magic, she told herself again. *And there are still the servants. Our belongings are worth something, even the smallest nightshift and corset; Balthasar will probably bundle everything up and send it back to his Treasury before Apolon has a chance at it.*

"Probablys" were no comfort, though. She opened the door to her cell and closed it behind her, wishing that she could have word with anyone, the lowest servant in the palace if need be.

I told Verit I could not imagine anything I had left un-done, and now I recall this, she thought glumly as she composed herself for sleep she no longer craved. *What more will I remember that I have not done?*

And how fatal will it be to us and to our plans?

§ 17 §

LEOPOLD

Leopold woke with the dawn, as he had every morning since early adolescence. He could not remember ever sleeping later than the rising of the sun even when he had stayed up long into the night at his father's meetings. Only illness kept him abed past the hour when the birds themselves rose.

He had but a single squire and a single page to tend to his few needs, unlike the long trains of servants others—notably, Apolon—required for their comfort. Nor were his quarters much more impressive than those of his officers; like them, he had a tent tall enough to stand in, divided into two portions: a sleeping chamber and a work chamber. In it was equally simple furniture: a chest for his personal belongings, a camp bed, a brazier to take the chill out of the air, a stand for his armor and weapons, a small folding table and chair. The few luxuries he owned were all birthday gifts from his friends and the few courtiers who felt secure enough to call themselves his friends. Rugs kept the damp and cold of the earth from penetrating the ground cloth, lamps provided warm illumination, and hangings softened the bare canvas of the walls; his bed was piled with fur blankets as well as good wool ones. Those were the only luxuries he claimed of all that his rank might have brought him. Always there was the knowledge that he was watched, and that too much indulgence might bring suspicion on him. He ate with his men and did not keep his own cook, as even some of his underlings did.

The moment he stirred, his page was ready with a basin of warm water for washing and the clothing of the day. The cherubic little blond child was something of a favorite of his, although he was careful never to let his preference be known. This was both for his own sake as well as the child's—favoritism would do him no good, and a noted preference would cause the boy to be assigned elsewhere, perhaps to a crueler master than Leopold. It had happened that way in the past. Still, in private, he took care to correct the child gently, when he needed correction, and smile upon him when he did not, making certain to always have a kind word.

He raised an eyebrow at the choice of clothing, though; court costume, as *he* wore it—rather more simple than that of most courtiers. A severe tunic of soft dark burgundy in heavy silk broadcloth, trimmed with gold and embellished with his father's crest upon the breast and back, matching trews, and high boots polished to a black gloss—there was nothing but the imperial coronet discreetly embroidered above the crest to show his rank. Any of the high-ranking officers would have a similar costume.

"Your imperial father wishes you to come to his presence as soon as you are dressed, my lord," the child piped up in a trembling soprano. "There was a messenger here before dawn."

That caused his other brow to rise. Normally the emperor did not require his son's presence so early—nor so formally attired.

"Thank you, Peter," he said quietly. "You did very well, as well as Klaus would have. I can dress myself; why don't you go see Sergeant Athold about your breakfast."

The page bowed and left, trying not to seem too eager, but he was a growing child and food played a major role in his life. Leopold smiled at the retreating back and set himself to making his morning preparations as quickly as possible. His squire, Klaus, appeared just as he finished; he assigned the adolescent to cleaning the parade tack for his horse—and as an afterthought, had the horse brought up to the tent, in case the gelding might be needed.

He strode out into the thin light of early morning with alacrity. Around him were all the sights and sounds of the men waking and getting themselves fed and clothed for the day. Here he was surrounded by his own personal troops, and he saluted individual men as he recognized them. They hailed him back; he was a popular commander, known to be evenhanded, just, and a good leader. In this alone he had not subverted his own talents to keep from arousing suspicion; he would not deny his men decent leadership, even if it meant that the emperor would watch him being cheered after victories with a frown.

There were enough bad commanders in this army; he did not intend to make his men suffer under one more.

He retraced his steps of last night, hearing voices within the tent even as he approached it. A guard held the tent flap aside for him, and he ducked a little to enter, turning it into a formal bow as he saw that his father was holding court just inside.

With the emperor was General Cathal, the actual leader of the Imperial Army, and Chancellor Adelphus, besides the ever-present Apolon. Cathal looked as he always looked: like an iron-haired, stern-visaged statue of marble brought to life and clothed in armor which he never put off, not even for state occasions. He nodded a curt greeting, and turned immediately back to the emperor. Adelphus, balding and bent, in his scarlet robes of state, gave Leopold a slight smile as well as a half-bow. He and Leopold had always gotten along reasonably well; he had no more ambition than the prince did, being perfectly content to do his administrative tasks (at which he excelled) and leaving intrigue to others. He recognized a kindred soul in the prince, at least insofar as lack of ambition went, and did his best to soften the emperor's attitude toward his son. Adelphus' only flaw was a touch of greed; he loved rich things, and generally found a way to appropriate objects that took his fancy.

The emperor grunted an acknowledgment of his son's presence, but did not wave him to a seat. "We have a task for you, Prince," he said brusquely. "We wish you and your personal troops to take charge of the city. Occupy the palace; survey the grounds for an appropriate place for a garrison and send Cathal word as soon as you have one so that he can send troops in. Prepare the way for our own occupation. We need an imperial presence in the city so that these fat merchants know whose hand is on the reins. Apolon reports too many of them think their queen is still the last word in authority."

Eliminate any possible subversion, he means, Leopold thought as he nodded in acknowledgment. But his spirits rose a little. A small task was better than no task at all.

"Apolon has sent his own men in already to seek out any possible subversion and deal with it, and to secure the city itself," the emperor went on. "I have given them a free hand to carry out some specific orders of mine; I want you to leave them alone and do not interfere with any of their actions. They are handling trouble among the merchants and registering the citizens, and they have their own lawkeepers in place. Just prepare the way for me, personally."

Leopold's spirits sank. So this was another do-nothing job; he was nothing more than a placeholder, a token of the emperor's attention, until Balthasar was ready to give the conquered city a look at her new master.

"Watch for any signs of the queen and the princess," Apolon put in peevishly. The scholar-mage looked particularly annoyed this morning, as if he had suffered a severe disappointment. "Somehow they slipped through our fingers last night. They can't have gotten far, but if you find them before my men do, you are to send them to me directly."

When Balthasar said nothing to contradict this, Leopold stifled an objection and only nodded again.

But the order raised the hackles on the back of the

prince's neck. There was something very wrong here. *Why is he so insistent on getting his hands on these women? It can't be for any good purpose!*

"Go—" Balthasar waved a hand at his son. "Get your troops ready, make a state entrance. Make sure you're in place in time to attend the Heart service sitting in the queen's seat; it's important that we show these people who their master is, and that will be the best place to start. These people are maudlin about their Temple, and everyone that can get free will probably be at the service."

"I hear and obey, Your Highness," Leopold said formally, bowing and taking himself out. His mind buzzed with unasked questions and unpleasant speculations.

He began issuing orders to his men as soon as he was within shouting distance; as always, they obeyed with commendable precision, leaving him to wait for his horse to be brought up, and to ponder the possible implications of the meeting in the imperial tent.

Father could be waiting to see if I try and take the city for myself, or if I obey him to the exact letter. But—this business with the missing royal women—I do not care for this at all! Apolon has some motive other than the obvious, some reason why he wants them in his personal custody.

His squire brought his horse just as the men finished their packing and began to fall into formation. He mounted easily, without a second thought, and sat in the saddle in an outwardly relaxed pose, waiting while they filled up their ranks.

Apolon is up to no good. Cathal—well, Cathal is always behind him. One might think Cathal some sort of automaton that Apolon had animated, if it were not for the fact that Cathal is a good strategist and Apolon so abysmal it is pathetic. The chancellor does not care what Apolon does so long as he does not get in the way of things running smoothly. All this, I understand. But what I do not comprehend is—why would Father fall in with this? It strikes me as something that could cause him a great deal of trouble with the people of Merina. Too tight a fist upon their throat—and, add to that, the extermination of the royal family—Father has forgotten something very dangerous. When you have people who have nothing left to lose, they have every reason to risk all for the sake of change, no matter how hopeless the odds.

If Apolon really *were* up to no good—if he meant harm to the women—

But Balthasar would say that it would make no difference. By then, he surely thought, Merina would be firmly under Balthasar's heel, and the people could do nothing.

That is a mistake. Desperate people make moves of desperation.

Leopold's horse snorted and stirred restively, reflecting his rider's unsettled state. *I do not like this. And I will* not *be a party to it.* There it was: his first real act of rebellion. But it was not rebellion against his father, was it?

No. It is against that cur, Apolon. However he has persuaded Father to this, it was nothing Father would have agreed to if he had taken any thought. No, Father is ruthless, but he is not—not evil. And Apolon means only evil to these women. I am as sure of that as I am of my own name.

He firmed his hands on the reins and calmed his steed, feeling just a little better, at least about his own part in this. Whatever Apolon planned, he would thwart it, however he could.

Which was what any man of honor would do.

✦ 18 ✦

LYDANA

Matild and Eel were awakened by the peal of the morn
bell, one of which was sounded in each ward of the city.

Matild had gone to bed in her shift, and she longed for
the deep basin of warm water which would have been
waiting for her in the palace. Water! They must put out
the barrel for the filling, as the wagon came early. Eel had
already slid from the bed with seemingly the same thought
in mind, for he was pulling at the big cask in the far corner
of the room, then pushing it toward the door.

Matild hastened to lend a hand. Together they got it
outside the door. She gave a glance up and down the
street. Yes, in so much it presented the usual view—the
barrels were out waiting, and she could smell, her stomach
faintly aching, the scent of baking from Berta's ovens on
the corner. She hunted out her purse and flipped a couple
of coppers to Eel.

"Two loaves of brown," she ordered. "And if she has a
crock of spread cheese, that also."

He nodded and was gone. Matild returned to her scrap of
mirror inside and surveyed as much as she could see of her
person. Such as she now was did not have too great an ac-
quaintance with water for cleansing, and she had enough of
lip rouge and the comb to prepare her for the day.

Just as Eel returned, she was swinging open the large

street shutters and he dropped his burdens on the table, quick to help her ease down the fold-up shelf which projected a little into the court, and on which she displayed her wares, giving a determined kick with his small, wooden-sandaled feet to set each leg firmly in place.

There were noises now beyond the ponderous roll of the water wagon. It would seem that her neighbors were recovering from the timidity of the day before. Max, the shoemaker, almost was ready for business, as was Lottie, who dealt in secondhand clothing.

They exchanged morning greetings, though it seemed to Matild that their voices were more subdued than usual, and she could see that their heads often swung toward the main street, however not with the eagerness of those awaiting trade.

The water-seller had his own budget of news—in fact, he was fair swollen like a great frog with it. Yes, neither the emperor nor most of his army had made any attempt to enter the wide open gates. But the emperor's son—now, he had come riding in within an hour of dawn, but only leading armsmen wearing his own colors, and had taken over the palace. It was thought that his father had decided Leopold was to hold the city while he was busied with other and more weighty matters. Though what those might be no one could guess.

Leopold, Matild thought as she and Eel cautiously worked the sloshing barrel back to its corner. What did she know of this only sprig of the imperial house? Though men for years had been full of the exploits of Balthasar and even spoken of his high lords in council, yet little had ever been said of the prince. Even most of the Marshals were better known.

"Out?" Eel had finished with eating, given a quick and impatient readying to the cupboard bed, and was now at Matild's elbow. She knew very well he must go out, for he could learn far more than she could hope to. Yet the thought of the black men hung heavy in her mind.

"Take care," she found herself saying, even though she knew that Eel needed no such warning.

"The guild houses?" suggested the other.

Matild nodded. The guilds controlled the wealth of Merina. Were the city now set up for stripping, those would be the first to attract attention. Then Eel was gone.

Matild fell to busying herself as if this was a normal day, unpacking her bead necklaces, arranging them on the sales table, snapping down the small clasps which would hold them for seeing but would permit no snatching. She took particular pains this morning to make sure that none she displayed were better than middling priced—rather than quality trinkets.

Having set up her display, Matild set herself on her high stool, steadying on her knees the divided tray in which there were piles of loose beads of every type and color. She threaded one of her needles, ready to work while she waited for customers.

"Ah, Matild—such pretties!" Kassie, on her way to a late visit to the baker's, gazed wistfully down at the strings. "That one," she stabbed a work-calloused finger at a string near the middle of the display, "that—that is what I would choose—the butterflies—they are like real!"

Matild spoke briskly. "A deal of work went into making them, girl. Cost you five coppers or a silver bit."

Kassie sighed. "Not likely to see either, not with that hard-nosed second wife of my father a-watching the purse."

"Bring Hughes." Matild smiled.

Kassie blushed and then slowly shook her head. For the first time she glanced over her shoulder before she answered. "Hughes—I have not seen him—not since three days now. He was called up when the council met, but he has not come home. This late, she'll have the broom to me. Give you a good trade day, Matild."

She hurried off. Hughes was a first-year member of the canal police. Matild slipped a red bead next to a copper one on her string. What had become of the regular guardians of the city? She shivered slightly. There was an unreality about this whole matter—Balthasar staying without the city, the men in black—

"Holla, dame!" She was startled as the open section of her table was darkened by another shadow. Looking up, she met the stare of one of those black coats. He was not alone, and his companion carried a roll of thick yellow paper which he held open with one hand, keeping a mark stick in the other.

"Beads, sir. You'll find the best—"

"You are a licensed seller?" The man was not frowning, but neither was he wearing the guise of a customer in the least.

Matild pointed to the somewhat askew framed strip of parchment which swung on a hook from one of the shutter strips.

She allowed herself something of a snap in her voice as she answered: "Use your eyes—there be my work lines, due signed by Master Garmage hisself, and with the seal of Her Own Good Grace, the Queen—"

He drew nearer and inspected the license. Then he spoke with a chill: "There is no queen in Merina, dame, have you not yet heard? You will need a new work permit and you will have to pay your dues for it at the Sign of the Three Cups before two days are out. Your name?" He barked that last.

"I be Matild Rankisdaughter and I be a beadswoman." She thought she dared allow herself some sharpness of tongue in reply. She had established a character and now was the time to live up to it.

"Matild." The one black coat nodded to his companion who scratched a line on the paper he held. "Six silvers for the half year for your license, woman. And we take no promises, only hard cash."

He had turned away, heading toward Max. Matild knew that she should not be surprised. After all, they had known from the beginning that Balthasar was out to wring all he could from the rich port city. But such a sum was far beyond raising in two days time by such a merchant as she appeared to be. Was it the emperor's decision now to loot the city in his own way by taxes none of the smaller merchants could pay?

She heard a raised voice from Max's stall. The shoemaker was a man of uneven temper. He was also one who pinched every copper bit before he pursed it. The one black coat moved quickly, and she saw him now catch the shoemaker by the loose front of his smock to give him a shake.

"Think yourself fortunate," the aggressor said, "that I am in a good mood, or you'd be caged for taking that tone with the emperor's men. You will pay or you shall not work, lout."

Matild continued to think. Shelyra was safe—so far—but these black coats seemed everywhere. And Saxon—what had happened to him? It had been her intent to contact him as soon as possible. Now she was sure that she must do so—if she could—in the most secret fashion.

Normally she would have expected her fellow tradesmen to explode into the street when the black coats left, with loud appeals to various saints and angels for aid against such exploitation. But the court remained quiet, too much so, and she was aware that there was very little sound from the street beyond.

If these hoodcrows had come to the nests of the poor, what was the fate of the guilds? She was to discover before the hourglass turned as Eel returned. Not at the usual headlong pace which suited his role, but keeping close to doorways, flitting from one to the next as if he expected to be picked up.

However, he was not breathing hard as he came into the bead shop, though his eyes still moved from side to side as if he expected some fate to be looming over Matild's own shoulder.

"They move—on the guilds," he began abruptly. "The black coats took all the masters to the palace this morning. They put one of their own people in each guild house and have brought in merchant scribes of their own, demanding all the ledgers. Nor will they let the journeymen and women continue working. They have locked them out of the workrooms and are questioning them about the business of each house."

So they did not only hunt the mice of Merina's merchant world, now they had made their attack on the top. She felt a strong need to get to her own guild house, to see just what was going on.

"They have brought extra men to the guild of the Tiger," the Eel continued. "Master Samenson and Master Kird were taken away. They are asking about the queen—"

Yes, that might be the first move of Balthasar's attempt to shake her out of hiding in her own city. But not even her most trusted work people knew of Matild's hiding hole.

The emperor would find a rich answer to his investment of *her* house! They had controlled the best of the gem trades for centuries, and it had been the hobby of many of the guild masters to put aside particularly fine or unusual jewels to be kept either for the house collection, or for very special orders. There was one such resting on her own worktable in the hall now, unless someone had the wit to hide it. It was an order for a marriage crown from overseas—one which had taxed her powers at creation. She shrugged—there was more than a piece of fine work at stake now.

"They plan a high ceremony at the Great Temple," Eel continued. "Perhaps the emperor will be there. There is talk of his making a speech afterward." That appeared to be the end of his budget of gathered news, for now he sat on his stool watching her.

"Saxon?" she nearly whispered the word. The aid of the captain was what she had counted upon. He would no longer be at the inn. Perhaps he had gone out to the harbor itself. She topped the small jars of loose beads in her work box as she thought of what move she could make.

"There is Jonas—" As usual Eel was following her thoughts.

Jonas—yes! Though Saxon was a prudent man, used to keeping his own council, yet he did trust the one-legged innkeeper—not the master of the Sea Dragon, but of the far less pretentious common seaman's grog shop. Jonas had served with the captain for some years, until he lost a leg at Ourse, and Matild was aware that he was indeed Saxon's source of knowledge concerning the less legal traffic in both the harbor and the canals.

But he could not be approached openly by day. Matild would have no excuse for closing her shop and seeking the streets, and she certainly had a firm idea now that any happening out of the ordinary would command the attention of the patrolling black coats.

But there was one thing— "When is the ceremony?" she demanded of Eel.

"At the nooning—today."

So. Well, no one could possibly question a woman seeking the consolation of the Temple after the shock she had had this morning.

"You will keep shop," she said. "I will go to the ceremony. If any asks for me, say truly where I am. I shall— I shall ask Berta to go with me."

She stopped at the bakery and found the plump mistress of it, tear stains on her round cheeks.

"Ten silver!" She greeted Matild with a wail. "I take in perhaps five silver a week—when others have money enough to buy. But there is my daughter Ella, and her least one is sick. She went this morn to the city dispensary and it was closed, with one of those hoodcrows at the door to say the sick could care for themselves—unless they paid. Matild—this evil is—"

"Worse than we feared it might be," the beadseller nodded. "They are having a High Heart ceremony this nooning. I go to ask the mercy of the Greater Will—come with me."

Berta clapped her hands and her second daughter looked out from the oven room.

"We go to the Heart," the baker said. "Look to the shop.

Even the black coats cannot keep one from the Great Mercy—"

Matild wondered about that as they moved off together. Her own idea seemed to have gathered other followers. There was a steady stream of people, mainly women. Matild wondered at the few men to be seen. There were some of an older generation, but the younger ones—surely the emperor's men could not have rounded up the whole manpower of Merina! There would be no place to keep them.

Once more she found the square before the Great Temple was fast being filled. But she ploughed ahead, Berta at her heels, and this time was able to win up the steps into the long nave, though once there they were wedged tightly into a corner.

The sanctuary lamp was burning and the choir had taken their places; the Gemen filed in, one robed and veiled figure like another. There were not too many of them left, Matild saw with a small touch of fear, particularly among the Grey Robes. Though other families beside the Tiger had the inborn gift, they had not run much to daughters during the past generation. And since the talent did not manifest itself until middle age, and those with it were sometimes not too long-lived, there was steady erosion through the years. Only about one quarter of their stalls had occupants.

She was shaken out of such dire thoughts by the procession from the sanctuary: the archpriestess in full robes, but instead of her usual brilliant scarlet, she wore the purple of mourning—mourning for a city already lost.

Those about Matild knelt. She did quickly also, as the Ever Flame was carried carefully to the altar. There were still the two chairs of state, one to either side of the altar. The queen's chair, until yesterday Adele's, was occupied by a young man in his late twenties or early thirties—Prince Leopold? There was no sign of the emperor.

Nor did he arrive as it had been rumored he would. The service was full, but the archpriestess gave no sermon. She only left her own high chair and knelt before the altar, being steadied by one of the Gemen, in silent prayer. And Matild, seeing such a departure from the usual form of service as she had seen only at the death of her father, was fearful for Adele. She could only pin hope on the strong bonds of the three of them—if Adele was gone, she would certainly have known it, perhaps even the moment of her mother's passing.

Once the service was over, she caught Berta by the arm. "I would seek council." She nodded toward the confessional booths. The baker nodded. "I also, neighbor."

Matild had to wait until the Great Temple was partly cleared before she could approach the special booth. She knelt reverently for a moment facing the Heart and then pushed past the curtain to squat on a low stool, her face even with the coarse mesh of a screen which effectively hid all but the outline of the figure coming into the other side a moment or so after she had entered.

She spoke the time-hallowed words for beginning a confession. "Reverend One, my heart is not at peace."

"Speak child," came the ritual whisper, "for thy Mother listens." Was it Adele? She could not be sure.

"There is trouble in the city, Reverend One—" she began. It was difficult to get into her real problems when she did not know to whom she spoke.

"There is indeed trouble, daughter,"

Matild smiled joyfully. "Mother!" she whispered.

"Watch what you say—we do not know if we are observed." She had not heard such a stern note in her mother's voice for years.

Swiftly Matild relayed all she knew. Then she asked:

"Have you any later word of Shelyra than mine?"

"I have heard from the Gypsies that so far she is safe. But the child is impulsive, and what is going on now with those black servitors of Apolon—"

"Apolon?" Matild interrupted.

"Yes, the black coats are evil fungi grown from his sowing. They have served him, and, through him, the emperor; so well that Balthasar has given the policing of the city over to them. Apolon"—for the first time her voice gave a small quaver—"is more than a mage, daughter. Even as Verit is more than one of the Gemen, so is he also in a position of command. Though as yet he has not made any move save those which serve his master, we believe he has plans beyond those of the emperor. They have taken the guild masters for ransom—taking two-thirds of their stock in return for what they call liberty. Our law-keepers are captives, and they are taking any young man they come across and sending him to the emperor's camp for heavy labor. There has been a rumor that they will even send them back to Balthasar's other conquests as slaves. The gifted among us are beginning to spy now, but we dare not use too great a power lest we attract Apolon's full attention—power draws power, as you well know."

"Who wears the ring?" Matild asked softly.

"It was taken by the herald—perhaps it is now on the emperor's fist. Remember, daughter, with that and those ill-omened gems you play with fire."

She must not stay too long. Bending her head, she repeated the proper words:

"Give me Heart blessing, Reverend One, for I would be about the business of the Greater Power."

"So be it," she heard her mother sigh. "What must be done, we shall do."

❦ 19 ❦
ADELE

Gemen Elfrida finished her hours of hearing confessions deeply troubled in mind, a trouble even the familiar ritual chants could not entirely soothe, although they did remind her of the Goddess' presence and Her care for Her children. But against the misery she had encountered in the confessionals, the Goddess' compassion seemed faint and distant.

Fathers, brothers, and sons had vanished, either into thin air, or into the hands of Apolon's black coats. Taxes and licenses far in excess of anything a business ever took in had been levied against smaller merchants and large alike—with the warning that failure to pay meant closure of business. Was Balthasar trying to strangle the city? Was he trying to stir up rebellion, so as to have a reason to crush it? Or was he just looking for a way to loot beneath a thin veneer of legality?

More than ever, she regretted that they had left the city to Balthasar's hands. But what else could they have done? To resist meant a quick death at the hands of his troops—

And now, did they face a slow death, instead, by strangulation?

So much misery, so many tears, and all of those seeking the confessionals asking the same question: Why? Why had this happened to *them*? Why had the Goddess abandoned them? Why had the queen abandoned them? The last had hit hard, and hurt deeply.

She could only tell them what she herself had been told: sometimes terrible things happened to good people, not because the Goddess was indifferent or was putting them to the test, but only because that was the way of things on earth. If the Goddess answered every prayer, though She was omnipotent, the contradictions involved would bring more trouble than there had been in the beginning. She used a simple example: if one woman prayed for the tree beside her house to grow and give her porch shade in the heat of summer, and the woman next door prayed for a blight to kill the same tree that was destroying the foundation of her house, which prayer should the Goddess answer? Or another—if a storm came up and destroyed a fishing boat full of honest men, was the Goddess responsible, or punishing them for something? There was no heavenly malice involved in what was happening in Merina—

Though there was certainly earthly malice.

Have faith! she told herself firmly as she headed for the refectory and her lunch. Perhaps food would help her feel a little better.

And perhaps it would lie like a lump of lead in her stomach, as most meals had thus far.

This was not working out the way she had thought it would. It had all seemed relatively simple, three days ago. . . .

"The threat of the Evil One is division and despair." The words echoed in Elfrida's head in a woman's voice, one she could not quite place. The thought was certainly timely, but where had she heard these words?

Midway through the meal, which was, as usual, eaten in silence, she remembered. It had been a sermon delivered several months ago by one of the Brown Robes, a woman who in addition to her healing gifts had a natural gift for preaching. It had been at one of the Lady's High Feasts, and the Dowager Queen Adele had been in attendance. Verit had presented the Gemen to Adele after the service, and Adele had asked how she found time to prepare such a sermon with all her other duties. Verit had laughed, telling the dowager queen that the Gemen had been informed only an hour before the service that she would be giving the sermon.

Perhaps I should ask Verit to have her preach again, Adele thought. *She is truly inspired, and her words show both wisdom and sense. Division and despair are exactly what Apolon is trying to induce in us, and we must fight against them with every power at our command.*

Lunch was uncommonly serious; Elfrida was not the only Gemen to have stood duty in the confessionals, and it seemed that everyone had heard similar tales of woe.

And I must return to the booths after lunch, she thought reluctantly. *They are still open for three hours, and someone else might want to contact me.*

As she had feared, the food she had eaten lay uncomfortably in the pit of her stomach as she took her seat again in the third confessional. She could tell through the coarse cloth of the screen that her first postulant was a man, though that was all she could tell.

"Reverend One, my heart is not at peace," said a deep, pleasant voice, but before she could give the ritual answer, the voice continued. "The root is deep, the tree stands tall, the great cat walks her way." As he spoke, the shadow of a hand came up and pushed something small through the loosened corner of the screen. It dropped to the floor with a tiny clatter and she picked it up. It was an earring, a sapphire earring, the blue stone glinting from the fierce eye of a mythical beast. She knew it, too—it was Shelyra's, and she had worn it to the meeting with the council before they all three vanished down their separate escape routes.

"Speak, child, for thy Mother listens," she replied automatically, a little stunned, then added quickly, "Although, if you have not suddenly been shape-changed, you are no child of mine!"

"Nor grandmother, though a certain young lady wants

to be certain that *hers* is still among the living," the man said cheerfully. "Some call me Thom Talesmith, Reverend One."

Thom Talesmith—the rogue Lydana sent to watch over Shelyra! "You may tell her that tales of a demise are certainly exaggerated. And you may tell *me* what is happening in my city!"

"The fellows with the black feathers are everywhere," the man said briskly. "You've heard tales of their doings already, I've no doubt. Reverend One—there's something uncanny about some of them. . . ." His voice faltered for a moment. "It's hard to explain, but some of them—don't seem right. They don't seem like proper men. Like— they're single-minded, but all of it for something I don't understand and wouldn't want to."

She frowned. "They are Apolon's men, and he is a dark mage—more than that, I do not know. But I would walk carefully near them. He may have granted them powers we are not used to dealing with."

The shadow nodded. "There's something new for you— the big general, that one called Cathal, he's moved his own special company of mercenaries into the city, and I'm not sure that the prince, who is supposed to be running the place, knows they're here yet. Cathal's quartered 'em in some of the warehouses and the old garrison down by the docks. I've seen some of 'em—I know their kind. There's going to be trouble from 'em, Reverend One. They didn't get their fight, they didn't get their loot, and they're looking for a way to get both." His voice turned pleading. "Can you spread the word among the people not to provoke 'em? Speak soft, say yessir, nossir, keep the eyes on the feet? Otherwise— they're looking for blood."

And they would find it, soon or late. Elfrida nodded. "I can say as much in confessional, and have the other Gemens do the same." At least here was *something* she could do, something that might make a little difference.

"As for the girl—" He hesitated, and coughed. "Reverend One, I was supposed to spirit her out of here."

"And she won't go. I expected as much." In spite of the sick feeling behind her breastbone, she had to chuckle a little at the bewilderment in his voice. She guessed that this man was used to having his way with women, used to having them court him. He was not used to a girl like her granddaughter. "I think you will find that you will do more with her if you try to persuade her rather than insist that things be done your way. I do not think you will get her to move from this city, though. She is of the House of the Tiger, and the bones of Merina are our bones; her canal water is in our blood. We will stand by her until there are not two stones standing atop one another."

"I made a pledge as a blood-liege—" Odd. He sounded plaintive. As if he was ashamed of not being able to fulfill his pledge.

"Give it a week of trying; if you cannot move her by then, I absolve you of it," she replied quickly.

"Thank you." He sighed. "She said to tell you she hasn't learned much. The prince isn't living in the palace yet; he's staying with his own troops in what she called the 'little garrison.' "

"That would be the barracks on the palace grounds where the palace guard lived," she told him. "That's interesting. I wonder if he is searching the palace for traps and tricks before he decides to move in."

"I would if I were in his shoes," Thom told her. "You people gave in without a fight—and if I were as used to treachery as these imperials are, I'd figure you had planned to let the palace do your fighting for you."

"Hmm." That in itself told her a great deal about the prince and the way he thought. And yet, despite the fact that he was her enemy, her initial impression of him had been cautiously favorable. If *he* had been the one truly in charge, she thought that she would have had no misgivings about the safety of her city in his hands.

But he was not; he was only a puppet for his father—
—and for Apolon.

"That's all I have to say, Reverend One," Thom said into

the silence. "And since I made my peace in the Water Tower, the only thing I have to confess is that I've wanted to strangle that girl a half dozen times a day."

"You are not alone in that," Elfrida told him, holding back a smile. "And if you controlled your temper, that is penance enough. The peace and blessing of the Heart be upon you, child," she finished in the ritual phrases. "Walk in Her shadow and know that She hears you."

And with that, Thom Talesmith bowed his head, murmured his thanks, and slipped out of the confessional booth.

Elfrida turned her attention to the next to confess, but part of her was still blinking in astonishment. Whoever would have thought it! Thom Talesmith—thief, rogue, ne'er-do-well, smuggler, drinker, and wencher of legend— was pious! He had meant that last as an actual confession from the heart! She knew sincerity when she heard it, and it had been there in his voice!

She had no doubt that he *had* made a full confession in prison—and had meant it, too.

And for some reason, that relatively insignificant revelation gave her a tiny glimmer of hope and caused her spirits to rise again. For if Thom Talesmith could turn out to be a true child of the Goddess—

—then perhaps anything was possible. Even saving the city.

⚜ 20 ⚜

LYDANA

If Berta had received any more comfort from her own visit to the confessional, she did not show it as the two women paid boat fees grudgingly, being in a hurry to reach their homes again.

Matild walked into trouble. One of the black coats was holding Eel, and was slapping him first on one side of his face and then the other with a brutal force while another black coat stood by.

"What's to do?" Matild demanded. "What has the lad done?"

The cold-eyed man who had interviewed her earlier looked at her measuringly. "He does business without a license. He is a rogue and will be the better put to honest work—"

Matild's one hand had slipped under the edge of her bodice as if she were clutching her heart in distress. Her fingers touched the ruler's stone from her signet, and a warmth from it raced into her.

"He is my own sister's lad." She set herself squarely before the black coat. "As such he is apprentice-bound to me under the law. He is no rogue, and if he keeps the shop it is because he has been told to do so."

"While you gad, beadseller?"

"While I go to Temple services as is right and proper.

Is the Temple now to be closed to us of Merina? I think the emperor would not have it so—they speak of him as a loyal son of the Temple."

The man blinked, and his lips moved as if he would say something but was biting back words. Loosing Eel, he threw him against the wall.

"Best keep to your shop—while you still have it." He spat; a gob of spittle struck full on her faded license above the royal seal.

They went, and Matild watched them out of the court and away with narrowed eyes. Then she looked back to Eel; both his cheeks were scarlet from the blows he had suffered. He would have bruises to show later. In her, all the anger which had been building broke. To quietly sit and take abuse was not the way of the Tiger—their fearsome crest had been the badge of their courage and fury. It was time that more must be done than just listen to rumors and try to plan any sense out of this chaos.

She led Eel to the back of the shop and rummaged in the hanging cupboard for a jar of herbal paste which was not too old to be used. As lightly as she could, well aware of the winces the other could not suppress, she painted the swollen flesh.

"What brought them?" she asked as she finished her task. Her arms were about that slender young body, enfolding it as if she could so save it from any pain.

"They came as if they had business." The words were muffled by puffed lips. "At first they asked prices—but they had other questions about you, about the shop—they looked through all the amulet necklaces as if they hunted for something. Then they threatened—and you came."

"The amulet necklaces!" Matild, her arm still about Eel's shoulder, came back to the display board. It was plain that several of the strings had been tugged on and only the guards she had devised had kept them in place. One was broken and the beads had rolled out into the street.

She had never really dealt in amulets with any belief in

their purpose. From time to time she had selected some of the various pieces of strange design because they went well with the patterns she held in mind. Here was the Double Heart in tarnished silver, a Sea Eye in copper, a representation of the Flame formed by small red beads glued together—and several oddities which had come from travelers who had exchanged them for her wares.

The Temple did not altogether favor the wearing of amulets—though those of approved design were often used to center a string of prayer beads. Those who clung mainly to a belief in the power of such pieces were not fervent followers of the Heart. And many used them for purposes closer to the actions of a mage—

Mage!

Apolon—a mage—the black coats were truly his men. Matild was open-minded enough to know that certain objects, when concentrated upon, could convey emotions—if those receiving them were also talented in some fashion. What did Apolon fear that he must send his black coats hunting for amulets even in a stall such as the one she tended? It was yet another piece to be somehow fitted into the pattern.

"They did not look at the Temple pieces." Eel had slipped out of Matild's hold and gone around outside to pick up the loose beads from the cobbles, his head and shoulders showing suddenly above the edge of the display table.

Matild stared at what still lay in full sight. There were five such necklaces: three had Temple-approved designs, and the fourth was the one with the copper butterflies held together with rose crystal beads which Kassie had admired so longingly. The first held the Sea Eye—but that was a very common sight in any port city. Most sailors wore such, perhaps not quite believing in their potency, but still feeling that they needed any extra luck they could garner.

Since the black coats had broken only the chain of the

Sea Eye, she must believe that their attention had somehow centered on that.

Or—a sign? As the ruler of Merina, she had been well aware of the activities of smugglers—a certain amount of such activity could never be entirely suppressed and she had not expected it of Saxon. Those were small-fry. It was only when some sly and competent leader put together a gang and worked on a larger scale that the government moved in. It could well be that certain amulets were tokens of introduction among these scavengers.

Since the black coats seemed very well advised, they must also have heard that many of her customers were seamen, and the reputation she had built up over the years of friendliness with mariners might now be a deficit rather than an asset for her.

She gathered up the loose beads and the amulet and returned them to her box, placing a very simple chain of jet and crystal in its place. She must get to Saxon!

Though they kept the shop open all afternoon, there were no customers. Matild allowed Eel to go shopping for food, enough to last for several days. Meanwhile, she kept her hands busy stringing beads and her thoughts shifting, weighing, and striving to put into patterns what she had learned.

There was no chance now to call upon the resources of the guilds. But she still had not only the jewels of ill-omen but a work box of settings into which they might be placed. However, as long as the shop was open, she could not engage in any such work.

It was late afternoon before anyone crossed the court. Max's shop had been open, and she had heard the steady rhythm of his hammer off and on, though he had not shown himself. It was as if a great fearsome shadow had settled down upon them all. Then Kassie burst out of the house at the end of the court.

Her round, childish face was wet with tears and she smeared her hands back and forth across her cheeks as she came running blindly. Matild was on her feet in a moment and stepped out of the doorway just in time to intercept the girl as she blundered past.

Kassie clutched at her, throwing back her head and giving forth what was almost a howl.

"Kassie." Matild held her and then gave her a small shake to catch her attention. "What is the matter?"

The girl's eyes, between swollen lids, were wild; she was like some hunted animal. Kassie was often the butt of her step-mother's jealousy and hard dealing, but Matild had never seen her in such a state before.

"What is the matter?" she repeated more loudly.

"Hughes—" she choked on the name even as she tried to say it.

"What is it with Hughes?" Matild asked, pitching her voice sharply to get the girl's attention.

"They—those hoodcrows came to the smithy—they told his father—Hanz—they have taken him—to be one of their slaves! All the law-keepers have been taken."

Matild felt the chill of fear. She had been so sure somehow that they would have a chance to do battle—even in the shadows. But it seemed that the enemy now moved so fast, they could not foresee where the next attack might come.

"They—they brought in a smith of their own—he is to take over the smithy and Hanz is to be only their servant—in his own place!" Kassie had calmed somewhat, but she still looked wild-eyed. "Please, dame, why do they do these things—we did not fight. Perhaps—" Suddenly her head straightened up and she rubbed her hand across her eyes for the last time. "Perhaps we should have. Now they take our men like animals to the butcher and—and they—they have hung a man—right before the Temple—"

"A man hung—for what act?" Matild was fully chilled now.

"Was Master Linos of the Metal Guild—they—they say he would not obey them."

A guildmaster hung! No, she had dallied long enough without any real plan of action. The Tiger—her head straightened proudly—the Tiger stalked his own trails and none disputed his passage. So it had been—so it was!

She soothed Kassie as best she could, and then came back to the shop where Eel squatted on a stool, waiting, shopping done. Swiftly Matild began to retell what the girl had said, but he was before her, adding details—of young men in chains being marched out of the gates, of shops wrecked because their owners in some way annoyed the black coats.

§ 21 §

ADELE

Archpriestess Verit came in as they were finishing dinner and pulled Gemen Elfrida aside. The hallway leading to the dining hall was wide enough for the rest of the Gemens to file past without intruding on a whispered conversation. "Prince Leopold wishes to pay his respects to the Dowager Queen Adele," she said in a low voice. "Can you pretend to be ill, or do you need to really get sick again?"

Elfrida sighed, feeling the weight of responsibility that seemed to come with the persona of Adele settle over her again. "I'll have to pretend," she replied. "I didn't bring any of the berries from the palace with me. But I don't think that he'll notice it's a pretense."

"Very well," Verit said. "How much time do you need to get into place? I stalled him through dinner—I fed and talked with him in my parlor—but I can't stall him too much longer." She looked worried, and a bit harassed. Her

long years as archpriestess, fraught though they had been
with all the odd situations any authority had to deal with
at one time or other, had probably not prepared her for
this.

Well, they didn't prepare me, either. Elfrida frowned as
she tried to guess how much time she would need for the
transformation. "Buy as much time as you can. I'll have
to get my cosmetics, and they're at the palace end of the
tunnel. Remember, keeping Adele alive was your idea—I
hadn't made preparations for it. But I ought to be ready
in half a candlemark at the longest."

Verit nodded, some of the worry leaving her—but not,
by any means, all of it. "That wasn't as bad as I thought.
I'll warn the infirmarian to expect you. You can return
through the meditation chamber; the people in it are to
be trusted." She hurried off toward the infirmary to prepare the infirmarian for the deception, and Elfrida headed
for the lower tunnel, feeling her muscles knot up in her
shoulders with tension.

She made the best speed she could back to the palace,
where she lit the lamp, grabbed up her cosmetics box and
her most elaborate bed robe, and wrapped them in a dark
shawl. *I think I am beginning to hate Adele.* Carrying the
lamp and making a mental note to move her dressing table
to the entrance to the meditation chamber when she got
the chance, she returned to the Temple, extinguishing the
lamp at the end of the tunnel just beyond the meditation
chamber. The bundle seemed unexpectedly heavy—or was
it just that weight of responsibility again? The entrance in
the chamber came out to one side of the altar, behind one
of the twin pillars set against the wall to each side of the
altar. There were four robes hanging in the tunnel outside
the hidden entrance, one for each color of the Orders.

There were two people in the chamber, ostensibly meditating; a man in red robes and a woman in brown. Elfrida
recognized both of them; the man was Gemen Fidelis,
whom Gemen Elfrida had worked with a few times, and
the woman was the one whose sermon Gemen Elfrida

had been remembering earlier. Unfortunately, she still couldn't remember the woman's name. That troubled her, obscurely. It made her wonder if her mind was going— which at this point, could spell disaster for everyone.

No, it's just stress, and the fact that I only heard her name once. Surely.

Both of them looked up briefly from their prayers, just long enough to recognize her, as Gemen Elfrida came out from behind the pillar. Gemen Fidelis nodded briefly to her before both of them returned to their prayers, paying her no further heed. She might have simply walked through an ordinary door, rather than materializing out of the wall. Verit had certainly picked her people well.

Elfrida made her way to the infirmary unnoticed— doubtless by the mercy of the Goddess, she thought. In fact, there wasn't anyone in the long stone hallways at all, despite the fact that there were generally a few people about at any and all hours. The infirmarian guarded the door while she shed her habit and bundled it into the cupboard, along with the spare habits that had been occupying Adele's place in bed. She quickly put on enough cosmetics to change the shape of her face *and* make herself look really, truly at death's door, fastened her hair in two loose braids, and put the bedgown on over her shift. Hearing voices in the hallway, she quickly climbed into bed and concentrated on making her breathing sound shallow and labored. After her recent journey to the palace and back, gasping for breath wasn't difficult. So many things could go wrong with this farce—

She hoped her face was done properly, but reminded herself that she had done this many times over the past two years. *The change to Adele should be automatic; it was until yesterday, and I don't think I've forgotten it overnight. It's just that I didn't expect to do it again.*

The situation could have been funny if it hadn't been so dangerous.

The infirmarian entered, followed by the Archpriestess

Verit and Prince Leopold. "You can't stay long," the infirmarian said firmly, and with an authority even a general would quail before. "The Reverend One tires quickly."

Adele had no fault to find with that statement. Suddenly she felt completely exhausted. *Be alert, be alert—you daren't slip, here. He can't notice anything amiss.*

She held her hand out, and it shook all by itself. It looked particularly fragile and transparent in the candlelight. Prince Leopold bowed over her hand, every inch the polished courtier. Adele looked him over, not bothering to hide her scrutiny. She was old and dying, after all—what had she to fear from the invaders?

I am an old woman about to pass the Veil, and no mere mortal can threaten me. And I am an interfering old woman who has never hesitated to speak her mind. The first was a façade, the second genuine, and both gave her courage to regard him without fear.

Prince Leopold was a plain man, with dark hair, dark eyes, and a rather homely, bony face; he had none of the boldly handsome looks his father was said to possess. There was a faint line between his eyebrows as if he was always worried about something. His body was that of a fighter, not a courtier, though—but not as powerfully built as Balthasar was said to be. He was also simply dressed, with no signs of his birth or high rank in his clothing. Although the fabric of his uniform was fine, it *was* a uniform, with none of the braid and decorations most royal "warriors" affected, whether or not they deserved such decorations. Balthasar's dress uniform was purportedly so heavy with braid and gold bullion it took two squires to lift the tunic.

Apparently he didn't take after his father much.

And his face was kind, which surprised Adele. She had not expected to find a man like this in the emperor's train. But, of course, the emperor's only son would not have many choices; his father would make such decisions as to where he went and what he did. Presumably the emperor had ordered him into the army; perhaps to keep an eye on him. *Did the emperor order him to see how I do?*

"Your Grace, I am most sorry for your illness." He said the expected words courteously, but Adele could tell that he truly meant them. Whether he was here by his own will or by another's, he was sincere in his sympathy. When he had bowed over her hand, he had held it gently, and he had set it down on the coverlet with equal gentleness.

I like him, she thought with faint surprise. *I really like him. He is a good man. I could have wished there had been someone like him in our own court, instead of all those ambitious, callow, self-serving puppies. This is the kind of man little Shelyra could have had respect for.*

She gave him a faint smile. "Death comes to us all in our time, Your Highness," she whispered. After a few careful shallow breaths she continued. "I do not fear for myself . . . but for my people—and my family. My family, most of all. I have heard nothing . . . of Lydana and Shelyra."

And that is the truth, she thought with triumph. *I have heard from Matild and Raymonda.*

"If I find the queen and the princess," he said firmly, "I shall see that they are treated with the honor due their station. I shall see that they are protected, as they should be, for the queen offered this city in honorable surrender."

Adele inclined her head. Something in his voice concerned her greatly. He wasn't speaking just to her, and he wasn't quite speaking to himself . . . it was as if he was preparing to take a stand in a bitter argument. *Who wants Lydana and Shelyra, and what are they wanted for?* Judging by the grim set of Prince Leopold's jaw, she feared it was Apolon. Then she looked into his eyes, and she *knew* it was Apolon, as surely as Leopold did.

If Apolon wants them—it is for no good purpose.

Suddenly she did not have to feign feeling ill. She collapsed back against the pillows, barely able to breathe. She scarcely heard the infirmarian firmly escorting her visitors to the door.

She wasn't sure whether she swooned or simply fell

asleep very suddenly, but the next thing she was conscious of was Verit's warm hand on her shoulder.

Her voice was full of concern. "Can you get up, Gemen? You've missed the ritual for the ninth hour; if you miss Vespers as well, it may be remarked upon. Even though we divided the orders only last night, people already know who else is supposed to be in their group."

Gemen Elfrida pushed herself upright, feeling strength coming back into her. "Apolon searches for the women of the Tiger," she said. *As I feared . . . as I feared.*

Verit frowned, and bit her lip. "Yes, I caught that, too. Prince Leopold isn't happy about it."

"He seems a decent enough young man," Elfrida observed, standing up carefully and going to the wash basin to remove the cosmetics from her face. "Not what I would have expected from the emperor's son. I believe I know what he was thinking. He feels that the women of the Tiger should be protected, but he's afraid he doesn't have the power to do it."

Verit nodded in confirmation. "I think the Dowager Queen Adele can die very soon, as soon as possible. In fact, I think she had better, before Apolon realizes he might lure Shelyra and Lydana out of hiding if he takes Adele prisoner. I don't want you anywhere near the infirmary when it happens—I'll arrange it for when you're at a ritual."

Gemen Elfrida changed back into her grey robes, feeling all that heavy weight drop from her spirit as she put off the bedgown. *No more divided life, or divided heart. At last.* "All right," she said. "I'd best be going to vespers. Do you want me to hear confessions tomorrow?"

Verit shook her head. "I think you should be as visible as possible. I do not want anyone to connect Gemen Elfrida with you."

"No more do I," Elfrida said fervently. "In fact—I will never be happier than when Adele is safely dead."

§ 22 §

LYDANA

Matild, her mouth a straight line, set about shutting up shop, though it was far from sunset. She would waste no more time; she must move tonight. And to visit Jonas would be her first move.

They ate hurriedly: bread, cheese and the coarse ale that was the district's drink. Then Matild pulled out the upper of the two drawers installed beneath the cupboard bed. There were piles of clothing within, but she knew what choice she would make.

It took time, and she was impatient enough that she found her fingers fumbling at ties and clasps, but at last they had stripped down and redressed—again in those tight-fitting body-covering suits of a gray so dark they seemed black. There were also the hooded cloaks to go with them. Matild transferred her skirt-knife to the belt sheath, then twisted around her a length of black silk into which she fitted the stones of ill omen.

Eel opened a box and brought out two sets of metal rings. With delicate precision he fitted these over the fingers of each hand. From every finger now protruded a knife-blade thicker than a large needle—as deadly as a beast's claws.

Matild shut the outer door after the shutters were tightly fastened, and barred it. From all appearances the

shop was closed for the night. She put a lamp where its
faint glow might be noted by anyone taking the trouble to
try to peer through the lattice of the shutters.

With Eel's help, the table was moved, and the tallest of
the stools set in its place. Again she felt above her for the
release chain of the trapdoor. Eel had a coil of rope ending
in a large hook over one shoulder. Once the trap door was
open, he took Matild's place and hurled the hook with its
trailing rope up and out. A stout jerk assured him that the
hook was caught fast, and he climbed to disappear into
the dusk above. The rope swung back again and Matild
took his place. Though she had practiced this several
times in the past for no other reason than such a use as
she must put it to tonight, it was a struggle to draw herself
up until she could hook one hand over the edge of the
aperture. Eel's two hands closed on her shoulders, and his
wiry strength was put to the utmost to bring her out. It
was a narrow scrape which she could never have made
wearing ordinary clothing. Eel had already busied himself
with a second line, which was looped about their two
cloaks to raise them, and Matild crouched, turning her
head slowly, as she made a detailed survey of all that was
about her.

Though the small area of the beadshop was tightly
crushed by its two court neighbors, it was only one story
tall. However, the houses on either side loomed higher.
Eel did not attempt to climb either of those, but went to
the wall at the back. That projected no higher than Matild's shoulder. In a moment she had followed him,
crouching on the rough surface of that barrier. Below
there was a stretch of rubble where court dwellers must
have dumped the debris of house repairs for years, and
this slanted down to the last of the inner canals.

"The skiff—" Eel's whisper was the slightest of sounds.

She could see easily enough, even in the dim light, the
small, battered boat. Unfortunately there were two shadowy figures beside it, one already tugging at the mooring
rope.

Eel uttered a snarl not unlike that of a hunting hill-cat.

He leaped outward and down, his knees thudding home on the back of the closer of the two men. Matild did not hesitate in following. She had already provided herself with a loose stone from the wall top, and landing rather unhandily on the slope, skidded down toward the boat. The man who had been busy with that turned quickly, only to meet her rough weapon full-face. He gave a small cry and fell.

Eel had risen from the one he had pulled down, and now gave the body a kick so that it rolled over. Matild caught a glimpse of a white face from which startled, glazing eyes stared up at her. She did not need to see the growing runnels of blood from that torn throat to know he was near death.

"We can't leave them—" By main force of will she held to logic and need.

"Boat." Eel was on his knees by the water's edge, swishing the blooded points of his claws in the turgid flow. "Take them—then—over." He made a tossing motion.

Matild felt a sickness she fought fiercely. This was war and the sight of enemy bodies was not going to defeat her so easily. She had never killed before, but then, there had never been any reason to do so.

Together with Eel, she dragged both of the bodies into the skiff, which was weighted down perilously when she and her companion took their own places within. She felt for a pulse at the throat of the man she had battered. There was nothing. And they were both black coats.

If they were to be found near here, all those of the court, even of the street beyond, might be under suspicion. Eel was right: they must be taken away as far as possible. They had nothing to weight the bodies—however, one found floating in the canal might have been dumped there at any point along its length.

She took the sculls and headed close to the embankment on the left. Not too far away was one of the tie bridges, and near there would be a good place to get rid of their perilous cargo. The buildings thereabout were warehouses, and she knew of no residents who could be placed under suspicion.

She fought the water until the bridge loomed near them. Dusk had now become night. Up and down the edges of the canal were the reflections of lanterns, but those could be avoided.

Somehow they got the bodies into the water, though Matild feared twice the skiff would overturn and dump them also. Now the light boat bobbed much higher. Some trick of the current took the two nearly submerged bodies out closer to midstream—and *up!* She had forgotten the sea tides, the force of which in turn fed the canals. But there was nothing she could do now, except hope they did not come ashore where they would make trouble for the innocent.

Her own desire was to get away as quickly as possible, and she put what was left of her strength to the oars, sending the light craft skittering seaward.

Had these been ordinary times, there would have been large night-lanterns lit at intervals along each shore. Matild thanked fortune that some attributes of a world turned upside down did favor them in so much.

"Boat—" Eel hissed. Instantly she strove to head for the left bank. Her companion leaned outward and caught at a trail of vine which had crawled out of some neglected garden. With even so fragile an anchor they were able to bring the skiff close in. And this was just such a pocket of darkness as she would have sought—fortune indeed favored them this night!

Fortune—that would be the first answer—but there was another and stronger influence which must be working for them. She could not see Adele and those other Talented Ones at their prayers and "seeings" but somehow she was very sure that there was a mantle of some protection about them this night.

The boat they had so eluded was much larger, nearly the size of a barge, and it bore no more running lights than they did themselves, signifying that those aboard would pass as unseen as they could. Smugglers—river scum—sneaking out of their holes with the customary canal patrols withdrawn? Or were these more black coats about evil business? There was no way of telling.

She and Eel waited until they were well away. Even then Matild did not first take to oars again. Instead, as Eel was doing, she gripped the wall vines and tugged. Their advance was slow, but it had the advantage of being noiseless.

The vine curtain did not last too long, and she had to return to the oars. Her shoulders were beginning to ache now from the unusual strain being put upon them, but she refused to allow such a minor discomfort to slow her down in any way.

They came at last to a culvert meant to carry the excess of the summer's torrential rains into the canal and away from the city streets. She knew well where they were now—two-thirds of their journey behind them. Awkwardly she swung the skiff into that opening; even Eel had to duck as the rounded top curved over them.

It was only a short distance until the skiff scraped bottom against the stone. Luckily there was no great push of water to send it back into the canal, and they could hopefully leave it here out of sight.

Matild hunched as she splashed into water which carried the taint of refuse in it. She gathered her cloak about her waist to keep it from soaking up that noisome liquid. There came a small pinpoint of light ahead; Eel held a striker on to give them some idea of footing. He knew this path even better than Matild, and she had no fear that they would take the wrong turning.

Twice they passed smaller openings from which the smelly overflow of drains entered the culvert. Then they came upon a ladder reaching from the water to what was manifestly one of those manholes down which repair men and cleaners could come when necessary.

Eel hoisted himself up and pushed, half bent over, with the strength of his shoulders. Matild knew a flutter of alarm. What if it was somehow locked on the other side? Then there was a grating, and it gave. She tugged at Eel's leg.

"Let me try!" she ordered.

He dropped from the ladder so she could take his place, and a moment later she was straining in much the same position he had just held. There was an opening above her—then something gave way and the manhole clanged back and down.

The noise sounded as loud to Matild as a bell peal. She clung to the ladder and tried to listen past the reverberation of sound for any other noise. But there was none.

"Me—first—" Eel was tugging at her. Though she wanted to refuse, Matild knew he was right and yielded to him. He was smaller and far more used to night-slinking than she was. Then a moment or two later, he was looking back down at her.

"All clear."

Again Matild had that feeling that they were being favored—that they were on an errand approved by the Greater Power and that Talents were being woven about them. She came out into a narrow alley. Not too far away hung a night lantern, dangling from it a rope twisted in a complicated pattern. Jonas' own sign! They had come to their goal—or at least to the door of it.

Matild whirled her cloak about so that the inside was now the out, and showed stains and patches. Eel did likewise and produced boldly so a badly mended tear. Muffled by these garments, they slipped to the alley opening and looked out. Again Matild was surprised at the quiet which held here. Usually by dark this section of the city was awakening to its own kind of business. Yet there were dim lights in only a few windows, and only one or two figures kept to the shadows, making haste on whatever errands drew them out of their holes.

Even the front door of Jonas' tavern was closed—something which only occurred during the heights of the great storms. And his shutters were up. Matild was so astounded at this lack of hospitality that she nearly stopped in midstep and lost her balance. Then she caught the narrow glint of lamp light through the shutters and knew that the place could not be altogether deserted.

There was no knocker on the great door, but she dared thud home her fist, twice, then paused, and then four times in quick succession. She and Eel had drawn close together and as far into the overhanging shadow of the doorway as they could. When she had almost given up hope, she saw in the dimness that the door was beginning to open, moving as noiselessly as if every one of the great iron hinges had been recently oiled.

However, it opened no farther than a crack, and there was a hoarse-voiced demand from within.

"Who comes?"

"Twelve arrows and a shield." Matild shaped the words carefully. That *had* been the password that Saxon had lately mentioned, and she trusted that it was one which would still suffice.

The slit at the door's edge became wider and she was able to squeeze inside: Eel was even quicker to get within. The smell of old ale, of slaplick cleaning, and of clothing which needed a good dousing, caught them.

"So—'tis you!" The doorkeeper brought out a lamp he had been hiding behind himself. His tone hardly suggested that they were welcome guests.

"Yes," Matild returned. "We need your aid—"

"As one might expect," he returned, the surly note still thickening his voice. Jonas was usually a philosophical soul, not hunting for any trouble but living in peace until he was fully aroused. "Come, then—"

They followed him away from the door into the wide open serving room. Matild heard a rustle, the thin hiss of whispers.

Then she saw there were at least half a dozen people gathered there, some men, a couple of women wearing the half-masks that were fashionable in this section of town. As these were all grouped about the long table, she guessed that they had interrupted some meeting.

But Jonas did not lead them to the table—instead he stumped along on his wooden leg to a darker corner farther away from the comfort of the fireplace and motioned them to stools. Turning his back on them, he returned to the large broached cask and handily held three tankards at once, well-balanced so they could be filled one after another. Returning with this refreshment, he settled himself on a short bench and stretched out the peg leg.

"They've taken the captain—that's what has brought you here?"

Matild tensed. "When did they get him—how—?" The feeling of being caught in an enfolding and dangerous net was pressing in on her. Saxon had certainly foreseen what might happen to the officials of the government when Merina fell—he surely had prepared a bolt hole even as the three of the Tiger had.

"You might well ask—" Jonas grated. "Dimity?" He raised his voice, and one of the women at the long table turned her head. Jonas jerked a thumb in their direction and she slid off the bench and came to them.

"The captain—" Jonas said, and slapped his wide hand down on the table.

"Message." The woman was as laconic as the innkeeper. "Sealed with the queen's seal—reached him as he was leaving for the harbor. He stepped aside to read it, and those hoodcrows had him—they used throw-ropes and bundled him up before he could pull a weapon."

Her seal—the queen's seal! Her hand went to her breast now to feel that which she still had pinned against her heart—that had been the false seal. By her own supposed cleverness, she had brought down Saxon—well that jewel might be considered one of ill omen.

Her hand slid down now to the first of those lumps in her sash. Ill omen—it seemed that those she would aid were targets. Yet with all her study, she was sure that these could still be weapons if safely used. Nervously she drained her tankard, as did Eel.

"Where did they take him?" she demanded.

The woman shrugged. "They had a barge, chucked him in like a roll of rugs or such. Simpkin—he saw it, too— was waiting to take the captain out, but he dove overboard when the hoodcrows came at him—Simpkin is half seal-dog, they never put eye on him. I think he followed their barge. Would be like him to hook hold on it somehow and follow. At least he ain't back yet."

"The Water Tower—" Matild wondered aloud. If they did hold Saxon there— But it was only a chance.

"There's been someone else askin' for you." Jonas' ale-heavy breath puffed into her face when he leaned closer, as if fearing to be heard. The woman who had been standing beside him turned quickly and went back to the company by the long table.

"Who?" Matild prompted when he did not appear ready to add to that statement.

"Give us a candle inch," he motioned toward where one of the hour-marked candles stood burning steadily, "and we'll get him for you eye to eye."

"Well enough." She nodded. "But Jonas, what of the captain?"

He showed yellowish teeth in a hound's snarl. "That we was just takin' up when you came." He waved his hand toward the company by the table. "We wait—for another couple of candle marks. If Simpkin has news for us, he will head here and I promise you no hoodcrow will sniff out the trail he takes. Lakin?" He raised his voice again, and this time one of the men crossed from the long table.

"Pass the word that you-know-who is wanted—and at the double."

The unshaven, greyish-skinned man stared curiously at Matild and Eel, then slouched toward the door.

"The captain," Jonas was suddenly becoming confidential, as if he somehow sensed in Matild an ally, "he's sent word to the Brethren—expected to join them this night, he did. He's dealt fair and square with 'em, and they know that them as follows him does well for themselves. Those black devils has taken the harbor guard and put their own men in. But they don't know waterways too well. Several of them," now his grin was very broad, "have already gone swimming here and there—never came back, though. Swimming in these waters ain't for them as haven't the feel of the two tides in their bones."

Somehow before she thought, impelled by an impulse she could not understand, Matild spoke.

"Jonas, tonight we killed two of those guards."

He stared at her, and then grinned again. "Now that's a bit of news as one wants to hear. We'll drink us a toast to that."

He was gone before Matild could stop him, returning with their tankards, frothy foam high at the brim.

Though heretofore he had shown no sign of his recognizing her rank, he now leaned once more closely over the table to say softly, "Got rid of the bodies, I'm in hopes, m'lady."

His casual attitude aroused further Matild's dire thoughts of what they had done. It was Eel who answered, matter-of-factly, "In the canal with them."

Jonas was grinning again. "Proper work, youngster. Floaters tell no tales of where they took to the swim uninvited like."

"There will be vengeance." For now, time and events were moving slowly enough that Matild could really think.

"Aye. Them hoodcrows will see to that. We've fallen on hard days, lady."

"Not as hard as will come to be." The newcomer had slipped as silently and as formlessly as a shadow, looming up now behind Eel. It was plain he had not entered by the door. And she knew him well.

"Thom!"

He was scowling at her. "No names, no hanging ropes around one's neck. And a merry task you have pushed on me, lady."

"Shelyra?" She was quick to catch his reference.

"Shelyra—" He accented the name heavily. "She-tiger, more likely. Short of taking a fist to her jaw and laying her out to put ropes on her, no man can control that one. Right back at home, m'lady. She's slipped me twice, and each time she makes for the palace, swears she knows ways as those rats will never nose into. Having a fine time, according to her, watching this fancy-nancy of a prince rule. I'll swear she's got ears clean around her head as to what she has been picking up, listening where they think there are no ears but their own."

There was no use, Matild realized, in hectoring Thom. She knew her niece only too well, and Shelyra's exploration of hidden palace ways would lead her back to that form of gathering information.

"What has she learned?" she asked steadily, aware that Thom must have braced himself for a tirade concerning his lack of control over the princess.

He drew a deep breath. "Well, she had a good bundle of scraps. We've been trying to fit them together when I can get her back into safety. There is some mouthing among the guards that Leopold is more or less of a figurehead, that he is kept from taking any real part in affairs. I think the old cock has no wish to let the younger one do any crowing."

Matild nodded; that fit with what she had seen—the black coats doing as they willed, despite the promises the prince made.

"They've shuffled off the old chancellor to see he doesn't kick over the traces. Old 'Delph is no fighting man—his job is running the territories as the emperor grabs them in and making sure no ambitious member of the court puts a knife in him. He never appears without two bodyguards—and they are rough, overseas fighting men. Leopold hasn't faced up to him any, at least, not while Shelyra had him under watch."

The chancellor—she had a thought for him—

"General Cathal, now he's a nasty one. Only has come to the palace twice as we know—keeps with the army. He's all soldier, and a cruel commander. Most of the atrocities of the past, he thought up. Balthasar so far keeps him close. I think he is going to be held ready as a threat—if Merina don't conform in every way to any new law. Then the general will sit in the prince's seat in the palace." He stopped to draw to him Matild's untouched tankard and took a heavy draught.

"What of Apolon, the mage?" demanded Matild when he did not continue after several swallows.

Thom did not meet her direct glance, but stared down into his tankard. For a long moment he sat silently, and then asked slowly, "Lady, have you ever had your skin crawl as if a slime-worm sought you out? I watched Apolon from hiding, and felt so. This—this *man*—at least he has the appearance of a man—is of the Total Dark."

Now Thom raised his head and did look at her. "Surely I am no saintly son of the Temple, as you well know, lady. And I have had blood on my hands that did not spring from my own veins—but never was it the blood of the innocent and unaware. I am a thief, and you yourself saved me from a hanging to do your will. I have known the dregs of Merina, even the pirates of the coast—and I have heard and seen evil things. I have not heard this Apolon speak anything but platitudes, nor has he raised his hand against anyone—he lets his hoodcrows do that in the name of this new law. But there is such a depth of blackness within him that it catches at a man's throat when he looks upon him. This I will swear to. The evil which has entered this city is centered in this Apolon, and we have seen but the first of it!" His hurried speech carried with it the force of his conviction.

"And he is a mage—" Matild shivered, reached to draw her cloak about her. She felt as if she were suddenly at sea—as if high storm winds struck at her.

Both men were staring at her, and in spite of the low light, she thought she could detect uneasiness in their eyes.

"Lady," it was Thom who found a voice first, "all know the strength of the Tiger and how it holds from generation to generation. What powers may a mage invoke in turn?"

She spread her fingers on the table. Her right thumb felt light and empty without the ring. She owed them frankness; to be deceitful now would weaken all the forces she would try to raise.

"A mage is first, by our standards, a scholar, a seeker of old learning. Second, he comes to the stage where he now labors to put part of that learning to the test. But, as ever in this world, there is the way of the Heart and the way of the Dreadful Dark. Knowledge used to further well-being for others—that is blessed and true as the Heart's Blood. Knowledge used to engender power, to control, to kill—that is of the Dark. The House of the Dragon has in the past produced three mages. All of them entered the Temple when their Talent waxed alive. But there have been no more such now for two generations and I know of no others in Merina."

Except—perhaps Adele? And the archpriestess? The Temple held the secrets of who held power and who did not, and guarded those secrets closely. Now she was glad of it.

"It is this—until we try him, we do not know what this Apolon is, save he has chosen the Dark Way. And we dare not try him until we are sure that we are in as full strength as we can summon."

"While," Thom flung at her, "he can proceed to nibble away at what small chances we have."

Matild nodded. "However . . ." Her hands sought her middle and those lumps in her belt. Her mother's warning crossed her mind, but desperate times needed desperate measures, and she could no longer wait to move.

"However," she began again, "there is something we can use for a testing. Who wears the ring of rule—Balthasar?"

"Shelyra has not seen it on Leopold's hand. It seems the emperor does not think of it as a trinket to be thrown to his substitute."

"So, Leopold does not wear it. Now this chancellor who is so protective of his skin, is he also one who has a liking for riches?"

"He has taken a full quarter of the guild hostage-money for his own," Thom answered her.

"And the general—"

Thom shook his head. "I cannot tell you. Such eyes and ears as we still have can't cover him."

She changed the subject. "Where have they taken Saxon—the Water Tower?"

Thom grimaced. "They have turned the House of the Boar into their new *place of detention*." He accented the last three words. "Since they hung the guild master there, marched off his workmen in one of their slave gangs, thrust Lady Fortuna and her children into the street, they have made it their place of confinement for such as they consider prisoners of note. While they loot all Master Unois' stock and cart it away."

"Yah." Jonas rubbed his stubbled jaw. "The captain— men know about him—he's got better sea knowledge than three-quarters of the emperor's navy. Iffen they can just get him on their side, now—so perhaps they are speaking him soft, and trying to win him over."

Matild uttered a sound which was very close to a snort. And the burly man opposite her at the table nodded.

"Aye, but the captain is a cool one. I think he would not be saying yea or nay too quickly, rather listening to what they offer—or threaten—to see the chance to raise his sail flag again."

The House of the Boar she did not know too well—that was the center of the refined-metal trade of the city, and she had only been inside on high feast days when it was necessary to visit each guild in turn. Still, there was one thing she was certain of—even as the palace was riddled with hidden ways, each guild had secrets known only to the masters and their families, perhaps still unknown to the usurpers.

Eel stirred. The needled nails on his hands scored the table. "Lady Fortuna," he said.

"If she can be found—"

Eel grinned. "Ain't I one of the shadows? That I'll learn quick enough."

"If the captain comes free," Matild turned again to Jonas, "then will there be those who will take his commands?"

The innkeeper stabbed a fleshy thumb toward the party at the table. "Each of them there—they are sworn to the captain, and each of them can give orders to others. The captain had a good plan in the making and sent out the word just before he was took."

Once more Matild fingered the burdened sash. "Thom," she swung upon the young man, "you pride yourself on your thievery. Can you still bring out of the House of the Tiger something—"

His eyes were glistening. "They've got a double guard there, but that is not saying as how I can't loot in and out, too—this very night, if you are wishful for it."

Matild dipped her finger in the ale Eel had hardly touched and began to draw on the tabletop. "This is the walled garden," she explained as she worked, and then gave a small smile, "though I am sure you are well aware of all the precincts of *that* guild house."

His answer was a grin.

"Very well, by the fountain in the garden is a bench. It is deeply graven with the badge of our house. Dig well into the right eye of the Tiger's mask—right, as it faces you. That opens one passage. Now—" Swiftly, she drew more lines, this way and that, some crisscrossing and intercepting. He followed each with the knowing eye of one who has seen such crude maps before and profited by them.

"This brings you to my own workroom," she told him at last. "Therein is a table and in the drawer, a case, unless they have swept all clean. We can only hope that they have not. It is about this size." She swiftly sketched an oblong in the air. "That, I need."

He arose and his hand went to his forehead in a jaunty salute. "You shall have it." It appeared he had no thought of failure. Then he was swiftly gone. Matild nodded to Eel, and he too took off from the table.

"I will need a workplace," Matild announced flatly. "I think that the beadshop may be closed to me."

"You can have the storeroom, lady. Now, what will I tell them as to the captain?" Again, he indicated those at the table.

"That he will be with them as soon as we pull tight some ropes of our own," she returned.

There was nothing to do but wait, and now her body told her that she needed rest. At Jonas' suggestion, she found it in that same storeroom he had suggested, stretched out on a pile of ill-smelling sacks. Crude as it was, it was a bed of sorts, and she was ready to make good use of it.

She would rest an hour, two at the most, and then be back at the shop before false dawn. And as soon as the sun set again, she and Eel would return—until Thom managed to bring her tools and the rest here.

And then—then she would see what she could do to undermine the path the invaders walked, thinking they walked it unopposed.

§ 23 §

SHELYRA

From her spy hole up near the ceiling of the room Leopold was using as a conference chamber, Shelyra watched and listened to what was going on in complete comfort. It used to be the smaller ballroom, the one that the youngsters of the court once used to receive dancing lessons. Now Leopold had moved a small table in, one that could seat six people, and used it to receive reports and consult with the emperor's great lords of state. Evidently Leopold did not yet trust the actual audience chambers—she thought from the way his men were going over each room that he suspected traps for the unwary.

This was one of the more inconvenient passageways and it was only half-height; she had to crawl along it, as it ran above the level of the door frames. On the other hand, that made it far less likely that anyone would discover it.

She lay with her head pillowed on one arm and her eye up against the spy hole, and found herself feeling rather sorry for the beleaguered prince as he listened to the reports of two of his officers.

That's stupid. I should be glad that things are difficult for him! And I should be glad that he is baffled by how to fix them!

"Apolon's men are everywhere, sir," one of the captains concluded apologetically. "And anywhere they are, they keep us out. At a guess, I would say that Apolon replaced all of the local law-keepers with his own men, which makes us redundant at best."

The prince drummed his fingers on the table in the ensuing silence. From where she lay, Shelyra could not see his face, but it didn't take a mage to know he was probably frowning. "I can't do anything if they decide to exclude you, Kastor," he said, finally. "I certainly do not want you to try and force the issue. The best I can do is to tell the emperor, and point out that we will have a difficult time doing the job he ordered us to do if we are prevented from even entering some sections of the city by Apolon's men."

The captain sighed tiredly. "In that case, sir, perhaps we ought to be reassigned to the palace. At least we can be useful there, looking for any tricks that might have been left behind." He looked as disgusted with the situation as Leopold sounded. From some interesting shadings in his voice, Shelyra guessed that the black coats were almost as unpopular with the emperor's regulars as they were with the citizens of Merina.

Leopold nodded. "Make it so," he ordered. "We're holding the roads well enough; no one is going to get in or out of the city without passing one of our checkpoints. We've done that much of our job, at any rate."

The captain saluted, as did the other officer; they turned briskly and left.

The prince turned to the person on his right, a plump man in rich robes of plum velvet. "You see what I mean now, Adelphus?" he said with disgust. "No matter what I decide, I'm going to fail. If I order my men to do their duties and to hell with Apolon's lot, I violate the emperor's order to let Apolon's men do what they want. If I issue more orders like this one, I violate the emperor's orders to pacify the city." He threw up his hands in a gesture of despair. "So what am I supposed to do here?"

"Did you get in to see the dowager queen?" Adelphus asked, inconsequentially.

Changing the subject? Shelyra wondered. *But why? Maybe because he can't answer the question.*

"Yes." Leopold probably read the abrupt change of subject the same way Shelyra had. "If she doesn't die within the next day or so, I not only will be very much surprised, but I am going to request the services of their infirmarian for the troops, for the man is surely a worker of miracles. Whatever Apolon thinks is going on—well, I can only say that his vaunted powers must be failing him. That poor old woman could hardly breathe; if he thinks she's going to engineer some sort of conspiracy from her deathbed, he's out of his senses." His tone changed to one of profound but repressed anger. "I'll tell you something else— I am *not* sending my men out to hunt for the queen and the princess on his say-so, either. If he wants them found, let him send out his own men; he seems to have enough of them. For all *I* know or care, they both went out and flung themselves into the canals in despair after the abdication. It's what *I'd* have done in their place."

"Perhaps they did at that," the chancellor said smoothly. "I certainly cannot imagine how two insignificant women are managing to hide themselves so effectively from such a concerted manhunt. Either that, or they left the city and are heading across the sea, and of no consequence to us."

Insignificant women? Why that pompous, conceited, bubble-headed booby! Shelyra seethed. *Just wait until he moves into the palace and I get a chance at him! I'll show him who's insignificant!*

"The point is, the only place where I'm able to do the job that was set me is here, in the palace," Leopold said, adroitly turning the conversation back to the topic *he* wanted to cover. "What am I supposed to do? If I complain to the emperor, I'm going to look ineffective—if I don't, I won't get anything done!"

The chancellor sighed. "I suppose I'll have to speak to the emperor about the problem," he said reluctantly. "I'm supposed to be observing how you're getting on, and that is certainly an observation, and a valid one."

Leopold snorted and lurched up out of his chair to pace the floor.

He's done so much pacing there must be a trench worn away, Shelyra thought. *I wouldn't want to be in his position. He can't possibly win, no matter what he does, and he knows it. Either he's not very bright, or he's dreadful at playing politics; I can't imagine how he got himself locked into this situation.*

She should have been pleased, but somehow she wasn't. From everything she had observed, poor Leopold was a fine officer, courteous to all, conscientious of the welfare of his men—and absolutely ineffective. Not because he couldn't have done everything he'd been ordered to and more—but because no one was allowing him to do so.

She had found herself wishing, more than once, that Leopold had been on *their* side. With someone like him to rouse the populace and inspire them, Merina might have been able to defend itself even against the emperor.

Of course, if Leopold had been on their side, *he* would not have allowed the city defenses to rely on nothing more than the old stratagems of bribery, diplomacy, and alliance. He would have recognized the threat that Balthasar represented long before the emperor was in a position to think about taking Merina, and would have established a standing army—

Damn. I believe I'm beginning to like this man, she thought with chagrin. *He's worth two hundred Thom Talesmiths. His father is a fool. But—he may be honorable, he may be brave, but he can't be bright. Even an idiot could have seen this position was a trap.*

"Well," the chancellor said, after watching Leopold pace for a few moments, "I had best be getting back to the camp. The emperor will be waiting for my report."

"I—" Leopold began, then shook his head. "Never mind. As you can see, the great palace at least will be ready for occupation shortly. Just give me warning so that I can dismiss the servants and bring up the emperor's servitors from the camp."

"I shall." The chancellor levered himself up from his chair and ambled toward the door. "Stop wearing yourself out with that infernal pacing, Leopold. Go get some rest. I'm sure things will be better in the morning."

The chancellor's two bodyguards joined him at the door, a pair of burly blonds who looked as if they regularly threw cattle around to strengthen their muscles. What they had in brawn, they lacked in brains, however. Shelyra had observed more than once that the simplest of machines, like a snapfire, completely baffled them. If told to make a light, they invariably plucked an entire candelabra from a mantle and held the whole thing in the fire, with unfortunate results for the candles.

Strong like bull, dumb like ox, hitch to plow when horse dies. If someone actually attacked the chancellor—say, doing something really clever, the way an assassin would— it was even odds that these two gems would not *notice* that anything was wrong until he was stone dead and the perpetrator well out of reach.

Leopold stood beside the table for a moment longer after the chancellor left, then shook his head. "He's right about one thing," the prince said aloud. "I'm not getting anything done pacing."

He left the room himself, but Shelyra knew where he was going to go. He went there every night, just before he left the palace and retired to the garrison, where he stayed with his men. Only the palace servants stayed here at night. He was not trusting the safety of his men or himself to ground he was not certain of.

She levered herself up off the passage floor and took her own route to the palace chapel. There was a spy hole there, too, and Leopold had a habit of speaking his thoughts out loud when he was in the solitude of the chapel. Sometimes she learned something useful.

The chapel was a fairly plain room; it wasn't used much, since the Temple was so near. It didn't even have a representation of the Heart—only a many-rayed lantern over the altar, a stylistic version of the Eternal Light. Her aunt had ordered the lamp put up in place of the Heart image, and the queen was probably the only member of the royal family who *did* use the plain little chapel rather than walking to the Temple.

Leopold seemed to find some transitory peace here, however. He never failed to make this his final stop of the day, no matter how tired he seemed to be.

He had gotten there before her and stood with his hands clasped behind his back, looking up at the Light, in silence.

Finally he broke that silence.

"I don't really care for myself if I'm disgraced," he said aloud. "But my men—there isn't another commander I'd want to see them working under. Especially not Cathal. The man's a brute. There're stories about him—stories I can't even repeat without feeling sick. I've seen him when we've taken a city—did You know that his personal troops are all mercenaries, because the imperial troops won't suffer a man that vicious as their commander? What am I thinking, of course You do." He sighed, and one hand came up to rub his temple.

"The other thing—I'm afraid of what might happen in this city if Cathal gets control of it. Or Apolon, but I don't think my father is likely to put a mage who's never commanded more than a couple of servants in charge of a city. If Adelphus gets it—Adelphus would be all right. He understands money, knows you can't milk a cow till she drops and expect her to keep producing for you. He'd probably make things hard for people, but he wouldn't make them impossible. But Cathal—he didn't get his siege, didn't get his battle, didn't get to sack the place. He's fuming about that. You must know that, surely." His voice turned a bit harsh. "I always thought that this city was supposed to be someplace special for You—can't You do something? You don't have to help *me*, but You ought to help Your city!" His voice held a note of real pleading, a tone that made Shelyra hold her breath with surprise.

"There's something else—You might not be able to see into a heart as black as Apolon's—I've learned enough to know that if the queen and the princess are taken, *he* gets them. It's all set up; he's going to be the one put in charge of them. There's something he wants out of them; I don't know what it is, but it's going to be bad, very bad for them. He's even ready to break into the Temple and take the old woman if he gets permission from my father. I think he plans to use her as a way to bring the other two out of hiding. Now, that's breaking Your sanctuary, besides being repugnant and reprehensible— When I saw the dowager, I tried to warn her. I only hope she understood."

That revelation left Shelyra frozen in place. Leopold shifted his weight back and forth, as if he'd like to pace, but wouldn't do it here.

"I've done what I can, and still hold my own honor and my loyalty to the emperor," he said finally. "It's going to be up to You."

And with that, he turned and left the chapel, leaving Shelyra still standing at the spy hole, numb.

When she could finally move, she made her way down to the servants' quarters. If Leopold had *said* he'd tried to warn Adele, then that was exactly what he'd done. And Adele surely understood that warning. She wasn't stupid, and she certainly wasn't as feeble in mind or body as she was pretending to be.

But I'm going to the Temple tomorrow night anyway, she promised herself. *I'll warn her then.*

Not even Apolon was going to be able to get into the cloisters without a great deal of trouble, anyway. He wouldn't be able to simply kidnap Adele—he wouldn't know what cell she was in. That left force, and force meant a troop of his men.

And a troop of black coats marching on the Temple was going to be noticed in a hurry, even if they came from the palace rather than the city.

As she reasoned this out, she made her way down through the maze of passageways until she got to the area reserved for the single rooms of upper servants, and the dormitory rooms of the lower servants.

She had been trying to leave subtle messages there,

each night that she roamed this place. She would whisper the names of the rulers of Merina into the quiet air of the dormitories, reciting the lineages she had been required to memorize as a child. She left tiny tiger eye stones on the floor where they would be found in the morning when the servants cleaned. Sometimes she dripped water out of a particular spy hole at the eyes of an official portrait of some long-dead king, so that the portrait appeared to weep. At other times, she whispered phrases in a hollow, mournful tone—"How can you sleep, when Merina lies groaning beneath the conqueror's boot?" "Weep, weep, O my city! By the waters of the river, lie down and weep!" "Sorrow and woe, sorrow and woe unending, to the cowards who will not snap their bonds!" "The Tiger lies in chains, and her den is looted by greedy apes!"

She particularly liked that one.

The idea was to make it seem as if the long-dead kings and queens of the city were walking the palace restlessly, stirred up by the conquering interlopers.

She couldn't tell if it was working or not; by day, she was too busy tending the horses, keeping them inwardly healthy, but outwardly on the verge of foundering. The black coats had already been to Gordo's compound once, to assess his stock, and had gone away snarling with disgust but unable to dispute the evidence of their own eyes. Since they had already set the amount of his license to do business, they couldn't make it up by inflating that fee, either.

The fee for doing business *had* made Gordo swear and kick hay bales for the better part of a day. It was outrageous—a hundred times the cost of the same license under Lydana's rule. As an act of revenge, Gordo summoned the black coats to come fetch it themselves, claiming he dared not leave his sick stock for even a moment, and paid it to them in the form of the smallest copper coins he could lay his hands on. They'd been forced to stagger away under a pair of enormous, heavy bags containing the coins, and Gordo had arranged for the bags themselves to be weakened along the seams.

The guards apparently got nearly halfway to the city gates before the seams broke.

Shelyra wished she'd been there. Thom had been, and his description of the black coats scrabbling on hands and knees after the coins in the dust had even Gordo smiling again. They'd had to take off their handsome coats and use *those* as bags to get the coins to the emperor's treasury.

Finally she finished her whisperings, completed leaving her signs and portents. It was time to go back to Gordo's, catch a little sleep, and then doctor those poor horses again.

She yawned as she made her way down one of the escape-tunnels—there were things stored here that she hadn't left, which meant this was probably the one her aunt and Skita had used. That made her think of Thom, who had been conspicuous by his absence, claiming that he was making observations around the city.

Huh. He just doesn't want to be drafted into cleaning stalls. Sick horses do make more of a mess than healthy horses.

That was fine. If he wasn't in the compound, he wasn't nagging at her about going to the Horse Lords.

There are still things I can do here, she thought stubbornly. *And until that changes—I stay here.*

§ 24 §

APOLON

To his face, they called him "The Grey Mage." Behind his back, they called him other things. "Balthasar's Hellhound" was one of the more polite titles; many were considerably cruder than that. But whatever they called him, their voices always held a note of fear, and they looked over their shoulders when they named him, fearing he was somewhere near, listening.

The Grey Mage sat back at his ease in his comfortably upholstered camp chair, while his chief attendant recited the reports of all of his spies. Not everything Apolon did was by means of magic—he found mortal eyes and ears to be just as useful. It was those same mortal eyes and ears that had brought him enough information to convince Balthasar to attack Merina in the first place. Tales of its riches—and its lack of defenses—had made it an irresistible target for the emperor. The fact that it held something Apolon wanted, and wanted badly, had made him turn Balthasar's eyes to it.

"And Leopold has been asking questions about you," the attendant finished in a hoarse whisper. "Many questions."

Apolon frowned, for that was certainly nothing he had anticipated out of the insipid prince. "Questions?" he repeated. "What sort of questions?"

What could that puppy want? Not blackmail, surely—

he was too honorable and upright to stoop to such a thing. What did he think to learn? And what did he intend to do with the information when he had it?

"He has learned that you have been granted custody of the Tiger women, once they are taken," the attendant whispered. "He has been questioning what you intend to do with them—the arrangements you have made for them, and so forth. He has been talking with your servants, and I believe also that he is trying to gain an impression of how you perform your magics."

Apolon repressed a surge of anger, and another of apprehension. Of all of the members of the court, Leopold was the only one clever enough to deduce something of the source of Apolon's powers from descriptions gleaned from servants. He might be vapid, but he was not vacuous; there was a quick mind behind all the honor and sentiment. And Leopold was the only one intelligent enough to see that Apolon's arrangements for the two women were short-term at best, though they were certainly *secure* arrangements.

Put the two together, and suspicions would begin; if Leopold had gotten any amount of information, he could probably find a way to garner some proof of his suspicions.

Such as—sending a few men back to some of the imperial conquests, to put together lists of missing men. Not all of Apolon's conscripts had been culled from the ranks of the conquered. Sometimes he had not had the freedom to be that choosy about who he recruited.

"He learned nothing, of course," the attendant continued soothingly. "Those he questioned know better than to say anything to anyone about their master."

Apolon grunted. He was not inclined to be so dismissive, but there were steps that he could take now that he had been warned. "And what about the search for a place where I can work in freedom?"

The attendant bowed his head. "I regret to report, my lord, that the most suitable place has already been taken. We have not yet found one to match it."

"Taken?" Apolon said in astonishment. "Taken? What

is the place? Who took it? Not Leopold, surely—if one of those puling fools of Merina dropped a copper groat, Leopold would pick it up and hand it back to him."

"Not Leopold, lord," the attendant confirmed. "Cathal. General Cathal. The emperor has granted him the right to take the guild masters hostage and ransom them. Some of them have resisted—one refused to divulge the secrets of his house, and Cathal had him hung, then moved his men into the house. It is that house that is so suitable to your needs—the House of the Boar. It has all the aspects that you specified; no other place we have yet looked at has them all."

"Really?" Apolon considered that. "And why did Cathal take it?"

He did not expect the servant to know, but surprisingly, the man did. "There are rooms below, meant for the storage of costly weapons, that are suitable for the keeping of prisoners. But most of all, the place holds a blade said to be of some mystical power, and Cathal wants it."

Apolon dismissed that with a wave of his hand. "Cathal is welcome to all the toys he wishes. I want the house! Will he go when he has his plaything?"

The attendant hesitated, then said, "I believe that he will. There are better places to keep prisoners—and in any event, being Cathal, he may not keep them for long. They are too much trouble to him."

That was good enough. Apolon dismissed the eunuch with a wave of his hand and settled back in his chair.

So, Cathal now had his hand in Merina—and predictably, was reverting to his old habits. He just could not resist taking prisoners and holding them for ransom!

Then again, with all those mercenaries to contend with, Cathal needed a readier source of cash than the imperial payboxes. His mercenaries had been denied their looting spree, so he had to find them some other compensation. Yes, that was predictable enough.

That would pinch Leopold nicely. His own black coats had a virtual stranglehold on the common folk, and now

Cathal's men were milking the wealthy, who probably had considered themselves safe from harassment until now.

That left only the Temple.

Now *that* was a thorn in his side! He could not get his black coats in, not at the moment, and not without a great deal of sacrifice. Nor could he step over the threshold yet. His initial survey of the place had proved that to him. He had hoped initially that the Temple here would prove to be as corrupt and weakened as the one in Wolderkan— he had been able to stroll right across the doorstep with his army of servants and take the artifacts there for his own. But this Temple was held by those of the true and pure faith, perhaps kept that way by the effect of the Heart of Power . . . which made things a bit difficult for him.

At least, it would until he got his safe and secure working-place. At that point, he would be able to raise enough power to do anything he liked, including stroll across the Temple threshold. Once his staff was properly fed, there would be no barrier that could hold him out.

He closed his eyes to think for a moment—just a moment—

Quickly, he jerked himself awake, just as he was falling asleep. He felt a cold chill of fear, as he realized how close to unguarded slumber he had just come.

No mage of his kind dared let himself sleep an unprotected sleep. He must be in his bed, surrounded by talismans and guardians, and drugged, to prevent dreams from intruding on his rest and his mind. Mages who had fallen into a natural sleep had awakened mad—or never awakened at all. His own teacher had been one such, and Apolon had a hand in that fact. Every Dark mage had a hundred enemies or more, some of them not human, waiting for him to make a slip so that they could destroy him and appropriate his power. Apolon could not recall the last time he had been able to simply doze off without thinking about it.

He must be very tired to have slipped so far. It would

not happen again. Not now, when he was so near his ultimate goal.

Was there anything more for him to do?

Not at the moment. He ran over the list in his mind and could find nothing he had left out. Tomorrow he would have a talk with Balthasar about the way the boy was subverting the authority of his black coats. With any luck whatsoever, Balthasar would start wondering how long it would take before Leopold started subverting the *emperor's* authority. And Apolon would be there to encourage those thoughts.

Tomorrow he would also look into acquiring that house from Cathal. The first thing to do would be to find out what this toy was that the general wanted. If he had not already taken it, the object must be protected magically in some way. In that case, perhaps he could offer his own services.

Then he would look into finding a way to persuade the general to abandon the house, leaving it to Apolon. Once he had all secure, he could send someone into the palace to look through the rooms of the two missing women for artifacts with which to find them—but *first* he must find a way to replenish the ranks of his men.

He had a ship out in the harbor, loaded with some choice selections from the streets for his recruits, but the laws of magic made it impossible for him to work on a ship here, where all water was running water. No, he had to have a place in the city, earth-rooted, and the deeper, the better.

But the House of the Boar—that sounded promising. He rose from his chair and summoned another attendant.

Tomorrow. Yes. Tomorrow, many things would be set into motion.

✤ 25 ✤

THOM

Thom Talesmith was not a happy man.

Not that he was unhappy about being within the walls of this particular establishment; if he *had* to be inside Merina, he would just as soon be with the Gypsies and their Horse Lord allies and cousins. This was probably the safest place in all of Merina for someone of his reputation, for as yet, the emperor's men had not dared to force their way into this compound. Nevertheless, he was still *here*; and this was what made him so unhappy. He was just about ready to tear large hanks of his own hair out of his head as he stood over the princess and fumed.

The whole point was that they weren't supposed to be here at all, in any way, for any reason. Yet here they were, in a small, windowless room with two entrances, one obvious, and one not. They should have been well out of Merina, on the way to the endless plains that were the Horse Lords' stronghold.

Shelyra pointedly ignored his temper, as she had ignored just about everything else he had said and done since the two of them were shackled together by her aunt. She sat on the room's single stool, before the small table and mirror, and beneath a small oil lamp placed above the mirror on the wall. With no windows in this room, the lamp was needed by night and day.

Damn and blast the wench! Can't anything drive some sense into that head? Bad enough that she has to go back to the palace once—but to keep doing so, every other night? Has she no sense?

Evidently not. The princess finished tying on her shark-skin-soled, soft boots, and bound her hair up into a tight knot on the top of her head, pulling the hood of her black, tight-fitting tunic on over it so that not a single strand showed. She took two handfuls of soot and smeared her forehead and cheeks with the air of someone who has done such things so many times in the past that it was second nature. Then she surveyed the result in the mirror and nodded.

"We are *supposed* to be gone from here. We should be leaving the city while we still can, Your Greatness," he said for the twentieth time. "We should have gone as soon as that odd little servant of your aunt took your earring to her. The Horse Lords are perfectly willing to hide you, and the Gypsies can get you out, but we don't know how much longer those conditions will last. We *promised* the queen—"

"You promised the queen. I made no such promises." The maddening creature completed her preparations in a state of grim calm. "I am staying here. There is work to be done, if Merina is ever to shake off the collar of these imperial hound-masters."

"Then at least stay away from the palace!" Thom begged hopelessly. "The place is swarming with Prince Leopold's men, if they catch you—"

"They won't catch me." Shelyra raised an eyebrow in carefully schooled contempt. "They can't. There is no way to open up any of those passages by accident, not any-more. I locked most of them before we left the palace, and locked the ones we used to leave behind us. They can only be opened now from the inside. You can only get into them from the entrances outside the palace grounds, and I doubt that even the black coats would look for entrances there."

"They can still be opened with an ax," Thom retorted,

his neck hot as blood rose in him at her open contempt. "The walls are thick; it's only a matter of time before someone in Leopold's entourage notices just *how* thick they are and comes to the obvious conclusion! You're a fool, girl. The emperor is old in treachery, his dog Apolon older still—"

"And neither of them is here." Would the girl *never* let him finish a sentence? "Only the prince, who does not appear to me to be overly bright." She smiled cynically. "I believe I can protect myself from *him*."

"At least let me go with you this time," he pleaded. She only snorted. She didn't trust him; she'd made that abundantly clear. She thought he only wanted to learn the secrets of the palace so that he could help himself to the treasures there at a later date. Not that he wouldn't have done just that, under ordinary circumstances—

But not now. He shivered. He considered himself a brave man, but he had no intention of going into the palace now. Not while the empire held this city. There were some things that were just not worth the risk.

Shelyra rose to her feet and turned toward the hidden door. This door connected to what appeared to be a blind passageway in the part of the building reserved for storage. From here she could make her way invisibly to a postern gate down a noisome alley not even the black coats bothered to watch. And from there she would somehow get to the palace. She seemed very confident of her ability to do so undetected. She *said* she was a hunter, though how being a hunter could give one street-skulking skills he had no notion.

This sort of nonsense would have been enough to raise the hair on a saint. It had Thom tearing his out by the fistful.

She touched a hidden catch, and the wall panel swung open. He put out a hand to stop her, and she turned to face him for a moment with an expression of utter contempt.

She thought he was a coward. *Him!* He pulled back his

hand in an automatic reaction; she slipped through the panel, and it closed behind her.

For lack of anything better to do, Thom took himself down to the courtyard, where there was always a fire burning and folk gathered about it. Usually there were dancers and musicians from both the Gypsy families and the Horse Lord clan. Not that there had been anything to celebrate in the past few days, but musicians needed to keep in practice no matter what the circumstances were—and several of the dance styles were nothing more nor less than cleverly disguised fighting exercises. Naturally there were already edicts forbidding any kind of martial practice, but of course there was nothing to prohibit a dancer from practicing his—or her—art.

Just at the moment, the musicians were all men, and the dancers too, practicing the Horse Lords' stick-dance. *Very impressive, very exhilarating, especially in the firelight.* And no one who did not also know the Horse Lords would guess it was a refined form of stick fighting that was as deadly as it was impressive. It took years to master; Thom had never even bothered to try. A man could only master so much in a single lifetime.

As Thom stood there among the Gypsies, with the staccato clapping and drumming joining with his heartbeat, the thin white sticks flashing through the red-lit gloom, the pounding of feet on the ground, he suddenly felt eyes on him.

Someone was watching him closely.

He turned quickly, to find the odd little creature that the queen used as her messenger standing behind him and staring at him—now, as before, made up convincingly as a boy. She watched him with sharp eyes that revealed nothing of her own thoughts, and Thom thought that it would take a very clever person to recognize the tiny telltales revealing that the boy was really a dwarfish, slimly built woman. When she saw him turn, she jerked her head toward the stables and vanished into the shadows of the courtyard.

He stifled a sigh and shoved his hands into his pockets, turning to walk in the indicated direction. There was a single shadowed lantern burning just inside the door, sending a dim wedge of light out into the courtyard. The odd little woman was there before him, leaning insolently against the door frame, for all the world like a cocky adolescent.

She spoke first. "You're still here, but my box is not." A flat statement, but one with more than a hint of accusation.

He bristled a little. "As for the second, there wasn't time before dawn last night. And as for the first, that's hardly *my* fault," he countered. "I can't get the girl to leave! In fact"—the words tumbled out of his mouth before he could stop them, colored heavily with resentment—"in fact, she decided she was going to go spying in the palace every night, and nothing I can say or do would change her mind!"

"So, you can't control her, hmm?" Sardonic amusement lit the little woman's eyes, and Thom restrained the urge to throttle her. "Odd. I would have thought from your reputation you would have no trouble convincing her to do what you wished."

"Nobody told me I had to control her," he said sullenly. "That wasn't in the agreement, and I doubt you could have convinced the queen to agree to what I'd have to do to 'control' her. 'Get her out of the city,' you said, 'take her to the Horse Lords.' Well, she's with the Horse Lords, so half of my bargain is complete, and if *she* won't leave after all my arguing and persuading, I consider the rest of the agreement to be null and void."

The creature chuckled. "You could, of course, knock her on the head, bundle her up in a bag, and carry her out whether or not she liked it. You wouldn't have to tell the queen how you got her out."

The idea had a certain appeal—an appeal which was canceled by the certainty of what she'd do to him if he tried, or worse, succeeded! *Soprano is not my best range, and anyone accepted into the Horse Lord families knows how to use that gelding tool of theirs as readily as most people can use a fork.*

"That wasn't in the agreement," he repeated stubbornly. "You just go tell the lady that I'll get her box tonight, and that I wash my hands of the wench. I'll protect her where and when I can, but if she refuses to have my company and won't allow me to follow her, there's nothing I can do."

Now the little imp laughed aloud. "In that case, *you* still owe my lady half of your life. So, the way for you to redeem it is—fetch the box she asked you to get, and perform another little task, easier than the first."

"What?" he asked suspiciously.

"Follow me and find out," the infuriating creature said mockingly. "Unless, of course, you're as cowardly as you are ineffective. You still haven't gotten that box, which makes you one or the other to my mind."

Stung, he followed in the imp's wake as she scampered across the courtyard to the same postern gate Shelyra had just used. The stench in the midnight-dark alley was enough to knock a camel to its knees, and his feet slipped in puddles and piles of things he really did not want to think about. On the other hand, he also didn't want to think about running into any black coats.

The creature had an uncanny instinct for avoiding the black coats, holding him back or gesturing him on so that all he ever glimpsed of those birds of ill-omen was the tail of a coat vanishing around a corner, or the tip of a staff showing above a wall. He soon had his bearings; if she was going where he thought, she was heading for Stingray's Court, a place of small tradesmen, minor guild workers, and their homes and the businesses that supported them. At length she brought him to a shabby-genteel quarter of shops, all of them closed and shuttered tightly against the night and what walked it. After a furtive glance around, the creature raced across the street to a particular shop, knocked once, and gestured to Thom. She vanished into the shadows of the door, as Thom followed her example, scuttling across the street like one of the shadows.

The door was open a crack when he got there, and the creature nowhere in sight, but a hand reached through and seized his sleeve, drawing him inside abruptly. He did not attempt to fight, and stood blinking in the light of a lantern as the woman shouldered him a little aside to lock her door.

The room was as shabby-genteel as the exterior of the shop; what little furniture there was was worn, but of decent quality, and it appeared that the front window could be opened to make a display shelf for whatever goods were purveyed here. He recognized the woman who held his arm as the queen, but only because he had some small experience with disguise himself. He doubted very much that there were many people in this city who *would* know that the faintly overblown and shop-worn brunette had even a passing resemblance to the missing queen. Well, that answered one question; where the queen herself had gone. He didn't think she'd moved into Jonas' back room, and interestingly enough, she didn't appear to be any more eager to leave Merina than her niece.

So, that only proves they are both fools!

The lady's small creature was completing a whispered monologue as the lady herself locked the door, and the queen favored him with a disapproving glare as the tiny woman spoke her last word. He merely shrugged.

"If *you* can't control her, why should you assume I could?" he replied to the unspoken disapproval. "She does what she wants, and neither one of us can do anything about it now." He added something else that had occurred to him. "Her friends among the Horse Lords and the Gypsies are likely to take any attempt I make to coerce her very badly. My blood-oath isn't as strong as hers—and they place a high premium on personal courage. If they see me trying to stop her, I could find myself in serious trouble with them. They might toss me out, and then there wouldn't be anyone trying to protect her back or make her be cautious."

The queen grimaced and nodded grudgingly, as if acknowledging the simple justice of his statement.

"Don't think you'll get off without having to do anything to earn your life and freedom," the queen said then. "I still need that box, and I have another task for you." Her mouth quirked slightly. "It's one you'll find familiar, I'll wager. I need you to steal something else besides that box."

"Not from the palace—" he interjected.

But the Queen shook her head. "Not the palace, no. Not even someplace particularly difficult for someone of your fame to get into. Just the common workshops of the House of the Tiger. There is a certain wooden casket, so long"—her hands measured it for him—"so tall, and so deep. It should be among the tools at the third bench from the door in the great workshop. I need that. It holds more tools that I don't have with me. You can get the box I asked you for at the same time, I imagine."

He did not ask her what she needed it for. Without a doubt, she had her reasons. "And do I bring it to you?"

But she shook her head. "I will be—elsewhere. Eel will be waiting for it, just outside the house; Eel can guide you to where I am, or take both things from you if you've roused guards. That way, even if you are pursued and stopped, they won't find anything on you."

He raised an eyebrow. *Eel? That's what the dwarf is calling herself? Well, that fits, right enough.*

He offered a sketchy salute. "The box and the casket are as good as yours, lady," he replied, with a hint of his old self-assurance. "I'll have them out of there before dawn. I was planning on getting the box tonight, anyway. By the time I got out into the street last night, it was too close to dawn to chance it. I didn't think you wanted me to get arrested before retrieving your belongings."

"If you can get it in the next few hours, that would be best." No admiration, nothing but matter-of-fact acceptance of the fact that he was about to work a small miracle. Not even the acknowledgment that it *was* a miracle. He ground his teeth in annoyance, but did not allow his pique to show.

Instead, as he turned to let himself out into the street, he cast his own sally over his shoulder.

"While you're waiting, you might take some thought to how I'm supposed to 'control' that wench of yours," he said flatly. "Else she's likely to get us all killed."

And with that comforting aside, he vanished into the shadowed darkness.

✦ 26 ✦

SHELYRA

She would rather have died than admit it to that boaster, Thom Talesmith, but Shelyra had been terrified every moment of her journey across town. She was terrified every night, for that matter; she was not as confident of her ability to evade the black coats as she claimed. Only when she let herself back in through the hidden door to the tunnel beneath the garden did she breathe easier. In fact, she paused in that secret room she had used for her transformation into Raymonda to take long, deep breaths until her heart stopped pounding. She was not looking forward to the return trip. There had been far too many of those black-coated crows out there, and they seemed to be able to see in the dark as well as any owl!

But for now, she was here, and once again it was time to take the measure of their conquerors. They'd finally moved into the palace today, and she needed to see if there were any changes.

The public rooms, first, then the working rooms, like the kitchen. I want to see if they are holding any conferences, and I want to see how they are treating the servants. If they haven't turned all the servants out today, that is. I doubt that they are going to keep them much longer.

She slipped silently along the passageways, going first to the throne room. The palace was silent—uncannily so, even though it was very late at night. She might have been the only living thing in it.

She had expected to find the prince holding court from her aunt's throne, but the throne room was empty, with only a few lights burning, and it did not look to have been used since the abdication.

That was certainly odd, considering that the emperor had held the city for more than a week, and the prince had been in residence for a full day. Odder still was the utter lack of *noise*; she had also expected by this time to find drunken soldiers roistering in the halls and helping themselves to whatever they could find. By now the discipline imposed by being in strange and unsecure territory should have worn off. But as she traversed the maze of hidden passageways, she discovered only soldiers standing the nightwatch, in pairs, stationed on every corridor. Their officers were sleeping soberly, quartered in groups among the chambers once reserved for guests and their retinues. Searching for the common soldiers, she found them garrisoned in the rooms once allotted to the servants.

Everywhere she found only discipline and order. There was no sign of abuse, of looting, not so much as a single vase out of place. There was a lock on the door of the wine cellar, but nothing on the pantry doors, the implication being that a hungry man could help himself, but Leopold did not believe in putting too much temptation in the path of his men.

Eventually she came, once again, to a grudging admiration. Leopold, it seemed, had the respect and obedience of his men, if nothing else. He *had* turned the old servants out today, but that was to be expected. He could hardly trust them, after all, especially after some of the games she'd been playing here. Of course, that meant that nothing had been properly *cleaned* in the palace since the emperor took the city, but she doubted that a little dust was going to trouble a professional soldier.

Unfortunately, that meant there wasn't much to learn here tonight. Sober and quiet men did not let secrets fall from their lips. But the order here gave her a very odd and disquieting impression—as if the person commanding the black coats and the person commanding the soldiers quartered in the palace were two entirely different people. There were rumors reported by the Gypsies that the black coats were Apolon's men only, and not only not regular imperial troopers, but that they didn't even have to answer to the emperor for what they did. Could it be that Leopold commanded only the palace and not the city, that the black coats who reported only to Apolon not only ran free, but actually held the city itself? Could the enemy be as divided as all that?

If that was the case—perhaps she could sow further confusion among them.

Her own lips curved in a smile as she watched a pair of soldiers pace back and forth in one of the hallways. *I wonder if they find the silence and the emptiness as uncanny as I would? I've never known a soldier that wasn't as superstitious as an old maid. I wonder if I can't encourage them to believe that the palace is even more haunted than the servants have been claiming? Perhaps I should be less subtle in my "hauntings." And while I'm at it, I should haunt the Summer Palace, as well.*

The idea had its charms, it certainly did! If the palaces got the repute for being the residence of angry spirits, the soldiers might demand to be quartered elsewhere! And that would divide the prince from his fighters, besides giving her freer access to this palace itself. Originally, she had hoped to make the servants nervous, make them re-

luctant to serve their new masters—and spread the tale of
the "hauntings" in the palace into the city, in hopes the
tale would cause unrest in the city. But if she could cause
unrest among the imperial soldiers—that would be better
still!

*In that case—no more little signs, mere whispers and
noises in the dark, tiny changes where no one but a servant
would see them. Time to make the "spirits" manifest in a
much more obvious fashion.*

She spent the next hour or so—slipping briefly out of
hidden doors into empty rooms, preferably rooms she
knew were locked—making mischief. In one room, she
left all the chairs upside down. In another, she turned all
of the portraits of the members of the House of the Tiger
to face the wall. She piled ornaments into a pyramid in
the middle of a table, strewed beans all over the floor of
the kitchen, and in her aunt's bedroom, removed all the
bedclothing and carried it into the tunnel, leaving only the
embroidered coverlet, and soaking the featherbed with water. Everything would seem normal there—until whoever
usurped this room tried to go to bed!

She could not face her own rooms, not now, not when
she was certain that the invaders had gone through her
things at least once. Even though she had left nothing of
any real value there, except the state jewelry and the
things too valuable for Gordo to dispose of, the very idea
of some imperial officer pawing through her belongings
made her slightly sick. It felt like a violation when she
simply thought about it, and she did not want to have to
face that fact.

The last act of vandalism drained the remainder of her
energy, and she faded into the passageways again wondering what Leopold and his people would make of her
work in the palace. She had taken care to make no noise
during her mischief, assuming that silence would be more
frightening, when the damage was discovered, than the
sound of something tearing the rooms apart.

The rest of her work was not yet done, but she decided

to leave an excursion into the Summer Palace for tomorrow night. There *was* one thing she did have to accomplish before she made her way back to the Gypsy Quarter, however. She had to get into the Temple—more specifically, she had to get into the cloisters.

Fortunately, that was the easiest of all the things she'd done this evening. Adele had already shown her the secret passage that led from the queen's suite to the Temple itself. The archpriestess traditionally required that special access to the queen, who would in turn become the archpriestess in her own time. *And will the emperor require he be made secular head of the Temple as well as the city, I wonder?* she thought as she felt her way toward the less-familiar sections of the secret maze. *I wonder what he will think when they tell him that no man can head the Temple? Unless, of course, he is prepared to make a certain little personal sacrifice.*

To gain access to this final passage, she needed to squeeze her slender frame through a small shaft above the closet in the queen's bedroom and let herself down into a passage from above. Only someone as young and athletic as she could have managed it; most people would have entered through the secret door in the room itself rather than go through such contortions.

The passage ended in a thick, heavy wooden door, which she opened cautiously to find herself in a tiny room that contained only a lantern and four hooks, each with a shapeless robe hanging upon it, one of each of the four colors of grey, rusty-brown, yellow, and red. She peered through a spy hole into the next room, which held an image of the Heart, a prayer bench, and a single, brown-robed figure kneeling at the bench. She put on the brown robe and opened the door. The Gemen rose hastily as the back wall of the room opened.

The Gemen waiting for her there waved her hand to forestall her exit. "I know who and what you are and why you are here," she said softly. "I have been stationed here to take you to your grandmother." She smiled shyly; Shelyra thought that she must be about forty or thereabouts, her dark, graying hair was cut short as all those in the orders wore it, and she wore spectacles through which she peered earnestly. "This is supposed to be a cell devoted to solitary meditation. There are four of us privy to your secret, one for each of the watches of the day and night; only four and no more, and we will die rather than reveal it."

Shelyra stepped inside, allowing the door to swing silently shut behind her and hoping grimly that the Gemen would never find herself in the position where she would have to prove that assertion.

Shelyra drew the cowl of her robe up over her head to hide her soot-smudged face. A moment later, the two of them were walking sedately down one of the cool, echoing stone corridors of the Temple cloisters.

Shelyra thought that she would never have been able to keep track of who lived behind each of the myriad little doors along this corridor, but the Gemen seemed to have no such trouble. She tapped lightly on one, and at a murmured phrase too soft for Shelyra to hear, opened it.

She did not enter herself. "I will wait for you in the chamber," she said. "I will leave the door open so that you can find it. Come when you are ready to return or leave by another way and I will help you."

She hurried back down the corridor, leaving Shelyra to enter on her own.

If she'd had any doubts about the wisdom of this visit, they were dispelled the moment she saw her grandmother waiting for her, looking better and stronger than she had in the past several months. Suddenly, all the fear and uncertainty she had been telling herself to ignore rushed over her, and she flung herself into Adele's arms with a small cry of pain, like a wounded forest creature fleeing into shelter.

She did not remain there for more than a moment, however. This was not a time for weakness, and Adele undoubtably had troubles of her own to deal with. After a brief embrace, she pushed herself away with a bright, false smile on her face. "We keep hearing rumors in the city that you are sick, or even dead," she said to cover her lapse. "Even though Thom said he talked to you, and I knew better—"

"Even though you knew better, this must have been as much a relief for you as it is for me to see you," Adele replied warmly. "There are rumors here that you were caught fleeing by Apolon's men and they drowned you in a canal, and that Lydana is in the emperor's custody. Even though I know better, such things create terrible doubts."

Shelyra nodded. "I came to see if there is anything you need from outside the Temple," she said. "And to tell you that I am staying. I am as safe in the Gypsy Quarter as I would be anywhere, and I cannot leave our city to these brutes, not when there is a chance I can accomplish something here. I have complete access to this palace and the Summer Palace, and I intend to use that access to spy, if I can." She described the situation within the palace to Adele in great detail, while her grandmother listened intently.

Adele shook her head at the end of the recitation. "It appears that Leopold is not in command of anything except his own men, since the black coats are reporting to Apolon separately. What a dreadful situation for him to be in! It renders him doubly ineffective."

Shelyra nodded eagerly, hearing her own thoughts echoed so completely. "Do you think I could widen the rift? The more we divide the enemy, the better off we are!"

But to her disappointment, Adele shook her head. "Wait until I think the plan over, first. If Leopold is in actual charge of so little, the rift may already be so wide that we would waste energy and time better spent elsewhere. I *do* need some things from the Summer Palace, if you do have free access there. I did not have time to move all of my books, although I put them all under mage-lock last summer, before the emperor's armies drew so near. No one who is not of our blood will even be able to see the books for what they are, much less carry them off." She smiled wryly. "I had a warning; perhaps I should have paid more attention to it."

Shelyra shrugged. "If hindsight were foresight, we should never make any mistakes. Where are these books, and how do I get to them?"

"They are in my suite, in the small library," Adele told her. "And if you don't wish to bring them through the tunnels, take them to the confessional—the third confessional from the Heart on the right, as you know; I will endeavor to be there every day. Every second book in my suite is a volume on magic, but to the eye of anyone not of the bloodlines of the Tiger, they will only look like volumes of history and religious matters. *Very* dull reading, very typical for a silly old woman who thinks herself near death, and not likely to tempt anyone into picking them up for a closer examination."

Shelyra chuckled at that. "I will begin moving them tomorrow into the hidden room I found," she promised. "And from there I will bring them here, a few at a time. Or I will send them with someone to the confessional if there are too many for me to bring. I doubt anyone will suspect women coming to the Temple, holding chant-books. Even Gypsies need to pray."

"One would hope," Adele said dryly. "Although I have had my doubts, now and again. What of that thief who is supposed to have spirited you out of Merina?"

Shelyra sniffed disdainfully. "That was Aunt Lydana's idea, not mine—and, I suspect, not yours, either. I suppose we can trust him within strict limits, but he is more boast and wind than he is substance, and I do *not* trust him to be able to spirit so much as a turnip cart out of the city. He cares for nothing but himself, his profit, and his notoriety; not for Merina, not for the Tiger."

Her grandmother sighed. "It may be that you underestimate him, but he is a thin branch to trust our weight to; I think you are wise not to depend on him overmuch." She pursed her lips, and Shelyra sensed she wanted to say something more, but was hesitating. "I know that you are a practical child—" she began cautiously.

"Are you about to tell me that you have set angels to watch guard over me?" Shelyra asked, only half in jest. Adele saw angels and other spirits—or said she did. Shelyra had never seen anything out of the ordinary whenever her grandmother had tried to point these spiritual apparitions out, not even when she was a small child, and supposedly more open to such things. Adele's claims often made the queen acutely uncomfortable, although Shelyra herself had never been bothered. If her grandmother was deluded, there was no harm in such delusions, and if she was *not*—well, right now Shelyra would cheerfully accept the guardianship of any creature, be it angel, ghost, elf, gnome, or gossamer-winged sylph from a child's bedtime tale.

"Not—precisely," Adele said soberly. "The Light does not send Its messengers to do aught but warn or guide. No, I simply wanted to remind you that there is magic afoot, and much of it may be very dark, indeed. I will do what I can, but I am only one poor woman. Guard yourself; leave nothing that may be linked to you where an unfriendly hand may purloin it. I know that you can guard yourself well against the dagger in the night, or the bravo in the alley—but I have reason to believe that you are the focus of a hunt, and the hounds tracking you are not of this world."

Shelyra bit her lip thoughtfully. "I will do my best, Grandmother," she said at last, "but—these are not the weapons with which I am adept."

"Then find someone who is—perhaps one of your Gypsies," Adele urged. "I cannot be there and here, too. I would feel better knowing you had someone at your back who is a master of the weapons of the spirit."

Now it was Shelyra's turn to hesitate, for the Gypsies *she* knew who were conversant with magic were not of the same faith as those that worshiped in the Temple of the Heart, while the Horse Lords could not be coaxed inside the Temple by *any* inducement, preferring to worship their own horse goddess, Ekina. And while that did not particularly bother *her,* Adele might not be so pleased. . . .

"I will see if any are willing, and acquaint them with at least some of my secrets," she temporized. "I would not put such a task on anyone, unwarned of the real dangers."

Adele nodded reluctant agreement. "One other thing—no matter what you hear of me from the Temple, do not believe it unless one of the Gemen comes to you with this"—she held out her hand, which still bore her wedding ring, a band of white gold inlaid with tiny rondels of tiger eye—"or you hear it from someone in that third confessional who is not myself."

"I will, and now I must go," Shelyra said, quickly, before Adele could think of any objections. "Dawn will come far too soon, and I must not be caught by it."

Her grandmother rose and embraced her. "Of course; I lose track of time within these walls—here in the Heart all seems timeless. Go quickly, return safely."

Shelyra returned the embrace and left, hoping she did not seem too eager to be gone. The bespectacled Gemen was waiting for her in the meditation room as promised, and carefully shut the door to the tunnel behind her. From this tunnel, it was easy to slip over to one of the other exit tunnels, this one leading off the dowager's suite.

Just as well that I don't enter and leave by the same route. If anyone was watching me and saw me vanish, he'll never find the entrance unless he sees me come out again. She yawned; it had been a long night, and the energy bestowed by excitement was wearing off.

But as she slipped out by means of a tiny door on a dark and seldom-used canal, something else occurred to her. In all of her prowling tonight, she had not once seen any sign of Leopold himself.

If he hadn't taken either the dowager's suite or the queen's, where was he? Why hadn't she seen him? And what was he doing?

❦ 27 ❦

LEOPOLD

Leopold completed his inspection of the palace just as the sun was going down; with some idea of the various facilities he was able to assign quarters and duties much more effectively and quickly. He'd dismissed all of the servants today, of course, once he knew exactly what their duties were and where all the stores were kept; they were not to be trusted. At the least, they would perform their duties reluctantly and with ill-grace, and at the worst, they would be potential agents of sabotage. They didn't seem particularly reluctant to leave, either; his sergeants said there were rumors spreading among them that the palace was haunted.

He left it to the sergeants to assign the duties normally attended to by servants to some of the men. This would be purely temporary, of course; when the emperor finally took residence, he would bring a full staff with him.

When he finished giving out his orders to his officers, he stood in the hallway outside the royal suites, staring at a painting of some ancestor of the former royal family. A stern-faced man, who nevertheless seemed to have a glimmering of good humor in his eyes and a half-suppressed smile on his lips, he looked nothing like the official portraits of Emperor Balthasar. All of those were so stiffly formal that they could have been portraits of some lifeless statue. . . .

I would like to have a man like that for a father, he thought impulsively, and felt immediate guilt. What was he thinking? He was Balthasar's son, his loyal son. No merchant-kinglet could ever be his father's equal. . . .

"Where shall we take your belongings, my lord?" his squire asked, startling him out of a reverie he was not aware of falling into. "The suite of the qu— I mean, of the woman Lydana?"

He thought about that, frowning, the familiar tightness in his stomach starting up again. Until today he had quartered with the men, outside the palace, in old, disused barracks, but now he needed to take up residence in the palace proper. Cathal's mercenaries had been sent to take over the barracks, forcing him to move his men, and himself, into the palace. There it was, another trap, another pitfall in his path. Would he never be free of them, of the maneuvering, the machinations? *If I take the queen's suite, that could be construed as usurping Father's privilege. If I take the dowager's suite, Apolon will do his best to oust me. And somehow I do not care for taking the princess' rooms. It seems—ungentlemanly.*

"Take my things to the suite at the end of the hall," he said finally. "I know that it has not been in use for some time, but I am sure it will be fine with a bit of airing." That set of rooms had last been used by a male; he would feel a great deal more comfortable there. Perhaps it had even been used by the man in the portrait.

The squire bowed and made no comment.

After he left to bring up the prince's belongings—and presumably recruit some help for an extensive airing and cleaning session—the prince remained where he was, still frowning. There was something that was nagging at his mind, although he could not put his finger on it. Something to do with the Princess Shelyra? Something to do with the way Apolon was intent on finding her?

Yes. And something to do with her rooms.

He retraced his steps, thoughtfully, trying to pinpoint what it was that had disturbed him. He had ordered that *all* rooms be lit by at least one candle or lantern, although that might seem wasteful. He wanted the guards patrolling the hallways to be able to see if they heard a disturbance in one of these rooms. He would countenance no looting, and his men knew it. This was all the property of the emperor now, and stealing any of it would be stealing from Balthasar, and thus a capital crime.

He didn't truly think any of *his* men would be inclined to even think about theft . . . but his were not the only men in the city. If Cathal had not yet moved his mercenaries into the barracks, he would by tomorrow, and mercenaries would steal anything left unattended. There were also those black-coated dogs of Apolon. He did not trust them, and he did not want to find himself in the position of having some important or valuable object go missing while *he* held the palace. For that matter, *they* might be the origin of the rumors of hauntings, trying to clear the way for themselves.

It would be just like Apolon to try to arrange a theft, he thought with irritation as he entered the door to the princess' rooms. *Or . . . perhaps what he would have his men steal would not be valuable at all, except to him!*

That thought occurred as he glanced around the princess' comfortable chambers and once again had the odd sensation that their owner had just left and would return soon. To a preliminary investigation, it did not appear that Shelyra had taken anything when she vanished, not even her own clothing. All was as she had left it, down to the hairbrushes and containers full of hairpins and other feminine fripperies on her dressing table.

And *that* was what had triggered his sense of "something wrong." Not that the room had been left virtually untouched—but that Apolon might be able to use what was here, precisely because it was virtually untouched.

Leopold was no mage, but he knew some of the principles by which magic operated. Any fool knew better than to let something personal pass into the hands of a mage. If the magician could not use it to control you, he could at least use it to locate you and spy on your doings. But perhaps the royal women were not aware of the way that personal belongings could be used. Perhaps he had better deal with it himself.

Apolon wants the princess, and I am positive he would take any means he could to obtain her. There must be many things here that he could use to find her!

Well, Leopold could do something about that—and while he was at it, he could see to it that the rooms of the dowager and the queen were similarly denuded. And he could do it all legitimately, under the guise of "readying the rooms for the emperor."

He felt his lips stretching in a thin smile as the warmth of satisfaction spread through him. It wasn't often he had a chance to thwart the powerful Grey Mage.

He sent for two men to help him, and began with the bed, stripping it of linens but leaving the costly gold-embroidered coverlet in place. *That takes care of linens that have been in contact with her.* The cosmetic table and the cupboard of cosmetics were next; he had all of the jars and bottles bundled into the linens, and sent both away with instructions to clean them immediately and thoroughly, and return them to the household stores. The princess' brush, mirror, and comb he took himself when the men left; there would be some things he would see to personally.

When the men returned, he had turned out all the drawers, consigning the contents of the most intimate to the flames of the fireplace. The delicate linen and lace burned quickly—thin, glowing ghosts of the laces wafting up the chimney on the heat of the rising flames. The rest he ordered to be sent, not to the household stores, but to the company stores to be used as rags. Soldiers always needed cleaning rags, and he had ordered a formal inspection for the morrow. By tomorrow afternoon, every last scrap would be useless to a mage, contaminated by boot polish and steel-rouge.

Oddly enough, he got no sense of "person" from the wardrobe and the costly, gorgeous gowns there. Nor did any of the jewelry call up that feeling—and there was a great deal of it, as befitted a scion of the House of the Tiger, renowned across the world for their gems and jewelry. The former he ordered sent into storage in the attics, the latter he locked into a casket with his own hands and placed on a table, prominently, beside the bed. Balthasar would claim the jewels, or the chancellor would; Apolon would get none of those. And he doubted that Apolon would be able to tell the princess' gowns from the others in the attics. What mere male could ever tell what was in fashion and what was of the fashion of a hundred years ago? He himself had been caught by that trap often enough, complimenting a girl on her gown only to have her turn quiet and strained—and find out later that it was a made-over antique from a jealous step-mother who wished her to look ridiculous.

He sent the men off with the last of the clothing and made a final circuit of the rooms himself. He was about to leave when he suddenly had the sensation that someone was watching him. The back of his neck crawled, and goose flesh crept over his arms.

He whirled, for he had never known that particular instinct to be wrong before. Who could have gotten in here without him knowing?

There was someone standing beside the wardrobe. It was not one of his men; even in the dark, he would have known that.

In fact, he couldn't quite tell if it was male or female, although the beardless face was beautiful enough to make his heart ache, and terrible enough to make it race with fear.

He could not look away from those eyes, that face; his gaze was riveted there, as his feet were glued to the floor. He could not move, even though every instinct told him that no living human should be standing in the presence of something like *that*. He suppressed the urge to kneel and bow his head, but only because he was not certain he could ever rise again if he did.

He could not have told what the person wore; all he could see was the face, the eyes—

—and the hands, long, slender hands that pointed to the wardrobe, to a section he had thought was empty.

The creature's face was bright—brighter than it had any right to be, for the light could not be a reflection of the light coming from the fire and the two candles over the mantle. It brightened still more as he stared, until it was so bright it was painful, and he blinked away sudden tears.

It vanished as he blinked; between one moment and the next, it disappeared completely, as if it had never been there in the first place.

Except that his eyes were still watering and retained an afterimage in the form of a human-shaped, glowing blind spot.

He began to tremble with reaction and reached behind himself for the wall, for his knees did not feel as if they would hold him.

Was that—? Blessed heavens. No wonder the first thing They say to mortals when they appear is "fear not"!

But he was a soldier; soon enough he had himself under control again. He waited just long enough for the afterimage to fade, and returned to the wardrobe, pulling open the doors of the particular section and peering inside. When he saw nothing, he fetched one of the candles from the mantle and brought it over to help in his search.

That was when he found it.

As a bit of property, it wasn't much; practically valueless.

But Apolon, if he had been there, would have seized on it and carried it off with ill-concealed glee.

Leopold picked up the tiny piece of metal with a thrill of elation. It was a tiny silver horse, worn smooth with much handling, as if the owner had often fingered it as a luck-piece or a calmative. Only one set of silversmiths in all the world made horse-charms like this one, meant to be tied to the halter of a favorite mount to bring the blessing of Ekina, the horse goddess.

The Horse Lords. Leopold knew it the moment he spotted it. As a clue to the princess' possible whereabouts it was priceless. Until this moment, he had no idea she even knew who and what the Horse Lords were—and he doubted anyone else did, either. To Apolon, as a relic of hers, much handled, it would be almost as good as having the princess in his hands.

Which he would be able to achieve, and soon, with this in his grasp. Leopold tossed the tiny charm up and snatched it out of the air with the same hand, then shoved it deep into a pocket, frowning. *Well, he won't have the chance now! Not while I'm here.*

But who—or rather, *what*—had that apparition been? His first impulsive identification he doubted, for why would an angel appear to *him*? Was it a ghost, then? The spirit of some long-dead ruler of Merina? Or something— something far less "personal" and far more dangerous? Not a demon, surely—any demons would be on Apolon's side. That left only one thing that fit all the parameters . . . and once again, he trembled at the memory.

I won't think about it, he decided resolutely. *Whatever it was, it meant to help me keep Shelyra out of Apolon's talons. If it was an angel—*

He shook his head quickly to drive the notion out. It didn't matter.

What did matter was that he had two more rooms to clean. Those extremely personal objects like the hairbrush and the silver charm he would take himself and hide them in a valise full of seldom-used neckcloths in the back of his own wardrobe. Eventually he would find a way to "lose" them, perhaps in a canal somewhere.

The rest would be transformed by the use of soap and water into something Apolon could no longer use to find the women. If Leopold had the chance, he would even find a seamstress to take the gowns apart and reduce them to a pile of fabric, jewels, gold bullion, and lace. Everything that the three women of this palace had used or worn, he would unmake, removing every trace, until there was not even a cold trail for that dog of a mage to sniff out.

And he could do it all in the best interests of his father, the emperor, ridding him of useless feminine fripperies and turning the results into something of value in the marketplace.

With a determined stride, he moved on to the queen's room, confident that by the time he retired to bed, he would have accomplished his goal completely.

After all . . . it appeared that he had help, didn't he? Whatever the source, he was not about to refuse it, or ignore it.

There was one more thing he was going to do. He was going to start asking yet more questions about Apolon—pointed questions. Somewhere, surely, the Grey Mage had made a mistake. Somewhere he must have let someone see or know too much. Leopold only had suspicions about the source of Apolon's powers until now.

Now I shall look for facts, facts I can bring before Father, facts that Apolon cannot refute. There is a rottenness here, and the source of it is in the Grey Mage—and I will prove it. I must prove it. The presence of the Messenger proves that. I must uncover Apolon's secrets.

For if he did not succeed in this—something told him that Apolon would not tolerate *his* actions and interference much longer. . . .

♦ 28 ♦

APOLON

Apolon smiled, a thin smile with no trace of happiness in it. Happiness was for fools who valued such ephemeral pleasures. He smiled merely to reflect satisfaction in the progress of matters thus far.

Leopold was now in a position where he could be eliminated. There was no one directly supervising him, and such unwonted freedom would surely tempt him into rashly idealistic behavior. With luck, he would challenge Cathal, and if Balthasar had to choose between supporting the general who had wrought so many victories and his overly sentimental (and somewhat inconvenient) son . . . well, there was no doubt in Apolon's mind which way the emperor would move. At the least, Leopold would be banished to some far-off, barren outpost, where Apolon could eliminate the prince at his leisure. At the best, the emperor himself would slay the fool, on the assumption that Leopold was making a bid for the imperial throne himself. There was always the chance that those many hints he had planted, about young men and their impatience to rule, had finally taken root in the emperor's mind.

That much, at least, was satisfactory. The search for the three women of the royal family, however, was not going well.

Apolon lost his smile. Of all the three, the youngest, the

Princess Shelyra, was the most important to his plans, for it was she who held what *he* needed. Potential power— not secular, but magical power; all women with the Talent held it in a kind of trust until their life-change, but those of the House of the Tiger held it in greater abundance than any he had yet encountered. A man could practice magic at any age, as long as he remained chaste, but a woman's power was never more than a potential until she reached the end of her fertility. Then, as if in recompense for having been held so long in abeyance, it flowered forth, becoming stronger with advancing age, so strong that the women who bloomed so late often outstripped male mages who had been practicing all their lives. Adele, the dowager—she would be a full mage now, probably had been for some years, since she abdicated in favor of her daughter. Fortunately for Apolon, her health was said to be very poor; in fact, she had collapsed after the city had been signed over to Balthasar. She was *probably* mewed up in the Temple cloister, still, by Leopold's own report, about to die. Like all those whose power was born of the Shadow, Apolon found it difficult to look into the Light, and he could not determine numbers and strength when more than two mages of the Light were gathered together. But if his luck held, she would die; she could be dismissed out of hand.

The former queen, Lydana—if he could not have Shelyra, she would do. She must just be on the edge of coming into her own powers, though, so the energy of *potential* would be much, much less. All those years she had lived, that Shelyra had not yet enjoyed—those would make the profit from her far less than from a younger woman. And she had been wedded, so she could not be virgin, which was another fault as far as he was concerned. If he could not obtain the princess, he would look more seriously for the queen, but for now he would concentrate on the girl.

Yes, the maiden. He licked his lips, savoring the thought, but not for any carnal reasons. Apolon had no use for carnal pleasures; they were ephemeral and meant nothing, hollow façades to tempt fools. The only real, lasting pleasures were cerebral and temporal—knowledge and power. Shelyra would not go to serve any creature's lust; certainly not Apolon's.

First, the immense potential of the Talent, bottled up within her. *Second,* the energy of her unlived years—sixty or so, if one went by the long lives of her ancestors. *Third,* the energy of virginity, which was the reason why virgin boys and girls were so favored by the Shadow as offerings. If he could give the Shadow-Lord the tender, untouched Shelyra—

When he gave the princess to the Shadow-Lord, there would be nothing he could ask that would not be granted to him. All he had achieved until this moment would be as a handful of pebbles set against the imperial crown. From the moment he had conceived of this notion, the Shadow had been whispering in the back of his mind, whispering promises that made him faint with anticipation. Soon those promises would become reality!

Apolon sat back in his camp chair and reflected on the day when it would be a throne, and he would rule the empire in the name of his Master. That would be a good day; when his servants would bring him everyone who had ever thwarted him, ever insulted him, throwing the headless bodies down before him until the carpet was dyed red with the spilled rubies of their blood.

I shall keep Cathal, I think. He amuses me. And he does not care who holds his leash, so long as he is allowed his extravagances.

Well, enough of that. There was work to be done. He gestured at one of his servants, one of the black-coated minions who now infested the city, hunting for the three women of Merina and seeking out information of any kind that might be useful to their master. This one, who had been waiting for an hour until his master had time to hear his report, was living; fully half of his servants were. The dead were not as clever as the living.

"Have you found what I need?" he asked. "Have you located the women?"

The man shook his head, groveling on the carpet at

Apolon's feet. "No, master. They might not even have lived at all; there is no sign of them. But we *have* found you the other folk you wanted, and performed the other task you set us, and we have planted the Fire Flowers in each house as you ordered. You may make examples of them whenever you wish. These people will soon realize the folly of opposing you and the emperor's rule."

Apolon leaned forward and spread out a map of the city of Merina, with every street and canal marked clearly. He placed it on the carpet in front of his servant. "Show me," he demanded. "Name me their names, and what they have done, and describe them to me."

There was always the chance that one of those he had chosen to make an example of would be one of the missing women. They could not hide themselves properly, he was certain of that. They could not be meek and abide the bullying of his servants with the proper servile fear. They were not bred to servility; they would strike out, verbally at least. They could not help themselves.

As the servant began his recitation—*all* his servants had good memories, or they did not remain his servants for long—he listened carefully. But most of the rebellious citizens were men; there were only a handful of women showing any kind of spine.

"—Matild Rankinsdaughter, a Beadswoman, of Stingray's Court; she is of middle age, but slender and strong, and she is known to have frequent congress with sailors. It is rumored that she has counted Captain Saxon among her lovers. She has turned a scold's tongue on the men who came to collect the due, and she is defiant in posture when she is not defiant in words. Everyone else in the Stingray's Court is afraid of your servants, but she clearly shows no fear and might well organize rebellion at any point. She is known to frequent the sailors' taverns, where there is much unrest. The sheep of her quarter are clearly willing to take her orders, and she seems willing to order them about."

"This Matild—" Apolon leaned forward again, his brows creased in a frown. "Could she be Lydana in disguise?"

But the man shook his head. "No. She is black of hair and her aspect is of a woman who is very free with her favors. That meek and mousey queen would faint if ever one like Matild crossed her path. And she is too old to be Shelyra, too young by far to be Adele."

"So she is just another interfering hag. Well enough." Apolon waved a dismissive hand at his servant. "You have not done *well*, for you have not yet located any of the women of the Tiger, but you have not earned a punishment. Go—and be more energetic in your searches. I shall expect a better report next time."

The man left, sweating with relief. Apolon allowed himself another thin smile. His punishments were actually rather infrequent, nowhere near as often or as brutal as Cathal's, for instance. He had learned long ago that the *fear* of punishment was more effective than the actual punishment itself.

A cold wind whipped in through the entrance to his tent, which changed his smile to a frown. He did not at all care for this way of life, and it was difficult to practice his magics with any kind of security here where anyone could stumble on him in the midst of a ritual. Even if he had gained access to the princess's room, he would not have been able to use what he gained there; his rituals were all too clearly of the Shadow, for they all required the spillage of blood. He would have to find a way to get Balthasar into the city within the next day or two. He could commandeer that house, the one of the Boar—although if he could not get that one, perhaps that of the Tiger would be amusing—clear out everything and everyone, and invest it with his own servants and tools. Then he could work; find some object belonging to the women to use to trace them—provided that they weren't already protected against such things. He had not been too quick to use his magic to find them, simply because he had assumed from the start that they *did* have such protections. But what he really needed was to set up his "recruitment center" again; he was losing servants, a slow but steady drain as some of them were set upon by a few rebels and rendered useless to him, a few vanishing altogether, probably into the canals. He needed to replenish his supply, and for that he needed a secure and private space to turn dead fools into dead-alive servitors.

Balthasar was tolerant, but there were some things even he would not countenance, and necromancy was one of them. He might *guess* what his Grey Mage was doing, but he would never ask, so that he need not *know*. But if it became common knowledge that Apolon was not Grey but Black—well, the emperor would not tolerate, would not dare tolerate, a necromancer in his service. What Apolon did on a regular basis was counter to every law in the empire, and Balthasar would regretfully send for the executioner.

For that matter, if he were to find one of the two women he sought, he would need a house with a good, soundproof chamber in it, to call up his Master. One did not do *that* in the open air! The risks he took in performing the rite in secret were quite appalling enough!

So, that should be his immediate goal. Set off the Fire Flowers to cow these sheep with his power. Move Balthasar into the city and find a house for himself. Get Leopold out of the way. Recruit more black coats. Find the women.

In fact, if his servants located either Shelyra or Lydana, he ought to leave the women where they were until he actually had secured the house. No point in seizing them until he had a place to keep them; Balthasar might find out he had them, otherwise.

He nodded to himself, satisfied that he had the best possible plans for the moment. And satisfied that all would go according to his plans.

After all, he was not doing all this alone. He had help,

didn't he? It was in the Shadow-Lord's best interest to make sure his servant did not fail.

Apolon would not *ask* for that help, for that would put him further in his Master's debt—but when that help came, he certainly would not refuse it.

✤ 29 ✤

LYDANA

She was in water, not swimming, seeming rather to float sluggishly. Half-turning her head, she looked into a face of horror where the features were crushed out of all human form. Matild screamed, flailed out with her arms, striving to win away from that thing.

"Lady!" She was being shaken back and forth, and she tried to clutch at the hands which so held her, hoping to be drawn away from that floating thing.

"Lady!" She blinked up into the face of the woman Jonas had called Dimity and caught her breath in a half sob. "He was dead—" she choked out, "dead and I killed him!"

Though at the time her act had seemed the logical one and, even when they had set the bodies adrift, she had not felt she was actually loosing a man to the creeping tide—now it all settled on her.

Dimity no longer wore the half-mask she had used the night before—no, two nights before. Or was it longer—it was hard to keep these days and nights separate. They all merged into one nightmare whole, an endless round of work and deception, in which she got too little sleep. This double life she was leading was doubly draining: the stress of slipping unnoticed back into her shop everyday, the strain of watching the black coats eyeing her—all these were taking a toll of her strength. Dimity was one with a young and not uncomely face, but old, watchful eyes, and her warm grasp still closed on Matild.

"Your first, eh?" she asked. "Well, it takes us all so. But I will swear that you had no choice, did you now?"

How much had she changed? Twice in her life she had signed death warrants and felt only that it was her duty, but this was another matter. She wiped a hand across her trembling mouth.

Dimity had loosed her now and was indicating a tray balanced on the somewhat rickety table in Jonas' sanctum. "Best eat, lady. Thom and Eel have brought what you wanted, and Thom has gone again. There's work for all of us now."

Matild washed in the basin of lukewarm water the woman had apparently also brought and then, feeling still shaky inside, striving hard to shut out the memory of her dreams, sat down dutifully to eat.

It was coarse fare, but she found that hunger was a fine sauce for the most primitive of dishes, and she cleaned empty a bowl of lumpy porridge, ate a round of strong-smelling sausage clamped between two pieces of dry bread. Dimity nodded in reply to her thanks and vanished again, but Matild noticed now, along with the tray, the box and casket she had described to Thom.

Though the tavern building was old and certainly in need of the lawful repairs, she could not hear any movement in the outer room. There was no bolt or lock on the door; she would have to chance an interruption of entry.

Moving the tray to the floor, Matild edged herself as close to the table as the stool allowed. She had slipped off her sash and was fingering the pockets in it, remembering just where each stone now lodged.

The chancellor was a man of greed—therefore, what would assuredly tempt him the most would be some spectacular find: the Diamond of Asusars. Out of its hiding place she brought that jewel.

Matild, during all her long years of training, had worked with many diamonds, but she had never favored the stones, having a greater liking for colors, and even those stones lesser thought of—such as opals—fire-centered, ice-blue—even the rainbow moonstones over the surface of which color played, just as it was caught within the structure of the opal. There was jade, which slipped so smoothly through the fingers, star rubies, sapphires . . . Somehow, for a moment or two, she could envision all her favorites spread out before her in place of this single blazing gem, which seemed to emit a visible chill.

But it was, by market value, a gem over which humans would always battle. Were it to show itself rightfully, it would be red with the blood of several centuries of dead made for its gain.

For a greedy man, a stone which by legend was greed itself, greedy for the lives bartered for it. Matild opened her work box and the casket of tools. One of the compartments held a number of old—some ancient—settings for rings and brooches. Often such were traded for the metal they contained, but she had always inspected such finds, often appropriating some piece or other whose design intrigued her.

A ring—since it was for a man. She sorted over the half-dozen old settings. Silver—no—even to her those she held still were of value for their designs. Only blatant gold to suit what seemed to her the gaudiness of that lump of forbidding ice.

Now it depended on size—how it could be worked well into the setting. She chose a broad band of green gold, plain except around the bezel where she would fit in the jewel. That had been wrought with minute and careful craft into a network of threadlike twiglets. Matild picked up her first tool and set to work at the delicate business of forming a bed for the diamond within that nest.

She had put aside the diamond, now fully set and ready,

when a squeak of the floor brought her head around.

Eel, holding a large roll of bread and sausage at which he was chewing avidly, sauntered in. His eyes flicked over the table, and when he came to join Matild, he moved to her other side, as far away from the completed ring as he could get. In the early days, when Eel had become her most trusted ally, she had discovered he was even more alert to baneful gems than she, and sometimes spotted them more quickly in any shipment unfortunate enough to contain them.

"Being generous?" He got out around a bit of sausage. "Who's the unhappy new owner?"

Matild smiled. "Eel, I thought it proper for the chancellor. He is said to fancy such things."

Eel grinned. "Not if he has wits in his head, but whoever said that he did, now? But—I have a tale for you—"

He leaned against the edge of the table and took a moment or so to swallow the last bite—one well beyond what one would believe possible to manage.

"The captain, and some others, they are in the House of the Boar right enough. And it isn't the black coats who have the overseeing of them. Mercenaries—men of Lakqua, I would say. Like the general's guard. They've kept a few of the servants to kick around, but the dame and her daughters were out on the street the same time they dragged the master off to hang him. It's no rumor, they seem plain about it—he was hung because he would not turn over the Gideon Sword. They say a mage spell-locked it for all time, and they tried to get the secret out of him. But they didn't get it. Like as not, he didn't have it anyway."

Every city as old as Merina had its roll of ancient heroes and heroines, its precious relics of earlier days. Deeds might be distorted out of all truth, made miracles by the years and the retelling of them.

"The Gideon Sword—" she repeated softly.

Merina had once had an enemy in his way more devastating than the emperor had yet proved himself to be. A seeker of knowledge who was more than a mage—and adept—and one who had desecrated all sources of Light. There had been a man (or an angelic being who took human shape) who had fought a mighty battle with this Iktcar. The Dark one had been killed in spite of all his arts, but also their savior had vanished—only his sword had been left. Some wished it set in the Temple. But there had been two minds about that: a weapon (no matter how well it had served them all) was, in the opinion of the archpriestess of the day, not to be hung in a place of peace and serenity.

Since the man calling himself Gideon had been a workman in the House of the Boar until he had wrought his sword and gone into the last battle, those working in metal had claimed him for a saint and hung the sword with all the protection they could assemble in their guild house.

"The general. He's been twice to watch the workmen from the camp try to loose it. Now they think he will come again and shatter the case."

Matild looked at the doom stones. What if Cathal got the sword—and perhaps something more potent? There was a chance—

Then she remembered the master's widow. "Dame Fortuna?" Perhaps if her husband had held the secret, she would be willing to reveal it to bring down his murderers.

"She claimed sanctuary with the Servants of the Poor," the Eel returned promptly. "Has to stay within their gates because she is afraid of being took—or one of her girls—"

So—perhaps she did know more than they had expected. How long might it be before Cathal, infamous for his atrocities, might dare even the Temple to get her? She was sure the general was certainly no respecter of the Heart as the emperor at least pretended to be.

Again Eel picked up her thought. "They got a watcher at the cloister right enough, but not a black coat. So far she is safe."

Matild nodded. Her mind was already busied with her

second task. Another ring? No, the stone she had in mind was too large for the settings she had kept. But she had noted that the officers of the imperial crown each wore a heavy metal cuff on their left wrists—one very wide, which could be used in some types of hand-to-hand combat like a shield.

There was an archer's bow guard among her bits and pieces of settings; a stroke of luck she hardly dared hope for. She had kept it because the edge was so finely tooled in a pattern strange to her. Now she pulled that out and then drew forth another gem. She heard a catch of breath from Eel.

"That! You had *that*, lady!"

"The captain took it from Frisal when he cut him down on the quarterdeck of his ship at Graise. Yes, I know what it is—though not how it came into Frisal's paws. This is the Mouth of Vor."

The glimmering black stone was indeed cut oddly. On one side there were lines suggesting graven lips—the likeness of a closed mouth. On the other side it was a smooth oval. She began to work swiftly, but it was a lengthy job and required all her skills. When it was done, the smooth side fronted the world; the Mouth was hidden. She could not know the range of knowledge among the emperor's officers, but she did not think her ruse would be easily detected.

❧ 30 ❧

SHELYRA

Shelyra—or rather, Raymonda, for she was back in that particular guise—stood beside a lamppost, a little apart from the rest of the Gypsy group, and watched another dancer perform for a dispirited group of workmen. She yawned; it had been a long night, and even though she had slept a little later than she was used to, she had scanted herself on rest. Right now she was trying to gauge the temper of the city. It was not entirely satisfactory. She had hoped for some open rebellion by now, but Merina seemed cowed, resigned, willing to put up with whatever the emperor imposed upon her. The city absorbed each new blow, each new burden on her back, and only bent her head further beneath the yoke. Not only were the black coats of Apolon abroad in the streets, but there were imperial mercenaries of General Cathal's companies enforcing the general's particular whims in a few quarters. Leopold's men were somewhat in evidence, but not strongly; they made no attempt to either impose more restrictions or to restrain the mercenaries and the black coats from outrages. Merina was under not one thumb but three, and confusion had begun to set in as each of the three imposed his own particular rules.

"You there!" A hand suddenly seized Raymonda's arm from behind, and it did not take much feigning at all to turn her automatic reaction of *attack* into one of wincing away with fright. The man who held her arm was not a black coat, but one of the mercenaries. The former were deadly, but the latter were mad dogs and unpredictable. This one had a cruel face, a mouth full of broken teeth, and bad breath.

"What you want with my cousin, hey?" One of her friends among the Gypsies interposed his body between Raymonda and the mercenary, forcing him to let go of her. Bruno was a huge man, one who could handle the wildest of horses, control even a spooked and frightened draft stallion with ease. Even one of Cathal's mercenaries would give way before Bruno, at least temporarily.

"She stands around, she's dressed like a dancer, but she don't dance," the mercenary snarled. "So what's she out here for? We got imperial laws about her kind of woman— they gotta be in imperial houses, pay their fees, be where they can be watched—"

"She's not that kind of woman, *gajo*," Bruno spat. "You keep your filthy ideas to yourself! She don't dance yet 'cause we haven't played no northern music, hey sweeting?"

Bruno chucked her under the chin like a child; she fluttered her lashes and dropped her eyes shyly, then nodded.

"She dance northern style, no stamping and heel-clacking—" Bruno continued. "Music for that is different from *flamank* style."

The mercenary interrupted him. "So play northern music, pud, or I'll have her taken up for a loose woman! If she's really a dancer, she better be able to dance!"

Raymonda felt a trickle of fear and was glad she had not gone outside the Gypsy Quarter alone. This group was large enough to protect her—for now—but if she had ventured into the streets by herself—

Bruno assessed the temper of the mercenary, judged that he had pushed it far enough, and signaled to the musicians. "Northern *zigan*, boys! Make it lively!"

Make it lively—the faster I move, the less obvious my

mistakes will be, and if this bully does *know northern style, he won't notice that I'm not doing all the footwork if I turn quickly enough, make enough arm gestures.*

I hope.

Raymonda took a pose in the center of the group and held it through the introductory phrase. Unlike the southern dance style, which also began with a stylized pose, but one of proud carriage, she held her arms curved over her head, entwined, with her back slightly arched. Then the melody began in earnest, and so did she. She bent and danced like a willow in the wind; she twirled like a waterspout, her skirts swirling around her feet in an ever-changing pattern of color and movement. Southern music was mostly guitarra and a clapping accompaniment; northern mostly fiddle and tamborine. Southern *flamank* dancers challenged each other, challenged their audiences with proud posture and staccato barrages of footwork; northern *zigan* dancers yearned and entreated, implored, with supple bending and swaying, whirling away. If the *flamank* was all fire, the *zigan* was water and air.

One of the others, a man she hardly knew, jumped into the circle with her. Now the dancing was easier; he could set the pattern for her to follow, and he could help her with adroit lifts and turns. She put her dance into his hands, gratefully, and followed the minute directions his body gave her.

The pace increased, faster and faster, as the two of them whirled and bowed, circling around an invisible center holding them both tethered. She tired; she hissed out her breath through her mouth, a stitch building in her side, her lungs burning with fatigue. Sweat ran down her face and neck, and still the music continued, driving her and her partner on and on—

Until, at last, it stopped, and her strength ran out as the music ended. She collapsed at her partner's feet in the traditional ending to the *zigan*. She lay on the cobblestones, face hidden in her hair, panting and spent.

There was no applause, but she had not expected any.

She was just grateful to have come through it without any major mistakes. She simply lay where she was while she caught her breath and the stitch in her side slowly faded; about the time she felt ready to rise, a hand touched her shoulder, and she looked up into her partner's face to see him smiling down at her and offering his hand. She took it.

"You dance well, oathsibling," he murmured in the Gypsy tongue. "Almost as well as my wife. Remind me to have her show you some steps when we return to the compound." He glanced at the surly mercenaries, at the sullen crowd. "I think that will be soon. There is nothing for us here."

"You see?" Bruno's voice boomed into the silence. "She dances. Are you satisfied?"

Thwarted, the ugly mercenary lifted his lip in a snarl. "So? Mebbe I better take her in anyway. That girl Shelyra's gone missing—mebbe she's Shelyra—"

Raymonda went cold all over, and her hand crept toward her hidden knife. Her partner's hand tightened on her arm in warning.

But before anyone could even begin to take that suggestion seriously, the mercenary's own fellows burst into hearty laughter.

"Aw, Guntur, you got a touch of the sun, or swamp-fever, or something!" one guffawed. "Her? *The princess?* Where'd a lady learn to dance like that? How'd a lady get down here with these scum? They'd rob her blind and throw her in the canal and not think twice about it!"

Now it was Raymonda's turn to grip her partner's arm in warning as his face darkened at the insult and he took an abortive step forward. From the anger on the faces of the others in the group, they were reining their tempers in with the same degree of difficulty.

They just want to provoke us into a fight, so they have an excuse to imprison all of us—they want to get into our compounds and right now they don't have an excuse to break down the gates and get in.

She must not have been the only one to have that thought, for, once again, Bruno stepped forward and spat on the cobblestones of the street with contempt—but *not* anywhere near the mercenaries. "Pah! Only fools here, would not know a good artist from dancing bear. We go home, at least we get appreciated. Come, brothers!"

He stalked off in the direction of the compound, and without a moment of hesitation, the rest packed up their things and followed him, with Raymonda crowded in with the other few women, her partner holding her arm in the center of the group. She was sweating now, not from exertion but from fear, and felt faint with relief. That had been close, too close! Only quick thinking on the part of Bruno and the other man had saved her—that, and luck.

But with the jaws of the trap closing in, how long could she expect that luck to last?

❧ 31 ❧

LYDANA

She was not aware how long she had been at work. Eel had disappeared some time ago, as she was only vaguely aware. Most of the time she had to concentrate fully on what she was doing, but her thoughts kept circling back to Saxon and the Sword of Gideon. Saxon must be freed and the sword—the sword made into a weapon, or so she hoped—that might again be, in part, their salvation. She sat back and worked her aching fingers, straightened her shoulders, and was aware of pain and stiffness there.

Her mother had warned her against the use of these

stones of ill-omen. But she was not using them actively as would a mage, who, by incantations and the like, would strive to add to their power for ill. She was merely putting them in the way of men to whom they might well beckon, leaving to chance the Wish of the Eternal Power for the results of her work.

"Are you through?" Again it was Eel, being careful to close the door.

"Yes." Matild stretched wide, and wriggled her fingers again.

"Best come out and listen, then." He opened the door and motioned her through. Matild tied the sash around herself, making a protruding bundle of the ring and arm-guard.

She found herself looking out into what was certainly a busy tavern scene. Men and women both were seated talking, but one after another they got up and approached Jonas, who was by himself at a smaller table. He had a tangle of knotted string laid out on the board before him, and Matild recognized the record-keeping system known to seamen, who many times lacked either a writing tool or a surface on which to use it. When he saw Matild, he gestured to her. The man slouching away from his interview with the tavernkeeper favored her with a sidelong glance, but there were no introductions.

"There's trouble enough for a rare tangle." Jonas shook the bundle of cords before her. "Them black coats has the city sweating. Listen, lady, you know more of the old learning than any of us—have you ever heard of walking dead men?"

Jonas' face was screwed up, and she saw something else, a glint of something—could it be fear?—in those eyes so overhung by his bushy brows.

"Walking dead men?" A cold shiver struck deep in her— the old learning, yes. What is legend, what is truth after the passing of centuries?

"Kaster, now," Jonas was continuing as if he must get this dire information reported as soon as possible, "he is a sharp man, an' not one to see shadows in every wall corner. He saw a black coat yesterday as he would swear was a shipmate of his a year ago and was knifed in Ulpar in a fight with some of the bully boys from one of the emperor's ships. Kaster swears Guloper was a dead man— no one is going to take to his feet and walk with a slit throat on him. Yet Kaster came back here a-shaking himself near out of his boots when he saw Guloper on patrol around the Temple square. Kaster ain't drunk, and he ain't crazy—though he may be one or other 'fore the hour's out. Two of his pals had to take him over there," he waved to a table in the opposite corner of the room, "and get him drinking or he'd gone out of his wits right in front of us."

"Necromancy—" Matild's voice was hardly above a whisper. "But—such uncleanliness was long ago swept from the world when Iktcar went down under the Sword of Light."

"Don't know what you call it, lady—we calls it devil work. The boys," he rolled his strings back and forth between his fleshy palms, "they've been knocking off a black coat here and there—quiet like and when it can't truly be blamed on any as knows nothing about it. But you can't rekill a man if he's already dead—now can you?"

Matild strove to clear her thoughts. "This must be made known to the archpriestess."

She thought for a moment and then spoke more sharply: "Dimity—is she about?"

Jonas raised his voice to near a dockside bellow. "Dimity, gal!"

The woman slipped from one of the benches and came forward. Matild studied her critically. She was very plainly what she was—one of the dockside women—but the Great Power turned none aside when seeking the general good. No one would be surprised that such would seek the confessional at the Temple.

The woman regarded Matild as shrewdly as if she had at once guessed who wanted her.

"Well?" she prodded.

"Come with me." Matild arose abruptly and started for that cupboard of a room Jonas had lent her.

Once within and the door closed, she spoke swiftly. "Have you heard of this walking dead man?"

The woman blinked her dark eyes. Her right hand arose and she made the Heart-sign swiftly. "It is known to us all."

"But it must be known to others," Matild said. "There are those better armored against the dire promise of such things. Go to the Temple, find the third confessional to the right of the high altar. When the Reverend One comes to you say this: 'The root is deep, the tree stands tall, the great cat walks her way.'"

Dimity repeated the sentence swiftly and Matild nodded. She had from the first believed that this dockwalker was keen-minded, to be trusted.

"When the Reverend One acknowledges you, tell her Kaster's tale. This is for the Protectors to know."

Dimity nodded. "Easy enough, lady. The hoodcrows are round and about, but so far they do not try to keep any from the Temple." She hesitated, and then continued: "There is a mighty lot going there now—women whose men have been taken, others that are just afraid. The Heart's Promise—perhaps that is near all we have left. But we shall hold to the Light and the Heart, whatever."

She was gone with a whirl of her skirts. Best leave Dimity to her own project—Matild had one perhaps far more delicate staring her in the face. She glanced down at the suit she had worn constantly since she left the beadshop. That would make her too noticeable. Back to Jonas—

She found him talking earnestly with Thom, who rested his hands on the table and leaned forward so that only the faintest murmur of what he was saying could be heard. Jonas saw her and beckoned.

Thom was looking sullen when he raised his head to face her. "A hard lass you wished on me," he near exploded, yet still kept his voice low. "I warned you she was going to get into trouble. She'll take no warning from anyone. There's talk beginning that the palace is haunted, thanks to her."

Matild sighed. She had thought that Thom would be the kind of colleague her headstrong niece would accept, since the spirit of adventure was so strong in her. It would seem that they found their forced partnership abrasive. But anyway, she had a task for him. From her sash she pulled the diamond ring.

Thom gasped, and Jonas gave a small gulping sound.

"That's a general's ransom." Thom's one hand arose as if he would relieve her of such a burden.

"Or a gift for a chancellor," she returned calmly. "Take no pride in this, Thom Talesmith, one as well learned in gems as you must know that some bring ill luck and disaster to their wearers."

His eyes narrowed. "And the House of the Tiger," he said very softly, "has a cache of such. No, I would have none of such a stone."

"You are but to take it to Shelyra," she ordered. "Tell her to see that it gets to the chancellor. If she is ghosting in the palace, let her make the most of such a haunting."

He did not take it in his hand, rather grabbed up one of Jonas' strings to hold it by.

"There is something working which is not of our making," he said as he tucked the looped ring into his pouch. "The guildsmen are beginning to think like men and not timid tradesmen—there are weapons missing. Something is coming on Merina worse than any sacking."

Jonas grinned. "Well," he thumped his strings down on the table, "we'll muddy the waters as best we can. Lady, we need the captain!"

"Yes. And I go to take the first step toward that. Jonas, get me clothing one of the poor widows might wear. I go to the cloister of the Servants of the Poor. Dame Fortuna has taken refuge there. It seems that sanctuary is still respected."

"And the captain, he's in the House of the Boar." Jonas

nodded briskly. "Aye, look to your sightings before you set sail. As for clothing— Hi, Wanda."

The blowsy girl who had been carrying trays of bowls of steaming soup around set down her burden and came forward.

"Get the lady what she needs," she was bidden.

It was some time later when Matild ventured forth from the tavern. She was muffled in a dragging, street-stained skirt, a raveling shawl pulled well up over her head. Luckily the cloister was located where the Gemens were needed the most, in one of the meaner streets near the tavern.

When she caught sight of it, she saw a small company of street children—among them Eel—and one or two women gathering at the door, and realized that this was the hour when bread was given out. Since the Servants of the Poor had been high on the list of the charities which she had supported from the palace, she knew them all and was well acquainted with the Reverend One, Gemen Zenia.

There were black coats standing guard also, only the width of the street away. She adopted a rocking gait and reached the outer fringe of the waiting beggars.

The smaller door opened and Gemen Papania came out with a huge basket held before her. Matild noted that the guard moved in a little and was keeping his attention fixed on that door.

"In the Name of the Great One, peace be on you. She gives Her children food for their bodies and peace for their hearts." Gemen Papania recited the formal blessing.

There was a scramble for the basket, but no fighting over its contents—such unseemly conduct would have brought the Reverend One, and no one wanted to face her at her sternest. In a moment or two, Matild joined them.

The Gemen turned her head quickly—the wide wings of her wimpled headdress hid the glance she gave Matild from any of the guards. Then she took the beadswoman by the arm.

"Well do you come to those who serve Her, desolate one—and your lad with you. There is harborage within, as has always been promised by Her and those who tend Her altar."

Matild was ushered at once to the small cell which belonged to the Reverend One, Gemen Zenia, and as she let her shawl fall from her head, the Reverend One rose abruptly.

"Lady"—she was cautious enough to use the common address—"are you claiming sanctuary? So far they have not broken their way in, but they watch us day and night, and we cannot hope that in the end we shall escape their prying. There is a foul wind in this city."

"There is indeed, Reverend One. No, I come not to add to your troubles. Rather I seek Dame Fortuna, for it is necessary that I speak with her."

Zenia nodded and picked up a wooden clacker, at the sound of which Gemen Papania again came in.

"This lady would have speech—privately—with Dame Fortuna."

"The dame has been at solitary prayer, but if you can bring her any hope, Lady, it will answer those petitions. We shall go to the chapel."

It was a small chapel, and very plain. Above an altar which boasted no fine cloth or begemmed sacred vessels was indeed a Heart. But this had been carved from wood so long ago that the crimson of its paint was wearing thin, and even its outlines were faintly blurred.

On her knees before it was the woman Matild sought. She had known Fortuna in happier days as a round-faced, bustling mistress of a large household, a woman who ruled that household well for its own good. But the figure who turned her head abruptly as Gemen Papania came to stand beside her was nearly a stranger. Her eyes were red and heavy with much weeping, there were lines, seemingly drawn by years of sudden aging, about her mouth. Her cheeks were sunken as if she had been fasting for weeks.

"They come?" she asked with a dull note of resignation.

"I will go. Tell the Reverend One that I wish no ill to all who shelter here—but—Lys and Rommy—must they be surrendered also?"

"There is no breaking of sanctuary," the Gemen replied quickly. "But there is one with whom it is best you talk, dame. It may be that good rather than ill will come of it."

Fortuna looked beyond the Gemen to Matild, who had thrown back her shawl and raised her hands to gather up straying locks and brush them away so that her face could be clearly seen.

The dame squinted a little, as if narrowing her eyes would give her a better view, and then her mouth dropped open and she scrambled from her knees and started to drop into a curtsy, but Matild stopped her.

"We are sisters in misfortune, dame; here there is no rank. But yours has been the heavier burden, for you have lost your homemate. Be sure that he is now warm held within the Heart, nor shall his name be forgot by us for whom he kept the faith, lest a treasure fall into evil hands."

Dame Fortuna bowed her head, and a single tear fell to the stone floor.

"But time runs at our heels like a hound on the course, and it is this same treasure which may now serve us in another fashion," Matild continued.

Dame Fortuna had straightened; there was in her, growing ever clearer, that same sturdiness of spirit which she had always shown before.

"Lady—" The word seemed to come hard for her. "If there is anything which we of the Boar can do—then let me hear it and speedily."

They sat together on the short bench at the back of the chapel, placed for those too crippled to kneel. Matild was frank, more open than she wanted to be, yet the circumstances were such that now she had no choice. She watched Fortuna's expression change from avid interest to bleak refusal and set determination, but the other raised no vocal objections.

Patiently Matild repeated certain portions of her plan—pointing out that the enemy was already rumored to be ready to take far more decisive action to obtain what he wanted. She also unwrapped what she carried in her sash, turning the armlet around so that Fortuna, even in this dim light, could see the ominous mouth.

The woman shuddered, her eyes fast on the thing.

"The sword—it will repudiate such—such foulness!"

"Has not the sword done battle with such foulness before—and bested it? We move not against the relic, but against he who reaches to claim it. Let the sword decide, if you will."

Dame Fortuna looked down at her fingers, locked together on her knee.

"There are oaths which are not to be broken—"

"Even to save what is the most precious?" Matild asked, still patiently. She had rewrapped the armlet, put it away. It all depended now on Dame Fortuna. Would she agree that to gain one must lose?

"The mage spells are strong—the general has already found that to be true."

"Yes. But do spells stand up to hammers which can break through a glass case after a blow or two?"

"Thus—" the other spoke softly as if she measured the weight of the idea behind her words "—force can break a spell—is that what you would say, lady?"

"That is what I say and what I believe."

There was a long moment of silence between them, and then Fortuna sighed. "He died to keep it—and you would have me let it go."

"Fortuna, your man kept the faith that he was sworn to. But in the past the sword was a beacon to us of hope and victory; let it become so again."

"Let me look again at that—that thing—" Fortuna spoke sharply. Matild obediently unwrapped the armlet. Though she did not touch it, the dame leaned closer, studying it as a master craftsman studies a product, hunting for some flaw.

"It can be fitted just below the quillions where the blade enters the sheath," she said.

Matild felt the leap of a victory hard won. "So shall it be!" she promised. "And this, I swear to you, Fortuna, by the honor of the Tiger—is such a weapon that has not been tried before, yet I believe it will sink home."

"Then—" The dame leaned closer so that her mouth was not far from Matild's ear. She repeated words which the other caught in memory, making sure the very intonation of the other's voice was set in her mind.

Once more she wrapped the armlet well. Dame Fortuna arose jerkily, as one whose aged joints protest any change of position. "I shall pray—" She motioned toward the altar.

But if she was to add to that, she was given no time, for a vast, thunderous clap filled the room. Clap—no, it was a tolling, as a second peal followed. Matild stiffened.

Death of a Reverend One—she was counting the strokes aloud, but could not be heard over the lament of the bell. That was the great voice of the Temple and only sounded for—

No! Matild shook her head in denial. Adele was not dead! She would have known it, their heart-tie was too strong. Yet those strokes told off her mother's years, and the use of the Great Bell itself her rank. Adele, sometime dowager queen of Merina, had entered into peace.

❧ 32 ❧
ADELE

Gemen Elfrida was in her place in the Temple when the passing bell started to ring, just as the chanting of the third-hour ritual came to an end. Even though she had been expecting it for more than a day, the sound startled her, for Verit had not told her just when Adele would "die." She was not the only person to jerk upright at the first peal of the bell; all over the Temple, Gemen and townsfolk alike showed wide, startled eyes as they looked toward the bell tower. The somber notes knelled out, hollow in the silence, vibrating in one's breastbone. Everyone in the sanctuary sat in silence, lips moving, counting the strokes of the bell—as if they didn't know perfectly well who had died.

Or who supposedly died. No, Adele is dead, truly dead. Only Gemen Elfrida lives now.

When the last note died away, all the Gemen knelt, as if at an invisible signal. Elfrida knelt with the rest of them to pray for the soul of Adele, whose soul certainly had more need for prayers than the souls of those who *were* safely dead. The dead had finished their work; they could err no more. Gemen Elfrida was very aware of the fact that she could—and perhaps already had. All this had been happening too fast, without proper time for thought or careful planning.

How many things I have done or condoned that will cost lives, or even souls? Lydana is not the only one of us playing with fire.

The group of Gemen scheduled to chant the ritual next entered and quietly knelt in their places, but no one from the first group stirred. Whatever they would have done next was forgotten, swallowed up by their need for prayer. In a way, Elfrida was surprised by the show of devotion— it wasn't just "show," it was a demonstration of how people had felt about the dowager, both the Gemen and the people of Merina alike.

Perhaps she represents to them in these dark times the last glimmering of light from a brighter past. In mourning her, they mourn the loss of their lives as they have always known them. Certainly the faces of those who sat or knelt with eyes closed in prayer held more than a shadow of despair. Elfrida bowed her head, as her old eyes stung with tears. It was dreadful to be so helpless in the face of such anguish. . . .

It seemed no time at all to Gemen Elfrida before the Archpriestess Verit entered, robed again in purple, followed by four strong Gemen, one from each order, bearing the open coffin, which they set before the high altar, below the Heart. So, Verit had decided to make the occasion one for high visibility, lest anyone doubt that Adele was truly dead.

Someone had done a good job on the effigy; it bore a remarkable resemblance to the Dowager Queen Adele. In fact, the effigy looked more like Adele as she had been than Elfrida did now. Elfrida wondered inconsequentially if they had used her own cosmetics on the face.

Certainly I will have no need of them.

Several of the stronger men among the Gemen followed with the funeral screen and placed it between the coffin and the congregation. They were followed by four more Gemen carrying large candles, which they placed carefully at the head and foot of the coffin.

The Archpriestess Verit lit the candles with a wave of her hand, an exhibition of magic that she normally shunned in public. After an appropriate moment of silence, she announced that the Goddess had been pleased to call her handmaiden Adele to Her Light.

In fact, she made quite an impressive little speech, citing Adele's piety, her charity, her devotion to the people that the Goddess had called her to lead, her heartbreak at being unable to continue to aid them. Before it was over, Elfrida was rather impressed with her own record. And it did not escape her notice how delicately Verit suggested that being forced to surrender the city to the unkind hands of the emperor was what had killed Adele. She never actually said a word that anyone would take as treason—but oh, what she implied!

I wonder if the emperor has any spies in the congregation? If so, I wonder what they are thinking. I wouldn't think they could take exception to what is essentially a funeral oration, but they might. I wonder if Verit thought about that.

Whether she had or not, when the archpriestess was finished, she dismissed Elfrida's group back to their regular duties and bade the remaining Gemen start the singing and chants that celebrated the vigil of a Reverend One's passing into the hands of the Goddess.

Gemen Elfrida left the choir as instructed and, remembering Verit's instructions to remain visible, followed a group of Grey Robes to the scriptorum, where she had a desk assigned to her. She pulled out the manuscript she had been copying and set to work, not stopping until it was time to return to her place before the Heart for the next ritual.

Once she heard the bells for her group, she hurried to the Temple in order to be there a little ahead of the rest, and made a slight change in the place where she usually knelt. She positioned herself in the place where she would be most visible to the greatest number of people, then bent her head in silent prayer as the rest of her group arrived.

There were more people from the city in the Temple

than ever; if the numbers continued to increase, the Temple wouldn't be able to hold them all.

Why aren't they going to their local chapels? Are the emperor's men preventing them from doing so? Or do they feel they must see the body of the dowager to believe that she is really dead?

Or is it simpler than that? Are all of them moved to make their own farewells to her?

Halfway through this service, there was a stir near the doorway. Elfrida kept her head bowed, but looked up cautiously through her eyelashes. Whoever the late arrival was, he was making something of a disturbance.

Then, with a shock that made her falter for a moment in her chanting, she saw who the latecomer was.

Prince Leopold—with a token escort of two of his officers.

And wearing a black band of mourning around his right arm.

He made no effort whatsoever to ascend to the dais and the area beyond the screen where the coffin and the "body" lay, which had been her initial fear when he appeared. Leopold was an observant man, and Elfrida wasn't sure that Verit's ruse would pass his scrutiny.

He simply took his place with his two officers in the front pew and remained there, standing, with his head bowed and uncovered, during the rest of the service.

At the end of the service, one of the two officers approached the Gemen standing before the screen in the place occupied by the presiding Reverend One and murmured something. They touched hands, and something small and dark passed between them.

A purse! Elfrida was near enough to them to hear a distinct *chink* of coins.

Her astonishment could not have been greater if the officer had sprouted wings.

A funerary gift! The prince brought a funerary gift for Adele! In theory, since there were no relatives to defray the expenses of the funeral, it would all fall on the Temple, which might mean the funeral itself could be somewhat less impressive than Adele's position would call for. Leopold had just made certain that Adele would have the funeral due a dowager queen.

Nor was that the end of surprises. The officer returned to his place beside the prince, and all three of them stepped out into the aisle, but they did not move away. Not yet.

Instead, slowly and gravely, they turned to face the screen that hid the coffin. With deliberation and absolute formality, in graceful unison, they placed their fists against their hearts, in the full imperial salute, granted otherwise only to the emperor himself.

Then, and only then, did they turn and walk away. The crowd parted before them, the expressions on the faces that Elfrida could see a mixture of shock, surprise, and disbelief.

She sympathized with them; she felt rather the same way herself.

What did *this* mean? Why had Leopold made such an astounding gesture?

Did it signal some bold move on his own part, or was it simply the response of a gallant young man to an old woman he had met long enough to admire?

Or was he giving notice to someone else—Apolon, for instance—where *his* sentiments lay?

Whatever the reason, there was one thing she was certain of. The game had changed again.

§ 33 §

SHELYRA

Raymonda did not breathe freely again until they were all safe within the walls of the compound. Her dancing partner had not let go of her arm in all that time, and she was glad enough of his support. There was nothing romantic about his manner whatsoever; rather, his solicitude seemed very fraternal, as if he knew her and was waiting for her to recognize him.

He did seem familiar; a very thin man, made of wire and whipcord, with a great beak of a nose and flashing, dark eyes beneath an unruly mop of wavy black hair. She was not certain how old he was; his was the kind of face that would change but little between the ages of twenty and fifty. In the thin light of the overcast day, his eyes still shone with merriment.

"So, little filly, we come home safely again, and still you have no friendly word for your old partner," he teased as the gates closed behind them. "I begin to think you do not recognize me! I am devastated! I thought I was much more memorable than that!"

Little filly? That was her pet name from the days when it had been her father who had taken her among the Gypsy clans and the Horse Lords. There could not be more than a handful of people who knew her by that pet name. Who was this man? She shook her head with doubt.

He sighed. "And to think that all this time I have been repenting of my harsh treatment of you, thinking that it had caused you great hurt, and *you* never had a second thought about it!"

Harsh treatment— Now that did strike a chord of remembrance! There was only one person who could have said that to her! "Ilya?" she said, incredulously. "What are you doing here? I thought you lived in Belrus! That was where your clan went—"

"So I was, but a Gypsy cannot remain long in a single place, you know that," Ilya replied with a grin; his teeth shone whitely against his dark skin. "So you remember me after all!"

"How could I forget? You were so *very* cruel to me," she replied as the bittersweet memories flooded over her. She had not forgotten, no, though Ilya had changed greatly. Hardly surprising—he had been only eight or nine, and she a mere seven years old when they met.

It had been her father's idea that she should learn the customs and dances of their hosts, and Ilya had been appointed to be her teacher and partner. *He* had been less than pleased to be saddled with the *gajo* child and had made his objections known, shrilly and often. She was a foreigner, and a worthless girl at that; why should he waste his valuable time teaching her to sing and dance like a Gypsy? What was the point? She would only forget everything she had learned as soon as she returned home. Or she would make fun of their ways, parodying their dances to make her wealthy *gajo* friends laugh. He had even resorted to pinching her and stepping on her feet, when no one was looking, to make her give up the idea.

If Ilya had expected her to dissolve into tears at the barrage of abuse, he had gotten a severe surprise. Instead, she had squalled with fury and set upon him with fists, feet, and teeth. Laughing, their parents had separated them, and Ilya had indeed taught the young Shelyra as he had been instructed—but this time, bearing a black eye, bruised shins, and a new and wary respect for the foreign girl.

"Did you wed that childhood sweetheart of yours?" she

asked, teasing him a little. "It was she who you wanted to dance with, as I recall, which is why you fought so hard against spending your time teaching me."

"Of course I did!" he said proudly. "She could not resist me! But—" His face darkened. "I should not so forget our situation in telling tales. Things are falling out darkly, little filly, and for you, most especially. My beloved Maya sent me to you because she wishes to speak with you, and not about dancing."

"What—" she began, but he made a hushing motion and cast a wary glance over his shoulder. "Not here," he said. "There are invisible ears and eyes about, even where we think we are safe. These are matters of *drukor*. Will you come with me? There is one you should meet and speak with."

A faint chill passed over her as she realized what he was trying to say. *Drukor*—that was the Gypsy word for magic. She tried to remember anything at all about Maya, and could come up with nothing but a vague recollection of huge, shy eyes and a wild mane of hair. Had Maya become a Gypsy mage?

But how could that be? No woman became a mage at the young age Maya must be!

"Maya's grandmother has much she must tell you," Ilya continued. "It is she who told us to find you. More than that I cannot discuss here."

"I will come with you," she said, making her decision swiftly. Thom was nowhere in evidence, but that hardly mattered. He was no keeper of hers.

Ilya smiled whitely again. "Good. We quarter in our wagon, behind the stables. It is not far."

Indeed, it was closer than many of the other buildings, and they reached the wagons in no more than a few moments, walking across the courtyard and then turning to go around behind the stable. There were fully a dozen wagons there, each with a family living in it. Ilya's wife Maya—recognizable, for she still had her huge, dark eyes and wild, curly mane of black hair—sat embroidering on the driver's bench of the third wagon, frowning with concentration in the thin sunlight. She caught sight of them as they came around a corner of the stables and jumped down to run to Ilya with a little glad cry.

Maya had grown into a graceful woman, a dancer born—Ilya's claim that Raymonda danced *almost* as well as his wife could be nothing more than blatant flattery. The ersatz Gypsy Raymonda knew that she could never match the fluid grace of someone whose most common actions were a dance in miniature. Still, it had been kind of Ilya to say that.

Maya embraced her husband without embarrassment, then turned to her guest with a shy smile. "I know who you must be, and my grandmother wishes to speak with you most urgently. She is within the wagon; will you take our hospitality?"

"Gratefully," Shelyra replied. "In matters of—the unusual—I am as ignorant as a babe. We all face someone who is no babe—and no friend of any who love freedom. I will happily hear all she has to say."

With a grave nod, Maya conducted her up the steps and into the wagon, into the presence of a truly ancient woman, a crone so wrapped in shawls it was not possible to tell what her shape was. But as the old woman looked up, eyes exactly like Maya's beautiful dark orbs met Shelyra's, and the princess relaxed without conscious thought. She sat down on a bench at a tiny table built into the side of the wagon, across from the old woman. The gray light from outside streamed through the window beside the woman and lit her face softly.

But, of course, nothing could be done or said without the ritual acceptance of hospitality in the form of hot, sweet tea and cookies so sticky with honey they made Shelyra's teeth ache. Formalities over, Maya introduced her grandmother.

"This is Mother Bayan; among our clan she is known as a powerful *drukorin*," Maya said with pride as the old woman smiled deprecatingly.

"I am what I am, and what the small Talent that the

Two have given me makes of me," Mother Bayan said in a soft, and surprisingly sweet, high voice. "But you, little filly—no, we will not speak your name, for I am not so proud that I trust my locks and wards to keep all safe— you are in grave danger from the forces of the Dark."

Shelyra nodded, thought for a moment, and decided to risk all on a single cast of the dice. "I have been warned, and warned also to find someone who might safeguard my path. Dare I ask that of you? It is a great favor, and I would not ask had I any knowledge of who else might be of help."

"You not only may ask, but I may tell you that I have been *geased* to grant you that aid, little filly," the old woman said firmly—and surprisingly. "The Two have not claimed much of me until now—perhaps They were intent upon waiting until the need was great." She paused for a moment, and stared down between her hands; Shelyra caught a glimpse of something bright there, a bit of reflection, as from a mirror. "Your danger is not so great now as it was last night . . . ah! I see now." She looked up again, her eyes wide, but still warm with concern. "You have a friend in an unexpected place. As he has served you, so you may be called to serve him to save him from the Dark Powers that would devour you both." Her lips formed a smile amid all the wrinkles of her face. "I would tell you who and what he is, but you would not believe me. So I simply tell you to look for a friend among your deadliest foes, and you will find him when he is in need. *If* that future comes to pass, that is."

"If?" Shelyra was puzzled. "Why do you say that?"

"Because the future is mutable; what we do here and now may change what I have seen," the old woman replied readily. "I see only the future that is most likely, and even that can be altered. Your enemy-friend—I had not seen him acting last night, and your immediate danger then was much greater than it is now, your likeliest future one fraught with terrible peril and requiring great courage and protection. But"—she held up a warning finger—"I can also see the past, and *that* is beyond altering. And in that past—nay, in *your* past—is the Emperor's Hellhound, Apolon."

"Apolon!" Shelyra exclaimed with shock and dismay. "What has that hoodcrow to do with me?"

"He seeks you for the sake of the power that lies dormant within you," Mother Bayan said as a cold wave of fear settled over Shelyra, and she hugged herself to keep from shivering. "It is he, not the emperor nor his general, who wishes you found. And if you fall into his hands"—she shook her head—"your end will not only be worse than ever mortal could imagine, but it will bring the Black Dog such power as should make us all quiver with terror. Power in *that one's* hands means the end of freedom and peace for everyone within the bounds of the empire, and for most outside of it. This is why the Two have *geased* me to your aid, for all our people will suffer if Apolon gains what he wishes."

How—comforting— Shelyra thought with a touch of despair.

"Now, things have changed, although the threat to you from Apolon is still a great one," Mother Bayan continued. "The immediate threat has been eliminated by your ally. The glass shows me nothing, which means that at the moment there is no future that is more likely than any other." She took a scrap of silk and swiftly covered what lay between her hands before Shelyra could get even a glimpse of what it was.

"So what does that mean for me?" Shelyra asked in a small voice.

"That you must take great care, and that I must safeguard you as best I can so that Apolon cannot find you by the sign of your potential power." Mother Bayan closed her eyes briefly. "Now I must ask you to trust me most completely, little filly," she continued. "For I must ask you for a single hair from your head. Without that, I cannot weave protections about you, for so the magic I know is woven."

She opened her eyes and waited, expectantly, her hands folded over the silk-shrouded packet on the table.

Shelyra hesitated, recalling her grandmother's warning against permitting anything of that sort to fall into the hands of someone else. But—what else could she do? She knew nothing of magic, nor did she have any idea how to find another magician to help her. Even if she could find someone else, what guarantee was there that this mage would be more trustworthy than Mother Bayan? The odds were against it.

Ilya was her childhood friend; the Gypsies had given her shelter and physical protection. Surely, if they wanted to betray her, there were easier and more profitable ways to do so!

Resolutely, she reached up with her right hand, teased out a single hair, and with a hard yank, pulled it out by the root, wincing a little as she did so.

She handed it to Mother Bayan, who took it in her age-spotted hands carefully, as if it were the greatest treasure in the world. "I shall guard this as I would my own, little filly," she said gravely. "I shall take care to destroy it if there is any chance it might fall into evil hands. I swear by the Two that no harm shall come to you through this or through my actions."

"That is all I can ask for," Shelyra replied with equal gravity. "And you are granting me a favor I can never repay. Be sure that I know that."

"Pish-tush," the old woman replied with a dismissive motion. "I favor us all by protecting you. It will be a dark world for my people if that Hellhound should sink his fangs into you. This is only my duty, the repayment I make to the Two for the power They have granted me."

Shelyra bowed her head in acknowledgment of that. The Gypsies bowed to the Light in the form of two gods, not one; twins, male and female. She didn't know much more beyond that, for neither the Horse Lords nor their Gypsy kinsmen ever made any attempt to convert even those they accepted into their clans as brothers into their religion. While the Way of the Two was not secret, the religion was not openly discussed with outsiders.

"Then, for all of us, I thank you, Mother Bayan," she said softly. "And if we win through this—your work will not be forgotten."

There seemed nothing more to say; Shelyra rose from her seat and, with a murmured apology, took her leave. She sensed that the old woman would do nothing more until she left, so the sooner she did so, the sooner the "protection"—whatever it was—would be in place.

Ilya and Maya were nowhere to be seen as she stepped down out of the wagon, so she was saved having to make small talk with them. After all that had happened this morning, she felt herself overcome with the lassitude of sudden exhaustion, and all she truly wanted to do was return to her bed in the stable and sleep the rest of the day away.

Tonight she would have to begin her work in the Summer Palace, exercises less hazardous, but more physically demanding than her prowling of the Great Palace. If she could, she planned to get *all* of her grandmother's books into hiding in one night; as she recalled, the bookshelf in Adele's room did not hold all that many volumes. If half of those were on magic, that would mean twenty, perhaps thirty books to be stolen away; not a great number, compared to the huge library Adele had already at her disposal in the Temple. The real trick would be finding other books in the Summer Palace to take the places of the stolen works, so that it was not immediately evident there should be more books than there were.

I will have to take one or two books from every shelf in the palace, she decided at last. *That is the only way to ensure I don't reveal that something is missing. That will take all night, between evading the soldiers and fiddling about with the books themselves—*

But her reverie was interrupted at that moment.

At the first sound of the tolling of the Great Bell of the Temple, Shelyra's head jerked up. She stared at the tiny piece of the topmost belltower that was visible above the walls and the surrounding buildings. The Great Bell only tolled on the occasion of the death of someone very important. But who? Not the archpriestess, surely—

She counted out the age-strokes, then the rank-strokes; passing everyone that it *might* be until there was only one person who matched both.

Adele. The Great Bell was tolling out the death of the Dowager Queen of Merina, signaling that Adele had passed beyond reach of any enemy.

§ 34 §

LYDANA

The Reverend One Zenia was on her knees, slipping her prayer beads through her fingers, chanting the Farewell as Matild came into her small office. Seeing her, Zenia held out a hand as if to draw her closer for comfort.

"Dearest lady—" she began, when Matild interrupted her.

"Reverend One, of your charity can you provide me with one of the habits of your house? I must go to the Temple."

The Reverend One gave her a long look, then rose quickly. "Yes, that must also be done. What I myself have is yours."

There was a small cupboard against the wall, and she opened it to show one of the rusty brown robes of the order hanging there. It was well-worn indeed, with neat patches of a slightly different shade of brown set in the skirt. On a shelf above, snowy clean and neatly folded, lay one of the winged wimples.

The bell had stopped its troubling tolling. Matild was already jerking off her skirt and allowing the shawl to slip to the floor. Her slim night-roving suit would fit well under the habit Zenia was holding out to her. But it took the aid of the Reverend One to adjust the folds of the wimple with its outstanding wings—though those might well give her more masking if she needed it.

Zenia made the Heart sign between them. "Daughter," her voice now held the warmth of those who shared a common purpose, "go with Her hand over you. This is indeed an hour in which you must seek out the uttermost cloak of Her ever abiding mercy."

Matild bowed her head. "Petition for me, Called One, I weave a devious path—maybe to destruction—yet I believe by the Heart this I must do!"

"That is so," returned Zenia calmly. "We move to Her patterns as She needs in Her weaving." She picked up her clacker again, and Gemen Papania materialized as if that sound alone could waft her from the farther corners of the cloister.

"This one goes—since the Reverend One just passed is her blood kin—to pray at the High Altar."

There were no longer any beggars at the door, but Eel stood at attention, awaiting her. Matild let her hand rest for a moment on the untidy mop of hair.

"Heart-daughter," for the first time she felt free to say words which had been growing within her all these past days, "this I must do—alone. But you also can serve—as eyes and ears—as you have done so well in the past."

Eel's level glance met her own, and held so for a long silent moment. Then he nodded quickly, and slipped ahead through the doorway Gemen Papania had opened, and was gone.

There was a stir in the streets. The black-coated watcher of the convent took a step or so forward at Matild's appearance, but then spat loudly in the gutter and looked away. As she moved on toward the other part of the city, weaving a way which would provide her with footing over the bridges, Matild was aware of a strange feeling. It was as if Merina itself had suddenly taken on the guise of that great beast which was her own sign, pausing in some padding stroll to raise a head, to sniff, to weigh some chance of coming battle.

She joined an ever-increasing stream of people moving in the direction of the Temple. They were coming into the square in groups where the women wept, children marched hushed and awe-stricken, and the scattering of men showed dour faces.

For the first time there was a line of troops—not black coats but mercenaries—across the steps, and they funneled between them those who would enter. Matild saw, as she made her way, striving to keep her head down, her wimple half-mask well in place, that there was color aplenty. The cathedral orders, so different from the humble one whose habit she wore, were masses of color: there was the slate grey of scholars, who must have arisen from their desks to come and pay this last honor, the red robes, the yellow robes and the brown, the last of whom, besides being the helpers of the poor in the city, were also answerable for the upkeep of Her own famed garden and the place of beasts to which any homeless or injured animal could come for succor.

The funeral screen had been set up. Through its lattice Matild could see the coffin on its dais against the edge of the high altar itself, candles at the head and foot, and above, the great crimson Heart which seemed to pulse like a living organ. Priestesses stood to one side, but Verit herself was stationed at the foot of the coffin as if she were a sentry standing on guard. As usual her face was impassive, but her eyes were heavy-lidded as if she had recently known tears.

The cloistered ones were in their stalls behind their screen and from them arose flutelike singing, not of sorrow but of exultation. This was one of their own passing into the Great Mother's hands to know a peace and rest beyond all understanding. The song caught at Matild— No, she would not accept that Adele was truly dead, not even when she heard those hallowed words so caroled.

She had passed the screen. The coffin was not closed— and in it there was a body! She must know!

One of the grey robes pushed out before her. It was plain he considered her coming an intrusion. But at his move, Verit had raised her head and, boldly, Matild did likewise, so that their eyes met.

The archpriestess spoke, her words carrying clearly in spite of the song. "This Gemen was one of those favored by the charity of the Reverend One—let her come forward and take her leave."

Stepping back again, the grey robe let her pass, and the others massed there made room for her since Verit had ordered it so. Then she was by the coffin looking down at—Adele? No, this was her face, calm and peaceful, look- ing like one who had died in the warmth of the Heart. But it was—Matild's thought took a wild leap, a guess— And then within her she knew the truth. What lay here was an effigy. For some reason, Adele must have arranged what would be a final escape. But that meant that she had been under unusual threat and had been forced to put to use rituals it was near-blasphemy to use for such a pur- pose. Great must have been her danger.

Would Verit know—would she attempt to pass along what Matild now feared—that indeed darkness was falling fast on Merina? She went to her knees beside the coffin, her head bowed, her fingers entwining with the prayer beads fastened to the rope belt of her long, worn habit.

"Daughter—"

No, that mask above her had not spoken. But into her now was flooding the love and trust which was her moth- er's always. She was not sure of the range of Adele's Tal- ents—nor really of those of any of the cloistered. Perhaps speech of mind-to-mind was one of the gifts midlife brought them.

"Look!" That seemed like a cry— Startled, Matild raised her head, glanced from the grey robe on his knees to her left, to the elderly brown robe on her right. They were still deep in prayer, their eyes closed.

"Look!" That order came again. Matild raised her head. She needed to hold it well back so that the folds of her headdress did not at least hide anything immediately before her.

The shimmer of the Heart was glowing brighter, as if within it pulsed now not only life, but leaping flames. The red glow painted the casket, reached out to engulf those about it. Just as the final sweet note of the Farewell sounded, the Heart appeared to Matild to tremble.

Then, from its point, there came drops—bloodred, seeming to be blood itself. The rubies set there for so many years were breaking free. They struck on the high altar, rebounded to the casket, and one fell into the open palm that Matild had half reached forth. She gave a small, quickly stifled cry, for it burnt against her flesh as if she held a coal from a firepit. Yet she steadfastly closed her fingers about it and held on.

"The Heart—it bleeds—it sorrows," someone raised the cry, and it was taken up by others in the crowd around her. "A miracle! Praise be the eyes to see—a miracle!"

Matild pressed her closed fist against her breast. It was still hot, and now from within the layers of her clothing there came a steady answer—a life-spark glowed also in the seal-stone that had once graced her state ring.

There was scrambling about her as those nearest reached for the fallen rubies, gathering them up to be placed upon the altar. The rain of gems was done, no more fell to be gathered into those piles. Matild held to the one which had seemed to come straight to her. She did not know what she held, except that it was a focus of power— and as such might be the weapon most needed for what she must do.

There were sounds from the other side of the screen now. She heard voices raised, questions shouted with little

of the propriety meant for those within these walls. The
screen trembled as bodies apparently pushed against it. At
a signal from Verit, those gathered before her got to their
feet and went out into the now unruly congregation beyond. The word "miracle" was shot back and forth, repeated from lips to lips.

Matild remained where she was. Then Verit came up
beside her and spoke swiftly, "Your Grace, there is little
time—what has happened here is clearly not of our devising, but a Sign from Her. The Reverend One lives even as
you believe." (She, too, must have the power of thought
reading, Matild guessed then.) "But it was necessary that
he, who threatened us with worse than the emperor could
hope to devise, believes her gone."

He? Could she mean Apolon?

"He has suddenly concerned himself with you of the
Tiger blood, as if he has been advised that of all of our
powerful ones you are the most to be feared. It is known
that he seeks diligently for the princess—and for you.
Watch yourselves."

She had known that Apolon was looking for her—and
Shelyra. But she had not guessed it was for anything other
than their value as hostages for the city's good behavior!

"But the time of the Talent is not yet come upon us—"
Matild protested.

Verit shrugged slightly. "Who knows what an adept can
force upon one he uses as a tool? We must move with
speed—"

She was interrupted by a louder shouting from beyond
the screen. A woman screamed, and then another. With
one stride Verit reached the end panel of lattice work and
looked through.

"Soldiers!" Her voice was icy with outrage. "Soldiers,
armed and attacking our people—within the sanctuary itself."

She flung herself around the end of the screen, and
Matild quickly followed, as aroused as the Archpriestess.
What was being done here broke all laws, not only of hu-

mankind but of She Who Rules Beyond the Sky.

There were soldiers. Not black coats, as Matild had more than half expected. They had not yet drawn swords, but they were laying about them with the lengths of light lances, the blows falling on women and men alike, and there were bleeding bodies lying on the pavement.

The archpriestess sped forward to face the invaders. She Beyond the Sky had Her righteous wrath, and that now was visible in Her servant on earth. Without thinking, Matild was only a step or so behind her, and felt a swish of air as a lance passed through the air within a finger-breadth of her shoulder.

"Back!" The archpriestess' voice was a trumpet, gathering all the resonance of thunder as it seemed to resound twice as loud from the walls about them. Those who had been recently driven like cattle turned on the soldiers. Matild saw hate in their faces. Unarmed as they were, they were ready to drag down these enemies.

"Stop!" The cry was as loud as Verit's and it carried with it the snap of command. An officer leading a small wedge of fighting men had pushed through the throng to whirl and face the attacking force. He was young and of high rank by his uniform, and the anger in him was as raging-hot as that which fueled Verit.

"Out of here—" He swung a company leader's cane in one hand, first idly and then pointing it at one and then another of the soldiers. "This is holy ground— Who set you to this? Get out, report to barracks, and you will find there such an answer as you will not forget to the rest of your days. Get!" He brought the cane down with a fury now, and sent one of the soldiers stumbling back.

Another, hard-faced, and with the insignia of a half-company commander, stepped around the man to face the young officer.

"We have our orders, sir."

"Orders!" exploded the younger officer. "Whose? I command in Merina by the orders of the emperor himself! I have given no such orders, and you may thank your gods that my page brought me word of your attack before you actually harmed some person here, or there *would* be orders for a hanging!"

"General Cathal gave the orders," the other replied stolidly.

"I do not care if the Foremost Fiend of the Netherlands gave you such orders; here it is my orders you listen to. Out instantly, or I shall see you are taken by my own guard, and it will be much the worse for you!"

The lesser officer's jaw was stubbornly set, but it was plain that he was not ready to stand up to the younger man. Then he grinned, a most unpleasant grin, like that of the deep-sea man-killer, and waggled his own cane in a salute that was half mockery.

"Well enough, Your Highness. You and the general can have this out face-to-face; I do not speak for my superior. Form ranks." He flung the order over his shoulder, and the scattered squad drew into tighter formation. "March—" They withdrew, leaving the chaos of their attack behind them. Already the brown robes of the healing order were spreading out to aid those who had taken beatings.

The prince turned directly to the archpriestess and inclined his head courteously. "Reverend One, we are not barbarians—at least, not all of us. I do not know what lies behind this beastliness, but be sure I shall find out and reparations shall be made."

She stared at him as someone studying a complex puzzle. "Prince Leopold—as you know, General Cathal has the blackest of reputations. Now his men have listened to your commands, but can those commands continue to hold? Are we," she made a wide gesture comprising all about her, "the very Heart of the world to be ravished? I warn you—She Who Stands Behind the Sun can be a bringer of wrath as well as hope and peace. Provoke Her too much, and then you must take the consequences."

He had a thin face, mostly hidden by his helm and the cheek pieces. Yet he stood arrow-straight and there was a flat line to his mouth.

"The emperor's word carries above all—he shall be told—"

Verit took a step nearer to him and held up her hand.

"Prince, in this much will She favor you, for she sends you words of caution through me Her servant. It may be that there are pits cunningly set beneath the roads on which you march. To trust is sometimes to open the gate to the greatest fear."

For a long moment their eyes held. Then his lips twisted into what could have either been a snarl or a grim smile.

"I give full credence to what you say, Reverend One. Be sure no warning falls on deafened ears. But this I also promise and I shall hold to it: As long as I am commander in Merina this place is safe, and those who serve Her," he raised his wand in salute, "need have no fear from imperial troops."

"You speak truth—as you see it—" Verit replied. "This much does She acknowledge that—" The archpriestess sketched in the air the outline of the heart, giving him the blessing due all who came before the great altar with no dark thoughts within.

Matild, her hand still tightly closed about the Heart ruby, was able to win out of the Temple. There was no sign of the soldiers who had made that wanton attack; perhaps they had indeed made their way back to barracks at Leopold's command. But she was trying to assess her opinion of the prince himself.

There had been rumors in the past that he was no favorite of Balthasar. He had been known on at least two occasions to argue against the sacking of shore cities in the north. But they also said that the emperor allowed him very little true authority, that part of the army scoffed at him, and his father considered him no true son.

Perhaps he had even been made governor here so Balthasar, waiting for mistakes, could have reason to pull him down, degrade him to a useless hanger-on at the court. Though Leopold was the enemy, yet she felt a concern for this young man. Courts were often evil mazes of dark intrigue; a man could be webbed around and destroyed before he was even aware of his danger. Though Balthasar, because of his insatiable desire to conquer all the lands he could easily invade, kept no real court, he certainly had an inner circle even in his numerous war camps, full of those who would pull down their fellows to gain a scrap more of power.

On the other hand, a dispute between the prince and the emperor, though it would clearly be won by the latter, could perhaps ease some of the hard hold on the city. Except—the hoodcrows—she had seen none of them engaged in the confrontation. They were Apolon's men, and the mage might mix a brew of both emperor and prince and come out with an answer which would be his alone.

⚬ 35 ⚬

LEOPOLD

Leopold did not take the mercenary officer's word for anything, not after the man sent his soldiers to attack unarmed people on hallowed ground. He personally saw to it that Cathal's men proceeded back to their barracks, sending his officers to trail them to make certain they did exactly as he had ordered. Only when he was satisfied that the mercenaries were properly kenneled did he send for his squires and storm up to his own **quarters** in a barely suppressed rage.

The mercenaries were supposed to be acting as a local policing force and enforcing imperial law. But in the past two or three days he'd been getting reports of outrages committed against the citizens of Merina by those same mercenaries. When he tried to investigate the reports, the mercenary officers always had "proof" that their actions were justified—and, of course, there were no witnesses to the contrary. This time, however, was different. They had acted against unarmed citizens gathered to worship on holy ground, and there had been nothing done to provoke such an outrageous attack. *He* had been given no orders permitting Cathal and Cathal's pet scum-troops free rein in the city! And even if he had—

To attack unarmed civilians in the very Temple itself! The man must be mad! Is he trying to provoke rebellion?

On sober second reflection, that might well be exactly what Cathal was up to—for a rebellion would give him the excuse to sack the city he had probably been looking for. Cathal had not been pleased when Merina surrendered tamely; resistance would have given him an opportunity to exercise all the savagery in his bestial soul. More than once, Leopold had argued against permitting the general's troops to be first in a city, knowing that the result of such policy would be a bloodbath. Cathal's men, like their master, were beasts, who reveled in looting and rape. They, too, had been deprived of the opportunity to unleash their basest lusts.

He will get no such chance here! As his squires appeared, Leopold ordered them to bring out his dress uniform and have his horse saddled and brought to the front door. Before the officer in question had a chance to inform Cathal of what had just occurred, Leopold would take the situation to the emperor himself.

He changed into the stiff uniform while his older squire fetched his horse, and ran the entire way to the stables, still buttoning his high collar as he ran. He dashed out the door and down the steps, then leapt on his horse's back without bothering to use the stirrups, startling the poor beast enough that it jerked its reins out of his squire's hands as it danced backward.

No matter; he got it under control again with a word

and a leg, for it *was* a trained warhorse, and nothing startled it for long. He bent and snatched up the reins, gave the horse its head, and sent the gelding galloping out of the palace gates, heading back to the Emperor's camp.

By now, the citizens of Merina had learned to clear out of the way when they heard a horse galloping headlong through their streets. They stared at him from the shelter of doors or side streets as he passed, but no one made any move to impede his progress. The iron-shod hooves of his war steed struck sparks from the flinty cobblestones as people cleared out of his way in utter and unnerving silence.

Sentries shouted at him as he passed the outer perimeter of the camp; he flung the passwords back over his shoulder, but did not pause even for a moment. The pounding of the horse's hooves shifted from sharp staccato to dull thuds as the road changed from cobbles to packed dirt. He was all too grimly certain that if any version of the outrage other than his own reached his father's ears first, *he* would be the one to suffer the emperor's anger, not Cathal. His stomach was taut with tension, and he forced himself to keep his riding crop hanging unused at his wrist. The poor horse was already doing his best; no whip would make him move faster, no matter how much Leopold desired it.

He pounded up to the emperor's tent, reined his lathered warhorse in so harshly it skidded to a halt in the churned-up dust, rearing back on its haunches. He flung the reins to one of the startled guards as he vaulted out of the beast's saddle. As he strode swiftly up to the tent, he spared a moment of guilty conscience for treating the noble horse so poorly; it did not deserve such treatment.

I shall make it up to you, he promised silently; then he pushed aside the tent flaps and there was no time for any other thoughts.

The emperor was with the chancellor only, for a wonder. Neither Cathal nor Apolon was anywhere in evidence.

Both the men looked up, startled, at Leopold's abrupt entrance.

Leopold went immediately to one knee, his head bowed, so that there could be no question of his motives, his loyalty or his obedience. He waited for the emperor to address him first and give him permission to speak, even though his nerves were afire and his neck muscles strained with the effort of holding in his angry words. He *must* make every gesture of subservience; only if he did so would the emperor even listen to him.

"I presume there must be a reason why you burst in upon us in this unseemly fashion, Prince Leopold," the emperor said coolly. "Perhaps you would care to enlighten us."

That was permission enough to let loose the torrent. Leopold began with this latest of Cathal's outrages, and added the rest—the wanton murders of noted citizens of Merina, the license he had given to his men to stir up trouble in the streets. The rounding up of women to create imperial brothels; the beatings of anyone suspected of "disloyalty." He recited it all with a chill rage, but carefully controlled both his words and his tone, for that was how the emperor preferred to hear things: told dispassionately, at least on the surface.

But once he had done telling over Cathal's excesses, his anger got the better of him, and he continued with the evil deeds of Apolon's black coats.

He knew at once that he had made a mistake when a complete silence descended. But by then, it was too late. The words could not be unsaid.

He tried to salvage it all, by returning to the subject of Cathal, but his father interrupted him before he got more than a few words out.

"I believe," Balthasar said, slowly, "that it is time I made my formal entrance into Merina. This very day; within the hour. Let the city know whose hand is on her leash, and she will quiet soon enough. It is time that I made it clear who is the ruler of the empire. I expect that once I am in place, there will be no more specious 'miracles,' no weeping over old women whose time was past long ago."

For a moment, Leopold had cause to hope that Balthasar had taken what he had said to heart. That he would bring both the Mad Dog and the Hellhound to heel, show *them* the whip as well, and cow them into their proper places.

"I believe that the governance of the city has been too great a strain on you, Prince Leopold," the emperor continued smoothly, dashing Leopold's hopes. "A city is not a company of soldiers, after all. You cannot simply give an order and assume a civilian will obey it. You must show that your hand is made of iron, give these people a reason to obey, prove to them you will not be disobeyed."

I said one thing too many, asked one too many questions. He is taking the city away from me—

"Yes, I shall take command of Merina myself. As for my loyal commander Leopold," the emperor continued in a cool and silken tone, as Leopold stared down at the geometric patterns of the scarlet and black carpet he knelt upon, "it is obvious that more officers should have the understanding that he has. And it is obvious that his duties have been a considerable strain on him. I believe we can relieve some of that strain and inculcate some of that understanding in our younger officers at the same time."

Leopold's heart sank further. *No—he's not—*

But he was. "I shall take command of your troops myself," the emperor continued smoothly. "And you, Prince Leopold, shall retire across the river to the Summer Palace, to train the younger officers I shall have posted there. I shall send those to you whom I feel need instruction."

Leopold could not have risen if the emperor had ordered him to. He was frozen in place, numb. At one blow, he had been deprived of command, exiled, taken out of a position where he might be able to discredit Apolon or

Cathal, and deprived of any chance to fulfill his promise to the archpriestess.

Somehow I must let the archpriestess know what is happening! Perhaps she can convince the people of Merina to lie quietly beneath the emperor's hand.

"I shall send word to your squires, so that you can leave immediately, Prince," said the chancellor, destroying his hope of getting word to the archpriestess before Balthasar actually took control. "I believe most of your belongings are still in the camp?"

Dumbly, he nodded, still not raising his eyes.

"Good," the chancellor said heartily. "Why don't you go collect them and take yourself across the river now?" There was a rustle of cloth, and the chancellor moved to Leopold's side, touching him on the shoulder to indicate that he should rise.

He did so, still so shocked that he moved like one in a dream, hardly knowing that he moved at all.

"Go along with him, would you?" the emperor said; Leopold could not bear to look at him. "See to it that he gets whatever he needs requisitioned. We wouldn't want him to go off unprovisioned."

Somehow Leopold found himself walking out of the tent, the chancellor at his elbow. He must have made his bow to Balthasar, but he couldn't remember doing so—he must have, for the chancellor would not have let him skip so important a gesture—

"Pull yourself together, boy, this isn't so bad," Adelphus said as they left the tent. "Stop acting as if you'd just been exiled to the end of the world! Apolon is very popular with Balthasar right now; you made a mistake in attacking him, that's all. He'll make a slip, his kind always do, and you'll be back in favor. Just go off to this Summer Palace, do what the emperor tells you, and everything will be fine."

Adelphus went on at some length in the same vein, and Leopold stifled the urge to strangle him. Balthasar was going to do *nothing* about Cathal! And as for Apolon—

At least I've destroyed any hope of his finding the princess through magical means, Leopold thought savagely. But that wasn't going to do anything to help the citizens of Merina. Between them, Apolon and Cathal were going to drive them into the dust.

§ 36 ❧

ADELE

Gemen Elfrida was startled to see the crowd of townspeople in the nave as she arrived for her next vigil; she had been planning Adele's death for so long that it no longer seemed like fresh news to her. She was oddly touched to see people crying—she had not expected that Adele would be mourned so fervently and for so long when the people had so many other griefs. *Perhaps this is one they feel it safe to mourn visibly,* she thought.

She gazed up at the Heart, attempting to summon the proper serenity, trying to compose her thoughts for prayer. But even the Heart had changed. At the bottom of it, gold was visible—for the first time in decades, if not centuries—and there was a large handful of rubies neatly piled together on the altar below it.

She stared in astonishment. What had happened here? *Never mind. It is not yet your business. And there are other things more pressing to worry about.* Doubtless Verit would explain later. Gemen Elfrida pulled her attention back to her chant-book and forced her lips to sing the proper words, even if, at this moment, she could feel nothing in her heart.

But there were whispers, distracting whispers, out amid

the people gathered beyond the rails that separated them from the Gemen. Ordinarily, Elfrida would never have paid any attention—in fact, she probably would not have even heard them. But now—she could not concentrate on even the most familiar of chants.

". . . .miracle. . . ." "Soldiers attacking. . . ." ". . . .beaten in front of the very altar. . . ."

Soldiers in the Temple? Suddenly, for the first time since she had been a young girl, she was impatient for the service to end. She was to stand duty in the confessional again, now that she had shown herself in public enough. Surely in the confessional booths, there would be some hint of what had happened while she had been obliviously copying a manuscript.

The service seemed to take forever, but at last it was over, and she hurried to take her appointed place behind the screen.

By the time her watch in the confessional booth was over, she had a very good idea indeed of what had happened. There was no doubt in her mind that the bleeding of the Heart was a miracle; she had helped clean the Heart once, when she had been younger and more limber, and those rubies had been affixed with all the skill of the best jewelers of the Tiger. Nothing, short of melting the gold itself, should have set them free.

But as for the marauding soldiers—that was a new and very disturbing element to the unrest in the city. It seemed that now not only were there black coats to worry about, but a cadre of mercenaries answerable to the vile General Cathal who had been let off their leashes. One woman had come to the confessional weeping so incoherently it had taken her a long time to control herself enough to make her troubles known. Her nephew, a member of the law-keepers, had been taken and had not returned—and her only daughter, who she had long suspected of having negotiable virtue, had been scooped up by Cathal's mercenaries and incarcerated in a house guarded by and catering only to imperial troops.

I do not know my own city anymore, Elfrida thought in a daze as the woman went away, comforted only a little.

Then again, there was little enough comfort for Elfrida herself.

More people came, some with tales of strange fires that sprang up out of nowhere, reducing buildings—but only *particular* buildings—to ash. These fires never spread beyond the buildings where they started, and could not be quenched.

Elfrida left the confessional in a fog, feeling as if events were occurring too quickly for her to even begin to keep up with them.

She went to the refectory for dinner, wondering if the rest of her fellow Gemen had been the recipients of similar confessions.

By the stunned and overwhelmed looks on their faces, they probably had been.

There was only one thought in her mind as she ate food she could not taste.

What has become of my city? And what can we few Gemen ever do to combat it all?

But that was not the only strange thing she encountered in the refectory, for as she ate, for the first time in her knowledge, she heard the voice of dissension among the Gemen as the rule of silence was lifted.

It first came to her attention as someone a table over raised her voice above the usual low murmur as tension made her tone a bit shrill.

She didn't hear what started the conversation, but she certainly heard the middle of it, and so did everyone else at those two tables.

". . . .how can you say that, Gemen Patria? That is surely the rankest nonsense! Why, look how quickly the prince brought men to deal with the troublemakers! The emperor is a faithful son of the Goddess and he will *always* see to our protection! Why, he is the *ruler!* It is his duty to do so!"

"Just because he's our ruler doesn't mean he's a good

one—or that he cares a tinker's damn for us, Gemen Althea," came the acid reply. "If you ask me, he just sees us as another rich place to loot—we're just a nut that's slightly more difficult to crack than a house."

The Gemen who had first raised her voice stood up abruptly, face crimson. "Well, no one asked you, Gemen!" she cried. "And I think you ought to speak to the Reverend One Gemen Verit for such—such—*blasphemous* and *treasonable* thoughts!"

And with that, the offended Gemen—and *not* one of the younger ones, Elfrida noted—abruptly shoved her stool away so that she could leave the table and stalked off.

Treasonable—well, I suppose so, if you accept that whoever is holding the reins is the "rightful" ruler. But "blasphemous"? How could speaking against the emperor be considered blasphemy? Elfrida watched Gemen Patria walking stiffly out the door, and she was not the only one whose eyes followed that indignant back. Most of the watchers wore looks of stark surprise. Some wore looks of mingled patience and disgust.

But some, much to Elfrida's unease, wore expressions of approval.

Gradually, the hum of conversation returned, and Elfrida strained her ears shamelessly to hear what Patria's outburst would ferret out of hiding—and some of it came as a distinct shock.

There was a faction, a minority faction, but substantial nevertheless, of those who felt precisely as Gemen Patria: whoever was the titular leader of the government of Merina was the proper recipient of their loyalty just by virtue of the fact that he was in charge. And that no matter who or what that leader was, the Gemen of the Temple were perfectly safe in their cloisters, and no one would hurt them. This faction claimed that the stories of woe in the city were all grossly exaggerated, perhaps by would-be rebels trying to stir up trouble for the emperor. And as for the invasion of the Temple itself—that they explained away as either a mistake on the part of the officer in charge, or shrugged away as a case of mercenaries attempting a little freelance trouble-making.

One or two were so stout in their defense of the purity of Emperor Balthasar and his motives that Elfrida had to look down at her plate, clench her jaw, and say a full string of beadprayers to keep herself from hitting them over the head with their own wooden trenchers in the hopes of pounding a little sense into them. These, like Patria, were not the youngest members of the Gemen, either. Most of them were numbered among the eldest, in fact.

And that might well be the explanation, she realized as she forced her temper to cool. *They've lived in here so long that the outside world no longer seems real to them. They can talk blithely about the notion that the stories of deaths, disappearances, and kidnapings are all invented or grossly exaggerated, because they simply can't imagine anything like that happening.*

They didn't *want* the world to change, so they would argue until they were blue that the world *hadn't* changed. And until something happened right in their laps, something they could not ignore, they would continue to believe that way.

But that meant that the Temple was no longer heart-whole. And there was no question but that would cut into their strength . . . like a thin shell of porcelain, their power would only be strong enough to withstand attack from without as long as it was seamless and perfect, without a crack or flaw.

And here is the flaw, she thought unhappily. *Just as neat as Apolon and Balthasar could wish.*

She shivered as a cold wind seemed to come out of nowhere, chilling her with a dreadful foreboding.

§ 37 §

LYDANA

As she hurried through the streets, she again began to
see the black coats. There were none near the Temple,
but then she sighted squads of them along some of the
streets, though they showed no interest in the houses on
either side.

Eel flitted out of a doorway to join her, in his usual
fashion of seeming to appear out of nowhere.

"Best forget Matild Beadswoman," he stated abruptly.

She did not lose a step, but she now expected a new
blow.

"What has happened?"

Eel scampered to keep up with her. "The shop is gone.
Yet the neighbor buildings show no signs of burning.
There is nothing but ashes and an evil smell between them
now—open to the sky."

Destruction of the shop. Did that mean they were indeed sniffing close on her trail? She clenched her hands
into fists hidden by the wide sleeves of her robe. That ruby
droplet was still like a burning brand, but she endured it
gladly, being sure that it was a promise of aid that one
could hardly hope to gain without the full favor of the
Great Presence.

"Those about—Berta, Kassie, Max—" she demanded.

"They keep well within. But so far they are safe," he

told her. "They say that this happened in the night, that there was a sound like the heaviest drum of thunder, and then flame shot high. But it was contained within the shop, as if it were a hearth and it was a properly set fire."

She frowned. "Set by who?"

Eel shook his head. "No sign of any open attack. Berta is nearly frightened out of her skin, but I learned that much from her."

"A mage device," said Matild slowly. "Such could have been sent whenever we were gone, to be activated later by a spell—I have read of such. Ah, we are indeed returning to ancient dark learning if that is true. But why destroy the shop?"

"We left it by the hidden way, as we always have," returned Eel calmly. "For all the fire-raiser would have known, we were snug in bed and now are wind-blown ashes. Which might be a very good thing—that we are dead as far as they are concerned," he elaborated.

Indeed it might, though they had no proof that their tracks were so well-covered. The cloister—she must not endanger the Gemen. If that which sought her could trace her— Yet she had to make contact there again. She quickened her pace.

They gained the cloister. She noted that the guards outside had been increased to three men now, and they stood openly, quite close to the doorway, though they made no attempt to stop and question her. And she had sent Eel on to Jonas to pick up any information the taverner's own lurkers had been able to gather about the approaches to the House of the Boar. For there—she drew a deep breath—there she would make her own strike.

Once inside the cloister walls, she was again ushered straight to the room of the Reverend One, who was seated by her desk table. Between her two hands, flattened on the surface, was a dull square of what looked to be opaque glass. She was staring as one caught in a vision.

Matild's palm burnt from an upflare of the ruby, until she uttered a small cry she could not stifle. The Reverend One blinked and looked up. Her eyes were as wide as one who had witnessed something that could not possibly exist.

"The Heart—bled!" she said in a soft, awed whisper.

Somehow Matild could no longer stand. She sank to her knees on the opposite side of the table and held out her fist, opening it slowly to show what lay on her palm.

There gleamed the ruby with more fire than any common gem could possibly show. It stirred a little as she freed it from her fingers' grasp. Below it, seared into her palm, was the Heart-sign, as if she had been branded.

Zenia looked at the stone and the sign it had left. Her hands moved in the double sign of the Greater Blessing.

"Chosen One—greatly are you favored! There is no Will before Hers when She chooses to express it! What are Her orders?"

Matild looked at the stone. Now that she had loosed her tight grip upon it, she no longer felt a burning. Nor did the scar it had left look raw—it might have been set upon her long ago.

The ruby rolled across her fingers. It tumbled, to touch the plate on the table. There came a flash of light, bright as the sun in all its glory, which made both women cry out and shade their eyes, blinking, trying to clear a sudden blindness.

When she could detect more than a crimson haze again, Matild was staring down at the plate. It was no longer drably dull, but rather had cleared, so that she might be looking through an unpainted window into another room. She put up a hand and jerked at the confining wings of the wimple so that she could see the better.

The background was still a swirl of colors, as if a rainbow had been entrapped, clear and steady. Adele stood before that, looking out and up at them. Her lips moved—Matild caught not sounds but thoughts:

"Those who follow Her have cried peace and patience. This we can no longer do, for this Serpent, come out of the Nethermost Hell, crawls freely. We have proven him truly a necromancer, able to summon the dead to fight again, even against those they once held in their hearts. We are coming fast to a final battle, nor can any foreseeing give us the word of its outcome—for when Light and Dark confront each other in full power no human soul can comprehend the forces so unleashed. We build now our strengths against that day and hour."

Matild's lips moved, but she could utter no sound.

"My daughter, take the gift of the Great One, use it as She puts into your mind. We must raise armies—not wholly against this deluded emperor but that fearsome shadow behind him."

There was another flash of light, and the glassy plate was dull and dead once more.

Zenia's hands were locked in prayer; Matild, her senses perhaps heightened by what she had seen and heard, could feel the fervent force of that petition reaching out. But her way was not prayer—though she now offered a plea for strength in the hours before her—but rather action.

She got up quickly, then plucked the ruby from where it touched the slab; she opened the laced bodice of her habit and the tunic beneath it. When she unfastened the brooch of the seal, she had to bend the clasp somewhat, but discovered that she could, in truth, hide the sacred stone within the hollow backing of the seal setting.

She did not disturb Zenia, but went quietly from the small room. From the chapel she could hear the chanting of the Gemen sending their wishes of happiness for the Reverend One.

Stepping into Gemen Papania's small niche beside the outer doorway, Matild put off the habit, freed her head from the confines of the wimple. She made sure of the tight pinning of her braids. The ragged garments which she had worn were carefully laid to one side, and those she used once more to clothe herself.

She felt a stab of hunger. It had been a long day, and she had not eaten regularly. There was no good reason to go fasting, not when she needed her full strength. She went to the kitchen and sawed a large hunk from a long loaf of bread, was glad to find a pot of sustaining honey which could be dipped over her slice, and ate slowly, washing it down with the fruit juice and water mixture she found in one of the bottles.

While she ate, Matild thought. There was certainly no way the invaders could stop the story of the miracle. And, judging by what she had seen on the faces of those being beaten away from the altar by the soldiery, this happening had been a mighty goad against frightened acceptance. Jonas had his eyes and ears, and Jonas knew fighters who moved by stealth and could not easily be met in open conflict.

But Saxon—ah, Saxon could do even more. He had always had a tightly bound following—loyalty was a shield and sword in his hands. It was Saxon they needed now— a fighting man and a planner of devious strategies, as he had shown many times in the past.

Therefore her object had no question. She must bring Saxon out of confinement, and arrange her trap for Cathal into the bargain. Matild glanced out of the small window. Though it gave only on a shadowed courtyard, it was enough to show her dusk was drawing near. The courtyard was without another outer gate, but a shed for gardening tools stood against the far wall.

Deliberately waiting to eat a second round of bread, Matild studied that shed. She was sure it was the answer to her problem.

The dusk was coming very fast—she heard the distant mutter of thunder. A bad night—what could better serve her purpose? She gave a last look around her and her eye fell on a stout kitchen implement carved of wood, intended for the rolling of dough. What better weapon could any woman wish for—easy to carry, noiseless, and familiar to the hand.

She was out in the garden and had reached the shed when there was such a thunderclap directly overhead that she could almost believe whatever power the mage used for destruction was now aimed at the cloister itself. But what came after was a flash of lightning, and by that time she had herself well plastered against the shed wall.

Matild was a tall woman, and though many of her interests were sedentary, she knew hard exercise. Had she not sailed on storm-tossed ships and climbed the near-sheer cliffs of the Yark Isles in search of bird-bone opals found only there? Though she was hampered by her bedraggled skirt, she made it to the top of the shed, from which she could look into the narrow street beyond.

Those lanterns meant to burn from sunset to dawn here showed wild flaring tongues of flame as the rising wind caught them. One after another, she saw them flicker out. There were certainly no signs of any watchers here, and no corners or doorways in which they could go to earth.

Matild let her homey weapon thud to the pavement outside, and dropped after it. Jonas first—she might have the knowledge, but she did not have the backing yet for her visit to the House of the Boar. Also—the Great One forbid—her quarry might well have been moved during this day.

The black coat seemed to rise out of the very pavement ahead. He had a rod aimed at her, and before Matild could move, a thin pencil of sickish yellow light speared out from the end of it, aimed to strike full at her breast.

Only the beam never touched her body. Her old shawl smoked, but the fire-tongue reached no farther. The black coat—she could only see his face as a white blur in the darkness—swung the rod up to aim at her head. But he was already too late. Too many years of careful practice in the arms court of hands-on attack had toughened Matild. Her improvised club crashed down first, and she heard a sound which sickened her as he slumped to the ground. She had killed again—she was as sure of that as if she had seen his life escape. But she made herself approach him to scoop up that rod. Some weapon of the mage, and so to be distrusted. But at least she would see this would bring no more harm.

The blaze of pain against her breast was so sharp Matild reeled back against the wall and leaned there, her eyes wide with terror. The fire which signaled the ruby's awakening did not abate. She felt that she must get it away from her skin and groped within her garments, worrying at the clasp of the brooch.

On the pavement, the downed man began to move. She did dare to stagger out a little and kick that rod away from the reach of his arm and groping fingers, though he continued to lie facedown.

He was levering himself up as far as his knees, making no sound, not even looking in her direction. His face— just as she had seen that stone-crushed face of the man by the river, so now she could see that his head was an odd shape; one eye was squeezed shut, and the other stared straight out before him.

He stumbled forward a step or two. Though he did not bend his head to view the pavement beneath him, the arms which hung loosely from his shoulders were swinging back and forth, as if he were indeed bent over and was sweeping the pavement for his missing weapon.

Matild gave a gasp—there was something so repulsive in this creature out of the night, she no longer thought of him as a man, and she could not completely stifle her horror and fear.

He turned; that horror of a head was now facing her. But though he moved, she knew in her heart that this was something of no clean world. At that moment she could not move, so frozen was she by sheer horror. He did not seem to be looking at her, yet in some fashion he must have sensed her presence, for he lurched forward, both his hands up as if to encircle her throat. And he still made no sound.

Matild's hand, the seal and the ruby in her grasp, swung up—a useless gesture to defend herself against this shambling horror.

Where the rod he had carried had a lightning's swift strike, from her hand spread a haze, a shining gaseous globe, growing ever larger as it spread outward. Red as the blood of the Heart, it deepened, and there came from it a droning hum.

The thing stalking her rocked back where it had halted for a moment. For the first time she saw expression on that white rag of a face. It staggered back, but already the outer edge of that spinning light encompassed it, encased it.

Matild did not hear the sound with her ears—it seemed to thrum through her whole body. It was not a cry of pain, of hate, of fear—but an emotion she could not put a name to.

The black coat fell again, his body moving into a tight curve, as might that of a child in deep slumber. Then it was gone, save for some smears of ash and a bundle of clothing.

She had seen the Great Heart bleed this day, now she had seem something else—the movement of forces beyond her comprehension. Perhaps Adele and those with the Talent could accept such sights and stand unmoved, but she felt weak and sick—she was no Talented one. And dimly, very dimly, in her another thought stirred: perhaps, against all tradition and training, she would never be able to accept that such forces would be a part of her own life.

She moved a little forward from the wall, and her boot sent the rod spinning. Moved by an impulse which was sent by no conscious thought, she stooped and swung the ruby seal brooch above the length of that strange weapon.

The rod twisted like a living thing—it tried to crawl from her as might a snake. She was ready for it, turning the brooch so that now the full flare of the ruby struck it. It coiled, twisted, fought in its own dark way, but apparently whatever force it carried was sealed within. Then it, too, collapsed into a mass of dull metal just as the full force of the storm broke, with drops of water large enough to sting as they struck her flesh.

The rain beating down brought Matild back to herself, and what lay before her. She must deliberately put from her mind what had happened here. This might later be relayed to Adele whose knowledge would encompass it, but Lydana was not of the holders of visions—rather the doers—and tonight she must do.

Girding up the flopping skirt to give her freer stride, Matild headed for Jonas. She was always ridden now by the feel that time hunted her down. And she was sure that tonight must see her foray at the House of the Boar.

She rounded a corner into the wind's push, having to fight against its fury. All the better for her purpose. There would be few abroad on patrol this night. The lantern marking Jonas' door still showed a spark of flame as she entered, giving the password which brought her into the large room.

Tonight it was truly crowded, and out of that throng Eel slid at once to her side. She could see Jonas at the other end of the room with a handful of others, all of a certain cast of countenance and agility of body which labeled them for what they were: river rats.

Some of those gathered there looked at her as she pushed her way toward the tavern-keeper. She had thrown aside both skirt and shawl within the door, and her form-tight stalking gear might mark her as assassin as well as thief.

One of the men by Jonas moved, and the taverner looked up to catch full sight of her. His round face was stern set, and she thought he was in the midst of planning some ploy of his own.

"What do you bring us?" He gave her no name or title as she fetched up facing him.

"A key into the House of the Boar," she told him without elaboration. "We can have Saxon out this night, if you can provide the men—"

Jonas gave a harsh cackle of laughter, his eyes sweeping about the group which he centered. "Hear that, bully boys. A key— It seems that Fortune favors us indeed. It was in our mind to try to storm the place this very night," he added in Matild's direction.

"Good enough," she returned. "What had you in mind?"

"Brock, here," he laid hand on the arm of the man beside him, "he is a water man. The south canal takes a swing in the right direction. None of these thrice-damned invaders has enough skill to attempt the waterways in a storm. So—having the weather on our side, how can we poor sailor men do better?"

"In no way, as I see it." Matild had recovered the full strength of the purpose which had brought her here. Now she had the tools for her undertaking before her, and in spite of what they had been, what they might be, in this hour she trusted them.

⸙ 38 ⸙

APOLON

The Grey Mage stared at the empty drawers that *should* have held the most intimate of feminine personal garments, whirled to glare into the closet that contained nothing more than impersonal court gowns, each worn once or twice at the most. That was not enough to impart the aura of "personality" to a garment that he required to be able to trace the wearer. He had been robbed, robbed of the things he needed most at the time he needed them most!

There was nothing—*nothing!*—here in the Princess Shelyra's room, nor in the rooms of her aunt and grandmother, that had any more than a casual connection to the women of the Tiger. That was not enough, not nearly enough, and rage boiled up inside him.

"Who did this?" he demanded of the soldier who had brought him here. "Who ordered that the rooms be cleaned?"

The soldier shrugged. "The emperor, I suppose; he expected to be able to move into the queen's room immediately, and assigned this suite to you and the dowager's to the chancellor. He must have ordered the rooms be stripped."

The soldier repressed a smirk, but Apolon caught it anyway. He knew what had caused it. Someone had stripped the bed in the queen's room, soaked the feather mattress with water, and carefully remade it. The damage had not been discovered until the emperor's servants arrived; by that time the featherbed itself was a mildewed mess, and the wood of the bed beneath it was covered with mold and black with rot. The smell was unbelievable, and the entire bed had to be removed.

Apolon turned back to the barren drawers with a snarl. This was just the last frustration in a long and trying day.

Just as the emperor's entourage had entered the gates, to the weak cheers of an audience rounded up by Cathal's mercenaries and Apolon's black coats, the sky had opened up and the entire assemblage was drenched to the skin. Instead of a triumphal procession to the palace, a procession meant to instill fear and respect into the dogs of Merina, Balthasar led his sodden officials in an ignominious dash, while the citizens scattered to the shelter of their homes and not even the presence of the mercenaries could deter them.

And once the emperor's people actually reached the palace, they discovered that nothing was ready for them. By sending the prince packing so precipitously across the river, Balthasar and Adelphus had forgotten that there would be no one to issue orders to prepare the place. The prince evidently had lived as spartan a life in the palace as he did in the camp, and very little had been changed since the queen abdicated. According to his officers, Leopold ate soldiers' rations with his men, spent most of his waking time supervising his men, and until very recently had slept in the same garrison as his men. He had indulged in no luxuries from the palace kitchen, and in fact, the entire kitchen staff had been dismissed before any other servants.

Perhaps that was why he had not noticed the depredations to food supplies. It wasn't theft—it was spoilage; or rather, it was sabotage.

The fine, white flour used to make the kind of manchetbread that the emperor preferred was alive with weevils. The butter and lard were all spoiled, the good cheeses covered with mold. There was no meat; it had been devoured by a small army of rats. The sugar and salt were now bricks; they had gotten damp and hardened into a form that would not be usable until the scullions had pounded and crushed them again. The root vegetables had all been rotten. And although Apolon was not entirely certain how *this* could have happened, every bottle of wine in the locked and sealed wine cellar had turned to vinegar.

All that was left was the coarse fare used to feed servants—dried beans and peas, barley, coarse wheat and rye flour, salted fish, dried meat, a very little honey, farmers' cheese.

The wood cellar had sprung a leak as well, and every bit of wood in it was wet. So the emperor would be making a scanty supper on soldiers' rations, going to bed in unaired bedding brought down from the attics, and doing so in a chilly room with a smoking, sputtering fire in the fireplace.

There were rumors that the palace was haunted, that spirits played tricks in the night, wreaking havoc in silence and vanishing without detection. Apolon would have suspected a human hand at work—except that all the servants had been dismissed before the tricks began, and there was no earthly way that a servant could herd rats into the kitchen or make hundreds of bottles of wine go sour. . . .

He felt a chill on the back of his neck for a single moment.

Then anger chased it away again. Natural or supernatural, *he* would deal with the perpetrator! He would build shields not even an angel could penetrate, lay traps even a mouse would trigger. There would be no more of this nonsense now that the Grey Mage was in charge—

Reality reasserted itself.

He could do all that—assuming he could get the time, find the magical energy to do all of that and tend to his own plans as well. He was still losing servitors at a slow trickle, but every slave he lost was lost forever, and took precious resources with it. He *had* to replace them. He could not continue his work without them. He *had* to find the princess. He needed what she represented.

"Bring up my servants with my things," he told the waiting soldier abruptly. The man must have seen something unnerving in his expression; he left, quickly, with a haste Apolon had not expected, given his insolent manner.

The man was one of Prince Leopold's troop, of course. The prince had been entirely too familiar with his underlings, encouraging such insolence. Now that the emperor had turned them over to Cathal, the fellow would soon find himself tied to a whipping post for such behavior.

Somewhere in this city he had to find a private place, a place where he could practice his art in absolute secrecy and security. That would not be possible in the palace.

He had thought that once the emperor brought his entourage into the city, everything would fall neatly into place. Instead, his path had become strewn with far more obstacles than he had ever anticipated. It was as if some unseen force was working against him, invisible as the scent of the canals and as all-pervasive.

Well, there probably was an "unseen force" working against him, in the form of those interfering old biddies, male and female alike, up there in the Temple.

His servants appeared at that moment, gratifyingly silent and obedient, and laden with his belongings. He took himself into the sitting room and waited for them to arrange his things. They carried off all of the princess' property except for the chest of jewelry that had been on a table in the bedroom. *That* had been confiscated by the chancellor's people. There had been three such chests, one in each room, all taken away by the chancellor's servants to add to the treasury.

That was fine. Apolon cared nothing for gauds, which fact endeared him to the chancellor.

As he sat, waiting for his rooms to be made ready for him, he formulated a plan of action. Since he had been frustrated in his attempt to obtain the princess, he would have to resort to other ways of finding her. In order to do that, as well as to be able to create more black coats, he would have to have a secure and secret place to work the darker magics. So that must be his first goal: find a good building, and take it over.

Next—recruit more black coats. Then locate Shelyra, for by then he would need the power her death would bring him in order to bring his other plans to fruition.

But before he could actually use her, he would have to do *something* about those fools in the Temple. For that, he needed a great deal more cooperation from Cathal and his people. Their efforts this very afternoon had *certainly* been notably less than successful!

If it hadn't been for Leopold . . .

Apolon ground his teeth in frustration again. Damn Leopold! The fool might as well be in the pay of those pious idiots in the Temple! And damn him twice for calling attention to himself before Apolon could get to the emperor and steer things in the right direction!

He had wanted Leopold out of the way for a long time; the boy kept reminding Balthasar of earlier days, and every time the prince did that, Apolon had to repair the damage as Balthasar backslid into dangerously altruistic behavior. But he wanted Leopold banished to a place of *his* choosing.

And the last place in the entire universe he would ever have chosen was the Summer Palace!

He had not yet located the magical library he knew must

be in the possession of the House of the Tiger. It was not anywhere in the palace, and not in the guild house of the Tiger. There was only one place left, and that was the Summer Palace across the river—which was where that interfering idiot Leopold had been sent!

Leopold had already been asking far too many questions about Apolon's activities, and Apolon was half inclined to think that it was the prince, and not the emperor, who had ordered the so-thorough "cleaning" of the rooms. Not only was it going to be impossible to find the books and get them out without Leopold knowing, but if by chance the prince started to *read* those books, he stood a better than even chance of getting enough clues to deduce exactly what Apolon had been doing.

If Leopold found out just how Apolon had been recruiting his black-coated servants, he might also deduce Apolon's ultimate plan.

It was time, and more than time, to exercise some of his influence on Cathal. Cathal should be able to arrange a suitable training accident.

But first, there was one small detail he ought to take care of. Chancellor Adelphus was showing a decided partiality to the prince, and he might decide to interfere in the staffing of the Summer Palace. The chancellor had outlived his usefulness as a free agent; he no longer had any original ideas, and his knowledge could be exercised as easily by a puppet as by a thinking man.

"Your rooms are ready, master." The servant entered noiselessly and stood before Apolon in a gratifyingly subservient pose. This was not one of his puppets, but the man was so cowed by his master that he might as well have been. He scarcely dared breathe without Apolon's permission.

"Fetch me Chancellor Adelphus," Apolon said shortly. The man bowed deeply, and retreated; the puppet-servants padded in and waited for further orders as he left.

"Build up a fire in the fireplace and prepare my special equipment in the bedroom," Apolon told them. The fire was hardly satisfactory, being built of the same wet wood that everyone else was using, but it was better than no fire.

At least *he* could mend the situation a little with a tiny breath of magic, so that all the smoke went up the chimney instead of into the room.

He waited in a chair beside the fire for some time, patient as a spider in her web. He could afford to be patient. The chancellor did not dare to ignore his invitation entirely, and eventually he *would* be here. And the outcome of the meeting, when he finally arrived, was predestined.

§ 39 §

ADELE

It was not until after the first of the night rituals that Verit was free to explain exactly what had happened that day. A great storm had begun outside, but within the Temple complex, the howl of the wind and the rumble of thunder was barely more than a murmur. Gemen Fidelis pulled Elfrida aside as they left the presence of the Heart and indicated silently that she should follow him. Since she had seen him earlier in the meditation chamber and knew that he was one of those whom Verit trusted, she accompanied him to a chamber near the archpriestess' rooms.

The chamber was a small room of bare stone, with a stone altar at its center. The altar was a cube which came up to Elfrida's breast and occupied most of the floor space. Much of what remained was taken up by four wooden chairs, high backed and with arms, but bare of ornamentation. The Heart which hung above the altar was the size of a human heart and made of some sort of crystal with a red tint to it. *Lydana would know exactly what it is,* Elfrida thought. *I do hope she is well, and Shelyra also.*

Gemen Fidelis seated himself in the chair to the east of the altar and gestured Elfrida to the chair to the north. She sat quietly, wondering what was going on and why she was here.

The Archpriestess Verit entered a few minutes later, followed by the brown robe who had been in the meditation chamber with Gemen Fidelis. They seated themselves to the west and south, respectively. Verit made the sign of the Heart, and the other three followed her example. Then she began to speak.

"These are dark days which have come upon us," she said, "and darker nights. I have chosen the three of you to work with me that we may avert the evil that seeks to destroy us and turn the Heart to its own ends."

"Apolon," Elfrida said. "Mage and servant of the Dark."

"If he serves the Dark," the brown robe asked, "is night the best time to work against him?"

Verit sighed. "Gemen Cosima," she said patiently, "are you suffering from the delusion that I had any free time today?"

Cosima shook her head. "No, Reverend One."

Verit shook her head. "In addition to the arrangements for the dowager queen, and the unpleasantness with the soldiers, I have spent much more time than I care to listening to those of our Temple who are convinced that the emperor and his followers mean us no harm."

"No harm?" Cosima gasped. "How can they say that after this afternoon?"

Verit rolled her eyes in disgust. "They feel that the soldiers must have been searching for one of the townspeople who had done something wrong."

Cosima shook her head in disbelief, while Elfrida nodded in confirmation. "I heard some of them myself, in the refectory," she seconded.

"Your point, however, is well taken," Verit added. "Normally night would not be the ideal time for this work—the servants of Darkness find Light painful to behold. But we wish to see what Apolon is doing, and *he* is more likely to be working now than during the daytime." She pulled a sheet of glass from a shelf beneath her seat, stood up, and placed it on the altar between the candles that burned near each corner. Fidelis and Cosima stood also, and Elfrida hastily followed their example.

Verit looked around at each of them. "Fidelis and Cosima, I believe you know Elfrida, at least by sight." Both of them nodded. "I have asked her to join us, even though she is new to the work of the Flames, because I believe she has skills which will be vital to us. I trust her implicitly, and you may do likewise."

She indicated that glass on the altar. "Elfrida, I trust you are familiar with the principles of scrying, even if you have not done it before." Elfrida nodded. "Let us see, then, what the Lady wishes us to see." She made the sign of the Heart once more, then reached out to take the hands of the people on either side. Everyone else followed her example, so that they stood handfast in a circle, all looking down at the glass.

It seemed to Elfrida that the glass fogged before her eyes. Then it cleared and she could see a room, which she recognized as Shelyra's room at the palace, where a man in dark gray paced angrily back and forth, yelling at the soldier who stood before him.

"It was a perfectly simple order, Cathal, and you botched it beyond belief! It's bad enough that your soldiers can't find either the queen or the princess, but when they fail to remove a dead body from a public place in which no one save themselves is armed—really, Cathal, why do we bother with your troops?"

"My men were doing well enough until Prince Leopold showed up and ordered them back to barracks!" General Cathal replied furiously. "Why don't you take your grievance to him, Apolon?"

"I'll deal with him when I'm ready," Apolon snarled. "Do you think perhaps you could find a few men in that great army of yours who can accomplish a simple task? Perhaps if you sent in a small strike force a few hours before dawn, when the Temple folk sleep between rituals, you could manage to get me that body?"

"What do you want with the dowager queen's body, anyway?" Cathal growled. "She's been lying in state since midmorning; I'll bet half the city has been through there by now. Everyone knows she's dead—it's not as though you needed the body to prove it!"

"What I want with the body is not your concern," Apolon said coldly. "*Your* concern is to get it for me."

"As you wish." Cathal shrugged. "But I'd take care if I were you, Apolon. After the scene you made this afternoon when the first attempt failed, half the army doubtless thinks you a necrophile." He turned and walked out, not waiting to be dismissed.

Apolon smiled grimly at his departing back. "Necrophile? No, not quite. But even those idiots may come closer to the truth than they ever suspect."

Verit broke the circle with a gasp and sank into her chair, leaning against its high back. Cosima knelt at her side and took her wrist, obviously checking her pulse. Fidelis sat down in his chair, and Elfrida did likewise, somewhat puzzled by Verit's agitation.

"Reverend One, what troubles you?" she asked.

"The body," Verit gasped. "Take it outside and burn it, at once."

"Verit," Fidelis said quietly, "it's pouring rain outside. We couldn't burn a salamander in this storm."

"The kitchen fire, then."

Cosima looked at her oddly. "We can't burn a human body in the kitchen fire."

"It's not a human body," Elfrida said.

"What is it?" Fidelis asked, his eyes round with surprise.

Verit was beginning to pull herself together. "Wax and cloth and wood."

Fidelis shrugged. "Wood and cloth we can burn. I hope the wax is the top layer and can be scraped off or we'll set fire to the whole kitchen."

"It should be." Elfrida stood. "Why don't we go deal with that while you recover, Reverend One."

"We'll all go." Verit rose, leaning slightly on Cosima. "We'll need all four of us to carry the coffin, in any case."

As they approached the main Temple, Verit said, "All of you, keep your heads lowered. It's best if no one sees your faces; the only person who should be known to be involved with this is me. Now, follow me." She walked to the altar with her head held high, while the other three followed her, heads bent and hands tucked in their sleeves.

Verit spoke briefly to the Gemen who stood at the head and foot of the coffin; they nodded and went to their places in the choir stalls. She blew out the candles around the coffin, then nodded to her group. Each of them took a corner of the coffin and they carried it out and down the hallway. No one followed them and no one was in the kitchen at this hour of night.

By the time they reached it, Verit was her usual self. "Elfrida, watch the door," she ordered briskly. "Cosima"—she passed over the hands and head—"this is the wax portion, please melt it down. We can use it for work candles in the recreation room."

"If you put cosmetics on it, wash them off first," Elfrida said without turning from her post at the door. She was glad that Verit was not asking her to help dismember the body; she was already feeling strange enough about this whole business. She had never realized that dying was going to be so complicated.

She could hear the crackling of the fire as they built it up from the banked embers, and the sound of the rain lashing against the kitchen windows.

"This dress won't burn," Verit muttered. "Too much gold thread and too many jewels."

"Consider it a donation to the Temple," Elfrida said.

"Shove it in a chest in the sewing room; it can be picked apart later."

"That's a good plan," Verit replied. "But for the moment, we'll put it in the tunnel beyond the meditation chamber. I don't feel equal to sneaking into the sewing room unseen; I've done enough skulking for one night."

"I should think we all have," Cosima said from her place at the stove. "Fidelis, do you know where the candle molds are? As long as this is liquid, I may as well pour it."

"Two cupboards over, the second drawer down," Fidelis answered. "Verit," he added, "what's wrong? Why are we in such a frantic hurry to destroy this body—aside from the fact that it's not a body? Does Apolon know it's a fake?"

"I doubt it," Verit replied grimly. "Apolon's a necromancer."

That produced three shocked gasps. "Are you certain?" Elfrida asked, turning her head to look at Verit.

"Didn't you hear him, Elfrida?" Verit frowned. "I thought you saw and heard what the rest of us did."

"I saw and heard Apolon yelling at General Cathal for failing to get the body earlier—when did that happen, exactly? I missed it and no one in the confessional was precise about time."

"So did I," Fidelis added.

"I wish I had," Cosima said grimly. "I got to help treat the wounded."

"At least no one was killed," Verit told her consolingly. "It's really been quite a day. I was hearing confessions this morning, when a girl came in with a story of a sailor who had seen a black coat he knew—the man had been killed in battle several years ago."

"Did you know the girl?" Fidelis asked.

"No," Verit replied, "but she gave me a password. The news she bore was a message from the queen."

"The queen is still alive and free, then," Cosima said with visible relief.

"Yes, I saw her later. She came to see her mother's body."

"Did she spot it as false?" Elfrida was careful to keep her voice merely curious.

"I'm quite sure she did," Verit said, "but then there was that business with the Heart, and the soldiers attacked, and she disappeared in the confusion before I had a chance to speak with her."

"What happened to the Heart, anyway?" Elfrida asked. "It looks as though it started to fall apart, and that can't be possible."

Cosima chuckled. "Elfrida, you have no sense of the miraculous. The Heart was bleeding—ask anyone who was there. They're calling it a miracle: the Heart bleeding in sorrow for the death of the dowager queen."

It was all too much; Elfrida collapsed to the floor laughing hysterically. "A body of wood, cloth, and wax, and a Heart 'bleeding' rubies. Was ever there a more unnatural funeral?"

"There will be real ones aplenty," Fidelis reminded them somberly.

The laughter died.

§ 40 §

APOLON

Apolon's servants had brought him an unappetizing dinner of pea soup and coarse bread, and built up the fire a second time before Adelphus finally appeared. The chancellor glanced at the tray on the table and made a face at the remains of the meal.

"I'm sending the servants to get better provisions before we break our fast in the morning," he said with a hint of apology. "They have orders to ransack the homes of the wealthy if they cannot find anything in the marketplace. We will not face another such meal, if I have anything to say about it."

"Do not apologize to me," Apolon said smoothly as he noted a new ring on the chancellor's hand, a huge, glittering diamond that Adelphus had never worn before.

Well. Well, well, well! So the chancellor was getting greedy enough to help himself now? Just as well he be controlled, before his greed interfered with Apolon's plans.

"I have eaten worse in the camp, after all," the Grey Mage continued in a cool pretense of affability. "I asked my servant to bring you here because there was something in the princess' bedroom I thought you ought to see, and it was something that could not be moved."

As he had expected, the chancellor immediately assumed that the "something" was valuable. "Oh?" Adelphus replied, a certain avaricious light in his eyes. "Just as well that you sent for me, then. Let's see this—whatever it is."

"Of course." Apolon smiled, rising from his chair and giving his servants a signal behind the chancellor's back. One went to the outer door of the suite and quietly secured it as the chancellor proceeded to the bedroom; another stood beside the bedroom door and closed and locked it as they passed the threshold, and the third and largest came to stand behind the chancellor.

"Well?" Adelphus said, gazing avidly around the room. "What is it?"

Apolon gave another signal, and the third servant seized the chancellor, pinioning the old man's arms behind his back before Adelphus had any idea what he was doing.

"This—" Apolon said as the fourth servant seized the chancellor by the throat and strangled him.

Adelphus struggled in the servant's arms, his face growing livid, then purple, as he fought for air. It was really of no use. This man had been prodigiously strong while he lived, and now that he was dead such minor problems as the pain from a blow no longer interfered with his ability to exert that strength. The servant doing the strangling had been a stonemason, and his hands were large and powerful. The end was as swift as it was inevitable; with a drumming of his heels on the floor, the chancellor exited life with far less noise than he had entered it.

Apolon had been waiting for that moment. The spirit had not yet left the body—and now it never would.

Apolon reached for a net of blood-dyed silk, copper weights made from coffin nails, and a hundred complex spells as the two servants allowed the body to drop to the floor. He cast the net over it, catching the spirit before it fled, and imprisoning it.

It struggled to leave—struggled longer than Apolon would have expected, considering the chancellor's checkered past. Quite often, once souls accepted the inevitable, they were not in any particular hurry to rush to judgment.

The chancellor must have been far surer of his reception in the afterlife than Apolon would have granted.

No matter. The soul was caught; now it would be bound.

Apolon walked slowly to the table beside the bed, and took a small, black-hilted dagger from his belt. With it, he opened a vein in his wrist, allowing a thin trickle of blood to fill a copper bowl there. He spoke the words of a Summoning, words that fell into the silence with a ponderous and heavy flatness.

This close to the Temple, he dared not speak a Greater Summoning, but the Lesser would do.

The silence deepened, any heat that had been in the air slowly seeped out of it, until Apolon's breath hung in the still quietude in misty puffs. The servants showed no such signs, of course, since they no longer breathed deeply, or warmly.

The glassy surface of the cooling pool of blood in the copper bowl ruffled, as if from an unseen wind, although there was no wind. A tiny whirlpool began to form in the center of the bowl, a vortex which slowly drank the blood contained in the basin, until the last drop had utterly vanished without a trace.

The bowl began to glow with a peculiar, sickly yellow-green phosphorescence.

That was what Apolon had been waiting for. He pointed to the body on the floor, still covered with the reddish-brown net of silk. "Bind," he said shortly.

The glow of light lifted up from the bowl, hovered in the air a moment, then sank down on the body. The servants backed away as far as the walls would permit them. They always did this, and sometimes Apolon wondered—did they recall, dimly, the pain of their own binding?

The glow covered the body, net and all, and a low moan issued from the livid lips of the chancellor's face.

The entire body shuddered, the heels once again drumming dully on the floor. Apolon waited as the shuddering subsided; slowly the chancellor sat up, then clambered clumsily to his feet, still swathed in the net.

Now Apolon reached out his hand and whisked the net off, gesturing for the nearer servant to come and take it. The glow remained on the former chancellor's body for a moment longer, as the lividity faded, the bruises on the throat vanished, and the appearance of life returned to Adelphus' visage.

Apolon spoke three more words of power; one that dismissed the Summoned creature, one that sealed corruption away from the body, and one that permitted Adelphus to speak when granted permission.

The chancellor stared at the Grey Mage with eyes in which pure horror showed through a dull glaze of befuddlement. Adelphus knew what had happened to him—and he knew he was utterly helpless to do anything about it.

"You will go about your regular duties as you remember them," Apolon told him carefully. "You will offer no advice to the emperor that you have not previously gotten from me. If he asks you your opinion on something outside of your instructions, you will say that you need to think about it first. If he asks you about Leopold, defer to Cathal's advice."

He thought for a moment longer, his thoughts a little dim and distant through a haze of weariness. He wanted the House of the Boar—he needed to know if Cathal still held it—and the last thing he wanted to do was to have to venture out into this storm, which bid fair to rage on through the morrow.

"Go to the House of the Boar and determine if Cathal still requires it," he ordered the chancellor. Minutia like icy rains and raging winds would no longer trouble Adelphus. "If he does not, requisition it for me. Then return and inform my servants of what you have done."

If Cathal still wanted the place, they could negotiate for it tomorrow. What he had to offer the general would certainly be a worthy trade for a simple building.

The chancellor bowed stiffly.

That should cover any immediate problems. Apolon would give the puppet more detailed instructions in the morning, after he had rested. He had given the Demon of Binding fully a half pint of his blood, and he felt a little faint and weak. Ideally, he would give the Demon of Binding someone *else's* blood, but he had not dared take the chance that the chancellor would cry out as his throat was slit.

"Return to me in the morning for further instructions," he finished as he grasped the edge of the table to keep from falling. "You may go."

The third servant opened and unlocked the door, and all of the puppets left the room, taking the dismissal to include all of them. Which was perfectly all right with Apolon; he disliked having the puppets undress him for bed unless his weakness after practicing necromancy made that necessary.

By holding onto the furniture he got himself safely onto the bed, and took off only so much of his clothing as was necessary for comfortable sleeping. The chancellor's soul was now bound to his body and animating it, but under the complete control of Apolon's will. Only a person of extreme piety could successfully fight such a binding, and Adelphus was hardly in the category of the pious. The drawback was that the soul no longer thought for itself, which meant that a creative person would no longer be able to create, only to copy what he had done in the past. Adelphus had once been a very creative thinker, although he had not shown those flashes of genius for some time. He certainly would not be able to evidence them now— but Apolon would be perfectly willing to think for both of them.

He had not taken over Cathal largely because he did not truly understand military strategy, and feared that making the general into a puppet would put an end to the string of easy victories that Cathal had won thus far. But he had enough hold over the general to control him; they shared similar tastes, pleasures that Cathal's position and rank made it difficult to indulge in. More accurately, Cathal liked to indulge, and Apolon made use of the results. Apolon was his supplier, and the general would do nearly anything to keep that supply line open. Cathal was far more useful as a free man than as a puppet.

Apolon climbed into the bed stiffly, shivering a little at the chill, damp sheets. The wind from the great storm outside howled at the magics keeping his fire going; he had a notion that if he had not taken that precaution, he would have been sleeping this night not only on chill, damp sheets but in a room with no fire, or one full of smoke. For a moment, his temper flared again.

But he told himself that it did not matter. Tomorrow, Adelphus would see to it that all was made comfortable again, with Apolon's comfort coming second only to that of the emperor. The situation was temporary, as his weakness was temporary.

And the end of all of this would be worth any amount of discomfort.

§ 41 §

LYDANA

The House of the Boar was one of the very few greater buildings in Merina which bordered directly on a canal yet had no walled garden or courtyard separating it from the waterway. The main entrance was on the other side of the building facing the street. However, above the canal was the wide loft door from which heavy gear could be lowered into waiting barges.

Their journey across town had been a wild one, and not under the command of Matild but one of Jonas' retinue whose handling of both boats and their motley crew aroused in her the highest admiration. There were some eight of the river rats themselves, well used to forays in the dark—and dark their journey had indeed been, for the night lanterns were dimmed by rain and wind—and there was Eel, as well as four of his street-wise companions.

Matild had waited for Jonas to raise some question concerning the boys, but the taverner seemed to treat their inclusion as a matter of course.

Yes, it had been a wild trip. Before they had taken to the waters, they had to lock hands in a chain at intervals, lest some one of them would be buffeted by the wind, blinded by the rain, and so lost along the way. Matild could only hold with a death-tight grip to the nearest plank seat, deafened and blinded by the madness which surrounded them.

But now their leader, one Dortmun, brought their craft under the blank wall of the place they sought.

"Git to it, younguns!" His terse order was nearly swallowed by the wind, but apparently he had already well rehearsed his followers in what was to be done. There was the swish of a rope through the air, thrown by a practiced hand. But it needed a second throw—which brought a few biting words from Dortmun, before the hook weighting its end caught on a hidden projection above.

A lightning flash showed Matild that there was a thin young body climbing, heading for the loft door. She also noted that some of Dortmun's trained knaves were now crouched at either end of the boat.

The next few moments seemed endless, lifted out of normal time. Then there flopped down upon them, striking Matild's shoulder a smarting blow, a rope. Dortmun had made his way to her side and now gave more orders, shrilled into her very ear.

"There be foot—handholds. I shall go first, follow straightly if you would be a part of this."

He swung up into the air past her. Glad that this night she was not hampered by any skirts, Matild reached above until her hand clamped on a looped knot. This was enough for a beginning, but with the wind full about them, swaying her like a banner in the breeze, she found that stretch of climb almost more than she could manage. Then she was pulled up by hands gripping her arms and shoulders, falling forward into a dark hole which smelled of oil and metal and general mustiness. And she remained where she was until the last of their party to appear had won into the loft.

Though her own craft had no need for the handling of large objects, Matild knew that nearly all Great Houses were fashioned on the same plan. There was a rattle out of the dark, and a hardly smothered exclamation, then a calloused hand closed upon her arm, slid down to her wrist, and she knew she must depend upon this as a guide.

They did not move swiftly—they could not—for they must weave a way among large obstructions. Matild heard grunts, bitten off oaths, and she once barked a knee painfully against a waist-high box.

Then there was the thinnest wedge of light showing ahead at floor level. A trapdoor set a-crack? They shuffled together in a group around it. She could see part of the dark shape of a head flat against the floor before the crack, and guessed that one of their party was scouting what lay before.

"All quiet," came a hissed whisper. "Jakkey, swing out the pulley beam."

Scrambling sounds came through the dark in instant answer. In the meantime that light-slit in the floor became wider and wider, noiselessly, just as the door finally came away entirely, having been steadied back to the floor with great care.

The light which had seemed so bright in the totally dark room above was now as dim as a single candle. Matild edged forward, determined to look down herself. She saw, heavily curtained by shadow, what might be a second loft. This was also piled high with boxes, barrels, and packets sewn into rawhide bags—cargo waiting to be transported.

She could even make out some of the cross-transfer signs of several different overseas countries crudely painted on the sides.

By a doorway at the far end was a thick candle in a protected lantern.

Yet there was no movement, certainly no sentry on guard. Once more, ropes, and their party slipped down, most of them with the ease of long practice. Once on the floor, Dortmun caught at Matild's shoulder with little ceremony.

"Which way?" came his hissed demand.

She called up all she had learned from Dame Fortuna. The top two floors for cargo, which could be then shifted straight down to the canal barges; then the living quarters of the family; the floor below that for the workshop. But where Saxon might be, she could not guess. She only knew where she must go first.

She whispered back such directions as she had, heard Dortmun grunt, and saw him turn to catch at another of his followers and repeat her instructions. But Matild had already moved on to the door, though she was not the first to reach it.

Eel stood a little hunched, his weapon-claws busy. Whatever latch there might have been yielded to his probing and he slipped through, Matild beside him.

"In the Great Hall of the Master—" But Eel did not need to hear that; he was already on his way in the right direction. The hall they traversed was a narrow one, giving on a stair wide enough to pass such bundles as lay above them. They could still hear the distant roar of the storm wind, but otherwise they might be lurking in a deserted building. At the foot of the short flight of stairs was a landing, which gave upon two doors. Here burned another of those candle lanterns. Matild gestured to the door on the right.

Eel knelt, ear pressed against the panel of the door. One clawed hand arose, signaling caution. The door was not locked, for he was already edging it open. Beyond was even greater light.

To see through the crack limited one's sight, but what Matild sought was on the wall directly across from the door, distanced only by the width of the hall, with its islands of heavy and ornate furnishings between.

Two of those tall-backed, tapestry-cushioned chairs were occupied by men—mercenaries taking a stolen ease. There was one on either side of a clear panel, seeming fused into the stone of the wall itself; the cover for the sword. It hung there in half shadow, dully, almost as if it were a sentient thing striving to hide from its enemies.

There was a warmth against Matild's breast. She felt there the awakening of the ruby's power, and cupped the now-doubled stone brooch in her left hand.

Eel was watching her, then his own swinging hand made a fist, showing all talons in response to the guards.

What she would do now, Matild knew, was the rankest folly—but it was so clear in her mind that her body might be moving by another's will. She slipped through the door and went to cover, heart beating wildly, behind a vast lounge piled high with cushions.

Eel did not join her, though he himself had moved—in the opposite direction—and Matild could well believe he would make the most of all cover to come at those two lazing guards.

"Old growl-guts comin' agin tonight?"

"Like him—wants to take us a-slackin' off. Bad night'll make him think we'd not be on watch." The fellow gave a heavy, beery belch.

"Ain't nobody gonna come out this night." The other seemed to be very sure of that. He yawned; a drawn sword rested across his knees.

The fire building in Matild's hand was a blaze now. Obeying the impulse which closed on her, she tossed the brooch so that it fell between the two lounging men, lying directly at the foot of the sword wall.

"What—" One of the guards lifted himself a little way

out of his chair and then slumped back. His gaze was fastened on the ball of red fire so that his head was at a sharp angle. Then he curved forward until that helmed head rested on his knees, and his fellow was only a moment later in taking the same cramped position.

Matild darted forward to press a palm flat against the stone on either side of the protecting panel. She drew from memory the mage words which both locked and unlocked. The panel misted, and then was gone. Matild bit her lip. What she did now might serve the forces of evil, but she had to take that chance. They had so few weapons, and they strove against a Darkness greater than they could measure or understand.

She made no move to lift the sword from its age-old hooks; rather she brought out that which she had crafted with such care.

"Great One," she shaped the words with her lips but did not utter them aloud, "this I do in Your Name, that those who are Your children can stand against the dark." She thought fleetingly of the man who was supposed to have forged that sword, and drawing a deep breath, she added, "If there be any ill in this, I take it on me. Let any dire fate be mine alone."

She reached forward and slid the armlet over the top of the unadorned pommel. It slid easily down and came to rest against the quillions. Oddly enough, coming to touch the dulled steel, it also dulled, and seemed to fade against its new bedding.

Once more, Matild sealed the sword niche, and then stooped and caught up the knot of fire, striding back and away. Eel appeared out of the shadow of another great chair and they were on their way toward the door, taking care to use cover.

"What's to do!" There was the crash of metal against pavement. One of the guards had straightened, and his sword had skidded from his knees to the floor. His companion sat up, blinking, and then with a small cry swung his head around to view the sword.

"Ain't no one touched it," he proclaimed loudly. "Don't know what—" He pushed up his helmet to rub his forehead. "Nothing happened." That odd shadow of unease faded from his face.

"Yeah—"

Matild and Eel had reached the shelter of the lounge again. They dared not try the door quite yet, Matild believed. The sentries (though they appeared not to know what had happened) might well have been aroused to a state of stronger alert. But Eel suddenly caught at her, pulling her yet farther down, urging her to crawl under the wide lounge, and she had just fitted herself in, when the door was flung wide open. The sentries seemed to have sniffed danger as quickly as Eel, as they were both on their feet, bared swords ready.

The leader of the newcomers was a tall man who lumbered forward like one of the high mountain bears—and like those dire animals, his eyes seemed red with inborn rage, his glances from side to side ones of suspicion.

"More light!" He snapped his fingers and two of his followers hurried past, bearing large oil lamps.

Flanked by those, he stamped forward until he faced the sword.

The line of vision for the two in hiding was strictly limited, but Matild was sure this was Cathal, come again to view what he wanted the most out of Merina.

"Get them in and busy!" He gave another harsh order. All that the two under the lounge could truly see was a number of boots, some such as were common to mercenaries, and several which might be those of townsmen.

"All right, smash it! Smash it, I tell you! Get that free, or I'll have the guts out of you to make bow strings! Get to it!"

The crashes which followed, close upon one another, so that the barrage was almost without interruption, were deafening even in a room as large as the hall. At last there came a shattering sound.

"Done!" The general's voice soared. "Get out of my way,

scum." There came a sound which could only be a blow, and a small grunt of pain.

"Angel sword, my foot!" The general's voice was pure derision. "Old tales. But I give you, this is a good blade. Here—what's this?"

Matild stiffened. He must have noticed the cuff. Would he remember that he had not seen this before—would he—?

But General Cathal was laughing with chest-deep force. "Captain cuff, eh? No—more like a high-rank, plain as it is. This angel—he was supposed to be a workman—but it seems he was a lot more. And if this Gideon found it a treasure—then it is certainly fit for the general of the emperor." There was a faint sound of metal-on-metal, and a click, as if the general had clasped that armguard about his own wrist. "Well, what is it?"

There had come a quick step from the door.

"So he's here, is he now?" the general said in answer to some news which had been whispered. "All right, I've got *my* treasure out of Merina—let him have what he fancies. I am not a greedy-guts like Adelphus." And again came that roar of laughter.

The heavy tread of the soldiers sounded across the room, their boots scraping on the once-polished floor. Then they were gone. Daringly, Eel squirmed forward a little toward the other side of the lounge to peer out.

"Gone!" The sentries' lanterns were still there, but as Matild pushed out of her cramped quarters and looked up carefully between two puffs of cushions, she saw that the chairs were indeed empty, and only the shattered glass splinters were spread across the floor.

"Come!" Eel pulled at her now. The door had been left open at the exit of the soldiers and their commander, but the brighter light of their lamps was gone, and now she heard the slam of another door some distance away.

She knew well the plan which they had devised. Dortmun and his river rats would free Saxon while she set her trap for the general. Her part had been done, and successfully. She and Eel should now retreat to the loft again. Only, how were the others to pass the general's party, which she had good reason to believe was on the way to Saxon? Would Jonas' chosen servants perhaps be caught between two parties? Though there was certainly nothing she could do to aid them when she had no idea which way to go or where they were now.

The loft seemed doubly dark after the light below—the single lantern candle too small to fight any of the gloom. They settled down prudently behind a barricade of boxes and crates to wait. Up here, the howl of the wind could still be heard; the storm had not diminished. A dozen years back, there had been such a night of raging blasts and torrents of rain and, when the tide came in, it had topped the walls of the eastmost canals, spreading floods down the streets. Matild was not seawise enough to reckon tide times, but she was certain that were they to take once more to the barge when that tide was on the flow, they would be swept, in spite of all their struggles, toward the inner city, away from even the small protection Jonas' tavern possessed.

๑ 42 ๑

LEOPOLD

Leopold had gotten himself, his two squires, and the three packhorses with his belongings across the bridge and safely into the Summer Palace shortly before dark. The chancellor had chivvied him along jovially every step of the way, even going so far as to send people to fetch the squires and whatever belonged to Leopold from the Great Palace so Leopold would have no excuse to return there. Perhaps he feared that if the prince's own intensely loyal troops learned whom they were to be serving under, they might protest, might even stage a minor revolt. He should have known better than that; Leopold trained his people in loyalty to the empire, not to any single commander.

The boys both knew the moment they saw the situation at the camp that Leopold was in disgrace, but both of them, bless their loyal little hearts, had stolen moments from the packing to tell him stoutly that they believed in him and would not abandon him for any other position, no matter who offered to take them on. He wasn't certain just what he'd done to merit such devotion, but he'd been very close to an emotional breakdown when the little one made the same speech.

So what else could he do but take them into exile with him? He had thought at the time that the sky looked threatening, but he had not anticipated the strength of the storm that now raged outside the windows of his suite of rooms.

They arrived to a rattlingly empty building. The emperor had not even sent an occupation force, since the land across the river, the Summer Palace included, was mostly home to peasant farmers. Balthasar never paid any attention to peasant farmers, since, for the most part, one ruler was the same as another to them, and there was a limited amount of goods and no money at all to be wrung from them. There were a few other summer homes, hunting lodges and the like, but the owners were all across the river in the city—and now were forbidden to cross the bridge, lest they escape before the maximum profit was made from them.

The Summer Palace and the summer homes of the wealthy and noble, unlike the Great Palace, had been left mostly untenanted; there was nothing but a skeletal staff, a couple of women to clean, and an old man and two boys to see to the stable and the pleasure horses therein. There *was* an extensive groundskeeping and gamekeeping staff, but they were all housed in cottages outside of the palace proper.

That solitude had actually suited Leopold fairly well. Frankly, the fewer people who were here to witness his downfall, the better. While no one had been ready for them, the staff here accepted their presence with a nonchalance that would have been unnerving had they not been so old. The housekeeper herself pledged to see that a suite was prepared for them while they had some supper, but had warned them that she was no cook.

It was about then that the storm broke, making the faint notion of sending one of the boys back across the bridge to buy a meal from a tavern an impossibility.

"Well," Leopold had sighed, "I suppose we will have to fend for ourselves."

The squires had turned up their aristocratic young noses at the notion of venturing into the kitchen to prepare a dinner themselves, but he had simply raised an admonishing eyebrow at them. The fact was, the idea of at last having a situation he had *some* control over made him begin to feel a bit more cheerful.

"What makes you think that you will always have a cook to prepare your meals on campaign?" he asked them. "Eventually you will leave my service to become warriors for the emperor—and you may well find yourselves in charge of a scout troop, living on what you can carry on your horses and glean from the land. And unless you *enjoy* raw squirrel and unpeeled roots," he added, as the truth of his words dawned on them, making the corners of their mouths draw down a bit, "you had better learn how to cook."

Their expressive young faces underwent enough changes at that point that he finally had something to laugh about in this miserable situation.

"It won't be that bad," he promised. "And I am a good cook, if nothing else."

With the help of another one of the women, who was listening to this conversation with every evidence of enjoyment, he found the kitchen.

He also found that it was fully stocked with non-perishables, perhaps in anticipation of a visit from the queen and her entourage that had never come.

It was a large and pleasant room, with brickwork walls and stone floors, a huge wooden table in the center of the workspace and many tall stools standing against the wall. If it had not been storming and night time, it would have been very light and airy, for it had large windows, glazed with thick, bubbly glass. He lit several lanterns he found hanging from brackets and built a fire in the smallest of the three fireplaces, the largest of which could easily roast an ox whole.

Everything in the pantry was in the nature of foodstuffs that were either preserved or would remain fresh for weeks or months at a time, but there was food in enough variety that he was able to give the two boys a handy lesson in rough cookery. Without eggs or milk, he could not make pancakes or some other quickbread, which had been his first choice, but eventually he found enough to give them a nice round meal. Sliced onions and whiteroots, browned in bacon fat, joined with fried bacon and sliced cheese for the main course, and for a sweet, which the boys both craved, he baked withered but still sound apples in honey and cinnamon in crocks on the hearth. To wash it all down, there was hot herbal tea laced with more honey. The boys looked doubtfully at the hearty peasant fare— they were used to soldiers' meals, but not this. After one taste, however, their doubts vanished, and so did the food.

As for Leopold, the mere aroma sent him back to happier days, when he had shared similar meals with his father's huntmaster beside the fire of one of the emperor's many hunting lodges. Things had been simpler then.

His melancholy mood was broken by the entrance of the old woman, who was much brisker than he had expected, given her apparent age. "The old king's suite has been turned out for Yer Highness," she said, bobbing a curtsy. "I see ye've made a good feed—there'll be eggs an' milk in the morning. I've ordered 'em brought over from the palace farm. No cook, though—" Here she faltered and looked at him doubtfully. "There isn't a cook hereabouts. The queen always brought her own."

"Never mind, old mother, we can manage until more of the men get here," he assured her. The two boys blinked at her sleepily, like two little bears, with their bellies full of honey and ready for a nap. "I expect them some time tomorrow, and there should be a cook with them."

Despite Balthasar's insistence on his being provisioned properly, the fact was that nothing had been sent that he had not brought himself. It appeared that the chancellor's real job had been to get him out of the city, and nothing more. He had expected nothing else, actually; it was a measure of how deeply in disgrace he was. Balthasar would not send any of his men until tomorrow afternoon at best, expecting the lack of servants to depress him, no doubt. And it would have depressed almost anyone else in his situation.

In fact, oddly enough, it had the opposite effect on him. He would have been utterly happy to have been left here alone with the squires and these few servitors who were so old that it seemed that it no longer mattered to them *who* they served.

If only he could simply be forgotten here! If only the emperor would just neglect to send anyone and, when he moved on to his next conquest, would leave without recalling his son! He could easily dwell here in complete content forever, taking the boys out to hunt, teaching them about the proper running of a home farm and management of game. If there were no imperial servants, soldiers, or other trappings here, there were also no imperial spies watching his every move. The weight of his duties and responsibilities had hung about his neck like the proverbial millstone for far too long—but for now, for at least a day and a night, they were gone, he did not have to wear a façade for anyone.

For the first time in many years, he was free—free for a little, anyway. Free to be himself, and free of any obligations, except the ones to the boys, which were the lightest of all of his burdens.

The little one nodded forward, almost falling, and jerked himself awake at the last minute. "We'd best get up to the suite then, dame," Leopold said with courtesy, rising and putting his plates aside in the sink. In that much, he would play the aristocrat; let someone else do the cleaning up. The boys scrambled up to follow his example, and all three of them walked slowly in the old woman's wake as she led them higher into the maze of the palace.

The king's suite proved to be an entire tower, perched on one corner of the main building; a cylinder of stone, with a room with two small beds suitable for the boys on the lowest floor, followed by a reading and reception chamber for him, then a bedroom, and last of all, an observation chamber on top. The first three floors shared a wall with the main building, and so only had windows on half of the curving wall, but the observation room rose above it and had windows facing in every direction.

Leopold saw the boys safely bedded down, just as the storm decided to take a definite turn for the worse. As the walls shook with each thunderclap, and the windows whitened with lightning, two sets of round, wide eyes looked at him imploringly.

Perhaps it was foolish of him, but there was no one here to see his folly. He tucked them both into bed and stayed with them, telling the stories that Balthasar's gamekeeper had told to him under similar circumstances, until full bellies and warm blankets overcame even storm fears and their eyes were shut tight in sleep.

Seeing to it that the fire in their fireplace was well banked and would burn through the night without tending, he blew out the lamps and left them to their dreaming. He went up the stairs intending to go to the observation room, drawn there by the sound of the wind howling about the tower and the thunder that vibrated even the stones of the building itself.

Despite its exposed position, the tower was remarkably cozy; the chimneys drew well, there was an ample supply of firewood at each fireplace, and the old woman had put hot bricks in each bed. She trailed after him as he climbed the stairs, her kindly face a little anxious.

"I didn't light a fire in this room, sir," she said doubtfully as he paused to have a look around the study. "Ye seemed so tired, I din' think ye'd be sitting up."

"Yes, that's quite right, dame," he soothed her. Poor old thing; she probably wasn't used to doing all this by herself. The queen must have brought over her entire staff when she visited here. "Seeing what you did for the boys, I'm sure you have done as well by me. Why don't you see to your own rest? You've certainly earned it, and this is a night to be in a warm bed, not tending to foolish young men and their whims."

She smiled at that, and was not at all loathe to take the hint. As she padded slowly down the stairs, he decided that he might as well have a quick glance around before traveling upward. He set down the lantern he carried and made a quick inspection of the furnishings—and felt again that twinge of nostalgia. This was clearly a man's room: heavy but comfortable wood furniture, well-padded with leather upholstery, braided rag rugs upon the wooden floor, a huge fireplace with an arrangement for keeping meals warm on the hearth. He would wait until morning to examine the books lining the walls, but he had the feeling that they were volumes he would find interesting. This was the kind of room he would have designed for himself, had he ever been granted that privilege and indulgence.

He picked up the lantern again and climbed the open staircase that circled up the blank wall to the next floor.

Here, as promised, there was a fire—burning clearly and cheerfully without a hint that the roaring winds outside could send smoke down the chimney. Again, the furnishings were simple: a wardrobe, a chair, a stand beside the bed, another with a basin and pitcher of water. The bed was of the old-fashioned, canopied sort, with heavy bed-curtains of a thick velvet. He had the feeling that tonight it would be a good idea to pull those snugly about the bed. No matter how well-made this tower was, there would be nasty drafts on a night like this.

But the thunder and flashes of light outside the bedroom's sole window drew him further up, although he left his lantern on the stand beside the bed.

Rain lashed the windows on the east and north aspects of the tower, making it impossible to see more than a blur of light in each lightning strike—but on the sheltered south and west, the view was clear and unobstructed. In daylight, the vista here was probably wonderful, but tonight, the storm held him spellbound.

He wondered how his men were faring, and felt sorry for any poor fool forced to patrol city streets in this maelstrom. Was this storm a sign of the anger of the Goddess, for the violation of Her sanctuary during the dowager's funeral? Was it a sign that She held the invaders responsible for the dowager's death as well? In a way, he hoped so—and he hoped that someone would say as much to his father.

Perhaps then he won't be quite so quick to let Cathal have a free hand to loot and savage where and what he pleases. My father does not fear much—but any wise man fears the wrath of the Goddess.

The thunder that shook the stone bones of the Palace was a primal force up here. The room was furnished with four chairs, one facing each window, and he sank down in one to sit and stare out at the fury of nature—

—or, perhaps, She Who Dwelled Beyond the Stars.

The storm held him mesmerized and mercifully allowed him to think of absolutely nothing for a while. He sat back in the embrace of the leather chair, while the thrum of thunder penetrated into his bones, and the scream of the wind filled his ears and his mind, while the sky-fire filled his eyes.

But the chamber had no fireplace—and the wind sucked warmth from the room like a thirsty leech. In time, he began to shiver as the cold penetrated his uniform and chilled him down to the bone. That, and not the storm itself, was what finally sent him back down to his waiting bed.

The room was comforting, welcoming, and wonderfully warm after the chill above. He stripped off his uniform and made a hasty wash in the water left in the pitcher, then blew out all of the lanterns, and by the light of the fire got into the soft and inviting bed and pulled the curtains tightly closed on all sides, muffling the thunder, and shutting out the firelight and the lightning.

The brick in his bed had not had time to cool, and the sheets were flannel, warmed perfectly. The room, the suite, the bed all felt—welcome. He felt at home here, comfortable here, as he had not felt since he was the age of his oldest squire. Perhaps he was deluding himself, but he would cherish that illusion of welcome, if illusion it was, for now.

And so, despite all that had happened to him on this

too-long and utterly miserable day, he fell asleep quickly and peacefully, and without any thought more complicated than to think how good it was to lie in a warm bed and listen to the storm outside rage unabated.

৭ 43 ৭

SHELYRA

If I'd known the Goddess was going to make her displeasure manifest with a tempest, Shelyra thought grimly as she bent her head beneath the onslaught of wind and water, *I'd have waited to do this until a quieter night.*

Shelyra had remained where she was when the bell began to toll for Adele's death, recalling what her grandmother had told her. Unless someone came to her, bearing her grandmother's ring, she had decided she would continue to assume that Adele was safely hidden in the cloisters of the Temple.

In fact, after hearing what Mother Bayan had to say, and remembering Adele's warnings, she had been inclined to think that this might be a ruse to throw Apolon off the scent more than anything else. A dead woman would be of no use to him—and he would not be looking for her interference, either.

So she had stayed in the compound, although others of Gordo's following had slipped out into the city to glean as much information as they could. She had curbed her impatience and her fears, knowing that she would hear what was going on eventually—and knowing, too, that with not only Apolon's black coats but Cathal's mercenaries roaming about, it was not safe for her to leave without a group around her.

Thom Talesmith, however, had not been so patient.

While "Raymonda" had brushed agents into the horses' coats to make them look harsh and brittle, he had paced the aisle of the stable, one ear cocked for the sound of people returning, and the rest of him fuming and fretting. She had ignored this, as she ignored most of what he did. If it had been a show meant to impress her with how deeply he cared about the dowager, it had failed. He knew what she did, and he should therefore have known that Adele's "death" was surely no such thing.

On the other hand, if it had been an expression of his own reckless, restless nature, she had been even less impressed.

"I'm going into the city," he had finally blurted abruptly, and before she could say anything, he had vanished.

"He's a fool," she had told the horse she was working on. The horse had flicked its ears at her and stamped its hoof uneasily.

Since Thom had not returned before she herself left the compound, she was more inclined than ever to think him a fool.

"You feel it too, don't you?" she had asked the horse.

She frowned now, and not because of the wild weather. There was something else in the air, and it wasn't just the storm. There was going to be trouble, and she had already had more than enough trouble.

But—it had occurred to her then that trouble didn't always stay where it started. . . .

She had left off brushing the horse, and went to the stall housing her bed and belongings, making sure that everything she needed was packed and ready to be snatched up at a moment's notice. If trouble had moved to the compound—as well it might have and might still— there was more than one escape route she could use, and she would.

She had set herself to watching the gate for the return of those who had left.

The Gypsies and Horse Lord folk who had trickled out into the city came back in a group, and with them, every other member of Gordo's household who had been on the streets this day. And then the gate was barred behind them.

One of the former was Ilya, and he had headed straight for her as soon as he saw her standing by the stable door. "What—" she had started to ask as he neared, but he forestalled her.

"Inside," he had told her, casting a nervous glance over his shoulder, and drew her into the stable.

"The dowager supposedly died in the dark hours before dawn," he had told her then, in what was very nearly a whisper. "They have been holding vigil for her. The archpriestess came to conduct the funeral service—and—and there was a miracle. I saw it with my own eyes."

He had looked so shaken that she could not doubt him, but— "A miracle?" she had repeated incredulously. "One that anyone could see?"

It had seemed unlikely then, and still seemed so, even after the testimony of many of Gordo's folks.

"With my own eyes, I saw it," he had said stubbornly. "The Heart, it began to *bleed!* A rain of red drops fell from it to the bier! Everyone saw it—and that was when the mercenaries attacked us."

She had felt the blood drain from her face, and her hands and feet went as cold as canal water in winter. "Cathal's mercenaries—attacked you? On hallowed ground?" She had been incredulous. Surely not even the mercenary scum General Cathal had as his personal troops were stupid enough for that!

Well, they are stupid enough to be on the streets in a howling storm, she thought grimly, for she'd been evading them all the way to the river. *I suppose they are stupid enough to attack the Temple.*

"In the midst of the sacred service," Ilya had affirmed

grimly. "They drove the people into the Temple, then began laying about them with staves and the butts of their spears. The archpriestess tried to stop them, but it was only when Prince Leopold arrived with his men that they ceased to attack. He sent them away and pledged to the archpriestess that there would be no more such incidents."

"Incidents!" She had snorted at that. "I would hardly call an attack on unarmed people on holy ground an *incident!*"

"No more would I," Ilya had agreed, his teeth gritted, despite the fact that the religion of the Temple was not his. "And the temper in the city is bad, very bad. Cathal— or his men—have been balked, and we thought it better to remain within walls."

She had nodded grimly, wishing she did not have to go out after those damned books—but there was no hope for it. "Thank you for coming to tell me, Ilya," she had said gratefully. "And—ah—if I were you, I would ask Mother Bayan's opinion about the dowager's death."

"Oh?" Ilya had replied doubtfully—then, "Oh!" he had said, as her meaning became clear. "Well, then." He had looked a bit more cheerful, but only a bit. "Still. The mood in the city is dangerous, and were I you, I would stay here."

"Or if I must go, I will go as the cat does," she had promised him, knowing she could not promise not to leave. "By darkness, and over rooftops."

Or over as many rooftops as the storm permits me to take! I do not dance upon wet tiles, thank you very much!

The storm began just after she did leave. If she did not precisely go over rooftops, it was at least by paths neither mercenaries nor black coats would be able to follow. Sometimes she took to tiny, threadlike alleys, sometimes she climbed over walls and through gardens, and in the immediate vicinity of the compound she *did* travel on the roofs. Fortunately, she was on the ground when the storm broke, or she might have been blown off of one of those roofs!

It caught her as she threaded a veritable maze of narrow passageways between buildings, a path that took her to a particular boathouse on the riverbank, near the bridge. And if she had not promised her grandmother that she would get those books, she might have turned back as the storm unleashed its fury on Merina and all who dwelled within the city. But she had the feeling that she *needed* to bring those books to Adele, a feeling that was as powerful as it was irrational, and she forced her way through the driving wind and rain until she made the shelter of her goal.

The boathouse appeared to be abandoned, although it was a substantial and enduring structure of brick and stone. The door was locked, but Shelyra had never needed a key for this particular building.

With a few fumbles, she managed to push the bricks in the proper sequence to let the concealed door in the brickwork swing aside, just enough to let her squeeze in out of the tempest.

She stood on the wide strip of internal dock, dripping in the darkness, for a long moment. The dock was much wider than it needed to be, but there was a reason for that. There was a boat here, a lean, dark creature, like a predatory pike—but this time, she was not after a boat.

In the intermittent light from lightning flashes, she felt her way across to the bridge side of the boathouse. Once there, she swung herself down carefully toward the water and felt for the first foothold with an outstretched toe.

The river was high, but not quite high enough to swamp the second boardwalk hidden beneath the first.

It was a narrow path that led back to the wall of the boathouse, the wall that faced the bridge, and by the time she reached that wall, the boardwalk rested not on pilings in the water but on good, solid stone, the same stone as the bank. This time, there was no complicated series of bricks to be pushed or pulled—just a plug of bricks to be removed, giving her entry into what had once been, and might still be, a smuggler's tunnel.

She wriggled her way inside, feet first, and dropped down onto the floor easily. She left the plug of bricks on the hidden stone floor of the boathouse, concealed under the boardwalk floor. The chances of anyone coming along and finding it tonight were remote enough she felt comfortable about taking that chance.

She felt her way along the brick-lined tunnel using both hands, not daring to strike a light. There was no telling who might be down here, although she had no reason to believe that anyone knew of this place but those of the Tiger.

Still, any secret passage outside of the walls of the palaces was subject to being discovered by outsiders. It was outsiders who had built this one in the first place, a fact she never forgot.

The tunnel smelled of damp and mildew, and really, so near to the river, it was remarkable that it stayed as dry as it did. Once in a while she walked through a puddle, or heard a distant drip of water, but that was all. After an interminable distance, her hands encountered a dead-end—and a series of iron rungs built into the bricks of the flat wall.

This was not precisely a tunnel under the river—actually, it was above the river, but hidden under the bridge. The bridge had two watchtowers anchoring it, one on either bank; this ladder led up inside the wall of the tower on this side of the river, and from there to a round tube that had been built directly under the roadway when the bridge was first constructed. The architect at the time had some notion of sending messages and parcels by dog between the two watchtowers, but it had been such a patently silly idea that entrances from the watchtowers had been bricked shut. The tube had never been used until smugglers learned of it and built this tunnel to connect with the shaft that led from the ground floor to the tube itself.

They used it happily enough, right up until the moment they were caught and encouraged to describe their methods by the queen mother of the time, a lady with persuasive charm and formidable Talent in magic to back it up.

So far as Shelyra knew, after that, the tunnel remained a secret of the Tiger. Certainly she had never seen any evidence that anyone besides her was using it.

She climbed until her reaching hand met air, and wearily pulled herself up into the mouth of the tube, still in total darkness.

Then she began her crawl down the tube itself. It was a long and tedious journey, all of it made on hands and knees, for there was no room to stand here. She felt the bridge vibrating around her from the force of the river roaring against its supports.

Finally, once again, her seeking hand met air, and she groped and contorted her way down a ladder that was the mirror-image of the one in the other tower.

At the bottom, she rested for a moment, then began the next part of her journey. This time, her hands touched the surface of a simple wooden door after a few moments, a door with no trick mechanisms; she opened it and closed it behind her, and reached with gratitude for the lantern and striker that were always on a shelf at shoulder height on the left-hand side.

Now, at long last, she dared have some light!

It dazzled her eyes after the long darkness, but it was a relief as well; she might be used to traveling molelike through the darkness, but that didn't mean she preferred such conditions. The next part of her journey would be much easier, for this tunnel, which led to the Summer Palace, had been built by artisans of the Tiger. The smugglers had needed nothing more than to get goods across the bridge and into the city without paying duties on them. The house had needed an escape route from the Summer Palace as good as the ones from the Great Palace.

Now that she could see, she stepped up her pace to a brisk trot. Although she was not exactly winded when she reached the next entrance, this one another concealed door hidden in the bricks of an apparent dead end, she was rather tired and glad to see her goal.

She turned a particular brick, then reached inside the resulting hole and tripped the release, allowing her to pivot the dead-end wall on a central point and slip past. And as the door pivoted back in place, she scanned the floor carefully for bits of paper, for she was just inside the entrance of the Summer Palace, and this was the only place besides Gordo's compound where she had a confederate.

The housekeeper here was her old nursemaid, who had been Lydana's nursemaid before she tended Shelyra, and Adele's private maid before that. Her given name was "Nan," but after she was put in charge of the nursery, it inevitably became "Nanny."

Nanny was to be trusted above anyone else—but most of all, she deserved to know what her beloved ladies were doing and how they were faring so that she didn't fret herself to pieces over rumors from the city. Shelyra had not had any second thoughts on that; it wasn't fair to the old woman to keep her in the dark. The other servants were just that—servants; they might be loyal to the Tiger, but their primary concerns would, of course, always be their own well-being. Nanny was family.

So when Shelyra had first gone to the Summer Palace to cache her gear, she had told Nanny what was going on—and gave her a way to leave messages, for sooner or later the invaders would come here as well, and Shelyra wanted to know when they did before she blundered into them. And in return, she had promised to keep Nanny informed of what went on in the city.

There! There was a tightly rolled scrap of paper lying on the floor—a spot which was beneath the removable eye of a carved Tiger in the front entranceway! Shelyra snatched it up and unrolled it.

"Kum to mee beefour yew set foot in Palace!!!" it read. *"Danjer, heer."*

A chill ran up her back. Something must have happened, men must have arrived—Shelyra only hoped that it was the emperor's men who had come here, and not Apolon's. . . .

She threaded her way through another maze of passageways until she came to the servants' quarters. Nanny had a small suite to herself—and a door from the passageways that Shelyra had showed to her, in case she needed to flee. There was a second scrap of paper there, just inside that door, saying basically the same thing as the first.

Shelyra blew out her lamp and cautiously cracked open the hidden door.

"Nanny?" she whispered into the darkness.

There was a hearty sigh of relief and the sound of a striker—a lamp flared into brightness, shining on the wrinkled face of the old woman waiting in the bed, hair neatly tucked into a cap, and a woolen shawl about her shoulders. "I've been waiting in the dark, hoping you'd come, dearie," the old woman said, her face reflecting the tension that she must have been in. "The rumors—and there's men here from the emperor—"

"Many?" Shelyra asked quickly, and at Nanny's headshake, gave a small sigh of relief of her own. "Well, let me just tell you what has really happened, then you tell me about these men."

She told over her full budget of news, and Nanny nodded wisely at the word that Adele was not dead. "I thought as much," she said quietly. "I never had the Talent your grandmother had, but there was a bond between us, and I felt nothing amiss when the bell began to toll."

She said nothing more, but Shelyra took her at her word, for Nanny *had* known every other time that something had gone amiss for Adele, several of which incidents Shelyra herself had witnessed.

Her eyes went wide and round at the word of the miracle, however, and she made the Heart-sign upon the breast of her nightgown.

"That's all that I know," Shelyra concluded as she finished with the story of the prince defending Temple and Gemen against General Cathal's troops.

"Ah!" Nanny exclaimed, her face displaying sudden animation. "So that explains it! Your young prince has landed himself in deep disgrace, my love. It's him who's here, and with no more escort than a pair of squires too young to be of any help." She smiled. "I pretended to be a plain old countrywoman, with accent to match, so he wouldn't think I could read and write, and wouldn't be suspicious of me."

"Leopold's here?" Shelyra exclaimed. "What happened to him?"

Nanny shook her head. "That I can't tell you, but I suspect he got into trouble over defending the Temple. He came trailing across the bridge with all his things and a more hangdog expression than I've seen since the day you got caught putting frogs in your governess' bed and sent to your room for a week to think on your sins."

Shelyra blushed a bit and smiled at the same time, trying to imagine dignified Leopold with the expression of a sulky child.

"He's in the king's suite, up in the tower," Nanny continued. "And I must say, my love, he's the sweetest man I've laid eyes on since your dear father left us. Any other man would have had a fit that there was no one here to wait hand and foot on him. Any other noble would have starved, or shouted me down into the kitchen to make some kind of mess for him—then shouted at me because I'm no cook. He made no fuss at all, went down to the kitchen and fed himself and the boys with his own two hands, then saw the lads tucked into bed and told them stories till they slept, so the storm and the circumstances wouldn't give them night-fears. *Not* the kind of man I'd have taken for that Balthasar's son."

"I'd noticed that," Shelyra admitted. "There's a kindness in him—and I can't imagine where he got it, since there isn't a drop of kindness in the emperor's body."

"He'd make a good father, that one," Nanny said med-itatively, then shook her head. "Well, he's out of the way if you need to get at anything, though I won't vouch for what might come here tomorrow."

Shelyra made a sour face. "If he's in disgrace, the em-peror will be sending men of his own to watch him. I *did* come to get something for Grandmother, Nanny, and I'd better get it now. I probably won't have a second chance."

"Can I help?" Nanny offered immediately. "I don't sleep much these days."

"Why, yes, you can!" Shelyra replied gratefully. "Do you think you could find me about—oh, twenty or so books, take them from places where they won't be missed, and bring them to Grandmother's suite?"

"Easily," the old woman said firmly. "And it will be a pleasure, finally being able to do something! I may be old and feeble, but it drives me wild not being able to help you."

She levered herself out of bed and put on a robe; She-lyra took to the passageway again and headed for Adele's chambers.

She keyed open the door here, which was actually a part of the bookcase she was to loot, and found that the books Adele wanted were as easy to recognize as Adele had claimed—although she had to open each volume and ac-tually begin reading it to determine what it was. She had found at least half of the magic-books when Nanny came shuffling in, her arms full of silly books of legends and flowery poetry. They were not the sort of thing that Adele would have read, but the invaders wouldn't know that.

She set her gleanings down on the bed, then began plac-ing them in the empty slots in Adele's bookcase. She sur-veyed her results as she placed the last book on the shelves, then without another word, went off in search of more books.

By the time she returned, Shelyra was certain she had found all of the books Adele had left behind. They were stacked up inside the passageway, safe for the moment, and she helped Nanny replace the missing books with the rest of the decoys.

"There," the old woman said, tilting her head to survey the result. "That looks reasonable enough."

"Nanny, I could not have done this with any speed without you," Shelyra told her gratefully, and she leaned down to kiss the old woman's wrinkled cheek. "Thank you!"

Nanny chuckled with delight. "It's good to have something to do at last," she replied. "Now—you'd best be off, or you'll never get into the city before daylight." She made a shooing motion with her hands, and Shelyra obeyed her with alacrity.

It took three trips to carry all the books out of the passageway; she didn't want to leave them there, for fear that they might somehow advertise their presence to another mage. Thus far, no one had discovered the secret passageways, and if Apolon came here, she didn't want to give him any clues as to the existence of the hidden ways. She left most of the books in her secret room, taking only the few she could carry easily while crawling beneath the bridge and protect inside her clothing from the rain. She had reason to believe that the room carved into the bedrock was shielded against magic; that was why she had brought the most important pieces of her "equipment" here. At least now the books were safe from the hands of Apolon; that was the important part. She had little doubt that at least one of the people the emperor would send to watch his son would be a toady of that evil mage.

Poor Leopold, she thought as she began her return trip. *For all the hardship and the danger—I would not trade my place for his for anything anyone could offer me. He is the one who needs a guardian angel, not I.*

ᔥ 44 ᔥ

THOM

Of all things, inactivity drove Thom Talesmith to distraction. It was inactivity that had driven him out into the city again, looking for news in all of his usual haunts.

He had thought about going to the Temple, but after consideration, decided that would be a mistake. There were rumors that the emperor's men were sweeping the streets for able-bodied men, pressing them into Balthasar's service, and he didn't want to get caught up in such a sweep.

Instead, he took to another haunt of his; not Jonas' tavern, but one of a similar ilk that catered to the land-locked equivalent of Jonas' river rats and wharf-skippers. He had not been back there in several days; there should be a mort of news waiting there for him.

He found that the rumors were true; he saw more than one set of black coats or mercenaries dragging off half-conscious or protesting men, all of whom were able-bodied and most of whom were young. He managed to avoid the press-gangs by simple dint of hiding at the first sounds of firm and "official" footsteps. It did occur to him, though, to wonder just what the emperor thought he was doing. At this rate, there would soon be no one to do the work of the city—and with no dock-workers, no craftsmen, no laborers, the wealth that Merina had once possessed would vanish without a trace.

Unless, of course, the women somehow managed to find a way to perform the work that their men once did.

He snorted in scorn at that notion. Women? Not likely! Hard to heave a bale of goods onto a barge when there were brats clinging to your skirts! And that would be if the woman was willing to take on such hard and dirty labor— No, women preferred to sit soft at home; he couldn't see any of the women of Merina having the gumption to move into the breach formed by the loss of their men. They'd probably just sit at home and wring their hands and wail.

He moved across town to the opposite end of the city from the docks—the area where the overland caravans entered Merina. Like the docks, this was a district of warehouses and workers, and like the docks, there were sections of it where you had better walk with one hand on your knife and know where you were going. To go there at night as he was doing—if you were not a known element there—was the height of folly.

The Angel's Arms was advertised by a pair of petrified pigeon wings nailed to the doorpost. To reach it, Thom went down a narrow, noisome alley full of rats, cats, and yelling brats until he came to the stairs leading down to the cellar of the most dilapidated building on the block. He reached the door just as the sky opened up. He was glad enough to duck inside as soon as the door was opened to his knock.

Inside, the effluvia of unwashed dishes, unwashed bodies, unwashed floors, burned food, and beer was enough to knock over the unwary. For Thom, however, the odor was a reminder.

This is where you came from. This is where you'll end up, if you aren't careful and clever. Better, far better, to die at the end of a hangman's rope than to eke out a pitiful existence of cadging drinks in the corner of the Angel's Arms, or some other place like it.

No one hailed him; no one would. Names were dangerous, and no one used them without permission. Thom took a seat at an unoccupied table and waited until one of the slatterns whose services were all purchasable came to take his order.

Except—it wasn't a slattern, sloe-eyed and all invitation. It was a frightened, round-eyed child of indeterminate sex.

It stood trembling beside his table and whispered. He couldn't quite catch what it said, but he assumed that it was asking what he wanted.

"Whiskey," he said, throwing a coin on the child's tray. "And bring Ard here. Tell him Thom wants to talk."

Ard Arnson was the owner of the Angel's Arms; Thom had spent more than a little coin on the information Ard had to sell. Ard would be happy enough to see more of that coin that he would probably forgive the abrupt summons.

In fact, Ard himself brought Thom his whiskey—that being the only drink potent enough to render the glass it came in sterile. It was very bad whiskey—but Ard's beer was worse.

Ard brought two glasses, in fact, and sat himself down across from Thom with a grunt.

"Where're the girls?" Thom asked brusquely.

"Impies," Ard groaned. "Came through, swept 'em up, hauled 'em off to some Impie house. Got every girl on th' street as didn' hide first." He gestured at the children waiting tables. "This's all I could get fer downstairs. Keepin' the couple'a wenches I still got safe-hid upstairs."

"Huh." Thom tossed down his drink, knowing better than to allow it to touch his tongue on its way to his throat. "Tough."

"Believe it." Ard followed suit. "Press-gang's been collectin' the boys, too. Ain't gonna be no one left but old men, wimmen, cripples an' kids. Bad fer trade. Real bad fer trade."

Thom considered this. "Makes a man start to think about dumping a few Impies in the canal," he offered.

Ard gave him a withering look. "Them as has, finds Impies under the bed in the mornin'. They got patrols marked out, an' if one'a theirs goes missin' overnight, they know where he went missin' *from*. Then they come to make reckonin' with the neighborhood. Strung up five men on Glasdon Street this mornin', just by way of an example."

"Did they now?" Thom toyed with his glass. This was not looking very promising. The imperial forces were one step ahead of anything the citizens of Merina might do to combat their depredations—and they weren't being fair about it, either. Evidently justice had no place in the imperial lexicon.

Ard might have been reading Thom's mind. "It ain't fair," he complained. "A man comes t' expect that the law is gonna be law-abidin', and it ain't fair when the law don't play by the rules no more."

"That it isn't," Thom agreed, then hazarded something more. "You think that the Temple—"

"When has the likes of them had time for the likes of us, when the knife's at their throat, too?" Ard demanded. "Oh, I heerd about the miracle and all, but right after that miracle, here comes the Impies, pushing right into the Temple and no angels to stop 'em." He shook his head sadly. "No, Thom, it's hard bad times all over, an' I'll tell you what I bin tellin' the rest. Get out while you can."

Thom got a bit more information out of Ard, but it wasn't terribly useful. The imperial troops had put a stranglehold on even this neighborhood by sweeping through it periodically and carrying off every marginally able-bodied man unwary enough to be on the street. Some had been released, after proving that not only did they own a business or work at a job, they had already paid their imperial dues for that privilege. The rest were dubbed "indigent" and taken to work in labor gangs. Where, Ard didn't know. Or why.

Thom mulled that over after Ard was gone, trying to put the pieces together. But none of them would fit—

No, that wasn't altogether true. None of them would fit *if* you assumed that the emperor wanted to keep Merina and its potential for producing further wealth intact. No city could function without its work force, nor could it function when its workers and merchants were being bled dry. Of course, merchants *always* claimed that the government was bleeding them dry, but they always found the money to spare for whatever else they needed.

Not this time. In order to stay in business, merchants had to pay over the equivalent of every copper of profit for a year—and all at once, for a six-month license. Some of them would have savings to cover the extortionate demand, but others? They would have one of three choices: cease business, find someone who had the money to take as a partner, or—

Or the third possibility. If they did not immediately close their doors, yet remained in arrears, they would find themselves with a partner, all right. Imperial soldiers would arrive on the doorstep with a warrant in hand confiscating their *entire* property, signing it over to an imperial citizen, and making the poor merchant or craftsman into the indentured servant of the imperial, all to pay off "penalties" accrued *by the hour* for each hour spent in business operation without an imperial license. Then the choices were even fewer: try to flee and take the chance on being declared "indigent" and swept up by a press-gang, or remain, a servant in your own house, a slave in your own business.

No, none of this made sense if Merina was intended to stand. But if, instead of simply fleecing the sheep, the emperor intended to take wool—then hide, meat, and bones, and never mind about wool in the future—then it made very grim sense indeed.

The emperor had never intended to do anything other than pillage the city. They had simply made it more convenient and less costly for him to do so by surrendering.

They should have fought. Now, it was too late.

There might be a city here when the emperor finally left—but it would be the drying bones of a city, with all of the wealth that sustained it, all of its workers, everything of value ruthlessly stripped off and carried away. It *would* be a city of women, old men, cripples, and children—

For that matter, it might be only a city of the old, the cripples, and the babes and toddlers too young to be useful. By the time the imperial forces stripped that much away, what was there to stop them from taking all marginally nubile women as imperial camp-followers, and the youngsters to fetch and carry for the army?

Nothing, except a sense of decency, which, it seemed, the emperor rather blatantly lacked.

Thom turned the whole construction of assumption, conjecture, and fact over and over in his mind, trying to find some flaw in it. Unfortunately, the more he looked at it, the more solid it became.

Outside the tavern, the wind howled like a thousand lost souls, and thunder shook the old building and rattled every loose board so continuously that the noise drowned any talk further away than a few feet.

Thom sighed and looked down at his empty glass. He hardly wanted to make his way back to Gordo's in weather like this—but this was also no place to wait out a storm. The Angel's Arms had flooded before, and from the amount of rain pouring down, it might well flood tonight.

He threw a copper on the table for the child coming to fetch his glass, pulled his coat tightly around his body, and got up. No one looked at him, or paid any more attention to him than they had when he had first entered.

He had to force the door open against the raging wind, and it tore out of his grasp once he was outside, slamming shut again. The wind was even worse when he got up to street level, and the rain lashed at exposed flesh with fury, chilling and numbing it in moments.

This was definitely the worst storm Thom had ever been in, and he wondered if it was an expression of the wrath of the Goddess at the violation of Her Temple. Or—could it be at the use of Her sacred ceremony of burial to conceal the fact that the dowager was very much alive?

Not that he knew that Adele was still among the living

for certain—but the lady in the confessional had been quite lively, and Shelyra had shown no sign of anxiety whatsoever when the bell began to toll the dowager's death. Put those two together, and add in the fact that the imperials *knew* that the dowager had taken refuge in the Temple, and you had a very good case for a phony funeral.

And why not? No one would look for a dead woman, no matter how much they wanted her.

Well, he *hoped* this storm wasn't an expression of the Goddess' anger at the perversion of Her sacred rites. It would be much better if She was making it clear that the imperials had transgressed.

"It would be even better if She decided to take a hand in things Herself," he muttered into his coat collar as he slipped on wet cobblestones. "Without some *real* miracles, this city isn't going to survive the emperor's mercy."

Well, at least there was one good thing about this storm. There weren't going to be any press-gangs out on a night like this. Only an idiot, someone who was desperate, or someone who had no choice would be out in this torrent.

"And which am I, I wonder?" he asked aloud.

And at that precise moment, hands closed on his shoulders from both sides.

He reacted automatically, aiming to take one of his assailants in the gut with an arm, and one in the chin with a fist. Neither blow made any difference.

In fact, whoever had seized him didn't act as if they *felt* the blows!

He started to squirm out of his coat, intending to leave it in their hands as he fled, a ruse that had worked well for him in the past.

He never got that far.

He woke up again in cold and darkness, but not in silence. There were at least a dozen more men with him, perhaps more. They weren't speaking, but he heard the sounds they made as they breathed and moved.

He cleared his throat ostentatiously.

"Oh, the fresh meat's awake," said a harsh voice out of the darkness.

"He'd be better off to have one of us cosh him again," said a second voice dispiritedly.

"Where am I?" Thom asked carefully as he slowly sat up. He still had his coat, for what it was worth. His cell-mates hadn't stolen it from him, which meant that they weren't the usual run of gallows'-birds. He also had a lump half the size of his fist on the side of his head, so he didn't have to ask "what happened."

"Your guess is as good as ours, boyo," said the first voice. "Someplace dark, wet, and cold, that's all we know. That, and we was all brought here by black coats."

Black coats! What would a mage want with men?

"I've been here longest, and I've only been here about a couple of days," offered another. "And we're in a hole someplace—when they bring food and water or someone else, they lower him down from above."

That last voice sounded educated. "Like—a cistern no one's been using?" Thom hazarded. "Anybody but me remember the Jeckeral scandal?"

"What, those cisterns over in the metalworkers' district that leaked so bad they couldn't be used?" said a voice that was deeper than all the rest. "The ones that cost so much, and then they found out that the Jeckeral brothers had run off with all the money?"

"Looks like Apolon found a use for them," said the educated voice harshly.

Thom went cold all over. "That's who has us?" he asked. "Apolon himself?"

"Apolon himself," the educated voice confirmed bleakly. "He took me personally. And if you know any clever ways of escaping from the bottom of a cistern, stranger, you'd better trot them out now, before it's too late."

"Why?" someone else wanted to know.

"Because he's looking for a place where he can work his magics, friend, and Apolon is a necromancer." The educated man laughed, but it was a sound with no humor in it. "I know, because I found out about his black coats—the ones that don't speak, never feel the cold, and don't complain about being out all night. Unfortunately, Apolon found out about me before I could inform the emperor."

"You're an Impie—" There was a growling from the other men, and a sound as if they were moving closer to the speaker—

"*Was*," the man corrected, bitterly. "Now I'm just what you are, and if you'd kill me now, it would be a blessing, so don't think I'm going to stop you."

That stopped them all in their tracks.

"Why?" Thom asked into the silence.

"I told you, Apolon is a necromancer. Don't any of you know what that is?" He waited a moment, then elaborated. "He uses *dead men*. He binds their souls so they can't escape, and he makes them into his slaves. Why do you think he's keeping us like this? He's going to kill us and make us into more black coats."

"No—" someone whispered in horror.

"*Yes*," the imperial said. "And there is nothing, *nothing*, any of us can do to stop him."

§ 45 §

ADELE

Gemen Elfrida, asleep in her cell in the Temple, tossed restlessly; her sleep was vision-haunted again, and the vision would neither permit her to wake, nor to achieve true sleep. Her dream was a confusing mixture of images: the Heart and the ruby from the queen's ring circled around each other as if in a dance, but a sword flashed between them—a bright sword with a band of darkness about the hilt. The sword seemed to brandish itself before her eyes, threateningly, as if to make certain that she noticed it.

She woke suddenly, shaking with exhaustion and reaction, as if she had been working magic herself.

Blessed angels. Now what has come upon us?

She breathed deeply, concentrating on calming and centering herself, making certain that all of her was in her body, safe in the Temple.

Something is happening, or has already happened, she thought with absolute certainty. *Now I must find out what that something is.* She rose from her narrow bed and pulled her robe back on over the shift she had been sleeping in. Her cell had one small window, but when she looked out, she saw nothing but the rain lashing against it. It was as if the Sky Herself cried angry tears over the horrors befalling Merina. *It would have been even worse if we had fought,* she reminded herself sternly. Still, she didn't think

321

she was going to get any more sleep for a time. Not until she puzzled through the images of her dream-vision. Why would she, bound to the peaceful work of the Goddess, have anything to do with a sword? It was a *real* sword, and not a vision-metaphor for war or conflict, that much she was sure of. Where that band of darkness had not dimmed the glory of the blade, she had sensed the power of the Goddess about it—and She very rarely put Her hand to any weapon, unless it was also meant to confront dark *power* as well as dark intentions.

The Gideon Sword, she realized suddenly, *that's what the sword in my dream was! But what was the darkness?* She stared out at the rain; lightning lit the sky so often it would have been possible to read by it. This storm was far worse than any natural storm for this season.

Could Shelyra have anything to do with the dream? It's a nasty night for anyone to be out. I wonder if Shelyra has managed to get out to the Summer Palace yet? I hope she doesn't try to cross the river in this storm. She relaxed a little and let that thought touch her inner senses for a moment; she had the sense that someone of her blood was out in the tempest, but it wasn't Shelyra. Nor did she have the feeling that Shelyra had anything to do with the dream.

Then who did? And why the image of the pair of rubies circling about one another?

Rubies . . . stones . . . and who of her bloodline was messing about with stones? Who had access to objects of dark power? Who *certainly* had the queen's seal, and just might have been given a Heart-ruby?

The rubies! The queen's and the Heart . . . Verit said that Lydana was here when the Heart bled—does Lydana hold a part of the Heart now?

A sense of certainty overcame her at that thought, and all the pieces fell together. *It's Lydana, all right,* she thought grimly, *and the darkness must be another of her cursed jewels. I warned her to take care how she used them, but does she ever listen to me?*

She sighed, realizing that this was the complaint of

every mother since the beginning of time. *Ah well, the world goes as it will, and not as I would have it. And if she's done something truly dreadful to the Gideon Sword, we shall know soon enough. I must remember to tell Verit about it, though. It may be something we need to shield ourselves from.*

So much for being able to get back to sleep! She opened her door and looked at the night candle in the hallway. It would be a while before she was supposed to be back in the sanctuary, but she didn't want to sit alone in her cell.

I fret enough as it is. If I am going to be awake, I might as well be awake and doing something useful. If I am going to fret, it might as well be in prayer.

She slipped silently into the hallway, carrying her sandals rather than wearing them, so that her footsteps made no noise to disturb the others. The stone floor was icy against her bare feet, but she ignored the discomfort as she made her way downstairs to the meditation chamber.

The chamber was empty save for a kneeling figure in red. *I didn't think this was Verit's watch here,* Elfrida thought with surprise, kneeling quietly a short distance away from her. Verit looked up and their eyes met.

"You couldn't sleep, either, Elfrida?" Verit did not seem particularly surprised.

"No, not well," Elfrida admitted. "I dreamed, and it was not pleasant."

"Cosima was almost asleep on her knees here." Verit smiled faintly. "I sent her to bed. I could not sleep either, although I had nothing so concrete as a dream to keep me wakeful."

Poor Cosima! With this current crisis, the Brown Robe was leading as much of a double life as Adele had! "If she was healing the wounded today, she's probably tired from that," Elfrida pointed out. "And younger people do seem to need more sleep than those our age do."

"True enough," Verit agreed, "but I suspect that we shall all need as much rest as we can get before this business is done. What troubles you tonight? Is it Apolon? Is he testing our defenses, or have you a premonition?"

In an odd way, Verit's matter-of-fact questions were actually a relief to her. Elfrida had lived so long with Lydana's unease about magic that it came as a pleasant shock to be able to talk about mage-craft and premonitions with casual openness.

Elfrida shook her head. "Not directly—but I have had a premonition of some kind. I'm not altogether certain what it means, though. Tell me, when the Heart bled, could any of the rubies have left the Temple with anyone?"

Verit looked at her closely, hearing what she had not said. "The soldiers never got that far, but there was one who was beside the coffin and who left the Temple afterward." She looked at Elfrida in silent question and Elfrida nodded. She had already heard from Verit that Lydana had come to the funeral in the disguise of a Brown Robe, and only Lydana would have left the Temple.

"So," Verit concluded thoughtfully, a look of speculation on her face, "a portion of the Heart has gone out into the city. This may be good or bad; I know not which."

"Nor do I," Elfrida replied. "That part of my dream was not clear. I believe that I was only meant to know that the Heart-stone was in Merina, and in—that person's hands. At least it didn't fall into the hands of one of the novices."

Verit frowned at that, as if Elfrida's comment reminded her of something else. "I fear that you were correct about the novices, Elfrida. I have been watching them since we brought them all into the Temple, and there are several among them who are clearly reluctant to look at the Heart. I could not tell you if that is because of a Shadow on their souls, or nothing more complicated than a guilty conscience, but in either case, I am glad we have them under our eyes."

Elfrida smiled grimly. "I thought as much. What do you plan to do with them now?"

Verit returned her smile with one full of irony. "I have arranged the schedule so that all the novices spend every moment they're not at meals or asleep on their knees in the sanctuary. They won't see what they shouldn't there—

nor will they have much opportunity to slip away and re-port to anyone. Those whose souls are clear will be granting us their sincere prayers—and those whose souls are not will have ample opportunity to reflect upon their own unease and discomfort. Perhaps the Goddess will bring them contrition."

Elfrida nodded; there was certainly no harm in hoping for contrition, although she personally did not think it likely. But then, she was a cynic, with far too much ex-perience of the outside world. In the inner world of the Temple, it might well be that Verit's hopes had more strength and reality than her own cynicism. "Good. What of the houses of the healing orders scattered about the city? Is anyone preventing them from doing their work?"

Verit pursed her lips as if she had tasted something bit-ter. "The apothecaries and the secular healers have been forced to close their doors, but the healing orders have not—"

"Yet," Elfrida finished.

Verit shrugged. "So far they survive unmolested, al-though some of them are watched. The Servants of the Poor—the Reverend Zenia's house—has been watched constantly since Dame Fortuna and her daughters took shelter there, but thus far no one has sought to violate their sanctuary. I only hope that no one does—before to-day, I would not have even considered it as a possibility, but if those mercenaries will violate the Temple itself, I doubt that it is piety that keeps them from invading Zenia's cloister."

But at the mention of Dame Fortuna, Elfrida saw again the sword from her dream, dancing ghostlike in the back of her mind, with that shadow about the hilt. "Dame For-tuna is of the House of the Boar, is she not?"

Verit nodded. "Why?"

Now the last of the pieces fell together. Zenia's order was of Brown Robes, Lydana had come to the Temple disguised as a Brown Robe. Could she have had access to that disguise because she was visiting Zenia? If so, what other reason would she have had to do so—except to contact Dame Fortuna, who held the key to the Gideon Sword? "I dreamed of the Gideon Sword, and there was a darkness about its hilt." She bit her lip with vexation. "I fear that my daughter has done something to it with one of her cursed jewels."

Verit sighed and shook her head. "Blessed angels. How are we to keep our magics straight, with all of these other wild magics about? Well, I shall tell those who watch in the glass to be on guard for any sign of it." She closed her eyes for a moment, and her face mirrored the frustration that Elfrida felt. "Why would she have done such a thing?"

Elfrida sighed wearily, for she wondered the same thing. "She is still young enough to believe that evil may sometimes return good. And in her way, she is as impetuous and as impatient as Shelyra."

"You should have taught her better than that," Verit said mildly, in a tone of faint rebuke. "Evil can never be used for any purpose but to serve evil."

"I tried," Elfrida pointed out acidly, much more sharply than she intended, "but she always resisted learning anything of the ways of the Temple. It was as though our powers frightened her."

"We frighten her?" Verit said incredulously. "She can scatter jewels with curses on them about the city—and *we* frighten her?"

Elfrida shrugged, for at this point, Lydana's motives and actions baffled her so completely that her daughter might well have been a stranger. She understood Shelyra far better than she did her own daughter. "I cannot fathom it. And if we win free of Balthasar, I know not who will succeed me as secular head of the Temple. I cannot think Lydana suitable, and Shelyra shows no signs yet—"

"If we have to," Verit replied with a faint hint of teasing, despite the gravity of the situation, "we can always bring Adele back to life."

Elfrida rolled her eyes. "After her miraculous funeral?" she exclaimed. "Now how would we ever explain that? I am in no mood to find myself declared some kind of resurrected saint! At the moment, in fact, my lack of charity toward even my own daughter makes me decidedly unqualified for sainthood!"

"Be at peace," Verit said, the teasing look gone from her face. "The Goddess will take care of Her own. We will win through this, Elfrida, and perhaps we will discover that even Lydana's strange plans have had their purpose."

"I cannot see how," Elfrida grumbled.

"And that is why we are imperfect mortals," Verit reminded her. "And why we must pray for more perfect patience, and more perfect vision."

Verit could not have delivered a less-subtle hint if she had stuck a copy of the chant-book in Elfrida's hands. Elfrida nodded and took the hint, clasping her hands and turning her thoughts back to prayer.

At least now she knew what to pray for.

⚜ 46 ⚜

LYDANA

Waiting was always the worst of any project. Lydana cupped her hand about the brooch. It had indeed overcome the two sentries, but how great was its power—how many men could it reach at one time?

Sounds below. She tensed, and Eel, close to her side, became a stiff, small body.

A small figure squeezed through the narrowed door without sending it further open.

"Eel?" The name hissed through the dark.

"Here, Smert." Matild recognized the name of one of her companion's street-followers.

"They're a-bringin' th' cap'n. He's bad off—got to fix it so they can get him up to the trapdoor—" The new shadow was already tugging at a box nearly as tall as himself to bring it under the square above. Eel and Matild came to his aid, pushing and pulling frantically until they had put together a kind of staircase, which was the best they could do.

"What have they done to Captain Saxon?" Matild demanded, between gasps for breath as she gave her full strength to the task before her.

"They wanted him to talk—but the cap'n ain't the talkin' kind. They thought as how the black coats were a-comin' for him and they wanted to learn somethin' first. Don't know what!"

They had no more than gotten the last box into place before the door burst wide open and there was light enough from two lanterns for Matild to be able to see the crowding rescue party. Four of the company, with knives which winked deadly in the light, played rear guard; Dortmun and a tall ox of a man supported between them a figure with a hanging head, who was manifestly just barely able to keep partly upright.

"Up—an' out!" Dortmun half-snarled at her and the two boys. She climbed their unsteady stair and three of the men followed and turned around, once aloft, to aid in the transport of their prize.

Matild had only a glimpse of a battered face, the stubbled cheeks matted with blood. Both eyes were puffed shut, and his nose seemed to be a single dark smear. She caught a glimpse of a limply swinging arm, encircled by a dark bracelet of bruised and torn flesh at the wrist.

Wind and rain beat in upon them. There was no keeping any lantern, no matter how well-protected, alight in this fury. Matild could only feel her way directly into those blasts from the now wide-open loft door. Then she was seized about the waist before she could move to defend herself, a rope looped about her waist, and was shoved out into the wild night.

She fought for breath against the pounding of the wind, soaked quickly again to the skin before she had taken more than two of those hard-fought-for breaths. She swung back and forth in the hold of the rope until suddenly she was caught firmly about the knees and drawn down to the wildly pitching barge. That this could be done at all was certainly a measure of the skills of those who operated outside the formal laws.

Moments later, she was crouched down beside a bundled form, and by touch more than sight, was able to draw his head to rest upon her knee. Within her tunic, warmth began to rise; not the fiery torture she had earlier known, but somehow sustaining, raising her confidence that for all the recklessness of their wild endeavors they would bring this venture to a successful end.

On impulse, having no other comfort to offer to what she was sure now was a totally unconscious man, she brought out the brooch once again; and moving her hands over the already-sodden blanket someone had wrapped around him, she was able to slip her hand under the edge of that, cup her palm on the breast she could not see, so that the warmth of the two stones lay full against his icy flesh.

She was no healer, nor would they dare to seek any out—not in this city, this night. Nor was she deeply learned in the Talent. Though she had been trained from birth to believe that power lay asleep in her, she found herself less and less able to foresee herself following her mother into the Temple. Ever since the ruby had come to her hand, she had somehow begun to change—and certainly all that had happened in Merina was enough to alter any life. Though she had no Talent, she possessed a will, a surge of such determination to aid that she deliberately focused her mind on the stones beneath her hand. Heal—feel no pain—the words seemed to burn through the dark before her eyes like crimson flames. This was no regular heal-craft—but it was all she could offer. She willed strength, healing, and all the might she had earlier turned on the stones when she had set her dominance over the sentries in the house behind them.

So concentrating on what she would do, she closed out the night, the storm, the very barge which bucked and twisted under them, sure she must not lose what she was beginning to believe *was* a fragment of the Talent—or *a* Talent.

Matild was so caught up in her concentration that she was not at first aware of the pulling of hands on her shoulders. She shook her head and blinked. Ahead was a point of light which did not seem blasted by the wind, and they were steadily drawing closer to that—or as steadily as the storm would allow.

Then there were walls rising on either side, closing out the wind and rain. The pinprick of light became two, three—large ships' lanterns set on standards. This must be one of the old warehouses where deliveries could be made by water—there being no wide streets, only mazes of narrow alleys above. She did not know much of this section of the town, but that it was the warren of those with her now, she could well believe.

With no ceremony, she was pulled from the side of the captain, so sharply that the gem was shaken from her hand. Though she cried out, no one listened. With her patient shadow, Eel, she stood on that landing, watching them bring the captain up into the full light, still enwrapped in the blanket so that only his ruined face was visible.

Without a word, those carrying him hurried on, and Matild had to break into a trot to keep up with them. There were more stairs, and she discovered she had to draw herself up from step to step by a tight hold on the rail, so far was her energy depleted.

There was a strong smell of hides as they climbed, growing ever worse. But the room they emerged into at the top was bare of any such bales and bundles as they had found in the loft. Instead, there were unmistakable signs of living quarters. Around the walls were pallets, mainly collections of ragged coverings. There were two tables and a number of stools. And there was company—such company as made Matild think for a moment she had stepped into some nightmare.

She saw scarred faces, some hooks for hands, several wooden legs such as Jonas wore, while the women among them wore either the tawdry colors of dock-walkers or rags as tattered as those forming the beds. Here indeed were the dregs of Merina, and looking upon them, Matild wondered at her own complacency of a few weeks ago, when she would have sworn that such poverty was not to be found in the city.

Those lugging the captain took him to the left, where two of the women had hastened to pile two of the pallets together to make a higher, and perhaps more comfortable, bed.

There came a sound from him for the first time—not a moan, as she had expected from their unavoidable rough handling—rather—

"Sea Star!" The words were not too mumbled for her not to understand. Her name—or rather, that name her husband had given her so long ago. Sea Star—a beacon for the homeward bound.

Matild threw out her arms, pushing aside those around her, those who would keep her away from him, with the strength she thought she had completely lost earlier.

Then she was on her knees beside him, and feverishly she thrust her hand within the blanket folds. No, the ruby had not been lost—it lay still upon his breast where she had set it.

She left it where it was as she turned upon those around her. "Warm covers—get him free from this wet. Is there one among you who knows the care of wounds?"

One of the women cackled. "Do we look healers? Oh, aye, we can tend him as best we can. Rufon has gone for the Bark Hag—she be our best at the business."

As they stripped the limp body, Matild shook with rage at what she saw. His wrists had been so tightly wedged in irons there were bloody grooves in the flesh. And he had been viciously beaten. More than his face was battered and puffed into purpling flesh. Had she not known who they had brought out of the House of the Boar, she would have thought this to be a stranger—to be pitied, yes, and carefully tended. But she would not have known the red rage she now fought to control so that she could best serve him.

Eel nudged against her, and she remembered from that far past when she had ruled a palace that her small companion also knew something of healing arts. They worked steadily together with the cleanest of the rags their hosts offered, and a basin of hot water—Matild longed for the arts of the healers.

But it was not one of the Brown Robes who came to her. There shuffled into the full view of the lanterns they had set about to aid in their tending a woman whose cloak was patched, but not ragged or stained. The thrown-back hood revealed a face so creased by wrinkles that it seemed her eyes were nearly hidden, and her mouth was twice bracketed. A short fluff of yellowish-white hair covered her head, and she leaned on both a staff and the arm of Rufon; one of the boys was coming behind her, lugging a basket he set down on the floor with a sigh of relief.

The woman glanced at Saxon, and then looked straight at Matild. Her lips unclosed in a grin which showed only a few stumps of yellowed teeth. After a long, measuring look, she turned again to the unconscious man and settled herself on a stool one of the women pushed forward.

Throwing back her cloak, she moved with more briskness than Matild would have thought possible. She wore a threadbare dress, but it was also clean, as was the small white kerchief folded about her wattled neck.

Suddenly her hand shot out and closed with a grip as tight as any iron's on Matild's wrist, drawing the younger woman closer; she opened her wrinkled, fretted eyes wide as she stared straight into Matild's.

"By the Three-Crowned One," she said in a voice thinned by time, "you have the old strengths, and the will and courage to use them. But take up your bauble now— he needs no more this night, but must rest."

Having had her hand released, Matild took the gem from where she had been careful to allow it to remain during all of their ministrations to Saxon. It still radiated warmth, and as she made a fist about it, she was aware of renewed energy once more.

Thus, by dawn of morning, she who had once been queen of Merina and she who only the outcasts knew, joined forces to save a life, and perhaps a country as well. And Matild knew that though this was no one she would ever find in one of the stalls of the cloistered in the Temple, yet her new battle companion was a favored follower of the Giver of All Powers.

§ 47 §

APOLON

What was left of the chancellor was waiting for Apolon when he woke, along with his chief puppet. Both of them stood quietly just inside the bedroom door. The wind still howled around the windows, and rain pelted the glass; it was so dark that Apolon would have thought it some time around dawn, if he had not known that it must be much later than that in order for him to feel relatively rested.

He ordered his chief puppet to mend the fire; by now

the wood had dried enough that he did not need to use magic to make it burn properly. Then he turned toward the chancellor.

"Give me your report," he ordered Adelphus. His stomach growled, reminding him of his entirely unsatisfactory dinner last night, and his hunger overcame his usual fixation on strategy. "What have you done about the domestic situation in the palace?"

"Not much can be done," the puppet droned. "The streets are flooded, there is no market today, and the servants report that they find it impossible to get out."

Apolon frowned; that was *not* what he wanted to hear, but he could not—yet—control the weather, and had no authority over the servants, so there was nothing to be done about it. "What about the House of the Boar?" he demanded. "Is Cathal still occupying it?"

This time the answer was much more satisfactory. "General Cathal has no more need of it and has turned it over to you," Adelphus said tonelessly. "He is much occupied with business of his own. His men are deployed on the streets on his orders."

"What business concerns him?" This was odd behavior, and odder still that the mercenaries would cooperate with such a venture. Cathal could not possibly have bestirred himself on behalf of the flooded citizens, could he? No— Cathal's mercenaries would have no concern for the plight of the citizenry, and neither would Cathal.

"He had a prisoner. The prisoner escaped last night. The men that permitted this fear his wrath more than the flood and the tempest."

Apolon emitted a bark of laughter, imagining Cathal's chagrin and rage at having a prisoner escape him. Between the lost ransom and whatever else Cathal lost when the prisoner fled, he must be incoherent. "Indeed! Well, I must say that I am not entirely sorry to hear that—although Cathal will probably take out his anger on anyone who gets in his way for the next two days. I advise you to stay clear of him."

The puppet nodded, but said nothing.

"What of my own prisoners?" the Grey Mage demanded. "Are they still in reasonable health?" He didn't want to move them if he didn't have to, but they *were* held in cisterns, and if for some reason those cisterns should suddenly begin holding water, he would have to send his men out *again* for more recruits, and able-bodied men were getting thin on the ground. The emperor had his own press-gangs out, so did Cathal, and Apolon's black coats only added to the numbers combing the streets for men. "And what of my black coats?"

"They remain in health and dry," said the other puppet. "They were examined this morning. And your black coats are at their usual posts."

So at least his servants were following his orders. Good. There certainly was an advantage to having servants and underlings with no wills of their own.

"You, Adelphus," he told the chancellor, "you return to your normal duties. If the emperor makes any comment about your manner or your appearance, tell the emperor that you are feeling slightly ill, and attribute it to"—he thought for a moment, then smiled—"to the unhealthy climate hereabouts. See to it that the domestic situation is rectified immediately. Just give the orders to your underlings and ignore their protests. Tell them you will send them to Cathal for punishment if they refuse to obey. You may go."

The chancellor nodded and walked ponderously out. Apolon turned to his chief puppet.

"First, I want a decent, hot meal," he ordered. "Go to the emperor's cook; if anyone can make something of this situation, he can. Secondly, I want to see General Cathal as soon as possible; find him and tell him so. Thirdly, I want my belongings packed, all but the things I have here in this room. We will be moving to the House of the Boar as soon as this blasted storm ends. Now go see to it."

The puppet followed in Adelphus' wake, leaving Apolon alone in his room. He debated the wisdom of getting out of bed, but until the storm ended—or at least, until he'd had his hot meal—there didn't seem to be any real reason to leave the comfort of the bed for the chill room. He would wait until after he ate, for by then the fire should have warmed the room sufficiently.

Strange; this storm had a positively unearthly quality to it. He didn't ever recall a storm raging for so long and with such ferocity. And the timing of it—the way it had blown up out of nowhere right after Cathal's foolish and abortive attack on the Temple. . . .

The fleeting thought occurred to him that this *might* be a manifestation of divine wrath, but he shrugged it off. Let this Goddess rage; he had Powers at his call that were a match for Her. As soon as he had the opportunity, he would begin placating those Powers.

No, it was probably the mages of the Temple, trying to cow him; this smacked of the kind of ploy that they considered to be clever. Well, if those pious fools in the Temple thought to raise the weather against him, he had weapons of his own that he could counter them with, as soon as he got into the House of the Boar!

He cast a proprietary glance at his staff, which leaned in solitary splendor just inside the open wardrobe. It was not all that impressive to look upon; to all appearances it was made of a dark wood, with a simple cylindrical head of brass. It was not until one drew very close to it—closer than Apolon would ever allow anyone else to get—that one saw that the head was not brass but gold. And that the gold had been engraved with a spiraling line of script, letters as fine as a spiderweb, words which made the eyes avert themselves without the mind being aware of it. . . .

Yes, as soon as he was established in the House of the Boar, he would be able to deal with those old women in the Temple. He smiled thinly. They would regret that they had ever considered interfering with him.

Of course—he would have disposed of them no matter what, for they stood between him and the Heart of Power. Still, if they had not insisted on opposing him so actively, he might have left them in illusory peace a little longer.

His puppet arrived carrying a tray of steaming food; unfortunately, it was not particularly appetizing food by Apolon's standards. Herbal tea with honey, porridge sweetened with honey, oat bread made into toast with more honey spread on it—all of it tooth-achingly sweet; too sweet for his taste with the honey, and too coarse and bland without it.

But it was hot, and it was well-made, which made it better than last night's mostly inedible dinner. He needed energy more than he needed a pleasing breakfast. It was hot; that was what mattered.

He ate it all fastidiously, trying to ignore the cloying taste of honey all over everything. When he had finished, he signaled to the puppet to take the tray away and finally stretched and swung his feet out of bed, carefully slipping his feet into sheepskin boots to avoid the chill of the floor.

He expected Cathal to appear shortly; after all, with this storm raging, there wasn't a great deal for the general to do. His men—or at least the ones who were not searching for the escapee—were not likely to volunteer to go help the poor, beleaguered citizens of Merina in their hour of need. And even if they did, the general would probably either laugh at them or order them punished for stupidity.

Frankly, Cathal's men, being mercenaries, were not likely to go out into this muck for anything short of triple pay or a threat to their necks. Therein Apolon had a distinct advantage over the general. His men would do whatever he told them to.

So he dressed quickly and neatly, assuming that Cathal would probably show up as soon as the general finished his own breakfast.

He was right; he had just enough time to get himself in place in the sitting room and arrange himself to look as if he had been there for some time before Cathal came blundering into the suite, more bearlike than ever.

Apolon looked up from the book he was reading, and although he did not allow the expression on his face to change, he frowned mentally. Cathal looked . . . odd. His eyes were narrowed in a very peculiar manner, but the pupils were dilated. His mouth seemed set in a snarl. The general had always reminded Apolon of a rabid wolverine, but now he seemed less in control, more dangerous. More bloodthirsty. Was the strain of inaction getting to him?

"I assume Adelphus told you of my request?" Apolon said, after they had exchanged wary greetings. Cathal had not enjoyed their last meeting—but then, Apolon had not enjoyed hearing of his failure.

"That you want the House of the Boar?" Cathal replied, and grunted when Apolon nodded. "Take it," he said ungraciously. "I warn you, I doubt you'll find anything you want there. I already took everything worth having from the place, and I have no intention of surrendering my earnings to anyone."

That took Apolon rather by surprise. Cathal had never struck him as the acquisitive type—not like Adelphus. Cathal looted for the pleasure of it, not for the gain. What would Cathal consider worth having out of the House of the Boar?

It had been the home of the master of the Metalsmith Guild—would Cathal's prize be a special weapon, perhaps something magical in nature? Surely he had not managed to acquire the Gideon Sword so quickly!

He took a long, hard look at the general, trying to recall if Cathal had ever worn anything special in the way of accouterments or weaponry.

He wore a sword at his side, but he always went armed, even into the presence of the emperor. Was the sword new? It might have been; Apolon did not know weapons well enough to tell one from another, and he would have to be in a position to examine it minutely and with spells to know if it was magical in nature.

But Cathal had never before been known to wear any jewelry, and *now* his right wrist bore an officer's cuff of workmanship unfamiliar to Apolon—and bearing a shining black, ovoid stone. It looked quite exotic, quite expensive. Was that cuff what Cathal had wanted?

He thought he caught a suggestion of magic about it. Had Cathal gotten more than he bargained for? Was this what had aggravated Cathal's already aggressive nature?

Apolon decided that it did not matter. Cathal was already rabid enough; a little more would make no difference. In fact, in the long run, this might make it easier to dispose of him. "Thank you," he replied with smooth courtesy. "That was not the reason I wished to speak with you, however. I have an idea regarding a certain interfering young idealist that will benefit both of us."

He did not mention Leopold by name, even though he was certain that in his own quarters he was reasonably safe. It did not do to be overconfident. The emperor had spies everywhere. Granted, most of them were in Apolon's pay as well, but there were always a few who could not be bought.

"Oh?" Cathal replied, his eyes narrowing into slits and his muscles tensing. "Truly? And what idea is that?"

Apolon spread his hands. "The young fool has been sent away alone in disgrace, alone, so that he can think over his disobedience—and we both know that the locals have been picking off our men whenever they are alone."

The general smiled a predatory grin. "I believe I understand. It would be dreadful if some hotheaded 'patriot' of Merina decided to try an assassination, wouldn't it?"

Apolon nodded, and folded his hands over his book. "And if that 'patriot' succeeded in his attempt—well, I would imagine that the emperor would order retaliation upon Merina for the loss of such an important officer. And the troops would undoubtedly descend to some—excesses—in their grief for the loss of such a noble comrade."

The general chuckled cruelly. "Without a doubt. I believe we understand each other."

Apolon bowed slightly. "I believe we do. I have a man I would like to suggest—"

"As have I," the general interjected. "Suppose we each send a man—to see to the young idealist's protection. We, who are loyal to the emperor, must certainly see to it that this young man is not left entirely unprotected."

"No—" Apolon interjected. "No, we should simply assign our men to the ones being sent by the emperor; I am certain they will be ordered off across the river as soon as the storm clears. There is no point in being conspicuous."

The general nodded slowly. "I can find out which squad is being sent out easily enough."

"And I can send you my man," Apolon replied. "Is that satisfactory?"

The general laughed. That was all the answer Apolon needed.

§ 48 §

SHELYRA

" . . . and Leopold is still alone except for the two squires," Shelyra said to her grandmother. "It's been two days since the storm started, and I don't know how anyone is going to get across that bridge until the storm ends, so I suppose he'll be there alone until then. I think we got the books out just in time."

"I believe you are right," came the sober voice from the other side of the confessional screen. "Events keep falling faster than we can keep up with them, I fear. At least in this one, we anticipated the danger early enough to do something before it was too late."

That admission on her grandmother's part shook Shelyra all out of proportion to the simple words. She'd had the feeling, off and on, that they were fighting a losing battle for the past three days or so. If Adele—a trained mage, a priestess, an initiate of the Temple—was saying that, then what hope had any of them for taking control of this situation, of taking back their city, of even holding their own against the enemy?

But Adele's next statement—or rather, question—took her completely by surprise. "How do you feel about this prince?" she asked. "Personally, I mean."

How do I feel about him? Her conscience gave her a severe jolt, so much so that she started, prodded by guilt. *Heaven save me, I like the man! I'd like to be his friend— or more—and he's the enemy!*

Now how could she admit that? "Why?" she asked in return, hoping to stall for time, and not entirely sure that her grandmother could not read her thoughts, or at least, her guilt.

"Because I feel very sorry for him, dear," Adele said, surprising Shelyra all over again. "I think he is a very good man caught in an intolerable situation. His loyalty to his father requires that he countenance everything that the emperor does, and yet the emperor has done things, and permitted his underlings to take actions, that Leopold himself finds absolutely repugnant. He is trapped between betraying his loyalty and betraying himself."

Shelyra sighed with relief. Adele had so perfectly summed up at least part of her feelings that it was uncanny. Once again, it seemed that she and her grandmother were more alike than was logical. "I feel the same way," she replied gratefully. "In fact, it's odd, but I almost want to—to watch over him, to try to see that he doesn't get hurt by all this. I know that's impossible," she added with a nervous laugh. "But that's the problem with feelings, they aren't very logical."

"It wouldn't hurt anything if you'd at least keep an eye on him," her grandmother said quickly. "He's in a dangerous situation, and you might be able to help him without hurting our own cause."

Shelyra's mouth fell open.

"You can probably learn as much at the Summer Palace as at the Great Palace," Adele continued smoothly. "And—I'd like you to keep clear of the Great Palace for now. We've learned that Apolon is staying in the designated daughter's suite. Please, Shelyra, do not take this amiss, but Apolon is very dangerous, both as a man and as a mage. He has been searching for you and for your aunt—we do not know why, but I have fears . . . and so does Verit. The magics that Apolon practices are of the blackest, and if he actually wants you—I doubt that it is as a hostage for the city's good behavior."

If Adele and Verit were afraid of what Apolon could do—her own imagination was quite able to supply a number of grisly things that Apolon could want her for. One of her weaknesses, which her aunt abhorred, was for common, sensational stories and ballads—many of which featured evil mages as the villains. And even though the storytellers and balladeers tailored their wares for the ears of Princess Shelyra, details were easy to fantasize.

I may be a bit reckless sometimes, but I'm not stupid, she thought with a shiver.

Adele continued. "While you remain at a physical distance from him, especially with running water between you, I believe he will not be able to find you—but if you are within the same walls as he—"

"Never mind," Shelyra said hastily. "I think if I just listen in the right places, I can learn almost as much as I would in the palace."

"Perhaps Thom Talesmith—" Adele began.

Shelyra snorted. She was *not* in charity with her supposed helper. "Thom Talesmith is even more useless than before, since he is nowhere about. He slipped off on his own business just before the storm broke, and he has not been back. I think he may have taken advantage of the storm to escape from the city."

But her conscience struck her then, and she added, "Or—to be perfectly honest, he could have been hurt or swept away. Or—well, there are gangs of the emperor's soldiers going through the city taking up every man they can find who cannot give a good account of himself, calling him 'indigent' and sending him off to work for them. He could have been caught."

He is certainly foolish enough to have been caught in such a way, she thought sourly. *It would serve him right, too—running off to avoid a little honest labor in the stable only to find himself working in a pressed gang!*

"The emperor is not the only one who has men sweeping the city," Adele said quietly. "Apolon does as well. And *his* gangs operate by night. Nor, so far as we can tell, were they hampered in their efforts by this storm."

A shiver went down Shelyra's spine, and she shuddered involuntarily. *But Thom evaded the black coats easily before—there is no reason why that should have changed,* she told herself.

"There is one thing more that I must tell you about Apolon," Adele went on. "You *must* pass this on to your people among the Gypsies. Apolon—is a necromancer."

Shelyra's heart spasmed, and she suddenly felt ill. *Everyone* in Merina knew the tale of Iktcar.

"There are reliable reports that men known to be dead have been seen walking our streets, wearing his black coats." Adele's voice shook; Shelyra could hardly blame her. No wonder she and Verit feared the mage! The last time a necromancer had walked the streets of Merina, it had taken an angel in human guise to slay him! "If you have heard tales of walking dead—well, they are true. Be very wary around anyone wearing a black coat."

"I will!" Shelyra assured her, hastily. She swallowed audibly. "I had better get back to the compound and tell them what you told me."

—and then to the Summer Palace, she thought silently. *I don't think Apolon is any friend of Leopold's. Perhaps Grandmother is right; I ought to watch out for him, at least a little.*

"The rest of your books will be coming in with the Gypsies as soon as the storm clears," she continued. "All of them old women. The young ones aren't leaving Gordo's without an escort."

"I don't think any young person, male or female, should leave Gordo's at the moment, with or without an escort." Adele sighed. "There are too many people combing the streets for victims. But thank you; having the books safely here will ease my mind a great deal. I would rather that Apolon have as little information about what we know as possible. Go with the blessings of She Who Rules the Stars, my dear. And with mine."

Well, Shelyra thought, as she made her exit from the confessional and bundled her shapeless rain-cape about herself. *That was mostly news I could have lived without hearing.*

With every passing moment, the situation looked worse and worse for the city. Shelyra ducked her head under the torrent of water that struck her full on as she exited the Temple—and it occurred to her then that trying to fight the emperor was a great deal like trying to hold back this storm with a leaky basin.

For a moment—in fact, for the first time—she was tempted to just give up. She could follow Lydana's original plan for her; she could go to the Horse Lords and encourage them to be uncooperative with the emperor. *She* would be safe—

But then her stubborn will rose up again. *Not while Grandmother and Aunt Lydana are here,* she thought, obstinately. *If they can risk themselves for Merina, so can I. There must be something I can do, and I'll find it, I swear!*

But the first thing to do was to get back to the compound. Gordo and Mother Bayan must both be told about Apolon, and quickly.

She saw for herself the truth of her grandmother's words about Apolon's black coats; they were out on their watches and patrols, despite the storm; for all intents and purposes, completely indifferent to the weather. That, if nothing else, convinced her that they could no longer be human.

And that was what convinced Gordo as well, when she made her way back to the compound at last, after several detours caused by flooded streets and bridges under water. Mother Bayan needed no convincing, however.

"Nothing you could tell me of that vile man would surprise me," she said firmly. "His evil hangs about him like a cloak of dark mist. I would not venture near him, were I you, under any circumstances."

It was the third day of the storm and Mother Bayan's warnings echoed in her mind, chiming together with Adele's in a chilling harmony, all the way to the Summer Palace. She really didn't feel easy until she was actually across the bridge and in the tunnel on the other side. It felt as if there were baleful eyes searching for her—she could sense them, scanning the darkness, waiting for her to make one foolish move. That one mistake would be all the owner of those eyes needed; he would find her, then, and—

Once again, the temptation to run—to use this opportunity to escape out of reach—was almost overwhelming. It would be so easy to escape from here, for she had everything she needed hidden away in her secret room. She could simply gather up her things, take a horse, and be gone.

No. No, and no, and no.

To flee now would be to betray everything she believed in. And for all she knew, that would be the "foolish move" that Apolon needed to find her!

It would be much easier to identify one woman with an expensive horse riding for lands the emperor does not hold, than it is to identify one common woman in the city. I am safer as Raymonda.

She searched for a message from Nanny, but there was nothing, either beneath the entrance hall, or on the other side of the door in the old woman's room. The two young squires were easy enough to find; their shouts echoed through the Summer Palace, and she discovered that they had independently recreated her favorite game when alone in the palace—

They had found what a wonderful slide the banister of the main staircase made—and how easy it was to build a soft landing place with the featherbeds usually stored in the winter linen cupboard beneath it.

Nanny was indulging them by pretending she did not know the mischief they were up to, just as she had ignored Shelyra when the princess had played the same game.

But Leopold was nowhere in sight.

I should try the king's tower, she decided. *If he's alone, he might start talking to himself again, and I might learn something new.*

Well, it was a good enough excuse to go looking for him, anyway.

She found him in the study of the king's tower, all right; from the looks of things he'd been there for most of the day. There were books piled everywhere, and the remains of a fairly hearty meal on a tray beside the fire. Her vantage point was a cozy one; the hidden passage here dead-ended on the fireplace, and heat from the fire made this nook warm and comfortable. She might even be able to get the chill out of her bones if she stayed here long enough.

But Leopold was neither reading nor eating; he was sitting in a chair she remembered as being her father's favorite, resting his head on one hand and staring at something she could not quite see from her current vantage.

Then he shifted his position, and she had a good view of it—and she blinked with surprise.

The object of his attention was one of the small portrait-studies that Master Leonard had done of her, before painting her official court portrait. This one was hardly more than a color sketch, but it showed her as she really thought of herself, for the stiffly formal painting of her in her high court gown always seemed to portray a stranger with her face. Leonard had sketched her as she sat in an open window on a windy day; she had been wearing her riding breeches and coat, her coat and shirt were open at the neck, and her hair was down so that the wind could move through it. Her grandmother had loved that sketch and had ordered it framed. She had kept it in her study, along with a portrait-sketch of Lydana at work on some piece of jewelry or other.

Leopold sighed, and she started. Then he spoke, and she started again when his first word was her name.

"Shelyra," he said, "I know this is foolish, talking to a picture—but this picture seemed so friendly, I couldn't bear to burn it the way I did all the rest of the things that seemed very personal. I'm sorry I had to do that, but I didn't want Apolon to get his hands on any of it." He chuckled sadly. "I hope you *like* the kinds of clothing that you're wearing in that picture—I'm afraid that all your daintier things are ash, and your gowns have been reduced to their component parts and stored in the backs of the attics. I did the same for your aunt, and your poor grandmother, may her soul be at peace." He chuckled again, this time with more feeling of amusement. "I wish I had been a fly on the wall when Apolon discovered what I had done. I imagine he wasn't pleased, given how badly he wants his hands on you. I hope you know that and are taking precautions."

Shelyra listened to this in pure astonishment. *Leopold* had done for her precisely what Mother Bayan had advised *she* do!

She said to be on the watch for a friend in a place where I would not expect one—but who would have guessed it was the emperor's own son? And the irony of it—that he should be talking to her portrait like an old friend, while she listened to him, all unknown. . . .

He rubbed his head as if it hurt him. "I needed someone to talk to, and I doubt that any confessor from the Temple is likely to be willing to come out here ever, much less in this weather." As if to punctuate that, the wind rattled the windows of the study, and a wash of rain hit the glass with such force it sounded like hailstones. "So, wherever you are, I hope you won't mind that I remembered the one friendly face in this city and took her out so I could talk to her."

She felt oddly touched. *Mind? How could I mind? Poor Leopold, Grandmother was right to feel sorry for you. Why couldn't you have had some other father?*

"Did you know that about six years ago, Father was thinking about arranging a marriage between us?" he continued, as if he was having a real conversation with her.

She stifled a cough. *Ah—no. No, I didn't. Wouldn't that have made an interesting scenario!*

"Nothing ever came of it, of course. Your aunt wouldn't hear of it until you were older—and I wouldn't have stood for it, either." He shook his head. "Imagine, sending a young girl to be the wife of a man in his twenties! Oh, I know it is done all the time—but I have seen the results of such arrangements, seen excited and innocent children reduced in the course of one night to terrified, speechless ghosts of their former selves. No, that is cruelty, even if it is cruelty by indifference."

Shelyra moved quickly to another spy hole, so she could see his face. She had never suspected him of being so sensitive before. This was certainly surprising. Very few men she had ever met were this cognizant of the feelings of anyone except themselves. None she had ever known would have turned down a bridal alliance because of the tender age of the bride.

He wore a grimace of distaste. "Father thought that the idea of a child-bride was perfect. He kept telling me I could mold you into anything I wanted. With an attitude like that—sometimes, lately, I've wondered if Mother didn't die just to escape him."

I could understand that, if I were wedded to Balthasar.

"But this—" He nodded at the picture. "This is the kind of lady I believe I could be friends with—I had a comrade who wedded his childhood friend, and I have rarely seen a union with more joy in it."

Perceptive, too. Is that age, experience, or both? Or— Another thought occurred to her. *Perhaps it is because he has been forced into the role of observer so often. He has had to watch life rather than participate in it. But he has learned from what he has seen.*

"I don't have many friends," he continued wistfully, "but I suppose that you know yourself that someone with 'prince' or 'princess' tacked onto his name can't have too many people he can trust enough to be a friend." This time he raised both hands to his temples to rub them. His head must be pounding.

He remained silent for some time, and when he spoke again, his voice was tight with strain. "Shelyra, I don't know what to think anymore. I'm supposed to believe that my father is always right, but this insanity of war after war after war—how big an empire does one man need? That's bad enough, but the things he's been letting Cathal and Apolon get away with—"

He threw himself out of his chair abruptly, and began to pace, still talking to the portrait.

"I haven't understood him since he made Apolon his advisor!" he said savagely. "The first two or three countries he took—there was some excuse. Berengeria was harboring huge bands of raiders and doing nothing when we complained through diplomatic channels about them. We'd had a border dispute with Allaine that went back centuries. And the king of Hergovia was so bad that a block of wood would have been better. But after that—it was almost as if he got a taste of blood and wanted more."

His fists were clenched behind his back, as if he wanted to hit something. "That was about when Apolon showed up, did a few parlor tricks, and the next thing I know, he's an advisor like Adelphus. Then Father promoted Cathal." He shook his head. "I can pinpoint the time, but I can't fathom the reasons! Is conquest a kind of drug for him? Is he so drunk on power that all he can think of is acquiring more?"

Shelyra listened to this astonishing soliloquy with both

hands supporting her against the wall. Never had she expected any of this out of the man she had privately considered just a bit stupid, although likable enough. Now, it seemed as if she had been completely wrong—Leopold wasn't stupid, he'd—

"I've just been deluding myself, Shelyra," he said, completing her thought before she could. He had stopped pacing and stood facing her picture with his hands outspread. "I wanted to believe in my father so much that I pretended there must be good reasons for everything he did. I tried to tell myself that he was just as honorable as I wanted him to be—that he had to do things that seemed outrageous because there were considerations I knew nothing about that he had to deal with. But I can't fool myself any longer."

And a good thing, too! she thought with mingled triumph and bitterness. *If you'd just come to your senses in time, we might not be in this situation now!*

But his head sagged, his posture reflecting defeat. "And now I am here, exiled. I will never be in a position to accomplish anything. I will probably be left behind here, conveniently 'forgotten,' with a squad of watchers to make certain I do nothing that might embarrass Father."

He sat down again, slumping in his chair, staring at the portrait. "I wish—" he said softly. "I wish things had been different, Shelyra. What am I going to do?"

She had the feeling he was about to say more—and she didn't want to hear it. She had already eavesdropped on more than she had a right to.

She retreated from her listening post with her stomach in knots. *He wants to know what he is going to do. Well, what am I going to do?*

§ 49 §
LYDANA

There was no way of counting the passage of time—in this large room there were no windows to show light of day, and from the beginning Matild and the Bark Hag were busied with Saxon. The younger woman snatched sleep on a pile of rags almost within touching distance of the one on which he lay uneasily, for he turned and tossed and tried to get up, so that sometimes they were forced to call on the help of some of those men who came and went to restrain him.

From the jumble of words he uttered out of whatever nightmares held him, Matild gathered a little. That his principle tormentors had been Cathal's men she was assured. But in addition, he mentioned from time to time a mage who had stood watching the spectacle. And, while there was rage in his scrambled retorts to interrogators they could not see, still he seemed to hold the mage in more fear than anger.

Matild ate what was put into her hands—mainly bowls of fish stew or gruel—and she helped the Bark Hag dribble into Saxon's torn mouth various brews the older woman concocted in pans set about a large brazier which she ordered brought to them.

Jonas came twice, staring down at the man cloaked in fever, looking to Matild or the Hag for reassurance. Matild remembered him saying something of a searching of the city and she only hoped they would not be driven from their present refuge, as lacking in comfort as it was.

The disguising swellings began to disappear from Saxon's face. Early on, the Bark Hag had carefully washed the ruin of his nose with two different liquids which gave off the pungent scent of herbs. And then, with Matild holding his head steady, wincing at every small moan he gave, she had reset the broken nose, coating it with a wax-like substance which held her repairs steady, being careful to clear out the blood-clotted nostrils. He no longer breathed noisily through his mouth when she was done.

Eel kept a watch on Matild, near forcing her to her bed, standing over her while she choked down the coarse, bad-smelling food. When Matild was pushed away from her place, she would always carefully lay the double-stoned brooch on Saxon's breast, as nearly above his heart as she could guess, and for all his tossing and turning, he never dislodged it until she came to claim it again.

How long had it been before that moment when his once again visible eyes opened, and he looked up at her? She could not have measured the time. But there were no fever-nightmares in those eyes now, rather recognition. His mouth worked, and she swiftly raised his head, so that the Bark Hag could get another pannikin of cordial in him.

As she settled him back, he put out a hand burdened with the heavy bandaging about the wrist and raised it unsteadily toward her.

"Sea Star—" Again that name she had thought so secret and had half-forgotten back down the years. "You—you bring me safe to port."

Matild felt the strain on her lips as she curved them in paths they had not known for a long, long time—a smile.

"You know me?" She so wanted to be sure that he had come back from that land of horror and phantoms.

"Your Grace—" The old formal greeting was not what she wanted now.

Matild shook her head. "The queen is dead," she said

swiftly. "What I am and what I do—I am another person."

His cracked lips attempted an answering curve and then he winced. "I am a sorry tool for you, lady."

"There are no tools; we ourselves are our weapons now." On impulse she brought out the brooch and held its ruby side toward those battered lips. He blinked, his gaze dropped to what she held, and then rose again to catch her eyes.

"The power has come to you—before time—" There was a note in that she could not understand. But she shook her head.

"No, the Talent is not mine—what I hold is a free gift from the Great One. Look upon it, warrior, and be healed!"

Again she felt her energy flow, be drawn, toward the ruby. She fought to hold her hand steady, not to shift her own position. Did she really see what came? She was never sure afterward whether it was sight of body or of mind, but a glow—like that of a fire welcoming a chilled traveler on a winter evening—rayed out from the ruby, not as a thrusting beam but in waves, each growing wider.

His face was crimson now. He might have been bathing in the very stuff of the sunset clouds. The waves spread down his body. He lay still under them, but his eyes never left Matild's, nor did her gaze shift from him.

Somewhere—very far off, like the echo of an echo—she heard a chant. Familiar in part, as she had heard it for many years at high liturgy, but also different, as if it were being now sung in prayer and entreaty before a more secret and secluded altar.

The waves rippled, joined with one another, and always his eyes watched her. One could not join minds—or could one? She had not grasped the Talent; she had no wish to. But in that moment she knew that through her this man was being restored—perhaps even more quickly than he could be with the aid of a true healer.

Then, as suddenly as it had sprung to life, the crimson

glow winked out. Her arm suddenly ached intolerably and fell to her side, as if she no longer had any control over flesh and bone. But—Saxon had levered himself up on the pallet.

The bruises were faint marks, the cuts closed cleanly, leaving but the faintest sign of scars.

"Aska, lady, neigjob varter—sebo larns—" The Bark Hag's head was bent in prayer at his other side. She twisted between her age-crooked fingers a length of red cord into which had been tied small nuggets of stone.

Perhaps she was as much priestess as Verit—though of an older faith, even closer to the Great One. Matild recognized none of those babbled words, but their tone was unmistakable. As the Reverend Ones told their prayer beads in their cells, so was this woman out of the far past giving her own praise, in her own way, to the same Power.

The man they tended was sitting straight, his head up, his shoulders back. There was no longer any sign of weakness or injury about him. Matild sighed and felt a supporting arm about her own shoulders as Eel was there again as he had been through all the time they had been fighting for Saxon's life.

Matild did not have the strength to get to her feet. There were men and women, those who sheltered here, crowding in upon them now, crying out in their excitement. Matild allowed Eel to urge her to her own pallet. There she collapsed even before the threadbare cover was drawn gently over her. She felt emptied, drained, and wanted no more than to retreat into the welcoming darkness which promised a safety she did not understand.

ॐ 50 ॐ
ADELE

Life in the Temple was less than peaceful over the next several days. Gemen Elfrida spent so many hours in the confessional that she started hearing the words, "Reverend One, my heart is not at peace," in her sleep. And the stories that followed that ritual phrase were enough to give anyone nightmares. These poor people were even beating their way through the storms to come here in the hope of a little hearts'-ease!

"I wish those idiots who are convinced that the emperor will deal fairly with Merina were hearing confessions!" she snapped to Verit when they met in the meditation chamber that night. Since there were only four of them to do the magical work they did, they had abandoned the work chamber for the meditation chamber so that it would not be empty if someone came through the passage needing help.

"An excellent idea, Elfrida," Verit replied. "I'll try assigning the more open-minded among them to the task. Of course, it will have to be limited to those who are ordained—we can't have novices hearing confessions, and I'll have to make certain that I don't assign anyone whose response to a person seeking consolation for outrages committed against him—or more likely her—is to say 'and what did you do to provoke this?'" She sighed. "The trouble is, in all of our recorded or remembered history, the secular leadership of Merina has always been benign at worst, and hand-in-hand with us at best. So many of our Gemen simply haven't the imagination to believe that an authority could *ever* be in the wrong, because secular authority has *always* been in the right. Gemen like that are simply going to assume they are hearing the confessions of a few malcontents, troublemakers, or at worst, would-be criminals. Only those who are still flexible enough to believe that things can change for the worse as well as the better will believe what they are hearing."

"That should limit you quite a bit," Fidelis said bitterly. "From the talk of many in my order at recreation, you'd think they had no more brains than the plants they tend."

"When do you find time to go to recreation?" Cosima asked enviously. "I don't think I've sat down outside of mealtime in days. Certainly not since the storm started, and that was four days ago."

"You must make more of an effort to go to recreation, Cosima," Verit said.

Cosima came very close to glaring at her. "Yes, Reverend One, I know that recreation is an important part of our daily lives—"

"At present," Verit added dryly, "it is also the best way to get a good idea of how the residents of the Temple are thinking and how much help or hindrance they are likely to be when matters reach a crisis."

Cosima nodded reluctantly. "I'll try harder—but I'm not going to leave a patient to suffer just because it's time for me to go and sit and gossip with the other members of my order!"

Verit seemed satisfied with that. "What of your order, Elfrida?"

"Most of them are ignoring all of this," Elfrida replied. "It's barely mentioned at all during recreation—and if someone *is* so 'worldly' as to bring it up, the subject gets changed in a hurry—especially after that outburst at dinner the other night. I think it embarrassed them. Most of that bunch won't care what Balthasar does as long as he doesn't burn the library."

Verit nodded. "The cloistered orders do tend to become unworldly, which is why hearing what the Brown Robes are saying is important. The Red Robes are of the opinion that Evil cannot enter the Temple; most of them think that we and our animals are quite safe as long as we remain within our walls." But she looked troubled.

"And the emperor won't harm us," Fidelis said in sarcastic tones, obviously quoting someone, "he is a faithful son of the Temple, is he not?"

Verit made a face. "I hesitate to mention this—but part of our protection may be eroding. When the orders are heart-whole, and are all praying for the same thing, our protections are at their strongest."

"I had thought about that," Elfrida said, after a moment of hesitation. "There are some writings to substantiate that. When we are heart-whole and praying for the same goal, 'the walls of prayer are strong and seamless'—but what happens when half of us are praying for the Goddess to save us from this fiend, a quarter are praying to be simply left alone, and a quarter are praying for peace at *any* price?" She spread her hands wide in a gesture of defeat."

"Oh," Cosima said as sarcastically as Fidelis, "the emperor is no fiend! He is a faithful follower of the Goddess and a son of the Temple, remember?"

"Anyone who countenances necromancy is not *any* kind of son of the Temple," Elfrida muttered. "I had six people come to me today, telling me that they had seen people they knew were dead among the black coats."

"What did you tell them?" Fidelis asked. He did not look surprised. Elfrida knew that he had been hearing confessions as well.

"I told them to pray for patience for themselves and mercy for the souls of the black coats, and to remember that She Who Lights the Darkness never abandons us, even though it may seem so when the world is dark."

"As good an answer as any, I suppose," Fidelis said, but he sounded dubious. "Do you believe it?"

"Yes," Elfrida replied firmly. "I believe that our prayers are answered when She wills it. And perhaps the Red Robes are at least partially correct." She paused to consider the facts, rather than the troubling commentaries she had uncovered. "Not even Iktcar at his most powerful tried to cross our threshold. Apolon has not entered the Temple—even on the pretense that he wishes to pray here. Nor have any of the black coats entered the Temple, and even General Cathal has not—he sent soldiers, but he did not come himself."

"The soldiers did harm enough," Cosima said quietly, her face shadowed.

"Not fatal harm," Verit pointed out. "Prince Leopold has been here the most, and some of his soldiers as well. The emperor and the chancellor have only come once: the emperor to sit in the High Seat—"

Elfrida winced. Having Prince Leopold there hadn't bothered her much, but the thought of the emperor sitting in her chair, even once, made her feel slightly ill. "I'll bet the chancellor spent all his time eying the rubies on the altar and the Heart."

"He did give the impression of a man taking inventory," Verit admitted. "But he came only once; the day after the herald's oath, and he hasn't been back since." She frowned. "Prince Leopold hasn't been here since he sent General Cathal's men away. Does anyone know why?"

Elfrida and Fidelis spoke at once. "He's at the Summer Palace."

"Relieved of his command and exiled," Elfrida added, "judging by what I've heard from his men. And—other sources, one who has seen him there."

"I agree," Fidelis confirmed. "A few of his men still manage to come to confession. Mostly they confess to anger about the way he's being treated and resentment of their new commander, the emperor."

"And what do you tell *them*?" Elfrida asked.

Verit spoke before he could reply. "I was afraid of this," she said grimly. "I tried to warn him, but I fear there was little he could do to avoid the traps in his path. Perhaps he is safer out of the way."

"So much for his promise that we would not be molested again," Cosima said.

"He never had enough power to keep that in the first place," Verit pointed out. "And he did have the wisdom to promise only that *while he was in charge* we would be safe. But thus far we have not been so troubled again."

"That may change when they think the rest of the city is under control," Fidelis said quietly.

Elfrida wondered if he had been a soldier before entering the Temple. Then she wondered how many of the Gemen had military experience. They might need it yet.

"Agreed," Verit said. "So let's see what Apolon is up to this night, shall we?"

There was no central altar in the meditation chamber as there was in the work chamber, so she set the glass in the middle of the floor and they all sat around it. It was not the most comfortable position for old bones, and Elfrida hoped they would not have to remain in it for long.

The vision came quickly, and Elfrida was the first to recognize Apolon's surroundings—she had made ceremonial visits to the various guild houses for years. "That's the House of the Boar. What is he doing there? He was living in the Designated Daughter's rooms in the palace."

"He certainly seems settled in here," Cosima remarked softly.

She was correct. The room held a large couch at one side, next to a writing desk covered with lists of some sort. There was a circle, with a small break in it, inscribed on the floor in the center of the room. A piece of chalk lay next to it. Inside the circle was a bronze tub half-filled with a liquid that looked suspiciously like blood. A wooden staff lay in the tub, and the level of liquid dropped noticeably as they watched, as if the staff were soaking it up.

But wood shouldn't be soaking up anything at such a rapid rate.

Apolon was standing near the door, talking to one of his black coats. "I want you to bring me my prisoners, and every able-bodied man you find on the streets between sunset and midnight," he ordered.

A normal person might have questioned this command; the black coat simply nodded and left the room in silence.

"I'd say that one's dead," Fidelis said, his voice barely above a whisper.

"I believe you are right," Verit said, dropping hands and letting the vision fade. "We shall meet here again to see what Apolon plans to do with the men he has gathered."

From the looks on the faces of her companions, Elfrida suspected that nobody was looking forward to that.

❧ 51 ❧

SHELYRA

There was another note in the tunnel entrance: *Sojers heer. Six. In sarvant korters. Bee karful.*

Well, she certainly didn't need that last warning. "Careful" was all she *had* been lately. Thom still wasn't back, and since no one had seen him, she was inclined to think he was either gone in the storm or had taken the opportunity to slip his leash. Gordo had sent word out to the Horse Lord clans outside the city to watch for him.

She had been making trips to the Summer Palace for the past three nights, and more often than not, caught

Leopold talking to her portrait. She was beginning to think she ought to ask Adele to have that little picture invested in the Temple, since it seemed to be serving as a confessor! A great deal of what she overheard made her both profoundly uncomfortable and extremely sympathetic to the prince's situation.

Leopold had been fairly certain that his father would let him sit and contemplate his sins alone for a day or two even after the storm cleared off, and he had been proved right.

Shelyra did not think that Balthasar would have been pleased at the results of that contemplation, however. With nothing to occupy him, he'd had ample time to think about the conduct of Balthasar, his armies, and his advisors, and he had been forced to admit to himself that, far from being admirable, it had fallen far short of acceptable.

He had not yet realized the extent of Apolon's evil, however. He suspected the Grey Mage of very dark sorceries indeed, but it had not yet occurred to him that Apolon could actually be a necromancer. But then, without proof, who *would* suspect someone as circumspect as Apolon of necromancy? The only sorcerers in the past who had been depraved enough to sink to those hellish depths had been flamboyant in the extreme and intent on conquering the world for themselves. They certainly had not trotted along tamely in the service of anyone else.

To Shelyra's relief, the Grey Mage himself had moved out of the palace and into the House of the Boar when the storm cleared. Oddly enough, so had the chancellor— and she had not thought that the two of them were that closely allied. Nevertheless, with both of them gone, she felt a little more at ease; it would have been a disaster if Apolon had somehow uncovered the hidden passageways, and worse if he had found the ones leading to the Temple!

At least she no longer had to worry about the possibility of Apolon finding some personal object overlooked by either herself, her aunt, or her grandmother.

She tucked the message into her boot for safe keeping,

and on the spur of the moment decided to check on these new interlopers. If they actually were men still loyal to Leopold—that would be an unexpected bonus. With even a few men to back him, the prince might consider making a real break with his father. That would divide the enemy forces again, as some of the army sided with the prince, and some with the emperor. She did not think that Leopold would actually fight against his father, but if all he did was take some of emperor's manpower away from him, it would be a plus for Merina.

There was only one spy hole in the servants' quarters, and it was not located in a particularly convenient spot. She had to lie on her stomach and press her ear to it in order to hear, and it was not possible to actually see anything from it, as it was hidden under one of the bedframes bolted to the wall. Her nose rubbed the floor, and she cushioned her chin on her hands.

". . . so he's still up there sulking?" said one strange, male voice, one that was oddly cold and expressionless.

A laugh. "He hasn't come down since the storm except to cook. Some warrior! In the kitchen doing women's work!"

That voice carried the accent of the mercenaries, dashing her hopes that these might be some of Leopold's own men.

"So he hasn't come down at all since the old man sent an army cook over for us?" The first voice showed neither scorn nor amusement. "That's going to make it a deal harder for us to get rid of him."

Get rid of him? Shelyra froze. Did they mean—

"If we're going to get the locals blamed for this, we'll have to lure him out somewhere that we can set up an ambush," the second voice agreed. "I've got everything I need to make it look good. I've even got a set of orders sealed with the old hag's seal to leave behind, but the stuff isn't going to work unless we can set up a real ambush. No one is going to believe a killing that happens here, in a house full of servants too feeble to chew their own food, where we're supposed to be on guard."

Her heart jumped into her throat and lodged there. *They're going to kill him! They're going to kill Leopold! I have to do something!*

But what? She couldn't materialize out of a wall to warn him! And even if she did, why should he listen to her? He'd be more likely to try and capture her! Just because he was talking to her picture, that didn't mean he would listen to the real thing!

She couldn't kill all the soldiers, either—she had no way to get them all at once, and the moment the first one died, the rest would know that their enemies had some way of getting inside the palace. And when they knew *that*— they'd kill Leopold and make it look as if she had done it!

What can I do? Oh, Goddess, what can I do? I have to save him. . . .

Then, all at once, a plan sprang up in her mind, as if the Goddess Herself had placed it there. And *she* had everything she needed to make it work, right here.

But first—she had to get to Nanny.

She got up, carefully, so as to make no noise, and slipped through the passageways as silently as a mouse, heading for Nanny's room.

As she had hoped, the old woman was there, this time sitting up with a light, waiting for her.

She tapped twice on the wall panel to warn Nanny that she was coming through, then opened it. Nanny was already on her feet, going to the door of her room to lock it against intruders.

"Those are the *nastiest* men—" she began, her face set in a frown, when Shelyra interrupted her.

"They're worse than you know; at least, two of them are," she told the old woman grimly, then described what she had heard in the walls.

Nanny went white.

"The poor lad!" she exclaimed immediately, confirming Shelyra's hopes that she might be able to get the old woman to help her. It wouldn't take much—but it was vital. "Shelyra, my very dear, we *must* help him! Could we get him out through the walls, do you think? Or—"

"I'll be getting him out through the walls, but not the way you think," Shelyra said quickly. "But I need you to help. I want you to go to the new men—warn them not to go into the village. Tell them that there's plague there. Tell them"—she thought quickly—"that there was a dreadful plague just like it that came right after the last terrible storm we had."

"The one when I was a girl." Nanny nodded, although she still looked puzzled. "But how will that help?"

"Nanny, if we manage to convince these men that there's a plague on this side of the river, they will do our work of saving the prince for us *and* they will be convinced that the prince is dead, at one and the same time," Shelyra told her. "What's more, with a bit more luck and the blessing of the Three-Crowned One, they'll flee back across the river when we've done our work. Now go quickly, act as if you are terrified, that you just got the news from the village. Then meet me in the kitchen."

She slipped back into the walls as Nanny began to fumble on a wrapper. Everything depended on speed now.

She literally ran to her secret room and abstracted three vials from her stores of tricks and poisons. She had no idea if these potions would be tasteless or vile; she had to take that chance. They *should* be tasteless; they were meant for horses, who would spit out anything really nasty. Hopefully, with enough honey, she could cover any taste.

She ran back down to the kitchen and waited for Nanny to appear. The old woman shuffled into sight soon after Shelyra arrived, and the younger woman came out through the back of the pantry as soon as she heard Nanny's footsteps.

"Well, I told them, and they're not at all pleased, maybe a bit nervy," Nanny announced. "Now what is it we need to do?"

"We're going to give the prince plague," Shelyra told her with grim amusement.

Now Nanny's eyes lit up with understanding. "In his bedtime tea?" she asked, and Shelyra nodded and handed her the three vials.

"All of it, all of them, and sweeten it to a fair-thee-well," she said. "And *don't taste it* yourself. These are powerful potions, Nanny, and I only have the antidotes for one person. Make sure the little boys don't get any, either."

The old woman had already gone to the kettle left to keep water hot on the hearth, and had gotten out two plates and three mugs. "I can do that easily enough," she said, nodding as she worked. "The boys favor hot cider, anyway. Tea for him and cider for them, and cakes for both. I'll take it up now."

"Good." Shelyra was sweating with nerves now, and striving to keep her hands from shaking; she had no idea how sick this would make Leopold. It might even kill him if all luck went against both of them. These were potions intended to incapacitate the horse of an enemy without killing a valuable beast—how they would work on a man, she had a guess, but no real experience. They weren't meant to be used together, either. They might counteract each other—or they might magnify all the symptoms by working together. "Leave him for about an hour, then come back up, as if you were fetching the crockery. If you find him sick, run and get the soldiers."

Blessed Lady, if you favor an honest man, watch over this one, she prayed as she slipped back into the wall, leaving Nanny to do her work. *He is a good man, and he deserves to live. Help me to help him!* There was so much with this plan that had to be left to chance!

Nevertheless, chance it she would. She had no choice, and he had no other hope.

The antidotes were in her pocket, but now she had to get equipment that would bring an unconscious or semiconscious man out of his room, into her walls, and then down to her secret room. This was not going to be easy, and she would have to do it all silently.

Rope, she thought as she slipped through the darkened passageways. *One of my pallets, blankets—the antidotes won't take for a good half hour, and he'll be weak as a kitten, after.* She could not take the chance that the men sent to kill him would flee the Summer Palace, and that meant she had to get him to safety, then make it look as if he'd wandered off in his sickness and fallen from the top of the tower. *Cochinel dye; that looks like blood.* She didn't think anyone would go looking for the corpse of a plague victim, but even if they did, as long as they found bloodstained clothing down there at the base of the tower, they might decide that wild animals had dragged the body off.

By the time she got all of this together, then brought it quietly up to the passage just below the prince's tower, Nanny must surely have delivered the brew. She climbed up to her nook beside the fireplace in the prince's study, and put her eye to the spy hole.

Her first thought was that she had spent so long in the darkness that her eyes were playing tricks on her—for the prince was on his feet, and holding the fatal tea with both hands, but he was staring at what at first sight appeared to Shelyra to be a man-tall *flame* rising up out of the carpet.

She opened her mouth to shout something, thinking that he had somehow caught the room on fire, but as she blinked, the flame disappeared. The prince continued to hold the tea for a moment, then, in a gesture as odd as it was apparently causeless, he lifted the cup in an ironic salute to nothing and no one, and drank it all down in a single gulp with the air of a man drinking what he thinks is a fatal dose of poison.

Did Nanny tell him anything? But why would she?

Then he sat down in a chair and clasped his hands over a book, as if he was waiting for something.

He did not have long to wait, as Shelyra had known would be the case. Within a half hour, he was delirious and semiconscious; sweating and lying on the floor where he had rolled out of his chair.

But—his face was also covered with livid, purplish blotches! And *that* wasn't supposed to be one of the symptoms of her potions!

But they're for horses, and horses have hair to hide their skin, she reminded herself nervously, her stomach in knots, her head beginning to pound. *You wouldn't be able to see purple blotches—I don't think—*

It was too late, anyway, for right on time, there came Nanny, who took one look at poor Leopold, gave a convincing shriek, and ran down the stairs as if for her own life.

Shortly after that, two men in hastily donned imperial uniforms came pounding back up the staircase, with Nanny and the two pages trailing along behind. They took one look at the prince writhing on the floor, and beat a hasty retreat without venturing any farther into the room, pulling the others with them, over the two boys' vehement protests.

"You'll come along and shut your face," snapped one man, hitting one of the squires with a *slap* that echoed up the staircase. "He's done for—you want to die, too? Shut up and move your little rump!"

The boys continued to protest, but the sound of a second slap followed on the first, and after that, the slamming of the door to the king's tower.

Then, to Shelyra's incredulous joy, after she had waited for many more agonizing minutes to be certain they wouldn't come back up to make certain the plague was doing its work—another sound echoed up the tower stairs. It was the sound of hammers on wood.

They were boarding up the door to the tower and nailing it shut!

Hardly believing her luck, she lost no time in springing

the latch and vaulting into the study, while the last blows still hammered on the door below. *I don't have to move him!* she exalted, while she bundled him up in the blankets she'd brought, hauled the pallet in and laid it beside the fire, then rolled him onto it. *Now—if he's not too sick, if I haven't killed him, if the damned antidotes don't kill him—*

The antidotes were already in liquid form. All she had to do was to tip his head up and pour them, one at a time, down his throat—shutting his mouth and holding his nose to force him to swallow after each one. He writhed in her grasp, but the potions she'd already given him had made him weak and unable to fight her. She got all three of them into him in short order, then laid him back down on the pallet to wait for them to work.

He looked awful; worse than she had imagined he would. His face was covered with those wine-purple marks, livid against the bloodless pallor of the rest of his skin. His limbs jerked and twitched spasmodically. He was sweating freely; his head tossed from side to side, and there was no sense whatsoever in his eyes. If she had not known what she had done, she would have well believed that he had the plague.

And he still might die of what she had done to him. . . . The next half hour would tell.

⚜ 52 ⚜

LEOPOLD

Leopold heard the old woman's footsteps on the staircase and her voice greeting his pages with a little irritation. He had been staying up here alone for a reason. He had hoped to be able to avoid the men his father had sent for as long as possible—and he really was in no mood to exchange gossip with that old woman, charming as she might be.

But he smoothed out his frown for her, and by the time she laboriously climbed the rest of the stairs to his study, he had a pleasant face ready to greet her.

He was glad that he had, when he saw she had brought him tea and a snack. It would have been boorish to be rude to her, when all that she wanted to be was thoughtful.

"I was a tad-bit worrit about ye, lad," she said in that charming accent. "Ye haven't eaten enough to keep a lamb alive."

"I haven't been hungry, dame," he replied, getting up and taking the tray from her. "But—thank you, thank you very much. And I hate to seem rude, but—well, I was meditating—"

It's not that far from the truth, he thought. *And she'll leave if she thought I was praying.*

She pursed her mouth thoughtfully and nodded. "Aye, then, I'll leave ye be, lad," she said, although she looked a little worried. "Just, ye drink that tea up, now. It'll help ye."

"I will," he promised, and she cast him another odd glance, then took herself off down the stairs.

Only then did it occur to him that she might have come up to his study for a darker purpose than to bring him a treat. He turned and looked at the innocent-seeming mug of tea on the tray. She had never done such a thing before—so why would she now? And why the insistence on his drinking the tea?

Am I being overly suspicious? he asked himself—then walked to the tray and picked the mug up, sniffing it delicately. *There is an awful lot of honey in this—and I don't recognize that scent of the herbs*— There was a bitter undertone beneath the honey—and one of the first things a soldier was taught about foraging for wild food was that anything that tasted bitter was probably poisonous.

He started to set it down, then thought better of the idea. He ought to find someplace to pour it out—perhaps out the window. He could wait, pretending to be asleep, and—

"*Prince Leopold,*" said a voice behind him, a voice so clear, and so pure, that if a bell could have spoken, it would surely have sounded like that. He started, turned— —and stared.

And sank down to one knee, his head incongruously bowed over the mug of tea still clutched in his hand. He had not knelt the first time he'd seen an angel—but that one had not spoken to him. The voice alone filled him with awe; combine voice and vision, and its power was irresistible.

The angel laughed, but he had no sense that it was laughing *at* him. "*Rise, prince, and fear not,*" it said to him in an uncanny echo of his thoughts the last time he had seen one of Them. He rose, carefully, and just as carefully raised his head.

The face, neither masculine nor feminine, shone with such power and beauty that his throat closed over unshed tears. It smiled, and its smile was joy personified, making his heart leap and race, filling his soul with illumination. It was draped in a robe of pure, white light, and light surrounded it and permeated it. He licked lips gone dry, as his heart pounded and his nerves sparked merely from being in its presence.

"You have friends where you least expect them, Leopold," the angel said gently. *"And deadly peril has entered your life this very day. Drink that which you now hold if you would avoid that peril—and if you would walk the path of Light and Honor, serving She Who Lights the Stars, trusting in those friends who would save you now."*

It smiled at him again, filling his entire heart and soul with its calm beauty—and vanished.

He stood there staring for a long moment, then as his fingers began to cramp from the grip he held on the mug, he looked down at the black liquid it held.

Deadly peril? Drink that which he now held?

But—

But what did he have to lose? If this was a potion meant to kill him—and despite the angel's reassuring words, it still could be that, for the angel could have been sent to save him from a far deadlier peril than mere death—what *did* he have to lose? His life was worthless now—he could not counter his father's errors, nor could he countenance the evil that the emperor and his underlings were doing. The best he could hope for was to live out a useless existence, constantly watched, constantly guarded, never free again. Even death could be preferable to a life as a powerless prisoner, forced to watch as the emperor's advisors committed atrocity after atrocity and Balthasar drank in power and blood as lesser men drank wine.

He raised the mug in ironic salute to the spirit, and downed it all in a single gulp, then sat down, in a strange and fatalistic mood, to wait and see what happened.

When it hit him, though, it was not what he had prepared himself for.

He began to feel a little lightheaded—then, suddenly, his vision blurred, his joints all turned to water so that he couldn't move, and he began to shiver uncontrollably. A moment more, and his teeth chattered, his limbs jerked spasmodically, and he slid helplessly out of his chair onto the floor. He tried to cry out, but all he could do was moan.

After that, he knew only terrible cold, as strange colors and sounds whirled around him. What he experienced could not even be called "visions," "nightmares" or "hallucinations," for they were without form or content. He "tasted" colors, "heard" the scent of the woodsmoke and the leather of the chair, "saw" the sounds of the crackling fire, of his own moaning. His limbs continued to thrash, and he could do nothing to control himself. Light and shadow, colors obscured anything that might have given him a clue to his surroundings. He could only endure it, lost in a whirlwind of utter madness.

He was aware of the cold leaving him first—then his limbs stopped shaking. Then all of his senses came back to their rightful places so quickly it felt like a dislocated bone snapping into place. It was a small eternity before he was able to open his eyes, but when he did, he was not certain that he was not in the grips of a different kind of hallucination.

A young lady with the face of his purloined portrait but dressed in the garb of a Gypsy dancer was leaning over him, one hand on his brow, a touch so light that he had not even felt it. Her eyes were shadowed with concern.

"Can you talk?" she asked, before he had even given thought to trying.

He licked his lips experimentally. "I—believe so," he replied hesitantly, his voice thick and hoarse. He spoke with caution. *I shouldn't let her know that I was aware the tea was—doctored.* "What happened? Am I ill?" Then, because he could not resist, "You *are* the Princess Shelyra, aren't you?"

"Shelyra, yes, but no princess at the moment." She looked relieved, and he wondered why. "As for what happened—I poisoned you, and I just gave you the antidotes."

Well, that was certainly blunt enough! *I didn't expect*

her to admit it—wait! She admits to poisoning and curing me?

He started to say something—he wasn't quite certain what—but she placed her hand on his lips to forestall him.

"Please. Listen to me, before you say anything," she told him. He would like to have leapt to his feet, but an attempt to raise his arm to move her hand away convinced him that he really had no choice but to listen to her. He couldn't even move a finger at the moment without breaking into a sweat of effort. Never had he felt this weak and helpless before—or more inclined to lay back and simply listen as he had been requested.

But she's the enemy! screamed one part of his mind. *She just admitted to poisoning you!*

Yes, admitted the rest of his mind, *but remember what the angel said. Are you going to doubt the word of one of Them? And who could the unexpected friend be but her?*

"The men your father sent here were not just sent to watch you," she told him fiercely. "At least two of them were sent to kill you. I overheard them plotting a way to lure you outside so that they could set up an ambush to kill you, one that would be blamed on the people of Merina and the queen."

Now *that* he did not believe! "My father wouldn't—" he protested, starting to sit up.

"No one said your father did," she snapped back, pushing him down on the pallet again. "Neither Apolon nor Cathal are particularly solicitous of your welfare—and with you out of the way, who do you think would be the next in line for the post of heir apparent?"

Now how does she know that? He closed his mouth on further protests. "But—" he began.

"I swear to you, by the Heart itself, I *heard* them plotting your death!" she repeated fiercely. "I would not lie about something like that—nor would I risk your life *and* mine on the chance that I could convince them you'd contracted plague!"

"Plague?" he repeated. "You poisoned me so they'd think I had some kind of plague?"

"Exactly." She sat back on her heels, a tiny glint of pleasure overlaying her concern. "It worked, too. They took your squires and nailed the door to the tower shut so you'd die in here. And a little while ago, I heard horses leaving, so I would guess that they've taken the boys and fled back to the city and the imperial physicians for safety."

And as if to confirm that, a more familiar voice quavered from just behind her, "Those exasperating men are gone, dear. I brought Jem and Lew up from the stables to get the tower door open again. Is that sweet lad all right?"

"The sweet lad has been better," Leopold said dryly, "but I thank you for your concern, dame." He tried again to sit up, and this time Shelyra let him.

It was obvious enough now how the old woman—and the young one—had gotten into his tower. A part of the bookcase beside the fireplace stood open, revealing a narrow passageway running between the walls.

And the sound of pounding and prying from below convinced him of one thing at least—instead of tending to him and fetching an imperial physician as they *should* have done, the men sent here ostensibly to protect him had barricaded him in here to die.

So that was how she "overheard" the men—and how she knows so many other things. These two palaces must be riddled with passages, like wormholes in rotten wood!

He sat back, bracing himself against the chair behind him. "Talk," he said, finally. "I'll listen. I won't promise to do more than that."

The weakness created by doses of six different drugs slowly wore off while he listened to her. The stableman and his helpers freed the door and presumably went back to their beds, since they did not bother to come up. The old woman took a more conventional path down to the kitchen and back up again, returning with hot brandywine and bread and cheese. He ate and drank while Shelyra talked, and what she had to say, unfortunately, made a great deal of sense. Worse, it tallied with things that he knew that he did not believe *she* did.

Of course, if she'd been lurking in the walls like a large-eared mouse, she might already know these things and be tailoring what she told him to that standard. But then again, why would she tell him that Adele was still alive and hiding in the Temple if she meant to deceive him?

"You don't have to believe me," she concluded. "Not without confirmation, anyway."

Interesting. Honest. And assuming that I am going to be suspicious.

"I can take you to a Reverend One at the Temple, if you'd believe her. She'll tell you the same things I just did, but—" She stopped and flushed.

"But I'm more inclined to believe a Reverend One than you, that is true," he said gently. *It does not matter if the Temple is in Merina; a Reverend One, at least, would not lie. I must believe that, or everything else I believe in is useless.* He got to his feet experimentally, quite expecting to fall on his nose. He was surprised and rather grateful when he did nothing of the sort. He closed his eyes for a moment. *The sooner I find out—* He was both anxious to learn the truth and wished that he did not have to. "We could go now, couldn't we?"

She frowned slightly in thought and tucked a strand of hair behind her ear. "I believe at least one of the Gemen I know will be awake." She sighed. "I hope you realize that what I am about to show you has been a secret within our family for centuries." She leveled a stern gaze on him as she rose to stand beside him. "I did not even reveal these passages to one of our allies."

He nodded, and realized then that he had not recovered as much as he had thought; the room swam a little when he moved his head. "Shelyra, I pledge you on my honor that I shall not make use of these passages without your presence or your permission. Will that satisfy you?"

He had reached out without really thinking about it and

taken one of her hands in his. She looked down briefly, but did not endeavor to remove it.

"If it were anyone else," she began, then shook her head. "Nevertheless, it is you. Yes, I will trust a pledge made on *your* honor."

He did not miss the emphasis on "your," and wondered whose honor it was that she did not trust. He smiled slightly, and lifted her hand to his lips to kiss the back of it before releasing it. She flushed, but returned his smile.

"Come on, then," she said, and led the way into the walls.

He wasn't certain why she was worried he might learn the secrets of the passageways, since he was lost before they had made more than three turnings. At some point he was fairly certain that they were outside the palace—and eventually, when the time came to go upward, he thought they might be moving up the bridge towers. When they crawled along a cylindrical tunnel that was only half a man tall, he was certain they must be under the bridge itself.

They emerged into darkness. He had never had the experience of trying to move across a city while avoiding patrolling soldiers; once again, his estimate of her abilities rose. Where had she learned these things?

Perhaps with the Horse Lords, he thought as he followed her evasive course around a pair of patrolling black coats. This was not precisely like the woman he had imagined—

But then, who said that she had to be? If she seemed a bit reckless, a little impulsive to him, well, in this case, it was all to the good. She would not have trusted him otherwise. If she had not been reckless and impulsive—assuming what she had told him about the threat to his life was true—she would not have saved him.

The trouble was, she could have manufactured the assassination attempt out of whole cloth, and the facts as he knew them would still have fit. It did not take a traitor to nail a presumed plague victim into his room—it only took someone who was afraid. And the bravest soldier in the army could be justifiably terrified of plague. So he still had his doubts, and many of them were deep ones.

Oddly enough, he actually regained muscle strength and control as they crossed the city, though he grew wearier. It took them a very long time to cross the city; it was false dawn when they finally reached the Temple.

Since it lacked only a little time before the earliest service, they were able to walk quite openly and decorously into the Temple itself. He had taken to wearing his ordinary hunting clothing rather than the uniforms of the empire when he had been exiled to the Summer Palace; he had not wanted to wear the uniform he was no longer certain he honored. Now that stood him in good stead, as he did not stand out from the thin crowd of worshipers in any way.

The service left him oddly comforted and calmed a few of his unsettled emotions. After the service, he followed Shelyra's example and went into the confessional she designated.

He emerged more than a little shaken. He had recognized the voice of the woman in the confessional; it was Archpriestess Verit. He would never forget that voice as long as he lived.

And he would never forget what she told him in the calm, dispassionate tone of one who has seen too much to be emotional about any of it.

She told him that, although she had no personal knowledge of an attempt to kill him, he could trust Shelyra to tell him the truth.

But that was not what had left him shaken to the core; it was what she had to say about his father's closest advisor and personal mage.

For Apolon was a necromancer; he had assumed that the Grey Mage had something to hide, but never had he thought it would be that!

There was no viler creature on the face of the earth than a necromancer. And everything that Shelyra had told him about the situation within his father's court was true; in fact, she had told him less than Verit did. The archpriestess was actually fairly certain that the emperor was not aware of Apolon's true activities and his source of power— but the fact still remained that the emperor had not bothered to find out.

He walked out of the Temple feeling as if the ground beneath him had suddenly become as transparent as air, as if the world had turned wrongways around and was still spinning. Shelyra took his arm as soon as he came out, which was just as well. He could not have found his way out of his own room at the moment.

"I'll take us somewhere we can rest," she said quietly.

All he could do was nod and let her lead him down the Temple steps, his mind a whirl of confusion.

❧ 53 ❧

APOLON

The storm had cleared away after three days of torrential downpour, giving way to four days of clear weather, which was all the time that Apolon needed to establish himself. Terror filled the House of the Boar, and in one large room in the cellars, the air reeked with the thick, metallic taint of blood. Apolon was in his element, and feeling quite well-satisfied. Finally, after so many things going wrong for him, the tide had turned in his favor. He had his stronghold, from which he could work without interference and in secrecy; Cathal was cooperating most satisfactorily. Now that Adelphus was a necromantic puppet, there was no more trouble from *that* quarter.

And very shortly, that inconvenient young fool Leopold would be out of the way as well. His agent had not yet reported by the time he had sealed himself in here to begin his work, but he was certain of success there. Life, on the whole, was good.

Now the Grey Mage was hard at work; the night was nearly over, and he had still not used up all of his prisoners. Half of them went to feed either the blood-demon that bound his new puppets' spirits to their bodies, or went to feed the entity residing in his staff. Human bodies and human blood alone would serve; neither was to be placated by animal blood. Those prisoners who were bled to feed either entity were useless as puppets afterward; both the blood-demon and the staff drew vitality from the body with the blood, which rendered it impossible to reanimate, though the spirit could still be bound to the corpse if he was quick enough. There was no reason to take that step, however, for a spirit bound to something that could neither move nor speak was fairly useless.

Although once he *had* served a particular enemy so, permitting the man to be found, apparently dead of heart failure afterward. He had taken great joy in attending the funeral, knowing as he did that the spirit was, for all intents and purposes, buried "alive," knowing what was happening to it and helpless to free itself.

The other half of his prisoners became puppets tonight, dying at his hands and sent off to replace the living and nonliving black coats who had fallen victim to the depredations of the locals. Most of those he had never recovered in any way; they had probably been dumped into canals and carried off to sea. What would happen to them, he was not certain; both salt water and running water did have the capacity to erode his spells after a time, and they might be freed of their bodies before sharks and other fish devoured them. He had released a few himself, when they had returned from patrols too damaged to serve any longer.

He was weary now, this close to dawn, and had saved those dregs of humanity that he was certain would be easy to subdue for the end of the night's work. They were criminals all, rather than terrified scum of the slums, or men who had been out after dark and had the misfortune of running into one of his patrols. The agents he had placed in Merina months before the invasion identified several choice specimens from the lot held in the cisterns. Most of them were so steeped in crime that it took very little to overcome their resistance; they were not interested in passing on to the next world, and one or two actually clung so determinedly to their bodies that the blood-demon had very little real work to do. Those made the best servants, when all was said and done. They retained a certain adroitness when it came to terrorizing the locals, as if they were still deriving pleasure from such behavior.

His last selection of the night should be the easiest: a thief and notorious profligate who called himself Thom Talesmith. From the stories about this man, he was probably a murderer as well, and certainly was so steeped in crime that he would work hand in hand with the blood-demon to remain earthbound.

He crossed his arms over his chest and took careful reckoning of the man as he was brought in, struggling and defiant still in the arms of two of Apolon's strongest puppets. He was a little surprised at the man's appearance; usually thieves with the reputation of one like this were rather scruffy and thoroughly hardened. This one was different. Handsome, young, he looked like any of the callow, innocent youths apprenticed to prosperous guildsmen—

For a moment, Apolon was overcome with an irrational anger, and his hands clenched involuntarily. If *he* had just possessed those advantages, he would never have needed to work, fight, and scratch his way to his current position—he could have used those callow good looks, could have seduced his way to power and wealth—

But he calmed himself quickly. If he had been handsome, he might well have taken the same easy path this lout had, relying on his looks to gull small-fry rather than using them to cozen bigger fish, and allowing his intellect to lie fallow. And in that case—he might well have found himself the prisoner of some other, cleverer fellow one day. He might have discovered himself awaiting the same fate as this Thom Talesmith.

Apolon always took the precaution of gagging prisoners who knew what was coming; they often shouted insults and imprecations and disturbed his concentration. Talesmith glared at him over the gag, but the human servants who saw to such details were adept at their business, and the best he could manage was a muffled grunt, an impotent snarl.

Doubtless, the fool expected Apolon to pontificate on the situation, outline in great detail the dreadful fate that awaited him, and explain what had driven the Grey Mage to such steps. He might even be expecting Apolon to boast about his current plans.

All of which would take an enormous amount of time—and was dreadfully inefficient. Apolon was nothing if not efficient.

"You'll understand everything shortly," Apolon said coolly, and took the ceremonial dagger from his sleeve, plunging it straight into the heart in a stroke calculated to kill quickly, but not so quickly that the blood-demon would not have time to act.

There was very little blood; with all the practice he'd had, Apolon was quite expert at killing without spilling much blood. He wanted the least amount of damage possible in his puppets; that made a great deal less that he would have to repair. He flung the special blood-dyed net over the body as it sagged in the hands of his puppets.

The puppets allowed the body to drop to the ground as the third puppet fed the blood-demon with blood taken from the prisoner before the thief, then all of them stepped away in a choreography so well-rehearsed he no longer had to give them orders. The thief's eyes were just beginning to glaze over, and the last breath rattled in his throat. The timing, as usual, was perfect.

Apolon raised his hands and his power, summoned the attention of the blood-demon from its feast, and pointed at the trapped spirit and body. "Bind," he told the blood-spirit.

And that was when his carefully laid plans fell apart.

Before the blood-demon could even begin to act, the trapped spirit of the thief rose up in the net and began to tear at the delicate weft of magic. Its struggles were very real, and far, far stronger than anyone Apolon had ever tried to bind before!

Apolon rocked back on his heels for a moment; never *once,* in all of the time he had used prisoners to make his puppets, had any of them tried to fight the binding with this kind of fierce determination! What kind of a man had this been?

He flung his own magic into the weft quickly, feeling the power drain from him as if he had an open, gaping wound. He turned his will on the spirit and strove to compel it; it threw off his compulsions as if it was shrugging away an unwanted hand on its shoulder and attacked the web holding it with renewed vigor and desperation.

He redoubled his efforts. *Still* the spirit fought him— and as the blood-demon moved in, powers and ethereal claws at the ready, it turned its attention away from the net and attacked the blood-demon directly!

The blood-spirit recoiled from the ferocity of the attack and tried to flee—and the spirit in the staff roused to sluggish interest.

For the first time in twenty years, panic rose in Apolon's dark soul, panic that reached up and grabbed him by the throat, that leapt upon him and held him in cold claws. If the blood-demon escaped his control, it would turn on *him,* and the entity in the staff might take advantage of the situation—

No, the entity in the staff *would* take advantage of the situation! His alliance with it was tenuous at best and based on his apparent power. If it perceived that he was losing power, it would move to attack him in concert with the blood-demon. And while the blood-demon alone could not harm him, the thing in the staff most certainly could!

Swiftly, he drew his ceremonial dagger and slashed his own arm, feeding the demon his own blood to placate and strengthen it.

With renewed power, the blood-demon returned to its attack on the struggling spirit. Apolon took advantage of the spirit's distraction to snatch up a potion and drink it to the dregs. He would pay for this—but not until after the spirit was subdued. He dared not release it now, not with the entity in the staff watching. He dared do nothing that smacked of weakness.

In a moment, the drugs in the potion released a rush of energy and power, and he now saw the auras of power that he could not with his own unenhanced senses. The spirit was a white light, flaring unevenly against the sickly green of the demon. He himself radiated a kind of blackness; if there could have been such a thing as a black fire, he would have been ablaze with it. He focused those energies on the spirit, intent on subduing it, no matter what the cost to himself.

In the end, it came to will against will, and it took a second potion for Apolon to win the struggle.

While the potion was still in effect, he bound the spirit into the body and set his spells to make it forget what it had been and obey only him once he issued his first verbal commands. The blood-demon he dismissed, satisfied and sated, and the entity in the staff lost interest in him, subsiding back to a steady, gluttonous drinking of the blood he had supplied it.

What had given this unlikely man the power to resist so strongly? He would never have expected Thom Talesmith, thief, lecher, debaucher of women, to be *pious!* Yet that was the only explanation that came to Apolon's exhausted mind as he bound up the wound in his arm and left his chamber of blood-magics.

The thief must have been—impossible as it sounded—
a good man, and a faithful child of his Goddess. He could
not have been saintly, or he would have merited otherworldly aid—but he was good enough that without Apolon's many resources outside his own powers, the Grey
Mage would never have been able to conquer him.

With one hand on the wall to augment his fast-fading
strength, Apolon hurried to his new bedchamber, which
was well-shielded with every protective magic he knew.
Tonight—or rather, this morning—he would need all of
them. He was utterly and completely at the end of his own
strength, and if anything made an attempt on him, he
would not be able to hold it off outside that protected
chamber.

Fortuitously, he had chosen a room not that far away;
he made it into safety before the last dregs of the potion
wore off, and literally fell onto his bed, fully clothed, consciousness fading with the effect of the drugs.

The four puppets left in the chamber of blood-magics
had been given no orders before their master fled the
place. For three of them, this was nothing to trouble their
dim and spell-fogged thoughts. Their master had left them
without orders before, and probably would again. And in
that particular case, their *standing* order was to remain
where they were until he returned.

But the fourth had been given no orders whatsoever,
standing or otherwise. In fact, he had not even been given
orders to obey.

So he would obey the last person he had pledged his
loyalty to.

He rose from the floor where he had fallen and stood
in the middle of the room. If there had been anyone there
to watch him, the observer would have seen the puppet's
brow crease faintly as it struggled to understand what had
happened to it through a fog of spells and compulsions.

There was something it had to do.

It took a tentative step toward the door and dimly felt

a sense of rightness. It took another, and another, and
followed the impulse out of the door and down the hall.
It had been clothed in the garb of a black coat before it
had been taken to the Grey Mage's chamber, so neither
the human servants nor the other puppets paid any attention to it. If it moved, it must be on the master's orders.
That was how it had always been; there was no reason to
suspect a change now.

There was someone it had to—

Had to—what? It fought to discover what it was it
needed to do as it walked out of the House of the Boar
and onto the front steps, into the thin, gray light of an
overcast day. What was it that it needed to do?

There was someone it had to warn!

Again, it felt that sense of rightness.

It stood on the steps of the House of the Boar for a long
moment, then, following a vague sense of proper direction,
turned to the south.

That felt right. Whoever had to be warned must be in
that direction.

It began to walk. It would know who it needed to warn
when it got there. It would know when it had gotten to
the right place when the place felt right.

It noticed that there were many creatures garbed the
same way it was now, all going in the same direction.
Lacking any other clue, it followed them. At length, as the
light strengthened, it came to a large building.

Temple, said a memory, and something about the building made the puppet want to enter it.

Badly.

It was in pain, dim and distant, but the pain went further than the body and it cut more surely than any knife.
The pain would stop if it got into the Temple.

But when the puppet tried, it found that it could not even
climb the steps. Something stopped it in its tracks; it tried to
move forward and couldn't. The pain increased as it tried to
move, and it knew that it was being denied something important, although it did not recall what that thing was.

Frustrated, it turned away—just in time to see a thin stream of people dressed differently from its fellow puppets leaving the Temple.

And among them was one it recognized, along with one it did not. It ignored the second, but the first was important—

In fact, the first was the one it *wanted!*

It started to walk, clumsily but quickly, toward them.

❧ 54 ❧

LYDANA

Matild came blearily out of sleep, feeling the dullness of one who has been reduced to the depth of exhaustion. Blinking up into the dusk above her, she felt confusion, that somehow her whole world had been turned awry. Then memory sparked in her mind like a snapfire.

Turning her head on a very lumpy support, she saw Eel beside her with an aura of being wrapped in unending patience. Meeting Matild's now open eyes, he smiled.

"Hungry?"

The word might be a key turned to loose the aching in her.

"Yes!" She did not try as yet to sit up, but from where she lay, she looked toward the other pallet where Saxon had lain. It was empty. In the ill-lit loft, she was aware of constant coming and going, of talk kept to hardly above a whisper.

Eel was back as quick as he had gone to drop cross-legged beside her with a cracked plate in one small hand

and a battered tankard in the other. Matild's nose wrinkled at the strong odor of fish.

Her servitor grinned. "There is a smidgen of bread also—been saving it for you. But now we live mainly on fish—"

At last Matild pulled herself up to take the plate. There were no utensils, and she decided that here one used one's fingers. She prodded the fish, flaking off some, and scooped those bits up with the edge of the hard circle she recognized as ship's bread. A hasty gulp of some very sour drink she could not put name to washed it down.

"The captain?"

"Out and about with the best of them. He and Jonas have been heads together for a good time and there has been a deal of coming and going since. We lie snug here—so far—"

Was there a shade of doubt in that?

"What happened in the city?" Surely the escape of Saxon had set some pots well to boil.

"Well," Eel squirmed a little as if in search of the most comfortable position. "The storm hit hard—as hard as the old one, which reached the temple square before. It kept the streets swept from any search parties for two days or more—"

"Two days! How long have we been here?"

"Some six days in all, perhaps more—hard to tell time when there is no daylight. You were busy with the captain during most of the first few."

Six days or more! She had been lifted out of action for that long—any disaster might have struck—

"You cannot hold off all of them." Again Eel caught her thoughts. "The black coats are out again and with them some soldiers—though they do not seem to work very well together. The young prince, now—one would take him to have some true thought for the city to have trained his own troops so well. His own men have been trying to aid where they could. Though aid from such is a chancy thing."

"Apolon—Cathal—"

"The mage has his black coats thick about the Temple walls, although as yet he does nothing. The general—he has by latest note gone back to the camp, probably to report to the emperor. He certainly has taken no visible interest in what has happened in the city."

There was a stir at the farther side of the loft and a party of their riffraff army came crowding in on the heels of two men walking together. Saxon was wearing light battle armor such as the seamen favored, and there was a dented breastplate spanning Jonas' broad chest, a bowl helm covering most of his balding head.

Saxon's eyes caught her in a side glance and he left his companions to come straight toward her.

"How is it with you, my lady?"

She looked up into his face, where the signs of that cruel battering were very faint now.

"How is it with *you*?" she countered. He moved easily, seemed alert and ready, as if he had never lain under her hands, eaten by fever and prisoned in pain.

"Well." He held out his hand, and without thinking she reached to grasp it, so he drew her to her feet and brought her over to the table, where one side bench and most of the stools were already taken, leading her to a place left beside Jonas where they both could sit together.

Jonas was already fingering his bunch of note-strings. "They brought in at least twenty more afore the storm was blown out. Lost 'em some hoodcrows doin' it—which is all to the good," his voice boomed. "We think as they have at least three of the big freighters crowded now. 'Course there were a good part of the fleet smashed up, but the fishers of the outer banks send word as how there is a fleet movin' in."

"The emperor's," Saxon stated rather than questioned. Then he said swiftly to Matild, "They have been bringing in men from the city, packing them into our own craft— the largest and stoutest ones—for what purpose we do not yet know. Perhaps this fleet comes to take them off—"

"Not many real soldiers," Jonas broke in. "Mostly hood-crows and some of them mercenaries as follows Cathal. There's a new story going round about him—thought you'd best hear it firsthand, Cap'n."

He turned his head a little. "Have him up with you, boys!"

Four of the water rats surrounded their prisoner so closely that Matild could not catch a true sight of him until they shoved him into the double-lantern light at this end of the table.

He looked almost as battered as Saxon had been, but he kept his feet, though he stumbled. His helm was gone and so was his mail and weapons, while across his shoulder, showing above the edge of his leather quilted jerkin, was the end of a bloody weal. He stared at their company and there was no hope in his eyes.

But—Matild stirred—he was hardly more than a boy! Though it would appear he was one of the mercenaries.

"We caught this one here," a man with a hook for hand, whom she remembered dimly having seen before, spoke like a squadsman giving a report, "in a skiff upaways. He says as how he ain't no man of Balthasar's anymore."

There was a flush on the young man's face as Saxon studied him.

"What brought on this conversion?" Saxon asked.

"He—he had Quin flogged to the bone! Potton as won the emperor's own Eagle for bravery—he—had the eyes out of his head and more—" He bit his lower lip and Matild saw drops of blood gather there. "I—" The flush had turned to a greenish pallor and he suddenly retched, his captors swinging him away from the table just in time.

"Give him a drink," ordered Saxon.

The mercenary was shaking. His captors stood a little away from him. Matild had seen men brought to dire straits, but this sickness was one, she recognized, of horror and despair.

"Who did this?" Saxon asked quietly after the man had had a flagon lifted to his lips, his arms being bound tightly behind him, and had taken several gulps. He was manifestly fighting for control.

"The general—Cathal. He's—he's gone mad. Picks out a man for no reason and brings his pet tormentors in to work on him."

"The emperor allows this?" Saxon continued in the same quiet tone of voice.

"The emperor—he don't know—or maybe care," exploded the prisoner. " 'Tis those black coats as are close to him these days—they and that mage! But Cathal—he's tormenting innocent men for no reason—like he's gone mad!"

"So, comrades of yours being so taken, you would be off?" Saxon nodded. "Well, I think for that no man can blame you. But Cathal keeps to his camp?"

"So far, yes. There's the emperor's guard—they don't take orders from him—but they have the hoodcrows to keep 'em away from the emperor hisself. The prince now, he's a decent fighting man, always treated his men right—stood up for them. But they all say—" He seemed very eager to talk now and Matild wondered if that flowed from a desire to please his captors, or the fierce hatred of his general. "They say as how the emperor, he keeps the prince away from him, and took his command also. Though no one can tell why—'less it is more of that mage's meddling."

"Tell me one thing, if you know it, armsman: What does the emperor plan to do with those men he seized out of this city and sent to be prisoned in the port ships?" Saxon leaned a little forward, his gaze holding the other's fast.

The young man shook his head. "We was told nothing about them, sir. That is some more of the black coats' work." Suddenly he shivered as if he had been enwrapped in a full blast of winter air. "That—Apolon—he has his servants and his men—we do not mix with them, nor does he ever try to take order over us. It's—it's like they is another kind of man entirely. Go in their camp place—there's no sittin' around the fire talkin' at night. They don't drink even when the victory bottles are passed after a battle—it's like they're not true men at all."

Dead men walking, thought Matild.

"And they are in charge of these prisoners?"

"As far as I know, sir."

"Lady," Saxon swung around to her, "you have that which can tell the truth or falseness of a man's speech—"

She raised her hand to her breast; under her fingers the concealed stones warmed. But she had never thought of using them in this way—why had Saxon? However, in that moment, she knew that his confidence in her tokens was correct.

She loosened the brooch and rested it on her flattened palm, covering that brand of the Heart which had bound her to a service she did not yet even partly understand.

"Swear you by the Heart?" She held the stones up, Jonas and Saxon pulling back a little so there was no one between them.

He did not even look down at what she held, rather his eyes were on her. Then, in a very low voice he answered: "Lady, who you may be I do not know, but—but there is that in you which cannot be denied. You seek truth, I give it. Yes, I swear that what I have said is the truth as I know it."

At Saxon's order they rid him of his bonds, and he was sent to a pallet in one of the loft corners while they were left to comment on what he said.

"Cathal has always been a man of blood, and one who delights in terror," Matild said. Then a thought struck through her and she knew a sharp sense of guilt. He was a monster, by all the war tales which had come to Merina in the past, but now he had in his possession a gem of evil so potent that its dark past was shunned by any normal human. Was that stone at work, building up Cathal's native-born cruelty into something worse? If so, that was her burden to bear. She closed her hand tightly on the brooch.

If I have sinned in this, she did not speak aloud, but her thoughts were clear and sharp, *then let me carry the sin. Turn it not against others who have done no wrong.* She half-expected the ruby to flare, perhaps even burn to a crisp the flesh surrounding it, but it did not. There was only a glow of comforting warmth, a rise of energy, a feeling that what she had done was part of an ordained pattern.

"We strike for the prison ships," Saxon was saying, and she heard a growling assent from those about her.

§ 55 §

LEOPOLD

Everything I believed about my father's honor was a lie. That was the single thought which ruptured the fundament of Leopold's world. *He may not officially know about Apolon—but he has willfully turned a blind eye to suspicions. He does know about Cathal, and he condones what his general does. He lives by expediency. Honor and truth are nothing more than words to him.*

He and Shelyra had not gotten much beyond the steps of the Temple when, despite his dazed and confused state of mind, his nerves shrilled a sudden alert.

This broke through his confusion; he had been a soldier long enough to heed his instincts immediately. A crisis of conscience could wait until he had security and leisure.

He took a covert glance around the square in front of the Temple, without making it obvious that he was doing so. It didn't take a scholar to know why his nerves were afire, once he paid attention to his surroundings. The area around the Temple was surrounded by Apolon's black coats, although there had been no sign of them when he and Shelyra arrived; they must have moved in during the holy service. Some of them were partially concealed, lurking around corners or peering from windows; others stood about openly and brazenly, as if daring the Temple authorities to challenge them.

And one lumbered toward them his gait curiously stiff and clumsy, as if he had been drugged, or had been sitting in one place so long that his legs had fallen asleep—

There was something else odd about this man; perhaps his own brush with death had made Leopold more sensitive to such things—but as the prince studied him, something strange came into focus about him. There seemed to be a shadow over the black coat, a dark, cobwebby miasma enshrouding him and obscuring his face.

The prince shook his head a little and rubbed his eyes, but the darkness remained, and what was more, it made him a little sick to look at it directly. And when he turned to look closely at one of the other black coats, he was astonished to see that same, shadowy darkness hovering over them all. Yet there was no such shadow enveloping the ordinary townsfolk, or even the imperial soldier or two he spotted.

Before he could say anything, Shelyra stepped forward to meet the black coat, her face blank with shock. "Thom?" she whispered. "What happened? What's wrong with you? Why are you—?"

Beneath the shadow, the man might have been handsome; he was blond and boyish, with the innocent good looks of a hero in a tale. The black coat tried to reply: his mouth writhed, his face working with strain, as if he was fighting some inner compulsion. And Leopold, watching him with the curious double sight, saw the web of shadow over him moving to further obscure his face, particularly his mouth.

Finally, after an interminable and agonizing moment of

struggle, the black coat managed to get out three words in answer to Shelyra's questions. "Warn—" he gasped harshly. "Warn—you—"

"Warn me?" Shelyra asked, shaking her head in perplexity. Leopold did not know what to make of her—was he the only one to see these sinister shadows? Or were the shadows nothing more than hallucinations? But if they were—why did he feel such fear when he looked on them? The longer he looked, the more his soul chilled, yet Shelyra appeared to see and feel nothing. "Warn me about what? Who?"

The black coat moved in closer, then stopped, swaying where he stood, his face contorted as he tried to fight whatever compulsion held him. "Warn—" he said again, and the darkness swarmed up and completely covered his head and shoulders, making him gasp. "Apolon—"

What horrible evil thing could be doing this? How could Apolon take such control over someone— Suddenly, a flash of intuition illuminated everything and made him sick to his stomach. Leopold seized Shelyra's arm and pulled her close so he could speak directly into her ear. "He's one of *them*!" he hissed urgently. "Don't you understand? Look at him! He's hardly breathing! Touch him, and his flesh will be as cold as canal water! Whatever he was the last time you saw him, he's *dead* now! Apolon killed him, that's what he's trying to warn you about!"

Shelyra whirled to stare, first at him, then at the black coat, and her face went dead white. Her lips twitched, and she held a hand up to her mouth as if to restrain sudden illness. "Oh, Goddess—" she whispered around her hand. "No—"

Leopold nodded grimly; he did not bother to explain the shadow he saw over the black coat's face. "Does he *sound* like the man you know?" he replied. "Does he look and act normal to you? How long has he been missing?"

"Long enough," she said numbly, and reached out to

gingerly touch the back of the man's hand. The speed with which she snatched it away told Leopold that his guess was right; the man's flesh was as cold as a frog's. He was dead-alive, a necromantic slave to his Master Apolon. How he had freed himself enough to warn them was a puzzle Leopold would probably never know the answer to, being no mage. The important thing was that he had, and that he had come to Shelyra.

She shook her head numbly. "What are we going to do?" she said, her voice full of distress and rising slightly above a whisper. She was talking to Leopold, who had to shake his head at her. He was no mage; how could he know what to do?

Her whisper was loud enough that the—creature—heard her and reacted to what he heard. His face contorted again, this time with a look of despair. He reached out with a clumsy, imploring hand.

"Free—me—" he gasped, and a single tear oozed from one eye and slowly rolled down his cheek.

That was more than enough for Leopold. This thing might be a necromantic puppet, but there was a human soul still trapped within it; he knew that with his heart, although he had no rational reason to make any such judgment.

"Free you?" Shelyra said to the creature. "Thom, what do you mean? How can we free you?" A faint light of hope touched her face. "Are you—is this just a spell, are you just under some sort of enchantment? If we free you will you come back to being yourself again?"

Leopold did not bother to explain what he *thought* the black coat meant; explanations could wait until later, when they were not standing in full view of twenty or thirty more black coats.

He wants us to free his soul from his body, to free him from bondage to Apolon. There are only a few people I know who could do that, and they're all in the building behind us!

"We have to get him into the Temple," he said in his firmest command voice. "But not openly—"

As he had hoped, she responded positively to the voice of command; she lost the panicked look and nodded. "Take his arm—I'll take the other one," she said. "I know a way in."

He seized the creature's right arm and she took its left, as if they were all the greatest of friends. They towed it along, as Shelyra chatted with the creature as if they were carrying on a conversation.

"Look as if we'd just realized he's a long-lost relative," she whispered to Leopold, under cover of her chatter. "I have to get him in the general direction of the palace."

He nodded and followed her lead. She knew where she was going—probably to find another one of those secret passages of hers. That was all to the good, for he was certain that not all of Apolon's black-coated servants were necromantic puppets, and the sooner they all got out of sight, the less likely it would be for one that was still human to think twice about a black coat with a pair of Merinan friends.

He hoped. At the moment, that was all any of them had to go on. Hope—and the Blessing of the Heart.

⚜ 56 ⚜

LYDANA

It seemed to Matild that they had spent all their time the past few days in conferences. A sudden memory made her interrupt the current conference for the first time since they had all sat down: "These black coats bear a powerful weapon—" Swiftly she sketched for them her meeting with the man who had turned that rod against her, to his own undoing.

Saxon rubbed his jaw with his hand. "A rod which spits power—" he mused. "Yet it could not touch you, lady. What was your defense?"

Regretfully she shook her head. "One which is mine alone, I fear." She brought forth the brooch and held it in the full light so they could see it.

"This," she held one side up, "is the seal of Merina— that which was surrendered was a far different stone." But she was not going to go into particulars about her own armory of crystalized evil. "And this," she flipped the brooch over, and there was a crimson radiance which seemed to puff upward. "You have heard of what happened in the Temple when the Reverend One lay in state. The Heart wept; this tear fell to me without my striving to take it."

Both Saxon and Jonas leaned forward, and she saw a faint reflection of the glow touch their faces.

"This—" Saxon said slowly, "this you used to heal me—is that not so?" he demanded of her almost fiercely.

Matild nodded. "It is a focus. How far its powers may stretch I have no idea."

His thought was quick. "Does it link you with the Temple?"

The ruby flamed up more brightly as if in answer to his question. Of course, her thought ran with his—it was of the Heart. Though loosened from it, still it would be tied in its own way, but she was not sure.

"I can only try."

Once more she cupped it in her palm. Almost she hesitated to make such an effort.

"But the Reverend One is not dead," Jonas said then, twisting his note-strings around and round in his fleshy fingers. Then he put forth one of those fingers, stabbed it into a drop of ale and, reaching forward a little, drew a very faint symbol on the table before Matild.

Perhaps he had already known—but she was sure that this man did not know the meaning of betrayal any more than Saxon.

"Yes," she said boldly, though her voice was low enough to be a whisper beyond the three of them, "it is my right." And she tapped a nail against the seal portion of the brooch.

He grinned at her. "They say as how the Tiger rules where he walks—or she walks. I say that Merina is not without protectors. What would you have of us, lady?"

She shook her head. "I am no war leader; what I can bring I will, but do not be mistaken—this Apolon is such as we have not thought to face. As for the planning—that I leave to my lord Captain, and to you and your liege men."

So she sat and listened as they planned. And it seemed to her that while they might be on the edge of a lost cause, yet they were such men as could wrangle victory out of the very jaws of defeat. It was only when they came to the final marshaling of individual duties and operations that she interrupted.

"In this I have a place, also." She tapped the brooch she had left lying on the table directly before her. "Do you deny that?"

"You—being what you are—" Saxon said slowly, his jaw firm set, "know what a prize you would be to this Apolon. Do we throw treasures at the enemies' feet and beg them to take them?"

Matild laughed. "My lord Captain, for years what men deem treasures have spilled through my hands. For their beauty I admired them, for their value I care little. Now, I have no beauty, but I may have more value—to you— than you know.

"Jonas," she turned to the taverner, "is there somewhere within this warren that I can be private for a while?" Now she did pick up the brooch and return it to its hiding place.

"There be the office of the checker—" he answered. " 'Tis much of a dumping place now and certainly not to be a place of comfort, but it is yours."

"Show me." Suddenly she had that feeling of need, as if she were on the edge of some action and must be readied for it. "Eel." She summoned the small figure close to her.

Saxon was frowning. "What would you do?" he demanded.

Again a new laughter bubbled in her. "Lord Captain, you have your mysteries, leave me mine. I will do nothing which will take me out of this safe room of Jonas', but it may be of value to us."

He was still frowning after her as she followed Jonas stumping across the wide warehouse loft, Eel pattering to match stride with her. The office was indeed a musty, cramped space and there were the remains of boxes and barrels which had been there so long that they were moldering to the stouter floor.

Matild chose a box, thumped it vigorously to make sure it would not collapse under her, and then sat down. She waved Jonas out, their only light being a candle Eel had brought along.

Talent—what was the Talent? No one through the years

had defined it. Rather, those who did not have it regarded it with awe; those who did never spoke of how they used it. She had not come to the years of Talent, but perhaps some other grace would be afforded her as so many had already. She spread open her hand, looking down at the Heart brand—it had so tied her for all time to its service.

Now she picked up the brooch. Her eyes closed, she was not inducing any trance; such was beyond her training and power. But her mental image of Adele began to form solidly, true even to the sometimes faraway look in her mother's eyes.

Adele—whose eyes widened suddenly and looked into hers as if they had indeed crossed the length of the city and sat knee to knee in this forgotten room.

"We move," her mind shaped the words. "We of the waterways. There is a need for haste."

She watched Adele's straight gaze probe even more sharply.

"There comes soon an ending—" The words seemed very faint and faraway. Then suddenly between them arose a dark shape like the curved side of a globe. And beyond that curve swirled a nauseous yellow-green like the slime given off by rotting fungi.

Instantly Matild broke concentration. Apolon—he had set guards or probes against the very thing she had tried to do!

"Lady." Eel's hold was on her, shaking her urgently. Matild nodded.

"Perhaps I chose ill, if that one has his ways of following thought. But I did not see *him*, and therefore he may only have suspicions."

Yet that was enough for her to return to warn Jonas and Saxon, only to find them and much of the company gone. She had thought that they would certainly have waited for her, and she knew a flare of anger. Was she to be so used—cut off from their venture?

It was as she paced angrily across the loft that she caught sight of the woman with whom she had shared her vigil over Saxon—she whom they called the Bark Hag. She was sitting placidly on a stool, her ever-present basket beside her, sipping from a bowl she held two-handed. On impulse Matild joined her.

The near wrinkle-hidden eyes met hers. Smacking her lips, the Hag held out the bowl to Eel. "Get me another good dollop of that, youngling. It warms old bones that ache from the water-cold."

As Eel obeyed without question, the Hag waved Matild to another stool. In a moment Eel was back, but the Hag ignored the bowl.

"Now—what lies in your mind, you who are not what you seem?" Her question carried a snap.

Matild studied the woman silently before she answered. As before, she was aware of the aura of power about this age-bent body. Involuntarily she raised her hand and sketched the Heart Blessing between them.

The woman gave a cackling laugh. "Fair greetings from the young to the old, is that it, lady? Well, you have the right of it. She who is Heart to you wears another seeming to me, but They are one and the same—though She was all mine in bearing in earlier days. You have been using the seeing—and you have had a fright—"

"You have heard of Apolon?" Matild was feeling her way. Her confidence in the Hag was growing stronger.

The woman's wrinkle-edged lips twisted in a grimace. "There will always be those twisted-witted ones who delve into matters they cannot begin to understand. Why, of Apolon I have heard and also of Iktcar, and before him—the Dark has its sons even as She has her daughters. Never is the scale even in this world. Sometimes it inclines one way and sometimes another. So—you know of Apolon—what knows he of you?"

Matild met that with the truth. "I cannot tell. Save—" Swiftly she told of her effort to reach Adele and of that barrier which had arisen between them. The Bark Hag nodded.

She reached down into that basket and rummaged,

bringing forth a handful of what looked like slender twigs, bound together with a silver cord which she swiftly loosened. None of them were longer than Matild's middle finger, and they seemed to wear the sheen of great age and much handling.

The Hag twisted them together between her palms, those eyes were now hidden by wrinkled lids. Matild saw her lips move, but could not hear any words. Then, with a quick turn of the wrist, the Hag threw her handful to the floor.

They did not scatter as Matild expected, rather they fell in a distinct pattern, and the longer she looked down at it the clearer it became. There was what could be the suggestion of a skiff, in it two stick figures upright. Fanning out from that rude representation of a boat were three thicker twigs, not unlike spears, aiming forward.

The Hag nodded. "So be it. You are called—by the ancient oaths your blood swore long ago. Men fight with steel and arrow—for those She favors there are other ways. Go you as you have sworn to yourself that you will—after the fighters. There will be that for you to do which is mightier than any sword stroke that great captain of yours can wield."

Matild swept her tongue across her lips. "Power draws power—the black coats already swarm at the harbor. If I call upon"—her hand flattened at her breast over the brooch—"Apolon can trace it—and me—and so be aware of Saxon and his men."

The Hag cackled. "Laws, what do they teach you younglings these days? Are all the old truths so much forgotten? Running water—running water, my lady—think of running water!"

Matild frowned; for a moment or two she could make no sense of that. Then a scrap of knowledge—such knowledge as had been largely pushed aside by the sages of the Temple—became clear.

"Evil cannot cross—" she said.

"Gather your wits, would-be savior." The Hag laughed

again. "Use what you have and take the old precautions. Now," she turned again to her basket, "let that youngling of yours bring a stoup of hot water—there is a kettle on the hob." She nodded toward the corner, where the fire was built on a brick hearth. "Bring also one of the flasks hanging there." Now she indicated a line of leathern bottles swinging from nails. "Rinse it twice, youngling, in the hottest of water, before you bring me it along with a stoup of the fresh."

She seemed to draw in upon herself as Eel sped to act on her bidding, her attention passing from Matild once more as if she were looking inward and not outward. Then Eel was back with a damp leather bottle and the stoup of steaming water.

Taking the bottle, the old woman sniffed at its interior and then seemed satisfied. Once more her basket yielded up something, this time a packet like a small linen bag. She bent over with a grunt, as if aching bones protested, and shifted a dustlike powder into the water of the stoup.

Picking up the container, she swished it slowly back and forth. Matild sniffed. Herbs, she thought, but a mixture she had never scented before. She drew a deeper breath as the steam from the stoup twirled in her direction.

This—this smelled like a fair morn in the country before the city gates—a spring morn with the perfume of flowers light on the air.

Carefully the Hag poured the mixture into the bottle. There was a little left in the stoup after she had corked the larger container. This she offered to Matild.

"Drink deep, both you and the youngling here. You will need to keep sleep at a distance in the hours to come— to hold full strength for what you would do. Drink and be sure that strength will be given you."

Matild had no hesitation in drinking; she knew well that if she were to follow Saxon's small army of misfits she must be awake. But she was careful to leave half the contents for Eel.

"Of Her bounty," the Hag said. "Your mighty thinkers

of the Temple—those who met with Her in the first groves could teach them a thing or two." Again she laughed.

"Well," said Matild slowly, "do I believe that, Reverend One." She did not hesitate to give that honor to this bundle of a woman in a patched robe.

"Reverend One—ha—they wouldn't call me that in that fine Temple of yours. Best give me the name I went by in my own time and place. I am the Hag—and none can rob me of that, for She Herself chose me."

The old triune! Matild was startled—Maid, Matron, Hag—She who was truly three in one and once had Her servants for each persona. The Hag held the accumulated knowledge of a lifetime; she could cure or kill, but only as it was laid upon her by the Greatest Power to do.

"Thanks are but words," Matild answered, "but feelings are heart-held. If She has chosen you to show me the way, I tread it—even to the Great Gate."

The Hag grinned. "Aye, a strong-willed one you are, but trust not too much in your own strength. You go to face that which stands against all light and life. There are many futures—those who swear they can foresee may, by chance, pick on one and swear it true. This much I tell you, queen that was: queen you may be again, but your fate is now tight-twisted with another, and you may never follow the trails the Tiger has always known. Rather you shall set fresh paths—though what may come of that, who knows?" She shrugged.

"I will take what comes, knowing that I am but one gem in a great setting—perhaps the least gleaming of them all." The younger woman hesitated. "You have given me much—what can I return?"

The Hag caught her eye to eye again. "Just this, Queen Lydana: do not forget the old when comes the new—there is virtue in them both. Now along with you. There is a battle to come, and it is yours as well as theirs."

✂ 57 ✂
ADELE

Elfrida and Fidelis sat in silence in the meditation chamber, waiting for Verit and Cosima to join them after the midnight ritual. She could not speak for her companion, but her stomach was in knots and she clasped her hands in her lap to still their trembling. After what they had seen in the glass the previous night, none of them could have the slightest doubt that Apolon was practicing necromancy—if any of them had held such doubts before. The House of the Boar now resembled nothing so much as a slaughterhouse. She was not looking forward to invoking the power of the glass this time.

"How many has he killed thus far?" Elfrida wondered aloud, not because she really wanted to know the answer, but because she could no longer bear the tense silence.

"Who's counting?" Fidelis asked. *He* sounded calm enough; she wondered how he managed.

She twisted her hands together. "I suspect he is," she said slowly, reluctant to voice her suspicion, but even more reluctant to leave it unsaid. She *might* be the only one to whom it had occurred. "I think he's working toward some goal we don't know about yet."

"Any idea what?" Cosima slipped into the room, with Verit a few paces behind her. Both of them collapsed onto the nearest bench, clearly wearied. Both of them looked as grim as Elfrida felt.

"No." Elfrida shook her head. "I wish I did. It's just a feeling; I don't know enough about necromancy to make an educated guess. All I can say is that there's something about that staff of his that bothers me."

"Other than the fact that he soaks it in blood?" Verit asked, her lips twisting in an expression of pain and disgust. "I can't imagine why he'd be doing that."

"It soaks up more blood than any wood I've ever seen," Fidelis replied slowly, his brows knitting in thought.

"That's what bothers me," Elfrida said, pummeling her memory for further clues and cursing the uncertainty that came with age. "I keep thinking I should know what that means—it's in one of my books from the Summer Palace, I think, but I haven't found the relevant passage yet."

"Do we have to watch him again tonight?" Cosima asked, her voice strained and profoundly unhappy. Elfrida did not blame her. It must be hard for a healer to watch so many deaths and be able to do nothing about them.

"We'll just take a quick look to be sure he's not doing something else," Verit said, patting her hand consolingly, "and then there are things we need to discuss."

They gathered wearily around the glass on the floor and took hands. It was the work of only a few minutes to see that Apolon was making more of the walking dead—and that he had enough prisoners to keep him busy until dawn, or after. Elfrida was nauseated by the vision, and she wasn't the only one; Cosima pressed her lips together tightly, looking decidedly green.

"So," Verit said after they had dismissed the vision. "*We* know what he's doing. How do we prove it to others?"

That seemed an odd question. "To whom do we wish to prove it?" Elfrida asked with a lifted eyebrow. "And why would it matter? The emperor may well know and not care, and he doesn't come here now in any case. Prince Leopold will be lucky if he lives through the year, given how things are going. Cathal would probably help Apolon kill, if asked. There's no one else—is there?"

"We need to prove it to our orders," Verit said. "We need to be united for what is to come. Division makes us easy prey, and we are quite divided—in spite of the fact that we've moved almost everyone into this building. Remember what you yourself told me about the orders being heart-whole." Her face was set and stern. "I believe you are right, Elfrida; we are about to face the final confrontation. We must stand together seamlessly and without a flaw in our faith."

Sober faces all around, and nods, proved that the others agreed with Verit's conclusion.

"Could we bring one of the black coats in and demonstrate to everyone what it is?" Cosima asked faintly. Her lips were white.

Verit shrugged.

"It's an idea," Fidelis agreed, "but there are several problems. First, not all the black coats are dead. Second, how would we get one? I don't think we can just walk out into the street and invite one inside, and I'd rather not try to grab one to force him in."

"We could try, if we were desperate," Verit said, "but frankly, the chances that we'd be killed in the process are high. If it was a last resort—but I don't believe we are at that point yet."

Yet. "None of the black coats has ever entered the Temple," Elfrida reminded them. "I don't know if this is because they don't wish to or because they physically can't."

"Do you think they'd dissolve into dust or something of the sort if they did?" Cosima asked doubtfully. She shook her head in bafflement. Elfrida didn't blame her. This all had an air of unreality about it—suddenly, with no warning, they had found themselves facing something out of tales and legends. But if this had been a legend, there would be heroes with magic swords waiting in the wings to save the day—

Unfortunately, unless Fidelis developed the prowess of a warrior thirty years his junior, they had no heroes waiting about. And the only magic sword in the city was in the hands of the enemy.

"I don't know," Elfrida said, feeling her spirits plummet.

"I don't know what they can and cannot do, and I don't remember anything in any of the books about them. I wish we knew more about them."

"Lady Bright, Elfrida, we know how to make them!" Fidelis protested incredulously. "Isn't that enough?"

Elfrida shook her head. "Not really. We know how Apolon makes them in a general way, but we don't know the specifics, and the specifics are what count. We don't know how he made the net he uses or exactly what the words he says mean and do. And it's more than likely that part of the spell is mental and we don't have even a clue to that. We only know what we see in the mirror, and that's not enough."

"Nor," Verit added, "do we have the character flaws necessary to truly understand that type of work." She looked at Fidelis. "Do we?"

"Of course not," Fidelis snapped. "But there has to be *something* we can do! Surely we can deduce how he achieves his effects so we can counter some of them!"

"He binds the soul to the body, that much is clear, and it must be necessary for him to do so in order to have something that resembles a living man," Cosima said after a long moment of heavy silence. "Verit, I have a thought—is there any way to free the soul?"

"He binds it with something that drinks blood," Elfrida added, with the feeling that Cosima's observation was the key to their desperately needed solution. "Does anything other than a demon drink blood? I never heard of anything else."

"Nor I," Fidelis said, raising his head like a hound scenting the quarry.

Cosima shook her head and spread her hands.

Verit frowned in thought. "You're right, Elfrida, a demon would be a reasonable explanation. If the soul is demon-bound, an exorcism should free it. The flaw is that I've never heard of anything but a demon drinking blood—but that doesn't mean Apolon hasn't."

"Could an exorcism do any harm?" Fidelis asked

sharply. "It's not as if we have anything else to try!"

"Not to the walking dead," Elfrida said. "It's hard to imagine anything that could make their condition worse." Now she added her own unpleasant observations. "They're in torment; I have no doubt of it. They are still aware of what's happening to them—at least at first; you can see it in their faces."

"But an exorcism can do considerable harm to the exorcist," Verit reminded them. "Especially if the demon breaks free of control, but is not banished." Her expression was grave as she looked about the group. "That is why it is not a rite undertaken lightly."

"If there were enough of us working together . . ." Elfrida started, but her voice trailed off. "I think we've just come back to the problem of being divided. It occurs to me that those who are not whole in heart with us could actually impede our effort."

"If we did the ritual in the sanctuary," Cosima protested, "we could draw upon the Heart for power. Couldn't we? Isn't that why the Heart is here?"

"But we'd be doing the exorcism in front of at least one quarter of our people if we did that," Elfrida pointed out, "some of whom are certainly working for Apolon. If *that* isn't being divided, I don't know what is!"

"What?" Cosima gasped in surprise. "What are you talking about?"

Elfrida stared at her, then bit her lip; she had forgotten that not all of the little circle were aware of her conversation with Verit.

"The next time you're in the sanctuary," Elfrida advised her, "look around. See how many of the Novices won't look at the Heart. That was why we brought them all here in the first place, to keep them from making trouble elsewhere."

"There are some," Verit admitted, "but not enough to interfere unless everyone else allows it, and there aren't that many idiots in my order—"

"Nor mine," Fidelis said flatly. "Quite a few, but not a majority. Elfrida?"

She shrugged. "Who knows? Mine don't discuss the situation, but most of them are sufficiently traditional that they'd certainly stop a Novice from interfering in any ceremony."

All of them looked at Cosima, and Elfrida wondered if she had followed their advice since the last time the subject came up. "Yes, I have been to recreation lately," she said. "And my order isn't cloistered the way the rest of you are. The healers have seen enough—and talked to each other enough—that we know what's going on in the city, probably almost as well as those of you who listen to people in the confessional." She raised an eyebrow. "From what I hear of *that*, you could run a spy network from one confessional."

"What an enchanting idea." Verit smiled for the first time that night. "If we're ever invaded again, we'll have to remember that. So what do the healers think?"

Her expression was bitter. "We're realists. Apolon and his servants are evil, General Cathal is a sadistic bastard, and the emperor is probably out of touch with what's going on. I've heard rumblings that we should never have let them inside our gates."

"Interesting," Fidelis said thoughtfully. "Would it be worthwhile to get the emperor back in touch, do you think? Or would it even be *possible*?"

"Probably not," Elfrida said with a heartfelt sigh. "When a ruler loses contact with his people, it's either because he doesn't care or because something has happened to him, like senility"—She paused as another thought occurred to her, and added slowly—"or—possession—"

What a hideous thought.

Fidelis whistled through his teeth, his face completely blank with surprise. "You think there's a possibility that Apolon controls him?"

"From what I've heard," Elfrida replied, "he's a bit young for senility." Then she added the observation only a parent would have made. "And no caring father would allow the way Leopold has been treated."

"If Apolon is running things," Cosima said slowly, "we *must* figure out how to unmake his black coats."

Verit was grim. "We'll try an exorcism if we get the chance, then. For now—our best option is to pray. Let's all get some rest and return after the morning ritual."

They met back in the meditation chamber after the next ritual; Elfrida had no time to speak privately with Verit, but something about the archpriestess' expression told her that Verit had some news for her.

Perhaps Shelyra showed up for morning service? In a way, she hoped so; she had gone too long without knowing what was going on with both Shelyra and Lydana. There were rumors that something was going on at the harbor, but at the moment there were nothing but rumors.

The glass showed no one in the workroom, and a search through the building revealed Apolon lying unconscious on his bed, still fully clothed.

"I supposed it's too much to hope that something went wrong," Fidelis said, dubiously. "He could simply have worked himself to exhaustion."

"Hope is something we should never give up," Cosima said quietly, but firmly.

Elfrida, still looking down at the glass, thought momentarily of her daughter and then her granddaughter, wondering what they were doing. She worried for Shelyra in particular, for it was obvious even to an old woman like her that the princess had become rather attracted to her putative enemy, Prince Leopold.

I wonder what she is doing now? If only we could somehow convince Leopold to come over to our side of this! He wouldn't even have to take an active part . . . I just would hate to see such a fine man harmed just because he's loyal to the wrong person.

The thought was enough to change the vision, somewhat to her surprise. A ruby-colored haze covered the glass, and when it cleared there was a new picture. The light was very dim, but she recognized Shelyra. She and another man whose face was not visible as he watched his footing were dragging a third figure between them along an underground tunnel. Elfrida recognized it as the one that led to the meditation chamber.

Who is that? And why is Shelyra bringing two strangers along the tunnel?

The third person was only a dark form, but Elfrida sensed something, perhaps from Shelyra. Terrible anxiety—grief—

Could that be a black coat? Did someone that Shelyra knows fall victim to Apolon? Are these two of her Gypsy friends?

"Do you see that?" she asked the others. "I think perhaps the Goddess is ready to demonstrate the power of Her Heart." She waved at the glass. "That is the Princess Shelyra, and I believe the man being carried is one of Apolon's victims."

"What do you mean?" Fidelis asked, staring into the glass. "Why do you say that the Goddess—"

"That is the secret way into the Temple this chamber guards, and they're coming toward us," Elfrida replied. "I recognize it. They will be here in a few minutes. I think Shelyra has found a way to bring us a black coat—I suspect the victim must be someone she knows."

Cosima gasped; Fidelis started, looking this time like a hawk with quarry in sight.

Verit broke the circle and handed the glass to Elfrida. "Put that in the chest in the tunnel and watch for them. That looked like Leopold with her to me. I just wish I knew who the third person is."

"Of course!" Elfrida said, dragging herself to her feet with the aid of the bench next to her. "I thought he looked familiar—but I know his voice better than his face."

Verit isn't surprised—which might be the news she had for me: that Shelyra brought Leopold out of the Summer Palace. I would bet that Shelyra brought him here to speak with Verit. If he wasn't on our side before that, he must be now! It was too early for elation, but for the first time this morning, she felt a stirring of real optimism—and with it a great relief. Leopold might not be spared in this conflict, but at least he would be fighting on the right side.

A moment later, the door in the rear of the chamber opened and her granddaughter and the prince stumbled through, laden with a black coat.

The black coat, face full of dim anguish, fell limply to the floor when they let go of him, as if he could not move on his own. That was when Elfrida saw his face and realized to her shock that she knew this man, and she understood the sickness on her granddaughter's face.

Apolon's latest victim was Thom Talesmith.

She stared at the man, not touching him, while the other three Gemen hurried the newcomers into disguising robes. *Poor Thom—how did you come to this pass? Were you just not as clever as we thought, or were you trying to impress Shelyra?* She did not know him well enough for deep grief, but her pity overflowed for him. There was something more in this man's face than she had seen in any of the others, even the ones in the glass when they were first taken over. He *still* knew what had happened to him—and he wanted to be saved. There was pleading in his face as he looked up at her. She could not mistake that expression, faint though it was.

He wants release. This is torture for him, more so than for any of the others.

Shelyra and Leopold were dressed as Brown Robes, Verit having pointed out that since Brown Robes came and went they weren't as well known to the Temple people as the members of the other orders.

"There's a shadow in this man's eyes," Leopold said to Verit as he donned the robe she handed him. "It's—I can't describe it. Before we brought him across the threshold, it covered his whole head and upper body, like a web of darkness, but once we crossed into the Temple, it recreated inside him somehow."

"I haven't a clue what he's talking about," Shelyra admitted, her face tight with grief and strain; but then she added staunchly, "but if Leopold says it's there, I believe him. I can't see this shadow of his—but this isn't Thom—or at least, this is Thom, but all of him isn't there. Or—something," she ended lamely. "I can only tell you that it isn't like the effect of any drug or poison that I know."

"And I suspect the lady knows quite a few," Leopold added dryly, earning him a ghost of a smile from Shelyra as she struggled to keep her other emotions in check.

But once Leopold had told them what he saw in Thom's eyes, the Gemen could all see it, too—even if Shelyra couldn't. "You should believe him, child," Verit said in a kindly tone as she stooped to examine the poor victim at closer range. "He's quite correct. Unfortunately, I believe that I know just what this shadow is."

But now Shelyra can at least tell that something is wrong, Elfrida realized with some relief, *even if she doesn't have the kind of sight the rest of us do. She may yet grow into it, if we all live through this.*

"You have to help this man," Leopold continued, with all the authority of a man who is used to having his orders obeyed. Then he softened it with an added, "Please—"

"We would whether you ordered it or not, Leopold," Verit replied crisply. "Of that, you may be sure. It is our duty to him as a suffering soul, to do what we can."

Leopold nodded, though his expression did not grow less troubled. He had not missed the fact that Verit had only promised to "do what they could."

Verit decreed that they would take Thom into the sanctuary to attempt the exorcism and began giving orders with the crisp efficiency of a general. "Cosima, you will explain to everyone what is happening. Just tell the story from the beginning: what we heard in the confessionals, what we saw in the glass, and what we are doing now. Your gift for impromptu preaching will stand us in good stead; I am certain of it. Go start now and set up the area around the altar—we will join you."

Cosima nodded and left, and Verit turned to Elfrida. "Elfrida, you and I will speak the ritual."

Elfrida felt a chill of fear as well as a thrill of pardonable pride that Verit had chosen her to assist; it was a great trust.

"Fidelis," Verit continued, "I want you and these two to hold onto the body. We'll use the floor in front of the altar—where the coffin was. He may fight quite a bit, but I think the three of you can hold him. If not, we'll recruit more help when the time comes."

"You want us to help?" Leopold said doubtfully. "But—we are not—sanctified in any way—"

"What I need are three sets of strong hands," Verit told him. "And I think perhaps it will help if two of those are hands that belong to people who care what has happened to him." She smiled faintly. "Intent plays a powerful role. And you both are firm in your faith, I believe. That also counts for a great deal."

Leopold smiled back shyly, and Elfrida decided that she liked this man even more than before. She also liked the way that he and Shelyra stood together, the way they oriented their bodies—there was attraction there, and the kind of understanding that comes with a partner one trusts, whether that partner be fellow warrior, simple friend, or spouse.

They arrived in the sanctuary just as one group was finishing its ritual and the next was arriving. Verit asked the first group to remain, told the second to take their places, and rang the bell to summon the rest of the Gemen. "I want everyone here," she said grimly, "including all the Novices." Elfrida saw that Cosima had cleared everything away but the two candles on the altar itself and the great book of rituals.

When everyone was in place, Cosima stood before the altar and began to speak. By the time she was done, the Great Silence of the day was punctuated by dozens of whispered versions of "I don't believe it" along with the occasional "I told you so." Verit, supervising the preparations for a full exorcism, ignored them all. Another stir ran through the assembled Gemen as Leopold, Shelyra, and Fidelis brought the limp body of Thom Talesmith in and laid it down where "Adele's" coffin had been. There were more whispers, this time only from those close enough to see the black coat's face. The shadow in his eyes was painfully easy to see, as if the demon binding him knew what they were about to attempt—but the expression on Thom's face was now the desperate one of a man in torture and looking toward freedom he dares not hope for.

Cosima joined the rest of them and picked up the heavy book which contained the ritual of exorcism along with several other rarely used rituals. She held it where Verit and Elfrida could both see to read from it, and Verit began, spreading her hands and inclining her face upward.

"O Thou that Dwellest in the Heavens, hear us and come to us."

Elfrida looked into her granddaughter's anxious eyes, smiled reassuringly, and took up the chant, following Verit's example.

"When we are troubled, we call upon Thee, and Thou hearest us." Not for the first time, she felt the real truth behind those words and sensed the comfort that came with them.

They spoke in turn, each of them taking a single line; it was Verit's turn, and she delivered her response with the sound of a trumpet in her voice. "Deliver the soul of this Thy servant from lies and from deceit."

Elfrida answered with the same conviction, but more pleading. "Deliver him from his cruel enemies, and rid him from the wicked man."

Fidelis swung a smoking thurible over the prone body. Shelyra and Leopold kept a careful grip on it as they struggled not to choke on the clouds of incense. The body twitched slightly, as if caught up in some internal struggle. Fidelis sprinkled it liberally with holy water, and the twitching grew stronger, almost to the point of convulsions. Fidelis added his to the strong hands that held

Thom's body in place before the altar. Verit and Elfrida together chanted the final hymn from the written liturgy, and Cosima joined her voice to theirs as she closed the book and set it aside. From here on, there was no set ritual; they would have to improvise, in response to whatever was happening.

Verit looked to Elfrida for suggestions, and Elfrida eyed the pile of rubies which had remained on the altar since the miracle of the bleeding Heart. The victim's struggles had slowed, and it occurred to her that they might need a physical link between Thom and the Heart. "Perhaps we should put those around him," she suggested in a soft whisper, "like vigil candles about a coffin."

"Good idea," Verit whispered back. She picked up two rubies, Elfrida did likewise, and they knelt at Thom's head and feet as they put the stones into position, then reached out to lay their hands on Thom's body.

Now, for the first time since the miracle of the "bleeding" Heart, the power of the Goddess manifested again. Lines of red light flashed from stone to stone, forming a box about the semiconscious semicorpse. A hazy glow spread out from the lines to cover the six people about him as Cosima dropped to her knees beside Fidelis and placed her hands on the body as well.

It seemed to be all the Heart had been waiting for. Rays from it spread to the stones and reflected back, until Thom and the six exorcists were bathed in so much light they seemed to be inside a giant ruby. The light grew until it seemed that everyone in the sanctuary would be blinded, but no one was able to look away. Even the Novices who wouldn't look at the Heart before had their eyes locked onto this spectacle; Elfrida could see, out of the corner of her eye, two of them she had noted from her time at rituals gazing at the group with their mouths open. She forced her concentration back to the task at hand. The heat was incredible; she could feel sweat dripping down inside her robe, and her hair was soaking wet under her veil. The light was so bright she was afraid that she would never be able to see in dim light—or even normal daylight—again.

Now Thom thrashed about under their hands again, making sounds that were somewhere between a scream and a whimper. A sickly greenish-yellow shadow covered his body where there were no hands on it, but whatever it was appeared to be in full retreat. The shadow shrank as it moved away from their hands, shrinking to a narrow band about Thom's neck—but she had no sense that it was hiding within him again. Now, this—thing—was being driven out, bit by bit, being forced out of Thom, out of this world, and into another they could neither see nor sense.

He spasmed once, violently, just as the last of the shadow disappeared entirely with an audible *pop* and a high, thin wail that did not issue from his lips.

Thom's breath rattled in his throat, and then he went limp, clearly dead in truth, lying on the floor in front of the altar, with a small amount of blood from a wound in his chest trickling down the white marble steps.

But there was a look of absolute radiant stillness on his face, as if he had lived a long and peaceful life which had come to a perfect end.

The power of the Heart was not quite finished, however.

The entity that formed above Thom's body was not quite an angel—for it was recognizably Thom Talesmith, and it lacked the blinding radiance that Elfrida associated with the messengers of heaven. But he was just as obviously not—quite—human anymore. *"Free!"* a voice exaulted in her mind.

He looked down at the six who had helped to free him, then out at the Gemen surrounding the altar. *"Thank you,"* said a soft voice in Elfrida's mind as her eyes met his. Then, in a louder voice, as the eyes rose to meet those of every Gemen in turn, *"Thank you all—"*

From out of the rosy light of the Heart four forms of white light coalesced around Thom. He smiled at them, a smile of pure joy that choked her throat with emotion, and held out his hands to them. They folded wings of light about him, hiding him from Elfrida's sight—then they all blazed up, and were gone.

The blinding ruby light faded to a pale rose color, but it remained like a canopy of protection above the body.

Cosima stood up in the thundering silence. "It is done. Come, Gemen, and pay your last respects to the soul of a brave man, a faithful servant of the Heart and son of the Great One."

The Gemen rose one by one and processed in single file past the body. No one spoke a word; Elfrida had the feeling that they did not dare to break the silence.

It took almost an hour for all of them to pass by, and Elfrida was glad to see that the suspicious looking Novices seemed badly shaken by the experience. Most of the Gemen and Novices were weeping, some in unnerving silence, some muffled in their sleeves. She noticed that Fidelis was regarding several members of his order who were crying with a mixture of relief and approval; she suspected that these were the ones whose brains he had compared to the plants they tended.

So, his people are finally coming to their senses. In fact, I think all of us are coming to our senses.

Some of the Red Robes were similarly affected, and she noticed that many of the Grey Robes regarded the body with horrified fascination, as if they were just now discovering that the things they had been hearing were true after all, and not merely obscure ancient legends.

Leopold stood beside the body as if at attention at a state funeral; Shelyra was crying openly. From the look on her face, Elfrida suspected a certain measure of guilt attended those tears, but that was nothing she could do anything about.

At the end of the procession Verit stood up and announced that the body would lie in state for the next day, so that the people of the city could see it as well. "—but it must be guarded by the strongest among us, lest we have another attack such as happened while the dowager queen's body lay here."

Several of the younger Red Robes quickly volunteered, arming themselves with the ceremonial shepherd's staffs they used for some rituals, such as Harvest, First Fruits, and the Blessing of the Animals. The staffs might be ceremonial in purpose, but Elfrida had hefted one once, and knew that it was quite as solid as the less decorative and more practical kind.

Verit then decreed that, in view of the upsetting circumstances, there would be an extra period of confession for the Gemen, immediately after the Midmorning Ritual— "which we might as well all say together now, since we are all here," she concluded, adding with a sharp glance at certain of the Gemen, "I believe that it will be a good thing for us all to affirm that the members of this Temple are heart-whole and no longer divided in our—opinions."

Elfrida saw that some of the Gemen flushed, and others bit their lips, but none looked away or bore the expressions of impatience or rebellion she had seen over the past several days.

As Verit chose the people to hear confessions, Elfrida noted that she was choosing the ones who had believed that the empire was benign. *The next few hours should be a real ear-opener for them.*

But for the first time since the invasion, there was no sense of dissension anywhere among the Gemen. Elfrida felt that burden, as well, easing from her soul.

We are whole of purpose at last! she thought as she lifted her voice in chant with the others. But then came the next, soberer reflection. *And I fear—it is only just in time.*

❧ 58 ❧

LYDANA

Distant bells were ringing incongruously for Midmorning Ritual at the Temple and nearer Parish Houses as the unlikely little band of warriors set off. This was very different from the trips Queen Lydana had made down to the seaport on official business in the years just past. She did not sit in comfort listening to the chant of a dozen men at the oars now. Her carrier was a leaky, fish-scented, cranky boat, though the two men who had been told off by the Bark Hag to handle it seemed able to keep it under some manner of control.

The first part of their journey had been a strange winding in and out among thick posts greened with sea moss, shadowed save for the light of the bow lantern. Matild guessed that this was one of the underwater paths beneath the warehouses, some nearly as old as the city.

When they broke into the open it was into a gray day, with heavy clouds overhead and around them and, having to be fended off quickly now and then by pole, some floating debris of the storm. The harsh cries of sea birds sounded above the lap of the water and the grunts of the men as they bent to their labors.

They did not seek the main stream, but kept as close as they could to the left-hand wall of the canal, as if that promised some protection.

At this hour the current was on their side, drawing them forward so that they used their oars more for steadying and steering than for progress.

There was a stiff wind still blowing inland from the sea, and Matild was glad of the cloak which had been lent her on her departure. She kept a sharp survey of both banks, turning her head from side to side. Normally these waters would have been alive with craft moving up or down, but they passed only one barge, and that was so full of water it was listing badly and seemed ready to turn keel up at any moment. Nor were there any guards at the two gates, and the fretwork of those gates, streaming long fingers of green growth, was pulled up to allow them free passage.

To Matild it seemed far too easy. Or had the storm wrought so much damage that the activities of the enemy were for a time at a halt?

She grew impatient and fought that impatience. There was no way she was going to hasten this journey. At last her need for something to do led her to test the Bark Hag's suggestion of the power of running water.

She beckoned Eel around until they were sitting knee to knee and she did not believe that the oarsmen could overlook her actions. Bringing out the brooch, she steadied it in one hand and reached out the other to Eel, who grasped it instantly in a begrimed paw. Though she had never drawn her young companion into such ways before, he appeared to know just what she wanted of him.

Staring into the ruby she tried to see only the stone, and then beyond its surface to the one she sought. *Adele!* called her thoughts. "Mother—"

The ruby appeared to swell in her grasp, almost to the size of a wirie glass. *Adele!*

Then she was answered. Her mother's face, strangely wan in spite of the vivid crimson which framed it, was there. And her eyes were seeking her daughter's.

"Saxon goes for the prisoner ships—then the fleet—" She tried to put her message as tersely as she could. "If She favors us, we shall head again inland."

Were those thoughts reaching the Reverend One? Now she saw a spark in the other's eyes.

"Use what you carry." The words appeared to be spelled out in ruby, aflame in her mind. "Give release—and then come, oh, come—"

Though Matild concentrated fiercely, that face faded and she could no longer sense any message.

Give release? Her hand once more tightened about the brooch. Did that mean that some power within the Temple had seen before them victory? But one did not pin too much on hope—that was the way of a fool.

They reached the bay and saw their first signs of life. Two of the great freighters had indeed suffered damage, but they were still afloat some distance apart. The bow of one was even driven up on a wharf. Beyond was a tangle of wrecked ships, fishing vessels, cutters of the harbor service, some coastal sloops. And the water was thick with floating menaces.

She could see movement on board the nearest freighters. There was no mistaking the black coats of the men at work there, cutting loose a splintered mast, striving to so lighten their unseaworthy craft.

Already the oarsmen had swung their own craft farther left, to where the longest of the piers extended. As they went, Matild found herself holding her breath; could they be seen from the freighter? She could picture in her mind one of their fatal flashes of fire shooting forth to finish them off.

A seabird screeched, and Matild saw one of her escorts purse his lips to answer with the same wild sound. A last swift use of a pole sent them against the wharf, or under it. She had just time to obey the whisper to "duck" as they slid again into semigloom.

There were walkways of planks, still slime-wet from the rise of seawater, along which men were moving. She was not surprised to see that Saxon was coming toward her— frowning grimly.

Matild swung up a hand to stop the hot words she was aware were swirling within him.

"This is my battle, Lord Captain. Would you have me cower in the shadows when such as those hoodcrows hold our men? I am the Tiger in this time, and as the Tiger I keep my own hunt." She stared at him, defying him to deny the truth of her words.

He frowned. "And if you die—or are taken?"

She shrugged. "That will be as the pattern wills. I have told you how these black coats answer to what I bear. How many have you brought down with sword or spear?"

His surprise was plain. "How did you know—know that they cannot be killed—or at least sent truly to their deaths by steel?"

"Walking dead men," grunted someone in the shadows behind them, and there was a tremor in that voice.

Matild stood still, concentrating on bringing all her wits and all her beliefs into line. "On which ship do they hold the most of our men?"

To her surprise Saxon actually grinned. "On but one now, lady. This past night we took the one farther off. It seems they may not have enough black coats for their army—thus there were mercenaries there. And our river rats are adept with claw and knife. We have kept that capture a secret so far. Two black coats came earlier with messages. Thurstan brained one before he could use that fire flasher of his, and Little Piet dumped the other into the sea. He landed across a floating spar and did not stir as long as we could watch him float."

"But the first—"

All humor was gone from Saxon's face. "We got his rod while he was down. But, despite that blow he arose—only it seemed that he was dazed, for he turned from us and walked away as if he no longer saw us. Nor did he head toward the ship where his fellows were. One of the prisoners told us that this has happened before—he had seen it in the city—a black coat knifed who rose and walked, not toward his slayer but away, as if seeking some comfort for his wound."

"There is no comfort for them," Matild answered slowly. "They are the servants of evil—the dead serving the orders of their lord. Yet do not find them the less for that."

"I don't!" he returned. "Marson died in their unholy fire-flash when he was careless. If we had a handful of those—"

Matild shook her head swiftly. "Not so. Let an honest man palm one of those weapons and he may be caught in Apolon's net! To touch pitch is to bring back blackened fingers."

"Then how?" Saxon asked. "We must clear out the last nest and soon. We not only need the prisoners aboard, but the fishers have reported that the emperor's fleet out-rode the storm by some fluke and is coming. Let them land forces here, and let him move the army he holds beyond the walls, and he would crack Merina like a nut, in spite of all his oaths!"

"He has not the Heart, nor has he what it can hold and disperse. Believe me, Lord Captain," she touched his sleeve lightly, "there is in my hand now more than any have carried against any foe since the Sword of Gideon brought down Iktcar himself."

"What would you do?" he countered.

"Battle," she replied. "Let me confront these black coats—now!"

He stared at her, his mouth twisted as if he would voice some oath. But she held him eye to eye, and in his gaze saw anger turn to uncertainty—and at last to surrender.

"So be it." He said that as if he were taking liege-oath once more. "They say many things of the Tiger, and perhaps some of them are true. On your own head be it—" There was anger in his voice again.

"On my own head be it," she agreed quietly. "If my hope is a shadow and quickly gone, yet I have given it a chance and chance is what we need this day. Eel, the flask!"

Almost instantly the leather bottle was in her hand and

she drank two drafts, feeling again that surge of strength and energy. Then, even as he had agreed, Saxon brought her to where she could easily get to the ship. The black coats were still at work. Then one looked up and gave a cry.

Matild held forth the brooch. She could still see the half-wrecked ship behind it. Then something else began to form in the air. It grew quickly, strongly. There hung the Heart even as it did above the altar of the Temple. And she felt the pull on her to hold it so.

Slowly, she took one step forward, and then another, and the Heart retreated by so much. She found footing without looking for it and climbed, passing over the splinters of a broken rail. The Heart was pulsing now, wide waves of crimson washing over the whole deck. There were black coats lying as if struck down in an instant. She saw the shadow of another burst from below, totter, and go down. But still she held steady, and there came no bursts of fire to seek her out.

But her concentration was slipping as she fought to keep the Heart in view. All at once, again the echo of an echo—a sharp voice in her mind—

"Well done!"

Now those washing red waves appeared to be sinking into the cluttered deck. Somehow she knew that there was a seeking—for the black coats—a fate sent to clear them from her path.

She took a step, felt a hand out to steady her, and knew that Eel shared this venture with her. But she could hold steady no longer, she was drained to the last of her strength.

The red waves of light appeared to flicker—then they faded. Behind her she heard the clamor of those who had dared to follow her.

"Lady!" An arm stronger than that of Eel was about her shoulders, steadying her against a strong, vibrant body. She tried to tuck the brooch back in its nest, and as she loosed it, her arm felt leaden, would have fallen to her side had her finger not caught in her sash. She was being guided to where the tangle of the fallen mast offered some support.

"Lord Captain!" The vigor of that shout shook her out of the haze which had filled her mind. "Look you at this one! He died of an ax—" The voice trailed away, as if the speaker was so astounded at what he saw that he could no longer find words.

Matild looked, as her companion must be doing.

There indeed lay one of the black coats sprawled on his back. She expected to see no outward sign of injury—but what she looked upon was the horror of a battle wound, a cleaving of skull. Beyond him was another of his fellows, and one of the river rats had gone down on one knee beside him. Daringly the man swung the body over. There was a gaping wound in the throat.

"But—" Puzzled, jerking back from the body, the man stared almost wildly up at Matild and Saxon. "We had no such weapons—they fell but not from any fight with us!" His hand arose and he sketched one of the ward signs.

Matild found her voice. She guessed—no, knew—what the Heart's Blood had wrought. "They were men already dead, now they show the wounds that made them so. Necromancer's evil plain to be seen."

The man got to his feet and shoved even farther back.

"Walking dead," he said slowly. "An evil—"

"Of the greatest depths," she finished for him as he paused.

"But the men—the prisoners—" It was Saxon speaking now.

"They are sons of the Heart, you will find them untouched." She staggered and he quickly lowered her to a seat on the debris.

"Get the hatch up!" His order was nearly a shout and men were quick to obey, struggling with the sodden fastenings.

As the barrier slammed back on the deck, Saxon moved

near to the very edge of the opening. "You below, men of Merina," he called, "up and out."

Ropes were dropped. They came up slowly. She saw among them the green livery of the water police, here and there a guard uniform, and the mass of varied colors of guildsmen, as well as some ragged jerkins such as covered the men now aiding them aloft.

The former prisoners stared about them at the wreckage in the harbor, and she saw that many of them were making the Heart-sign in thanksgiving.

But she was too worn by the pull of the Power to see them as more than figures passing before her. Eel was still beside her, his youthful strength a support. Then—then like a dream, it all vanished into dark as Matild's head fell forward on her companion's shoulder.

§ 59 §

SHELYRA

Shelyra could not stop crying all through the service although she had stifled her sobs in the sleeves of her borrowed robe; she had started when Thom had stopped struggling and his death wound had appeared. That was the moment she had realized that he wasn't just under a spell, he was *dead*, and had been dead all along, and it was at least partly her fault that he was dead.

After the service she had started to blunder blindly toward the confessionals, but Leopold took her shoulders and steered her in the direction of the meditation chamber. "I believe that you need to talk more than to confess, my lady," he said in a low and gentle voice, so gentle that grief choked her all over again. "I am hardly a confessor, but I am a willing pair of ears."

"And I." Her grandmother appeared at her left hand and walked with them toward the meditation chamber. Shelyra simply nodded, and let them take her where they would.

Once there, she sobbed out a confused tangle of self-recrimination and frustration—guilt that she had not taken better care for someone who was her liege man, anger at Thom for being so reckless, guilt that she was angry, frustration that he had not been willing to admit she knew what she was doing, more guilt that she had *known* that he was likely to go flinging himself out into the streets when she did not offer him safer scope for his talents or follow orders and allow him to smuggle her out of the city—

"This would never have happened if I'd just done what Aunt Lydana wanted!" she wailed at the end as she sat bracketed between her grandmother and the man who had been her enemy. "If I'd just gone to the Horse Lords—"

Adele started to say something, but Leopold beat her to the first word. "If you had left the city, my lady, the odds are that you would have been captured," he said firmly. "From the moment that the surrender of Merina was assured, there were guards on all the roads, the seaport was blockaded, and there were heavy patrols led by experienced trackers all through the countryside. The emperor assumed you would try to flee, all three of you, and he intended to hold you for the good behavior of the city. His advisor Apolon also wanted to hold you—for other reasons. Unless you know of more secret passageways beneath the hills"—she heard the amusement in his voice—"I doubt that even so clever a lady as you would have gotten past all that."

She nodded and his voice sobered. "Apolon *wants* you, my lady—wants you above all treasures. He would go to any extreme to take you. And I think after today, we may know why, at least in part."

"Necromancy," she whispered, but it was Adele who shook her head.

"I don't think so," her grandmother replied. "No, it is more complicated than that. In order to bargain with the—the creatures who serve him in his magics, he has to offer them something they want. Blood, of course, but also the power that comes from ending a life before its time, and other powers that depend on the type and the condition of a sacrifice."

Shelyra looked up, her tears still wet on her cheeks. "You mean—he'd just want me for a sacrifice?" she said, thinking oddly that it sounded like something out of a badly done miracle play.

But Adele shook her head. "Not *just* a sacrifice, 'Lyra," she replied, using the old pet-name. "You are something more than those poor men he was murdering in his workroom. In your blood is Power—the magical power that will come to you when you are my age. That would make you worth—oh—a thousand times more as a sacrifice than anyone else."

Shelyra shivered, thinking of other odd bits she had picked up among the Gypsies. *I'm a virgin, too—which ought to add to it. Lady Bright! No wonder Apolon wanted to get his claws on me!*

"So, you see, if you had done as your well-meaning aunt wanted," Leopold continued, "your city would be in much worse case than it is now. *You* would likely be dead, in a most unpleasant fashion, and Apolon would have used the power he obtained to make himself the equal of the emperor."

"No. Apolon would rule," Adele said crisply, and turned to Leopold. "I have no proof—but after all this, I have reason to suspect that your father is—not what he was. Apolon must have murdered several hundred people over the last few days, and not all of them were part of the rituals that made necromantic puppets. I believe that at least some of them went to serve the purpose he intended for Shelyra—and that your father, if he is not a puppet, is certainly under his total control. He might even be possessed."

Leopold blanched at that, and Shelyra reached out instinctively and took his hand. But his voice, though low, was steady when he replied.

"That—would explain a great deal, Reverend One," he admitted. "And it does explain more, if I assume that the Grey Mage has been exerting his power since he came into my father's service, working toward this day. And now I see the motivation for the fate this lady seems to have saved *me* from." He squeezed Shelyra's hand as he continued. "So—my lady, if you had followed your aunt's orders, *you* would be dead, *I* would be dead, and your city would be under the full control of a necromancer." He smiled at her, though it was clear that he smiled through pain of his own. "Personally, I must be entirely grateful that you have a rebellious nature."

"As for Thom Talesmith," her grandmother continued, her own voice turning matter-of-fact, "I will not speak ill of the dead, especially not of one who certainly redeemed his whole misspent life by struggling against the creature that held him to come here to warn us, but I must point out that you were not driving him out into the streets with a horsewhip. He knew the dangers; he courted them of his own free will."

Shelyra nodded, and began to feel the lump of guilt-born grief in her throat melting away.

"Mourn him properly, as a brave friend, my lady," Leopold said to her, "but do not take responsibility for actions you had no control over." He squeezed her hand lightly again. "I am afraid that is a failing of my own—I believe it is a part of being in authority over others."

She nodded and saw that her grandmother was watching Leopold with warm approval.

"Well, now," he continued, releasing her hand just a fraction before she would have felt it necessary to reclaim it, "we have several problems ahead of us."

"Apolon has to know what happened here—" Shelyra began hesitantly.

"Certainly," her grandmother agreed. "What is more, there is a battle going on at the harbor at this very moment, over the ships he and General Cathal have taken to use as prisons. It won't be long before word of that spreads over the city."

Shelyra did not bother to ask how her grandmother knew that. If the Gemen had been able to spy upon Apolon, they surely could have had a watch anywhere in the city.

"Open rebellion," Shelyra breathed, and Leopold sat up straighter.

"I agree—which means that we have very little time," he said. "Even if your people moved to take those ships in secret, it cannot remain secret more than an hour or two at most. Apolon will most *surely* come here."

Adele nodded. "That is why Verit did not dismiss the Gemen after the Midmorning ritual, I think. We will meet him here, in our own way. That leaves Cathal—and your fa—"

"My father is dead, Reverend One, following a long illness that began many years ago," Leopold interrupted her, with a face full of resignation that was somehow worse than grief. "The emperor is a man I do not know and cannot serve. He has forced me to choose between She Who Dwells Above and himself, and my choice must be with the Great One."

He bowed his head a little at that, and Adele reached out and laid her hand on it in brief blessing. Her touch might have given him some comfort, since Shelyra saw less despair and more determination when he raised his eyes again.

"Your place is here—I believe that mine—no, *ours*, if I may ask your aid, my lady," he said to Shelyra, "our place is at the palace. Cathal has always been a brute, but now he is a monster, and I must remove him. I may be able to—to deal with the emperor in a way that leaves him open to the aid of the Temple."

Adele had to shrug at that. "I do not know; we have not been paying a great deal of attention to what the emperor did." She smiled at Shelyra. "We have had other methods of learning his movements, and it did not seem efficient to use magic when we had perfectly good intelligence from other sources."

Shelyra simply raised an eyebrow. "So, the first thing, it seems to me, is that we need to get into the palace quickly, and see what we can do about getting rid of Cathal before he can go out and rouse up his men. After that—it falls as it falls."

"Battle plans rarely survive the first engagement with the enemy," Leopold agreed. "But I believe that it will be necessary to deal with Cathal by means of force. Unfortunately, the first problem is his mercenaries."

Shelyra pursed her lips. "I believe I may have a solution to that, and it is one I keep to hand." She reached for the large belt-pouch that never left her side these days, and brought out its contents: five small vials full of clear liquid, fifty tiny darts with needle points, arranged like sewing needles in a flat case, and the hollow tube used to deploy them. "This is a weapon that one of the Horse Lord groups uses," she explained as Leopold eyed the darts with interest. "And if you were ever curious, it is how they manage to raid the herds of their enemies with such impunity. The liquid is not precisely a poison, although it can kill in large doses—it mainly renders the target unconscious for an hour or more. The darts are only useful at a very short range—"

"But within the walls of the palace, we will certainly be working at short range," Leopold finished for her, looking more hopeful. "In that case, my lady, since this is a weapon you are familiar with, I shall leave it to you. What would like to do—" His dark brows knitted as he thought, which made his rather plain face look suddenly stern and unforgiving. "I'd like to eliminate the mercenaries guarding Cathal, then remove Cathal himself. Then, with luck and the grace of the Great One, we should be able to determine the situation with the emperor—if he has been tampered with—"

Shelyra bit her lip, then decided to make a countersuggestion. "Look, Leopold, if we can—incapacitate the emperor, there would be no one to know that he had not summoned you back to deal with Cathal and Apolon. Why not simply pretend that he has restored your authority? *Your* men would obey you without question, and as for Cathal's mercenaries, well, with him gone, they'll follow anyone who will continue their pay. That would put your men and his against Apolon's."

"Plenty of his men are rebelling already," Adele pointed out. "I know that morally you might find that plan repugnant, Leopold, but it is the one likeliest to save lives."

Shelyra held her breath as Leopold scowled then finally shrugged. "It is deception and dishonesty, but I cannot fault it, ladies," he finally said with a sigh. "You are right, Reverend One, it will save lives. Let us use it."

Shelyra let out the breath she had been holding. Leopold was pragmatic as well as being intelligent.

"We can always see that the emperor is restored to power once he is restored to his right mind," she pointed out, tactfully *not* assuming that Balthasar was probably in the same state that Thom had been. "You don't want the imperial throne, do you?"

He shook his head. "No. I never did," he admitted. "I was trained to rule and command, but an empire? No, that is too much for me. I should be happy enough to rule a smaller kingdom by far. . . ."

Like Merina? She didn't say it aloud, but felt a pang in her breast. She had skirted the edges of the thought before, but now she acknowledged it. *This is a man I could love. This is a man I would be proud to share a life and a throne with.*

He shook his head, as if shaking himself out of daydreams. "We waste time; every moment we dally is one more in which Cathal might learn of the uprising and vacate the palace, which would take him out of our reach."

"True." Adele rose. "I will go inform the archpriestess of your basic plan. Like you, I expect Apolon to confront us here. If you are able, or if you have the emperor in custody, bring him here. We will need every faithful heart—not just the ordained Gemen."

She smiled at both of them and her hands sketched a blessing over the two of them, and she left in a faint swishing of cloth on stone.

Shelyra repacked her pouch, then rose and triggered the catch that opened the door in the back of the meditation chamber. She and Leopold entered it and closed the door behind him, taking off their robes and hanging them on the waiting pegs. She had her hand on the second catch when she hesitated.

There was something she had to know.

"Leopold, did you—did you see anything, back there, when they performed the exorcism?" she asked.

He looked at her with a very puzzled expression. "Didn't you?" he asked.

She was used to hearing this from her grandmother, so it no longer made her feel as if she was a freak. In fact, as far as she could determine, there weren't many people outside of the Gemen who *could* see—what her grandmother saw. "Just light," she replied. "First red light from the Heart, then some white light, then the red light faded to pink. I thought—maybe—I heard someone say 'thank you,' but it could have been one of the Gemen." From the surprised expression he wore, he had obviously seen far more than she had.

But instead of answering her directly, he paused for a moment, as if gathering his thoughts. "Before I arrived here, I never once saw anything, not even light," he said at last. "I never really expected to."

"And now?" she prompted.

His expression turned inward, and the harsh lines of worry there softened. "I have seen—beings. I assume from their appearance, their actions, and what followed, that they are indeed angels." His gaze turned outward again and focused on her. "I was very suspicious of that tea you doctored, back in the Summer Palace. The old woman had never brought me tea before, and it smelled odd to me. Do you know why I drank it?"

She shook her head.

"Because an angel appeared and told me to." His reply startled her, and he smiled at her expression. "Truly. It said that I was in grave danger, that I had a friend I did not suspect, and that if I wished to escape my danger, I should drink the tea." She suspected from his expression that the holy messenger had said more, but it was his to disclose—or not—and she would not pry. "As for what I saw in the sanctuary—yes, I did see something. More than enough to tell me that your friend, as Gemen Cosima said, paid for every sin of his life with his heroic effort to warn us of Apolon." He laid a cautious but comforting hand on Shelyra's shoulder. "Believe me, my lady, I *know*, even as I know that the sun will rise, that your friend is held safely beneath the wings of the Great One."

Coming from him—a man as ordinary as good, home-baked bread—the words were more comforting than anything any of the Gemen had said.

She sighed as a great weight lifted from her soul.

"Now—we do have urgent business, my lady," he continued. "And it will not wait."

"Right." She nodded briskly and made certain of the contents of her pouch before triggering the door into the tunnel between the palace and the Temple. "Follow me, and watch what I do. You might as well know how to open them; if we're fleeing, I don't want you to find yourself stuck on the wrong side of one that's closed!"

§ 60 §

LYDANA

It seemed to her that even in that dark there was a coming and going which she could not understand. Nor did she greatly care. Once she thought she saw afar off the shape of the Great Heart, again a frail wisp of mist with her mother's eyes. And beyond her a flash of color without real form but which she knew was the life force of Shelyra engaged in some business of her own.

They left her at last—all those dream phantoms—and she was safely cradled in sleep. She awoke to sunlight in a bright pattern across the bed where she lay—no true bed, her bewildered eyes told her. No, rather like the pallet in the warehouse. Had she somehow been transported back to Jonas' hidey-hole?

There was movement beside her; she carried through the weighty business of turning her head.

"Skita?"

A child-sized hand was on her forehead, smoothing a path down her cheek.

"Drink, my lady." The other somehow boosted her up a little, and there was the rim of a drinking horn against her lips. There was a scent, faint and far off now, but memory stirred in her. Like an obedient child she drank.

The haziness in her mind was driven away as a wind drives even the darkest of clouds. She stared beyond her

437

nurse at a weathered wall. One could smell the sea now, hear its restlessness. And like a puzzle fitting itself together piece by piece, memory returned.

"What—?"

Skita smiled. Somehow she had shed the skin of Eel and was herself again, in spite of her dirty, ragged garments.

"What passes? Much. The lord captain is indeed a leader to be cherished. He has fashioned an army before the passing of the night. Now they work upon a trap for the emperor's fleet."

"A trap?" Lydana (yes, she was once more Lydana—not Matild the beadwoman—it was her city, her people for whom they fought) searched for the brooch, and now pinned it outwardly to the front of her jerkin, since she could not restore it yet to its original ring.

"The storm left much wreckage in the harbor," Skita was continuing. "The lord captain makes use of that. He prepared fire ships—"

Fire ships. Her memory spun back to earlier days—to the story of Ourse and their victory there. Suddenly all her strength and alertness was back, and she braced herself up. "I would see!"

"First," Skita was strong in her reply, "you will eat. That wonder-working drink of yours is gone to the last drop. You must keep your strength now as the rest of us do. Stay where you are—"

She was gone as Lydana looked about her. The room in which she lay was small, and it had a single unglassed window through which reached the smell and the sound of the sea. By the gear hanging on the walls she thought it a fisher cabin. Then Skita was back with a basin of water and a coarse towel. Thankfully Lydana washed her face, scrubbing hard at her cheeks, disgusted to see the streaking of the towel thereafter.

Skita had vanished again. When she returned the second time she had a tray—a tray of coppenwood with a beaten copper pattern laid therein, memento of some far voyage. On it was a plate of chipped pottery, beside a silver cup which might have come from some pirate plundering.

There was a stew in the bowl and beside it the favor of a spoon so she might eat in a civilized manner, while the cup held red southland wine of at least three seasons aging. The fisherman who harbored here did well for himself.

"Tell—" Lydana demanded between bites.

Skita settled down cross-legged; she held a length of ship sausage from which she nibbled from time to time.

"They make seaworthy—or at least as ready as possible if needed—three of the larger fishing boats. The hoodcrows and the others—they had guards on the stores, but they had not raided them. Probably they wanted them as loot for the fleet. So the lord captain has his pick of the best. They will stuff the boats with bale fire—"

Lydana swallowed hastily and tried not to think of the effect of bale fire.

"There are volunteers to crew them out—in fact so many the lord captain had to order that lots be drawn for the privilege. Those others have sent in two scout cutters. All they have seen is the wreckage and some of the men wearing mercenary armor as guards on board the freighters. They head in now." Skita took another bite.

Lydana waited until she had swallowed to hear the rest.

"The bay is awash with wreckage; they will come with caution. But the fire ships will seem to be taken ships—not only that, but in good order. The lord captain believes they will wish to send in prize crews to those. Our men will be hidden, and when those others allow their vessels their own courses, then—the bale fire! Those who deal with that are picked men. They have worked with it before and can be trusted to make the most of their knowledge."

"And if we so take the fleet?" Lydana asked.

"The lord captain does not believe that we can take them all, but if we take their flagship and three of the transports at least, we can make them veer off. After all, the emperor's fleet has never come up against our kind before. They took Gomba, yes, and it was a port city, but the merchants there largely depended on foreign ships for their trading and those scattered to the winds when they heard of the imperial fleet's advance. They have large ships—built so, I suppose, to emphasize the emperor's supreme glory," Skita's lip curled, "but such lack the mobility of those the lord captain used at Ourse. And Korsic, for all his piracy, was a better seaman, I would swear, than any on those ships out there. For too long Balthasar has been a victor—such a history of successes can make a man vulnerable."

"And overconfident," Lydana added.

Skita nodded. "Once the fleet is no longer a threat the lord captain will move his men cityward. We do not know what happens there, lady. But there is a pot boiling and we go to put more fire under it."

Lydana's hand went to the brooch. Dared she try to communicate again? Somehow she felt not. The Power which had fed her taking of the freighter might now be needed elsewhere and the slightest pull upon it might upset the delicate balance. Best wait and see how Saxon's strategy here worked.

With Skita in careful attendance she left the small room, one of two in a fisher cabin as she had guessed, and made her way to the towered building which had dominated all the harbor business for generations. They kept to the side, well away from the working men. There was a steady stream issuing forth from the lowest floor, each pair with a large canister between them. Bale fire had been a pirate weapon, but after Ourse, Saxon had had a supply put in their own stores, a prudent provision which was now paying off.

She did not see the captain, but Jonas' bellow could be heard, and now and then, she sighted the face of one of the river rats who had shared the warehouse quarters.

They took the upper door in and climbed to the tower, passing along the way men wearing the uniforms of Balthasar's mercenaries who had certainly never given liege-oath to him—or Cathal.

Some of them glanced at the two women, but no one questioned them and they felt as if in the activities of the moment they had been forgotten. Lydana entered Saxon's quarters near to the top of the tower.

There were signs that they had been ransacked. The natural neatness learned by a seaman usually quartered in a small space was missing. Torn papers lay about, and she saw her own official portrait pinned to the top of the wide desk, a knife contemptuously struck through each eye. She examined it critically and then wondered, were there a mirror on a wall somewhere about, if she would recognize her present self as even faintly akin to that regal woman in the full glory of fine robes and gems such as only the House of the Tiger could find in its coffers. But she had better than those gauds now.

Lydana's hand went to the brooch. She did not take the liberty of occupying the captain's chair, but she and Skita pulled a double-seated bench to the window looking harborward and there took their positions.

There were swirls of floating wreckage, perhaps some of it debris from the city, swept back by the tide-influenced canals. The large freighter was still anchored by its bow on the wharf, but one of those which had flanked it had been moved away.

"The black coats—" Almost Lydana expected to see those corpses still lying in plain sight. Skita gave a small sound—not quite a laugh, but in it such a grim undertone that Lydana glanced at her.

"They serve us!" The small woman thumped her hands on the windowsill and Lydana saw that she again wore her fighting claws. "The men were feared to have them about, but the lord captain, and Jonas, and Dortmun—they got an idea and afterward there were men to help put the idea to work. The bodies must be out of sight—they were too fearsome for some of the men. So, into the fire ships they went! Then those which bore no great wound signs—they will serve as visible crew. With them sighted on the ships, who in the emperor's fleet will raise a question—until too late?"

"If our men were afraid, then who carried out such orders?" Lydana wanted to know.

"The mercenaries—those the lord captain took in the first assault. They were as afraid as our people, but they were prisoners and so they had no choice and were put to work. The lord captain said as how fire must be used to cleanse such foul bodies from the earth and most spoke up that he was right."

So the fire ships would be crewed. Lydana felt for her brooch. "Great Mother of all, these were also your children though they have been forced into the ways of evil. Let them indeed go to a warrior's end and in that end find your mercy."

"So be it," Skita said. "If some soul-essence still lingers in their bodies may it find peace forever."

It was drawing closer to evening. Lydana saw three of the ships, their masts askew and trailing with loose ropes, being worked away from separate points along the numerous wharfs. Skita was right, black coats were to be seen on the decks, somehow lashed upright and, from a distance, seeming to be at alert.

Each of the small vessels was escorted by a pair of longboats, oared vigorously so that those heavy efforts brought the ships around and sent them outward as if they moved so sluggishly because of the wreckage about them.

"Lady—*look!*" Skita pointed with one of her clawed hands to the sea beyond. Some of the debris bobbed on the waves there, but beyond there was something else—moving bulks. The emperor's fleet—or else the forescouts of it! Already they had passed the outer isles, and they were making better speed than the fire ships.

Lydana's foreknuckle was at her lips and she bit hard down on flesh and bone. Was there one on those incoming ships who would suspect some bold trick? Who already had a farseeing glass trained on the three swinging ships?

Could such a glass center on a black coat and know him speedily for what he was—a twice-dead man, now serving their enemies?

It would seem that there was one wary captain at least within Balthasar's service, for those forerunning cutters were taking in canvas, slacking speed. There was a fair wind, and they had been making the most of it before.

One of the longboats beside each of the fishing vessels dropped behind, cutting the forward speed of those they escorted. Dropped behind, but did not head shoreward.

There were no storm clouds tonight, the fierce sharp-billed birds swung out and about those supposedly drifting boats. Lydana shivered, knowing only too well what attracted them. For the shore hawks were scavengers, and the signs of death they knew well. Would someone also see and suspect?

The foremost cutters were swinging aside, opening a path before the fishing boats. Now the wind was bringing on the fleet. How large it was she could not judge—or even if all of it was making for this landing.

"Hawks' meat." Skita almost purred the words. "See, they are pulling aside—opening a path. The black coats serve us very well in the end."

It was true the longboats had flitted back among the wreckage, leaving the ships they had escorted to surge forward, though what trick of wind or current served them now Lydana could not guess. Perhaps something greater than the men who risked their lives below was now in command.

Hardly daring to believe that this would come so easily, they watched the first of the fishing boats pass between the cutter scouts, which gave it wide berth—was that because of the black figures, now too small to be seen, who kept the deck? Perhaps Apolon's forces were as feared by the emperor's fighting men as they were by those who knew them for what they were.

The second ship was nearby the cutters. They were too far away now for them to see any action even if it were aroused.

Then—

There was no sound as she would have expected—only an upward reaching of flame-tongues. Fire—even bale fire—was part of the Great Power, one of the first gifts to mankind, and the fire enveloped the fishing boat just as it swung between the first two fighting ships in line. Those flames reached out across the water—and bale fire could not be doused by water: that was the greatest of its secrets. Sails and rigging caught, even as the second of the fishing boats bore in beside its fellow. The cutters tried to fend off the third, but were enwrapped with the red-yellow flashes.

Though it might be dusk by the hour lamp, yet out on the bay there was the fierce light of midday. Not only did the flames reach out, but by some trick of craftsmanship, round balls of fire arose to spin even farther ahead, bringing the bale fire to ships which might have deemed themselves safe and might have had a chance to run.

Lydana covered her eyes. This was a fearsome thing—down there men died such deaths as made her spirit cringe.

"It is true horror—" she said.

"Not as you think, lady."

Startled she looked to Skita. "Thus they would have served Merina had they been so ordered. I have seen what I have seen—there are those who delight in slaughter—"

She was still staring out to sea. And Lydana remembered—though Skita had never spoken of how she had come into a pirate's caging—it might have been by such fury as they were watching now.

Yet war or not, Lydana shivered. She dare no longer watch what her own efforts had brought about. The rage which had smoldered in her was being absorbed by that curtain of fire.

Her hand throbbed and she turned it palm-upward in the light. There the brand the Heart had laid upon her was glowing. She had asked that any vengeance be visited on her if she had done wrong. Was this a sign that her time for payment had come?

"Evil returns to evil," she repeated the old catechism she had known from childhood, "good feeds good. By Heart and Hand Merina lives—but only by the favor of the Great One. Even as I draw breath as You will it. Out of Your mercy take those who die now into Your peace, be they followers of Balthasar or men of ours entrapped in the fires they have set. Also—this I swear, by the Heart whose Blood I carry," her branded hand clasped the brooch, "that having thus served, I shall not so serve again. For the stain of what I have brought about will lie on me always."

Almost she expected some answer. But perhaps the Great One was through with her—she was a gem fast in its setting and there would be no more polishing and fitting to be done. Only she knew that what she had said was the truth—if there had been any welling of the Talent within her, that had faded. She had played with forces which were not hers to control. But at that moment she felt no loss, only as if she had set aside a burden not hers for the bearing.

§ 61 §

ADELE

Gemen Elfrida sat in her place in the sanctuary, intoning the chants with all the other Gemen. Verit had been right; a demonstration of what Apolon was really doing had made quite a difference in the atmosphere of the Temple. The few people who had not quite understood what was going on during the exorcism realized the true state of affairs fast enough once the Novices Apolon had tried to subvert started talking.

Apparently Apolon had not taken sufficiently into account the fact that anyone who could survive more than a month or two in the Temple was not the sort of person who could be expected to be anything other than horrified by the practice of necromancy. All but the newest one of "Apolon's Novices" had made full public confession and repudiated him and all his works.

The newest one, unfortunately, had not been in the Temple long enough to have become truly a child of the Heart. He had been blinded—at least temporarily—by the light from the Heart during the exorcism, and while he had not made a formal confession, what he had screamed out when he realized what had happened to him was just as informative.

Elfrida struggled to pull her wandering thoughts back to the ritual she was chanting. At the moment she was

446

unable to concentrate on what she was supposed to be doing. She was restless, and seemingly random thoughts chased each other through her head.

Except that—those thoughts were not really random; they were fragments of all of the dangers and problems that the Temple was about to face, and which had as yet no answers.

How long until Apolon showed his hand? The Temple was surrounded by his black coats, and they had begun turning people away who came to worship. How long until word of what Lydana and her ragtag army had done reached the emperor and his advisors—and what would *they* do when they learned of it?

Shelyra and her young—well, perhaps not so young— man had vanished into the tunnels of the palace a few moments ago, perhaps on the most hazardous mission of all. Elfrida was more and more certain that the emperor was a puppet of Apolon's. The Grey Mage seemed to have no taste for the outer trappings of power; such as he were perfectly content to let others be the figureheads while they ruled from behind the throne. If that was the case here, the emperor must certainly represent the acme of Apolon's skill. Balthasar must be able to speak and act seemingly on his own; that would take special magics to achieve, perhaps even a spell of purely mental control. Apolon had surely put great protections on his magics, as well, to prevent anyone from freeing the emperor as Thom Talesmith had been freed.

But Thom Talesmith was not freed by magic, she reminded herself. *He was freed by the Power of the Heart. Surely not even Apolon could counter that!*

But before Leopold and Shelyra could even begin to determine the cause of the emperor's behavior, they had to get past Cathal.

And they must, absolutely must, render Cathal unable to act. If they do not, he will surely ally with Apolon. We can probably meet an assault by magic, but we cannot put up any kind of defense against an assault by soldiers.

She tried to tell herself that all that was out of her hands now; that she must concentrate on what she *could* do, and trust to the Great One and the competence of those around her to handle the tasks they had assumed.

But it was hard, very hard. She was still too used to being the dowager queen, with her fingers in every pie. Old habits died hard.

She started, her heart leaping into her throat, as someone tapped her on the shoulder. She turned her head, and saw Gemen Fidelis, who laid his finger across his lips, then gestured for her to follow him.

Puzzled, she did so. He took her as far as the corridor before speaking.

"As you said, there was an assault on the prison ships in the harbor, and a further assault on the emperor's fleet coming into the harbor. Both were successful, and someone that Verit believes is Harbormaster Captain Saxon is gathering an army from the dockside end of the city."

Elfrida nodded; the walking pace that Fidelis set was too fast for her, and she saved her breath for keeping up with him.

"Now we have a problem; there is a loyal army moving toward us, but so are all of Apolon's black coats. It looks to me as if we are going to have fighting right on the steps of the Temple itself." Fidelis shook his head. "I'm still not convinced that the black coats—the living ones, anyway—can't get across the Temple threshold. So we need to think about a defense."

"Why are you coming to me?" Elfrida asked ingenuously. Fidelis gave her a withering look.

"Gemen Elfrida, I am aware that we leave our previous lives behind when we take our vows," he replied with a touch of acidity. "However, *I* am not blind, nor deaf, nor am I so inexperienced that I cannot see past a woman's cosmetics and costume to the woman herself. I stood and knelt within bowshot of the Double Thrones for the past five years, Queen Adele. I knew who you were the moment Gemen Elfrida entered the novitiate."

"*Damn!*" Elfrida swore, the word slipping out before she could stop it. "Does anyone else—"

"Cosima, I think. No one else but Verit, who obviously knows the identities of all of us." He raised an eyebrow at her. "So, Gemen Elfrida, you and I are probably the only two members of the orders in this Temple with real experience at warfare—or, at least, of conflict. It falls to the two of us to do what we can to ready the Temple against a physical assault."

She nodded briskly. "And just what were you?" she asked, acid entering her own voice. "If you have my identity, I would consider it a courtesy—"

"No one special, and no one you would have heard of, although in my day I did have a good reputation." He turned a corner, and she realized he was leading the way to the storerooms. Now that was a good idea; although strict accounting was supposed to be kept of everything there, in practice, the accounts seldom matched the stores for anything other than scribes' needs and foodstuffs. There could be things down there that would serve as weapons—things like the shepherds' staffs.

"I was a freelance mercenary captain," Fidelis continued. "You might have noticed my accent."

"Hmm, yes," Elfrida replied. "Northern?"

He nodded. "Venikia. I had my own company, until the day I woke up and realized that I was sick to my soul of fighting and determined to devote the rest of my life to something worthwhile. At that point, I got a rather convenient wound in combat that looked much worse than it was. I left the company in the hands of my second, and 'died' on the field." He shrugged. "There it is. There was no reason to come this far south, and yet I found myself drawn to the Temple of the Heart. Perhaps there was a reason for this."

"I suspect that there was, given the situation that faces us now," Elfrida replied soberly. "I suppose that Verit and Cosima have been scrying?"

Fidelis nodded, and stopped in front of the door to the

first storeroom. "We do have one advantage," he told her. "This is something that we had a hint of through the confessionals, and that Cosima has verified. Many of Cathal's mercenaries are deserting him—for atrocities he has taken to performing on *them*. Speaking as a former professional, I can't say that I wouldn't do the same in their place."

She followed him into the storeroom and immediately saw something of use. There was a row of ornamental pedestals cast of artificial stone; presumably they had once held statues or something of the sort. "We can use those as a barricade, or to hold the side doors shut," she pointed out. "That way we would only have to worry about watching the main entrance. So what this means is that many of Cathal's men will *not* join the black coats in an assault?"

"Good." He made a note in the little book he held. "Yes, that is precisely the point. So the numbers coming against us are fewer."

She had already spotted something else—leaning against the wall in a dark and cobwebby corner were some very old-fashioned banner poles, meant to be slipped through the tops of banners or tapestries so that they could be hung in the sanctuary for particular festivals. These poles had fallen out of favor because they had been made to represent spears—and were considered to be inappropriate for the Temple. Now that very resemblance might serve them.

"What about those?" she asked, pointing to them. Fidelis turned and peered into the corner.

"Excellent," he said. "Those are solid metal, aren't they?"

"I think so." She wormed her way into the corner and moved one experimentally. "They seem to be. Doesn't that make them too heavy to use?"

"Not if we're bracing them against horsemen trying to ride us down," he said with a casual air that made her blood run cold. "Too heavy to throw, yes, but we are *not* going to attack, we are merely going to defend. If they are stupid enough to run horses up on spears—" He shrugged.

She wormed her way back out of the corner as he made more notes. "That gives us a passive obstructive barrier, and a passive defensive barrier," he said vaguely. "I don't suppose there's anything swordlike around here, is there?"

"No," she replied positively. "The last real weapon here was the Sword of Gideon, and that left the Temple about twenty years after the defeat of Iktcar. Anything we find will have been made for a purpose other than weaponry."

He paused in his writing and scratched the side of his nose with the end of his pen. "You know—you're the obvious choice as archpriestess once Verit passes. You *might* consider offering one of the militant orders house-space here if we live through all this."

The calm of his words made her shiver with a chill. *Is he anticipating his own death?* she wondered. It was a logical thought. He was likely to be at the front of any real fighting that occurred.

"I'll do that," she promised. "As a whole, I don't care for the militant orders, but the Order of Holy Mikael has a good reputation, and they train their warriors to be healers as well."

"That was who I was going to suggest," Fidelis told her. "The times are dangerous, and the Heart is a relic of great Power. It's only a matter of time before another like Apolon begins to covet it."

That stopped her dead in her tracks. It was something that she simply had not considered. "Apolon wants the *Heart*?" she said incredulously.

"Of course he wants the Heart," Fidelis replied impatiently. "If I were in his position, *I* would. It's a reservoir of Power, and what does he need but Power?"

"But I would have thought he would not be able to use it," Elfrida protested.

Fidelis just grunted. "Maybe he can, maybe he can't. If he can, think how much farther ahead he is. If he can't, if it is too holy for him even to touch, he can still bargain with Dark Powers by offering to destroy it."

That, also, had never occurred to her, but of course

Fidelis was right. The Powers of Darkness would be only too pleased to have one of the major relics of the Light removed from the world, and would probably offer a great deal in return for such a favor.

Now much of what Apolon was doing began to make terrible sense.

"I don't see anything else here that's useful," Fidelis said as Elfrida stood there, rooted in place. "Unless you can think of something."

His matter-of-fact appeal to her practical side shook her out of her daze. She cast another look around, but all of the rest of the things stored here were nothing more than wooden and canvas decorations for various feast days, meant to be hung inside and outside the Temple. "Nothing that I can see," she said. "We'd better move on to the next room."

In the end, they came away with a list that included another two sets of pedestals, more shepherds' staffs, and a variety of odds and ends. There was more than she would have thought would be useful as weapons of defense—though most of the defense would be passive in nature.

There was no choice to that. The Gemen were *not* young, and most of them had never had any formal fighter training in their lives.

"I'm not doing something that is going to place a sedentary scholar in front of a trained man with bared steel in his hands," Fidelis said grimly as they parted—an assertion that relieved Elfrida quite a bit. "The Writ forbids murder, and that's just what that would be. If we can find a way to barricade ourselves in here, that would be best. *We* can afford to wait them out."

But as she left him to return to Verit, she wondered about that last statement. *Could* they afford to wait out a siege?

She didn't know. And her only hope was that they wouldn't have to find out the hard way.

§ 62 §

SHELYRA

For two days, Shelyra and Leopold had skulked about the secret passageways of the palace without being able to do anything. The emperor had created his own audience chamber out of one of the few rooms in the palace that had no passageways or spy holes around it. Their frustration grew with every foray into the palace. It was as if he knew about the passageways and was trying to prevent them from watching him.

He had replaced his personal guards with a mixture of six of Apolon's black coats and six of Cathal's mercenaries. Leopold's own regiment had been confined to quarters for insubordination after the men went out during and after the great storm to try and help the civilians of Merina. Evidently the emperor did not consider this to be appropriate behavior for his troops. Leopold had heard a rumor that Cathal had made one attempt to send one of his officers to their barracks to take command, and that the men had literally refused to hear him—they had, so rumor said, pretended that the storm had deafened them all.

And as for Cathal himself, the man had not set foot inside the palace in two days—but there were stories coming in from his mercenaries, men who had deserted his ranks, that appalled everyone who heard them. It seemed that when Cathal ran out of civilians to torture, he began using his own men to vent his frustration. Whatever control he had maintained over the years was gone, and at this point he was not even trying to pretend that the men he flogged, flayed, and strung up had actually *done* anything. They just had the misfortune to get in his way. Given that, many of his former troopers had decided that the best way to avoid him was to desert.

A few of these men had managed to penetrate past the gauntlet of black coats to get into the Temple; one or two of Shelyra's Gypsy friends had done the same. That was how they were able to get any news from outside at all. The Gypsies left once their budget of news was spent, but the mercenaries stayed, a development that had made Gemen Fidelis smile with grim satisfaction. Now Fidelis had a neat little squad of pikemen, armed with metal spears that had once held up tapestries on the Temple walls, who kept a careful watch on all the entrances. The mercenaries seemed perfectly happy to be there, but Shelyra wondered if they had any idea what they might be facing shortly.

One squad of pikemen was not going to do a great deal of good if the emperor brought men in force against the Temple.

Then again—perhaps those who came to join them had done so as a kind of penance. They certainly spent a great deal of time in the confessionals. They might very well know what it was they ultimately faced, and it might be that such a fate was preferable to one that came at the end of service to someone like Cathal.

It began to look as if the emperor—or rather, Apolon, acting in the name of the emperor—had elected to simply put the Temple under siege, assuming that sooner or later they would have to surrender. Or just perhaps, the emperor had more to worry about than a handful of old, scholarly men and women mewed up in a great, inescapable stone box. The mercenaries had also brought word with them that someone had successfully taken the prison ships in the harbor and had followed that victory up with the destruction of the ships of the imperial fleet which had come to bring supplies and reinforcements. The mercenaries claimed that the rebels now held the entire waterfront, and so far as they were able, the mages of the Temple confirmed that.

That was the situation as Leopold and Shelyra took to the tunnels just after dawn on the morning of the third day of the siege.

They realized that something was up as soon as they got inside the walls of the palace. The place was alive with activity. Men shouted and ran, their voices and footsteps echoing down into the hidden ways in a confusion of half-muffled sounds. Last night the palace had been so silent that it might have been deserted; this morning it resembled a disturbed nest full of very angry wasps looking for something to sting.

They traded glances in the dim light filtering down from one of the larger spy holes, and immediately took to the passageways leading to the emperor's audience chamber. Although they could not spy on the chamber itself, they had a single observation point within the chamber just outside it.

By now, Leopold knew the passageways that Shelyra had shown him as well as she did, and there was no fumbling around in the dark to get where they were going. Leopold had exchanged his military riding boots for the soft leather sort that the Gypsies and Horse Lords wore, so that they ran as noiselessly as a pair of rats in the walls, keeping track of where they were in the darkness by counting footsteps and trailing one hand along the wall itself.

Shelyra had been in the lead, so she was the one who reached the spy hole first. She uncovered it and put her eye to it just in time to see Cathal stride into the audience chamber, wrath in every line of his body, trailed by six reluctant-looking mercenaries. All six of them took up posts outside the door, three on either side; none followed Cathal inside. A moment later, six of Apolon's black coats came out, heading purposefully toward the exit. Leopold had already determined that all of the black coats attending the emperor were living men, not dead-alive ones. Not that it really mattered, for the living ones were sadistic monsters who took pleasure in the fear they inspired in people.

She reported all this in a whisper to Leopold before she surrendered the spy hole to him. He watched for a moment more, then pressed his ear to it instead.

Cathal must have sent the black coats out so that he could speak to the king in private. Whatever has happened, it must be important. Cathal never comes here anymore.

"Shouting," Leopold said quietly; in the near dark of the passageway, it was impossible to tell what his expression was, but she thought his voice sounded strained. "Not the emperor, though; it's all Cathal. It's muffled so much that I can't make out everything, but I *think* he's about to have an apoplectic fit because Apolon has just called in all of his black coats for some large operation of his own—and Cathal needs all the men he can get himself. There's something major happening down at the harbor that began around dawn—"

He was about to continue when more men came running in, interrupting him. He put his eye to the hole quickly, then switched to his ear. "Those were messengers," he whispered, the excitement in his voice rising. "And they left the door to the audience chamber open— there's an uprising down at the harbor! There are armed men coming toward imperial lines!"

"It's happening—" she said, her stomach turning to a knot between one heartbeat and the next. "Apolon is moving on the Temple, and the rebels are moving on the city. If we're going to do anything, it has to be now."

She sensed his nod, although she did not see it. A chill ran down her back; if they actually managed to eliminate Cathal and the emperor now, they would chop off two of the heads of this three-headed monster which had been devouring Merina.

"Can you get all of the guards from here?" he asked.

"I think so," she replied as she took out the blow-pipe and tiny arrows, and with them one vial of the all-important drug. She was very proud that her hands didn't shake, although she felt as if she should be trembling in every limb. "They can't be more than ten feet away. I can crack the door enough to aim and fire without their noticing."

The door into this room was at the back of a recessed alcove, meant to hold a life-sized statue. At the moment it held a rather silly artificial tree made of silk, since the statue of a former queen of Merina that had been there had not met with the emperor's approval. This was just fine for Shelyra's purposes, since the tree effectively obscured the back of the alcove without hindering her aim. With luck, none of the six men out there would realize what was "biting" them until she had scored at least one hit on all of them.

This was all such an incredible risk she could not believe that she was actually following through on it! *I'm certainly not the woman I was a few months ago. . . .*

The drug was very potent, but lost its strength rapidly after it dried. The darts were only effective for about an hour; after that, they would need to be redipped. One could immobilize a man for several hours, a horse for a third of that time. And, most importantly, she doubted that any of these mercenaries had ever heard of such a weapon. Even if one of them realized he had been hit by a dart, it should take them a moment to envision a dart as a serious threat.

She dipped the points of eight of her darts in the vial and discarded the vial itself; what was left would be as useless as water in a few hours, and it was too hard to reseal such a tiny bottle in the dark. Then she moved to the hidden door beside the spy hole, while Leopold kept his eye on the room.

Carefully, she cracked open the door; the light seemed blinding for a moment as she eased it open just enough to slip the barrel of her weapon through. The men were deployed in two rows, three on each side of the doorway, like a row of targets at a Spring Fair shooting contest. Someone came to slam the door into the audience chamber shut as she watched. That was a relief; it meant that she might be able to bring down the guards in here without Cathal knowing. No one noticed the open door behind the shadow cast by the artificial tree. By stooping just a little, she had a clear line of sight on all six of them.

This is going to have to be very quick. . . . She had become an expert in the use of this weapon, using the much less-potent drug the Horse Lords employed for taking game, but she had never been forced to take down so many targets at once. She only hoped she could get one dart into each of them before they realized that it was an attack and not an annoyance. The two things she had in her favor were the short range, and the likelihood that these men would believe the darts to be the bites of insects. At this range she seldom missed, and even though the darts were tiny, they were able to penetrate almost anything.

She loaded the first dart into the pipe, selected the man farthest from her as her target, and puffed into the pipe as hard as she could.

A heartbeat later, the man slapped his neck and swore.

"What's th' matter, Kappa?" the man next to him asked with a snicker. "That last girl you took have fleas?"

"Prolly," the first man said sourly. He didn't seem to have noticed the tiny dart; hopefully it fell inside his collar. Shelyra targeted the next in line. "Been slappin' bugs all night."

"Ye might try takin' a bath," jeered another as the second man responded to the second dart with a slap of his own.

"Damn!" he swore. "Git away from me, Kappa, them fleas is jumpin' over here!"

Shelyra hit the third and fourth while the first two were arguing; still her luck was in, for none of them had caught the little dart when they slapped at the irritating stings. Cathal was still bellowing in the other room, so he wouldn't hear the argument and open the door to find out what caused it.

The fifth stood aloof from the argument, until the dart struck him. That was when her luck ran out.

He slapped, like the others, but unlike the others, his hand came away with the dart in it, and he stared at it with a perplexed look on his face. Swiftly, before he could draw attention to his prize, she stung the sixth—just as the first suddenly stopped arguing, rolled his eyes up into his head, and collapsed bonelessly where he stood.

The others followed in swift succession, leaving silence behind.

She opened the door completely, and in a well-planned action, shoved the tree branches aside, ran to the door to the corridor, and locked and barred it. That would delay any aid from outside. Meanwhile, Leopold had run to the door into the audience chamber and was listening intently.

Shelyra armed herself from the fallen mercenaries; like all soldiers for hire, their weaponry was as varied as it was possible to be. They armed themselves at their own expense, and these six must have considered their weapons and armor to be secondary in importance to nothing. They might be in need of a bath, but their armor was polished, oiled, and without a trace of mending. Their chins were unshaven and their teeth rotting, but their swords and knives were of the best and finest make and materials and kept in immaculate shape.

Shelyra immediately seized on a dagger balanced for throwing, then snatched up the lightest sword of the lot. The rest were all heavier than she was used to, and that could be fatal in combat.

Combat— her stomach knotted. She had never been in real combat before, only the practices the Horse Lords held. *I might kill someone. I might be killed. I don't think I like this very much. . . .* When this had all started, it had seemed like an adventure. Now—now it was a very deadly business, and she just wanted it over with.

Leopold stepped away from the door long enough to seize a sword and dagger for himself. Then he nodded at Shelyra.

"Ready?" he asked softly. She swallowed and nodded. Oh, how she regretted getting into this, but of course, it was too late to back out now.

Leopold kicked in the door; it flew open, and he shot through it. She was right behind him, dagger poised to throw, ready to snatch her Horse Lord knife from the sheath once it was gone.

There were only three people in the room, and no guards at all: Cathal, the chancellor, and Balthasar. Cathal stood staring at the door, for once taken completely by surprise. Adelphus stood slightly behind the throne, his face blank and impassive. Balthasar sat on his throne, his expression a match for his chancellor's.

Cathal did not stay stunned for long; with an incoherent roar, he drew his weapons and flung himself at Leopold. Shelyra did not give the emperor a chance to make the odds against the prince two to one.

She flung the dagger in her hand straight for the emperor's throat, but he twisted aside, as supple as a snake, and it sank into the wooden back of the throne with a dull *thunk*. That seemed to be enough to center his attention on her, however; as she drew her Horse Lord dagger, the emperor pulled his own weapon from its sheath and advanced on her with great deliberation. She ran forward, and then to the side, to put herself between the emperor and Leopold.

She was already sweating with fear, a salt-bitter taste in the back of her throat. *I can't let him go after Leopold; I have to keep his attention on me.*

He was old—but he was also a seasoned fighter, and he outweighed her by a considerable amount. She was *not* going to let him close with her, even if she did have to keep his attention!

She also still had her blow-pipe and two darts; if she could lure him into the other room, she might be able to sting him with a dart before they became ineffective.

So she danced ahead of him, taking advantage of the fact that she was far more nimble than he ever could have been, staying just out of reach. That sounded easier than it actually was; Leopold and Cathal were engaged in a grim struggle all over the room, and she had to stay out of the way of Cathal as well as the emperor. She had no doubt whatsoever that if she happened to blunder into his reach, Cathal would grab her to use her for a shield.

So she ducked and swerved, and tried to keep track of how much longer the darts would remain effective. A miscalculation cost her the dagger, as she was forced to parry and lost it. That left her hand numb, but at least she managed to get out of reach before Balthasar could follow up.

The darts won't be good for very much longer, she thought, as sweat ran down her back and she narrowly avoided both Cathal's outstretched arm and the emperor's sword. Her breath burned in her lungs, and yet everything seemed preternaturally clear. *In fact, at the moment, all they might do is to slow these two down—*

Well, that would be better than nothing! Leopold was having a heavy time of it, and *she* couldn't avoid Balthasar many more times without slipping. Both of them were tired, and neither the emperor nor his general showed any *sign* of strain!

So she took a chance, dropped the sword as she ran, and pulled out the pipe. The remaining darts were in her collar; she reached for one as she leapt up onto the throne. She inserted it into the pipe as she turned, and blew sharply as soon as she had a target.

It happened to be Cathal, not the emperor.

She leapt down from the throne just as Balthasar's enormous, heavy sword came slashing down at her. She felt the wind of its passing against her skin and was mortally glad she was wearing her close-fitting, black "skulking" clothing.

But the powerful stroke also buried the blade into the wood of the throne—Balthasar struggled to pull it free, giving her a moment to whirl, snatch up the second dart, aim, and fire.

Cathal did not notice the dart, but she didn't really expect him to—not in the heat of battle. The second dart struck the emperor full in the throat—

And he did nothing about it. He didn't even bat at it in reflex, and on the softer tissue of the throat, that dart should have *stung!* She ducked around the throne, keeping it between herself and Balthasar—he kept swinging away at her, chopping huge gouges into the carved wood of the throne. In the back of her mind, a stray thought noted that Queen Lydana would have a litter of kittens when she saw it. . . .

He's terribly clumsy—why is he so clumsy? He was supposed to be an amazing fighter!

Then a thick, gluey voice came literally out of *nowhere,* and she almost lost a hand by not moving fast enough, it startled her so—because it wasn't Leopold's voice, it wasn't Cathal's, and it certainly wasn't the emperor's.

"Blood!" it blubbered, the sound oddly muffled. *"Feed!"*

She ducked around the throne again, trying to maneuver the emperor so that she could see the other two combatants as well as her own opponent. She had to choke back a cough as her breath rasped harshly in her throat and her heart pounded with exertion.

"Blood!" the voice shouted again, more insistently. *"Now!"*

Whatever it was, it came from the direction of Cathal! Could the general be harboring one of Apolon's blood-demons? But—the demon holding Thom had never spoken!

"Blood!" the voice howled as Cathal suddenly staggered backward, though Leopold had done nothing. *"Blooooooood!"*

Cathal stumbled into the wall and fell, his left hand clutching at his right wrist, as if he was trying to get rid of something. He began to beat his own hand into the wall as Leopold watched, dumbfounded; all he succeeded in doing was to force his own hand open, making him drop his sword, which hit the wall, then skittered across the floor a little in Shelyra's direction.

As if that had unleashed some dark power neither of them had suspected, the general screamed, pulled his own dagger from its sheath, and began to hack at his right hand with it.

Shelyra would have continued to watch in horrified fascination, but the emperor's attentions began to be a bit more pressing. In fact, in a moment, she knew that she was fighting for her life.

§ 63 §

LEOPOLD

Leopold would have moved, if he could have, but every muscle seemed to be paralyzed by the bizarre drama playing out before him. Cathal seemed to be trying to rid himself of an armguard on his right wrist, and Leopold had gotten the weird impression that the strange voice calling for blood had *come* from that arm guard.

It made no sense; it made no *sense!*

But as soon as the first drops of blood sprayed from Cathal's lacerated wrist, the entire scene, which had been strange enough before, took a more bizarre turn.

"Blood!" screamed that bubbling voice, this time in satisfaction rather than in demand—and Cathal shrieked, a high, terrified scream like nothing Leopold had ever heard come from a human mouth.

And even as he watched, Cathal's body began to collapse in upon itself like an inflated bladder losing air. All the while, Cathal himself continued to scream madly.

Lady Bright— Sickened, Leopold averted his eyes, and

found that he was looking at the sword that Cathal had dropped.

His gaze was caught, trapped, for now that Cathal no longer held it, the sword was no longer the ordinary, dull blade that it once had been.

Now it glowed with a pure, white light that Leopold immediately associated with the Messengers. He literally could not look away; in fact, it drew him, as irresistible to him as a flame to a moth.

Without thinking, he dropped his purloined blades and picked up this one—

Shelyra—he thought, belatedly. *Shelyra . . . Lady Bright! She's up against Balthasar!*

He whirled, made a short dash across the room, and stepped between his father and Shelyra with the blade held in both hands.

But as his father paused, staring at him with no recognition in his eyes, Leopold saw a new and different variety of shadow masking the emperor's face. Something held the emperor in thrall, but it was not the kind of blood-demon that had held Thom. This looked at him out of the emperor's eyes, recognized what he held, and did not like it at all.

He remembered Elfrida's suggestion, that Balthasar had been possessed and, moved by an instinct he did not question, reversed the glowing blade in his hands.

He now held it up between them, raising it like an icon, with the hilt uppermost.

Balthasar's eyes flickered from one side to the other, as if he could not quite look at the blade. Now a faint expression of uncertainty and alarm crept over his features, although they still registered no recognition of his son.

Leopold took a step forward, and the emperor took a matching step back.

All this time, Adelphus had stood quietly off to the side, out of the way of the combat, and had done nothing. Now, when Leopold glanced at the chancellor, he saw a shadow in Adelphus' eyes that was all too familiar.

Dead-alive. When had it happened? Just after he had been sent to the Summer Palace in exile?

At least that explained why Adelphus had stopped trying to help him. *Well, it doesn't look as if he is going to interfere. Perhaps he fears the sword—or perhaps he has no orders. I can leave him for the Gemen, I think.*

Cathal had stopped screaming, and Leopold did not want to look at what was probably left of the general. Instead, he concentrated on his father. Obviously Balthasar was not going to attack them, not while Leopold held this blade, but they couldn't just leave him like this. Was there *anything* he could do now? If he and Shelyra walked out now, that still left Balthasar in charge of the imperial armies, and able to continue the attack on the Temple with Apolon. Whatever held the emperor in thrall was intelligent enough to command soldiers, at least under Apolon's direction. And despite everything that had happened, he could not bear the thought that his father might die at his son's hands.

But—perhaps this sword might do something?

Whatever was in control of the emperor certainly seemed to fear it. Could the sword actually drive the possessing entity away?

It was worth a try, at any rate.

He took slow, deliberate steps toward his father, forcing Balthasar back into the wall, one stumbling step at a time. The emperor pressed his back against the wall as if he would like to press himself through it, his face still curiously impassive, but the shadow in his eyes was writhing away from the pure, white light of the sword in Leopold's hands.

Behind him he heard Shelyra panting heavily, but she said nothing. He continued to advance on the emperor as Balthasar turned his head away from the sword, fingers scrabbling uselessly on the wooden paneling of the wall, until finally there was only a single pace between them.

Quickly, before Balthasar could reach out to try to

knock it aside, he pressed the hilt of the sword against the emperor's face.

There was a soundless explosion of light—a choked cry—

And when the light died down again, the emperor was sliding down the wall bonelessly. He was not unconscious, but there was no sense whatsoever in his eyes, no expression on his face, and no strength to his muscles. He might have been an infant the size of a man—and in fact, as he slid down onto the floor, he curled up in a fetal position and stuck his thumb in his mouth, closing his eyes.

Shelyra came up quietly to stand beside him, staring down at what was left of the Emperor of the Known World. She said nothing, but her hand groped for his, and he freed one hand from his sword to take hers and squeeze it for a moment.

Movement out of the corner of his eye caught his attention, and he turned to see Adelphus bending over the wizened and withered remains of General Cathal. The general himself no longer resembled anything human, but the necromantic puppet of Adelphus—for surely that was what it was—didn't seem to notice or care.

Of course he wouldn't; he's not alive to care.

He dropped Shelyra's hand and took the hilt of the shining blade properly in his sword hand. Whatever had control of Adelphus would probably respond to whatever was in the blade—and even if all he did was to free Adelphus' soul—

He started to move, then froze as a bell-like voice rang out in the silence.

"Wait, Leopold. You are needed far more, elsewhere."

Startled, he looked around wildly for the source of the voice. It *sounded* like the kind of voice he had heard from the Messenger, but there was no one in the room except for himself, Shelyra, and what was left of Adelphus and his father.

"You cannot see me, Leopold, but you hold the blade that I forged to destroy one such as Apolon. The Temple is in-

vaded, and the Gemen are in dire straits; they cannot stand against the Powers of Darkness alone. You are needed there, and quickly, lest the Temple fall and the Heart of Power be turned to the Heart of Darkness!"

Leopold did not even stop to consider that the voice in his mind might be lying to him. Every word was so wrought with a feeling of truth that he could not doubt it, even for an instant.

He wavered for a moment as Adelphus reached for the unholy armguard that had sucked the life from General Cathal, but only for a moment. He could not be here, and there, too—but he sensed that no matter what the cuff created out of Adelphus, it would be a pale imitation of what Apolon was at this very instant.

He turned and ran for the hidden door, leaving Shelyra to dash along in his wake, certain that no matter how quickly he reached the Temple, it would not be a single moment too soon.

§ 64 §

LYDANA

"**S** o they turned tail and away with 'em!" Jonas, with a bandage tied rakishly around his frowsled head, had been consuming vast quantities of the sour drink at intervals. His gap-toothed grin was wide, and he was plainly in the best of spirits. Around his thick neck and slipping back and forth across his grease-stained tunic was a golden captain's chain of such fine fashioning it was a worthy piece of loot indeed.

"Hauled 'em out of the water right an' left, as the captain ordered. Lot of 'em would rather drown than frizzle. And them as did get caught are long gone."

It had been a long two days since they had sent the fire boats out, and for the past twenty-four hours those of Merina had been nosing in and around the site of the catastrophe. Most of what they garnered were men—some burned to the point Lydana could do nothing for them except suggest the old, old remedies. And those were dying fast. But their fellows were under guard in some of the battered ships, their armor and any weapons found going to arm Saxon's force.

Lydana had seen the captain only once, his arm wrapped in a greasy cloth, and he had worn the look of a man nearly pushed to the limit of his endurance. He was sleeping now in his old quarters in the harbor tower, having been forced earlier to surrender to his body's need by Jonas' and Lydana's combined urging.

There was a constant coming and going on the wharves. Those of the river rats who had managed to arm themselves, either from supplies or from their captives, were busied at trying out their new weapons—new to some of them—as well as acting in ragged companies. They all knew that the heart of the battle still lay before them within Merina itself.

There was a constant going and coming by canal, using all the tricks of the one-time smugglers, so that news from the inner city was fed to them—though how much was truth and how much only the embroidery of rumor, they could not be sure.

Those messengers reported to Jonas and Lydana. The taverner scrabbled away with his knotted strings while she hung over a map of the city—one of good detail she had found in Saxon's desk, marking out the various points of trouble.

She had made no attempt to reach Adele through the Heart's Blood ruby, for the report had come early that the Temple was under heavy siege and she knew that all the power of Talent must be now turned in that direction.

"So the crab-faces," Jonas remarked as he tightened another knot, "have turned their claws on Cathal. Well, mercenaries fight for the profit of it, and no man finds profit in being flayed, or blinded, or made handless by his commander's rage at the moment. They are not sworn liege men."

Lydana's thoughts flinched away from the pictures Jonas' words evoked. It did seem from the continued run of reports that General Cathal was acting more like one of those demons of ancient legend than like any human-born man. And guilt continued to prick her with the thought that the Mouth of Vor might well have something to do with these spurts of insane rage the general showed at increasing intervals.

"Balthasar," Jonas was continuing, "is kind of unlucky in his aide now, ain't he? Never thought as how he would give the old chancellor the kick. Seems as if they always got along well together. But they now say he was caught a-dippin' into the imperial pockets a little too deeply. At least the chancellor is under watch by Apolon, with most of his own household."

"Apolon—" Her thoughts had been following a different direction. Jonas lost his grin.

"Aye, that one. He seems better on course than any of the others now. Balthasar appears to have given him a full hand with the Temple. But the emperor—whatever's come over him—he's not acting like the emperor we've heard tell of for so many years. And it seems he's at odds with that son of his into the bargain. No one's seen or heard anything of Leopold, and Leopold's own men won't answer to the emperor, any more than the mercenaries will answer to orders. His own guard are now mostly black coats, and Apolon has his ear whenever he wishes."

Lydana chafed at the thought they had had no contact with the Temple, though she was well aware that those at labor there after their own fashion probably had neither time nor thought except for what lay about them.

Saxon's scouts were out each night, using their small skiffs and knowledge of the canals to get into the city. They kept the captain well informed of what was doing along their own portions of Merina, with now and then a bit of news from beyond that section. They had heard early that Thom had been taken by the black coats, and Lydana had had to fight hard against her own desire to use the Seeing to discover what had become of Shelyra. She could only hope that, since no news of the princess' taking had been as yet rumored, the girl had escaped whatever net had captured Thom.

She sat now as she would never have believed possible, say, two moons ago—in leather and light mail, only the tight coils of her hair betraying her sex. She had raided the stores to find protection for herself and for Skita, since neither of them were about to allow this motley army to row inward on attack, unless they were a part of it.

Nor could Saxon deny her that—though he insisted upon a bodyguard of six, handpicked by Jonas, to keep an eye on her. Yet though they were mightily busied putting their force together, it would seem that the captain did not yet judge the time ripe for action.

She let her thoughts fly cityward, paying no attention to those who came from time to time to report to the taverner. At last she went to stand once more at the window, looking out upon the wash of wreckage in the harbor. Save for two fishing boats she could spot from this lookout, there was nothing left of Merina's once proud fleet. The rebuilding—if they were favored enough by the Greater Power to win and rebuild—would take a long time. She found herself counting the costs of sending southward to Jamvar, where the most cunning of shipbuilders had their headquarters, to begin the long process of that rebuilding.

"Lady!" Skita had joined her in her usual silent fashion. "There is news—"

Eagerly Lydana returned to the table. She recognized Dortmun, talking very fast and waving his hands in gestures, as if to emphasize every word he spoke.

"Demons—that one has brought demons! He swears he will crack the temple as a fosbird cracks a nut! They still hold, but the black ones press in!"

"The army?" That demand was loud to interrupt as Saxon came up behind the man.

"They do not march—as yet." Now Dortmun turned to face the captain. "Lemmel, he got as close as their horse lines—there is more trouble with the mercenaries, and the emperor has ordered them disarmed by his liege men. There is fighting there also—"

"It is time." Saxon looked at Lydana. "If the Temple falls—"

"If the Temple falls, all which makes Merina goes also," she said, and caught fiercely at the brooch which now swung on a thong over her mail. "We can wait no longer."

He nodded. And then turned to some of those who had followed him in, with a rattle of orders which sent men running in different directions.

Jonas rolled up his string records and tucked them carefully into his belt. "It is but midmorning," he pointed out.

"So? Apolon is not likely to wait for night now just to favor us." Skita rasped her claws together, as if she issued a challenge here and now.

Thus the seaport defenders of Merina made ready to move in upon the heart of the city. Lydana was not questioned when she took her place in one of the foremost of the barges, Jonas at her side. Saxon was at the prow of its neighbor, and at his command, they cut loose and the big oars swung out, sending the boats into mid-canal. Lydana glanced back. There were others swiftly following, more than she had earlier realized were ready for the venture. Most of the men on them were armed; three-quarters of them wore mail or half-armor. They did not have the snap of disciplined troops, but she was well aware that they were perhaps, in their own way, more dangerous than the emperor's troops in close fighting.

The city, as they swept along, seemed to be deserted at

the edges. But, as they neared the site of the Sailor's Knot, smaller skiffs shot out to fall in with them, and news flew from boat to boat.

Cathal still commanded at least part of his rebellious forces, and although he was not with them, the force was marching toward the north gate, heading toward the struggle at the Temple square. The liege men of the emperor had held off so far, but no one knew how long that condition might last.

But that Balthasar had indeed turned directly to Apolon and Cathal for support was now certain. His guards were black coats and mercenaries, and he kept aloof from the rest of his force. In fact, no one had seen him outside the palace for some twenty-four hours now.

The people of Merina had for the most part gone into hiding, save those who had in the past served directly in the guards or with the marines at sea. Several of the guildmasters and their families had been openly seized and were held captive near the Temple square, their guardians black coats.

On Lydana's breast there was a flare of crimson; she could feel the warmth of that even through her mail. Was it a summons—or else the final upburst of power under great pressure?

Those from the harbor left their barges and formed into irregular lines. But they seemed to show no dismay over what lay before them. Perhaps her strange defeat of the living dead had in a way armored them against any terror of mage work. Lydana, her hand on the brooch, worked her way well toward the fore of the advance. Jonas, deterred by his peg leg, had lagged in spite of his efforts to keep up; but Saxon strode, bared sword in hand, his face half-masked by his helm, the sun glinting from his breastplate. Though they lifted no banner, it was perhaps that sight of their leader which kept the rest of their force in good order.

But there was something else. As they began to pass houses, there came others slipping through partly open

doors. No mail, no swords, but there were knives in plenty
and boar spears from hunting days, as well as less conventional weapons. Lydana saw one stout woman, her full
skirts kilted up, in her hands a long spit from some hearth-
side.

Now they could hear the sound of Merina's agony of
battle—a roar of voices mingled with the clash of steel.
Abruptly they came to their first skirmish, where some of
the mercenaries attempted to bar the way. Two other
swordsmen moved quickly up to flank Saxon, and there
were pikes at his back, their owners seeming to jiggle from
foot to foot to gain a good chance to bring their weapons
into use.

Lydana planted her shoulders against the closed doorway of a house and stood her ground, the light sword she
had found for her use ready. Out of the corner of one eye
she saw shapes pulling themselves up on the roof spouts
not too far away, knives clearly gripped between their
teeth. They swung out and down, taking the fighting mercenaries in the rear.

Resistance did not last long. Thoroughly beaten enemies were quickly stripped of their weapons—and whatever else the victors thought usable.

Now the sound from the Temple square, only a short
distance away, was deafening: screams and shouts, and
above all a droning which seemed to fill Lydana's ears and
make her head ache. She saw Saxon shake his head as if
to lose that sound, and one or two of those around her
held hands over their ears, their mouths opening in loud
howls of their own. Beneath Lydana's hand, the ruby fire
flamed ever higher.

Saxon wiped his blade on the cloak of the commander
of the force, now lying limply at his feet. Then he jerked
his thumb first at one house door, and then another, on
either side of the street. These were not the elaborate
dwellings of guild families of high rank, and shoulders ap-
plied sturdily to the doors smashed them in. Those who
had forced them sped inside. That the owners need have

no fear, Lydana knew, and she could guess what Saxon had in mind; either to use the back entrances, if the houses had such, or move over the roofs so that he could face what waited in the square ahead on a wider front. Men jostled by Lydana before she could get aside, and were gone.

Among the first had been Dortmun, and she was well aware of the trust Saxon had in him.

Once more, the main part of their sea army pushed forward. And once more they had to face the enemy. But this time it was Lydana who took command—for a blot of black coats was like a vicious stain across the pavement ahead. The ruby—it drew on the Heart, yet it was their only defense. She was torn two ways as she raised the ruby drop in her hand, and yet knew that she had no choice.

With a gasp, she called upon the power of the stone. There were indeed the crimson waves rising in answer, but this time they lengthened themselves into a point like a spearhead, to strike directly on the noisome creatures barring their way.

Struck—killed—leaving the mutilated bodies from some long-ago battles limp across the pavements for her and her companions to pick a careful path around. Now, just ahead, they could see the square, and masses of color through which threaded the black coats loyal to Apolon bound for the Temple steps.

Lydana had seen this square thronged before, but then it had been packed with almost immobile people. Now there were swirls of fighting up to the very steps of the Temple. There were the blots of black coats, their backs to the confusion behind them, facing toward the great door. Between the foremost ran now a long tube, which they were sighting on that same door.

At its other end was a round-bellied container almost like a tun of ale—yet with a greasy shine to its surface, as if there were not honest drink inside. Some further mage work of Apolon's, she was sure. Saxon, his head turning right and left to mark the coming of his own force, joined her, and she caught at his arm.

"The black coats—" She did not know what horror they were about to release, but she believed they had some super-weapon saved for just this hour.

She also knew that she dared not call on the Heart's Blood now. All the Power wrapped in the Temple must be holding guard—she dare not lighten it by even a fraction.

Saxon nodded and raised his voice, trained to outshout a sea wind:

"Holla, to me!"

They formed a fighting wedge of men. Those at the point where Saxon had taken the lead were armored and better armed, and they were lunging forward, united and so set on their goal that they cut their way in. Around them swirled mercenaries and the bright surcoats of the emperor's own liege men. Men fell, and their late comrades strode across the bodies to cut down their slayers and follow the captain. Lydana held tightly to her sword and thanked her husband in memory for the hours he had taught her its usage. All which was in her now was the need to reach the Temple steps.

Then, for the first time, she saw Apolon. Though he was only a man of middle stature who had heretofore effaced himself, there stood now before that door another being. Gone was the grey robe she had seen him last wearing.

Now he was clad in a screaming scarlet, close-fitted to his body, and over the blood-hue of that played smoky swirls, as if he were encased in a cloudy, secondary garment.

In his hands was a staff—Lydana's oath stung her own ears as she watched it act of itself. It writhed in his grasp, reaching with Dark Power from time to time, as casually as a man would reach for a grape—and where it reached, men fell dead. How had he gained that, and from what secret storehouse?

Still—she dodged a blow and swept low with her own blade. To stand and watch would mean her death, she realized. But they had won their way very close to the stairs now.

An elbow in her ribs near sent her from her feet, as Saxon's greater bulk rose before her.

"If you have Power—" The rest of his sentence was lost in the clamor, but she realized what he said. Before the door, Apolon raised his arm, and dropped it in what was plainly a signal. He seemed to have no thought for the struggle in the square.

Though the black coats held their pipe at his very back, he did not move, as from the mouth of it burst sickly green-yellow flame. It curled around Apolon, leaving him seemingly untouched, then hit and flattened itself against the door.

There was the stench of old death and evil. And—the very substance of the door which had stood untouched by time for ages, began to melt. Nor did Apolon retreat, but stood waiting for the barrier to be gone.

At the same time those about Lydana began coughing, lurching in sickness which brought racking vomiting. Even Skita clung to her, her small body shaken with the fury of the inner tumult which gripped her. Only the black coats showed no reaction. Nor did she, Lydana realized. Perhaps it was the talisman she wore. But she gently detached Skita from her hold and started up the steps. None of the black coats turned to see her; they were still intent upon their strange weapon and aiming the evil flames into the interior.

But Apolon marched inside, with all the arrogance of the emperor himself, in the middle of that flooding stench; then his host of dead men followed, tugging with ropes, while four held the pipe steady to bring up the barrellike source from which this effluvia came.

Lydana followed. This was the end, she knew. Cathal the emperor, they were on the outskirts of the battle here. For it was no longer being fought man against man, but Strength against Strength.

She reached the doorway herself, to look down the navat the high altar. There had been no guards on this side of the door—no visible ones. It was around the altar itself that the defenders were massed. And they stood as still as the statues of the Great Ones Gone.

The Heart seemed to have lost some of its glory. She felt a movement, a pull at the cord which held the brooch; it was standing straight out from her breast. She had dropped her sword before she entered this place of peace. Now she caught at the brooch and tried to dig the gem out of its setting, while the heat of the stone gnawed at her.

Apolon still marched confidently ahead, but his black coats had halted with the clumsy weapon. Apparently this last battle was on the part of their master alone.

The thong and ruby brooch it held was whipping about now in what almost seemed a rage. Lydana's fingernail broke, but the ruby was free. Free, but no longer in her hand—it was gone even as it touched her flesh.

There was a spark in the air—on it flew, over the heads of the black coats; and then it was gone, swallowed up in the distance to the high altar.

The Heart—it was glowing—higher, brighter. In Lydana there was an awe almost as great as fear. Suddenly she knew this last confrontation was not for her—that she was not one of the chosen and never would be. She turned swiftly, refusing to look back, though all about her there seemed to be a stirring, as if the Great Ones Gone were stepping from their positions, preparing to do battle for the faith in which they had lived and died. Lydana began to run, out of a place where she had no rights—

Then she was out through the ruins of the door, facing the turmoil in the square again.

§ 65 §

ADELE

For two days, the atmosphere in the Temple had been tense, but confident. Despite the continued state of siege, none of Apolon's black coats had even attempted to cross the threshold, and the few parties of mercenaries to make half-hearted trials at the doors had been swiftly repulsed by Gemen Fidelis and his tiny troop of spear-wielders. It began to look as if—now that the Gemen of the Temple were one in heart and soul—that the more confident had been right: Apolon and his followers could not cross the threshold.

But this morning, just as Leopold and Shelyra set off to make yet another foray into the heart of the palace, Elfrida almost called them back. She had a sudden premonition of peril, a sinking of the heart, and only the fact that she could not tell whether the peril was to the Temple or to the wall-skulkers kept her from calling after them.

She stared for a long moment at the closed door, as her feeling of trouble increased, and turned—only to find herself face-to-face with Verit. The archpriestess' grim expression told her everything she needed to know.

"Apolon—?" Elfrida faltered, and felt momentary relief when Verit shook her head.

"Not yet, but he is coming, in person." Elfrida's relief vanished as Verit continued. "We were scrying his work room, when he entered wearing some outlandish outfit and went straight to that—tub—to reach for the staff he had there. The moment he touched it, we lost the vision. When we try to scry for him, there is nothing but darkness."

Elfrida lifted one hand to her throat as real fear chilled her. It was a truism among the mage-Talented of the Temple that Light could *always* see into Shadow, by virtue of the illumination within itself, but that Shadow had a more difficult time looking into the Light, which blinded it. For Verit to have lost the vision of Apolon, there was only one explanation. Apolon no longer moved beside Shadow, but inside Darkness, the uttermost lack of Light, inside which there could be no illumination because it was Light's very opposite.

"But how did he—" She faltered. "Surely to gain such, the power required—"

Verit shrugged. "How many people has he murdered over the past two days? I suspect that his master originally demanded a sacrifice of quality, such as the Princess Shelyra, but has determined to accept quantity instead. It really doesn't matter now; what is important is that he is on his way, and now it is our turn to make the stand for our defenses."

Verit turned with a sweep of robes, and Elfrida followed in her wake. Already the scene in the Temple had changed. Fidelis had sent his mercenaries away somewhere—perhaps to one of the lesser doors, to make an escape if they could. The spears were now in the hands of the youngest Red Robes, who stood about the high altar itself in a square. They held their weapons braced with the points outward, forming a prickly defense against any purely physical force to come against them.

The Novices and those Gemen who had no magical Talent were grouped back behind the altar in a single mass of kneeling, praying bodies. If they could not contribute magically, they *could* contribute their faith, their strength, and their prayers. In the front of the altar, facing the main door and on their feet, were the Gemen of Talent—tried, or untried, it no longer mattered. If they survived this, they would have been tried in the only crucible that counted. If they did not—better to fall fighting than to fall into Apolon's hands. From outside the doors rose a clamor of voices and the sound of metal-on-metal that was rapidly eclipsing the hum of chants.

Elfrida took her place among the Talented, as Verit took hers at the head of the group. Above them, Elfrida sensed the power of the Heart, waxing now. The increase was slow, but suggested something of great weight gaining speed and momentum.

The only question was, would it wax to the fullest in time to do them any good?

Elfrida forced herself to dismiss such doubts and to hold her fears within her. She closed her eyes and joined her voice to the chants of the others, even as she joined her powers to Verit's.

Outside the Temple walls, the clamor of combat was very loud now; it sounded as if there was fighting on the Temple's front steps.

Suddenly, there came a strange, hissing sound that echoed harshly across the Temple and made them all falter for a moment. All eyes turned toward the front door, now closed and barred for the first time since Iktcar had tried to take over the city in the days of legend.

And the great bronze doors that had withstood that vile necromancer and his hordes were falling before a new threat.

An evil, greenish-yellow smoke arose from the doors themselves and seeped under the sills. *Something* out there was burning the doors away, as if they were made of nothing more than wood!

The Temple was large enough that air currents carried the smoke away before it reached the assembled Gemen, but Elfrida sensed that it would not be healthy to breathe it. Even as she watched, the doors melted away like snow-banks in the spring, revealing a mass of black coats carrying an odd weapon—and in front of them was Apolon, clad in eye-searing vermilion as unlike the muted scarlet of the Red Robes as could be imagined. Striding through the greenish flames and yellow-green smoke, he looked like nothing so much as one of the demons he cultivated.

The Power of the Heart above them took a leaping increase; Elfrida had not been aware of any physical manifestation of the Power before this, but now the Heart began to hum, a deep, thrumming sound that was felt, more than heard, and vibrated the marrow of the bones. At that moment, the rubies that had been lying on the altar levitated upward, leaping into the air as swiftly as slung stones, returning to the parent object that had released them.

The very air vibrated with power, and now the Heart bathed them all in rosy light, much as it had when the spirit of Thom Talesmith had been freed.

Apolon did not appear to be the least impressed.

His black coats remained outside the Temple bounds, but the Grey Mage strode across the threshold with no hindrance whatsoever. In his hands he carried the staff that Elfrida had last seen standing in a vat of blood. But now—now, even from where she stood, she felt its evil. Merely to have it across the Temple threshold was a pollution and a sacrilege.

Apolon surveyed the Gemen with a smile of faint disdain on his lips. He said nothing; he only rapped the butt of the staff three times on the marble of the Temple floor. Each tap of the staff echoed and reechoed across the Temple harshly, bringing pain.

Behind him, the wall of the Temple, the black coats, and their strange weapon all vanished. In their place was a billow of black clouds laced with scarlet lightning, and in the clouds, a door into the Nethermost Pits themselves, red and lurid.

Behind Apolon ranged a new and different army—an army of demons, imps, misshapen things that had no names. Yellow eyes glowed with nauseating avarice; dripping claws reached out eagerly, as if to snatch and rend.

Fanged mouths drooled green poison, and toothless, sucking leech-mouths oozed yellow slime.

From every mouth in the hideous army came the screams and howls that only the damned in their endless torment could have produced. Elfrida wanted to cover her ears, but did not dare to unclasp her hands. She felt as if a single movement on her part would rivet the attention of the horde on *her,* and she knew that she would wither beneath such scrutiny.

More than one of the Novices behind Elfrida fainted dead away at the sight of the demon horde; the chanting itself faded a little and grew ragged.

Verit's voice, clear and strong, rallied them all together again as she faced the demons squarely and without flinching.

Apolon raised his staff, and his horde cut off their cacophony. He spoke, his voice rising sharply over the chanting.

"Surrender now, and I will slay you painlessly," he stated arrogantly, his head lifted as if it already bore the emperor's crown. "Nor will I make any of you into my servants. Resist, and you will feel a thousand torments before you die, and a thousand more after."

In answer, Verit clapped her hands three times above her head in time to the chanting, each clap somehow sounding as loud as a thunderbolt.

The Temple walls to either side vanished, as did the vaulted roof above. The Heart hung between the floor and white, floating clouds above, all by itself, continuing to bathe the Gemen in its roseate Light.

But above the Heart, and to either side of it, were Angels in all Their glory.

Not the Messengers that had so often summoned Elfrida or given her words of warning or advice—oh, no. These mighty spirits were to those Messengers as a bolt of lightning was to a flickering candle. Their faces were actually too bright to look upon, and Elfrida was only glad that Their powerful gaze was not directed toward her. If it had been—she thought her heart would probably have stopped from sheer awe. No one could look upon these beings unmoved.

In Their hands They bore weapons—Elfrida could not force her eyes to examine those, either. These were *not* creatures for mortal eyes to gaze upon, and the souls of those still cloaked in flesh could not yet bear the presence of that much Power. These were the mightiest of the Spirits, and Verit herself fell to her knees, her face full of shock and surprise as she saw Them.

She must not have expected Them when she issued her summons!

Elfrida bowed her head over her hands, averting her eyes and concentrating on the chants, holding to the words as to a lifeline. They had answered the archpriestess' summons for aid, but the only thing that kept Them here was the condition established by the prayers of the Gemen, just as the only thing that kept the demons here was the condition established by Apolon and the entity in his staff. Break that condition, and They would be banished back to Their own reality.

With a shout of frustration, Apolon unleashed his horde. The angels required no such signal, for nothing had restrained Them from attacking but Their own wills. Both mighty forces met in the clouds above the altar, with the Heart marking the centerpoint of their combat.

Judging by the fallen bodies Elfrida saw out of the corner of her eye, fully half of the Gemen were either unconscious or dead. She herself was terrified beyond words, but besides that, she felt faint, weak, and fought to keep her hold on consciousness. Everything she knew told her that the presence of the angels above them depended on the strength of the Gemen below, just as the presence of the demons depended on the presence and strength of Apolon. She *must* hold; she and all those with her, or the Ones Above would fade out of this world, leaving the way open for Apolon and his horde.

She could not look upon the struggles above, so her eyes

went to the place where she had last seen Apolon standing.

He was no longer there; in the time between now and the moment he had summoned his demonic army, he had moved. He advanced on the great altar, staff held out before him like a weapon, face full of arrogant glee.

A quick glance around her showed Elfrida that there were no Red Robes left standing to defend the altar and the Gemen around it; they had been among the first to fall. All Apolon had to do to win was to physically attack and cut down the strongest of the Talented, and the rest of them would fall to pieces—

She shut her eyes convulsively. She was about to die, either at the hands of the necromancer or of his servants, and she did not want to see that death coming. She could not evade the Grey Mage, not and still keep up the chanting. She was too weak to do both.

"Hold!" thundered a new voice, from behind and to her left. Her eyes snapped open. *"Hold, spawn of Hell! Return to the foulness that gave you birth, or face the Sword of Gideon!"*

Elfrida nearly lost the thread of the chant at that. *The Sword of Gideon? But—Cathal had that—didn't he?*

The figure striding furiously out of the meditation chamber toward Apolon was not that of General Cathal, but of Prince Leopold. In his hands he carried the Gideon Sword, which glowed as hotly as the faces of the angels above them, and he carried it as one who knew very well how to use it.

Apolon laughed. "Oh, little boy, you should have stayed dead. What is that toy you have there? It is no threat to me!"

His hands spun the staff in the offensive moves of an expert, and he advanced another pace or two. "So, you would challenge me with that puny pot-blade of yours? Very well; it will save me having to hunt you down and kill you later."

Leopold did not waste breath on answering him; with a

face full of rage, he leapt into the fight as Apolon spun the staff to meet him.

Elfrida was not an expert on fighting styles; she had left that sort of thing to her daughter and granddaughter, who seemed to enjoy such arts. She did know one thing, though: in a fight between a man with a staff and a man with a sword, the odds were not in favor of the man with the sword. A staff fighter had additional reach and leverage, and provided that the staff was not one of fragile material that a good sword stroke would cleave or break, it was only a matter of time before the swordsman tired or lost his weapon to a clever blow from the staff.

Nevertheless, Leopold was giving a good account of himself, actually driving Apolon back a good dozen paces. The surprise, then fury, on the Grey Mage's face was proof enough that Leopold had startled him, and not pleasantly.

But the Grey Mage was hardly finished. Once he got over his initial surprise, he held his ground, the staff weaving a web of shadow in the air between him and Leopold, even as the Sword of Gideon wove a net of brightness between Leopold and the mage.

Apolon was no fool, and he had not gotten as far in the world as he had by being unobservant. It did not take him more than a few moments to deduce what Elfrida already knew—that the skill might be Leopold's, but the strength and endurance were the gift of the sword, and that without the sword in his hands, Leopold would be no more formidable than the Red Robes already lying sprawled about the altar.

Elfrida saw it: the moment when Apolon came to that conclusion. Abruptly his tactic changed from attack and parry to a concentrated attempt to disarm. He had the reach; he had the leverage.

It happened too quickly for Elfrida to see the blows clearly; she only saw a blur of motion from Apolon's staff and the result. The sword went sailing out of Leopold's hands, an arrow of brightness heading straight toward the meditation chamber; a second set of blows laid the prince out at Apolon's feet, stunned and unmoving.

Now Elfrida's chanting faltered, and she pressed her knuckles against her lips to keep from crying out. But her mind wailed in wordless anguish, and her heart stopped altogether. They were doomed . . . they were all doomed.

Apolon advanced, gloating, on the prone figure, the butt of the staff upraised for the final blow to Leopold's skull. "I cannot tell you how much this pleases me, Leopold," he said genially. "I cannot tell you how many times I dreamed of having you sprawled helplessly at my feet like this."

Leopold groaned, got one arm under him, and tried to rise, falling back to the floor with a gasp of pain.

Elfrida was paralyzed with fear and exhaustion—but there was a flicker of movement where the sword had fallen. Had one of the Red Robes recovered? Could he get to the sword in time to save the prince?

"I had to send my men to get rid of you when you were sent to the Summer Palace, but it really was not a satisfactory solution," Apolon continued. "Not when what I really longed for was to see your head splitting open beneath *my* weapon, to hear you weep in torment as my staff drank your blood—"

"Get away from him, you bastard!"

That was no male voice, screaming so shrilly that the words pierced the sounds of the battle above them—

Apolon looked up, expression blank, taken utterly by surprise—just in time to see the Princess Shelyra, face white with fury and sword clasped in both hands, covering the distance between them in the kind of all-or-nothing attack that only someone who was desperate would try. He barely had time to register that she *had* a weapon, when she was upon him with a final dancer's leap that began with a wordless shriek of hate, covered the last five paces between them in a single bound—

—and ended with her driving the sword up to the hilt through his chest.

⚜ 66 ⚜

LYDANA

Farther away from the Temple steps, knots of fighters still swung and strove to strike at their enemies. But closer by, people stood gazing dully around as if caught in a mist of bewilderment. The terrible choking stench had cleared, though the remnants of it were enough to set Lydana wheezing and coughing. She stumbled and was caught in a sturdy grip, found herself leaning against Saxon, who appeared to have recovered from the smokey assault to the point of roaring commands.

And his stream of such was bringing some order into the confusion immediately around them. Men and women straightened up and were shaken out of their momentary daze.

Standing on the step she could see the surcoats of emperor's men, the steel and leather of the mercenaries. Some groups of them still fought, but now Lydana in turn caught at her companion.

"Out and away!" she cried in his ear. She could feel a drumming in her veins, screaming in her head, the warning of what lay behind her. "Away from the Temple!"

He did not question her, but yelled his own orders. She felt rising heat behind her, as if the Heart pulled on its full power. Still beside Saxon, she stumbled down the steps and saw before her those turning toward the Temple, awe in their faces now tinged with a reddish glow.

Even the swirl of small fights which had still been in progress ceased as the edge of that rising power passed on and on, flowing outward, until the invaders stood beside the people of Merina, arms hanging limply at their sides, their attention for whatever strove there beyond any strength of their own.

Saxon's arm was around her shoulders when she stumbled over the legs of a prone body. Together they edged around to see. The whole of the Temple was growing hazy, as if it had been an illusion and was now drained of strength to hold itself visible. But there was color—the play of crimson, and shooting forth in filmy clouds the yellow-green of the flames which had won Apolon entrance to this final stronghold.

Lydana shuddered. There was enough of the Tiger in her to answer to that warfare, but the battle was no longer hers. She did not want ever to call and be answered again. The sturdy support of Saxon was real, and she held fiercely to that reality. From the corner of her eye she saw movements within the battling throng. People were on the move, slowly at first, and then on the run. The emperor's men, no longer in their precise formations, were on the heels of townsmen, the mercenaries elbowing past them.

Only those who had immediately followed Saxon did not move as yet, though Lydana read in their faces first their awe, then their growing fear. Here and there was a face she knew well: Dimity, a floppy mail shirt over her wharf finery and a long knife—stained—in one hand. Beside Dortmun, the man with a hook for a hand—

Perhaps in their own days they had seen enough of strange and deadly things that this could not scatter them.

The play of warring lights continued. And Lydana could not turn her back upon it. Rather she saw—or thought she did—forms moving in the light, forms which gathered the light about them like robes to make their forms visible. Or perhaps it was only an illusion born of the naked rage of Power.

But there was beginning to be a change. Those writhing

snakes of yellow-green did not rise so high, they coiled and lashed, but it seemed as if they were meeting a barrier, while the crimson light raged on.

Then, as suddenly as if it were a candle snuffed out, the vicious flames were gone, the crimson blazed heaven-high and also vanished.

"It is done." She need not stand upon the inner battle-field to know that; victory was high in the very air they drew into their lungs. Whatever Apolon had been was gone as if he had never existed. Those dead-alive who served him must be released at last.

She heard Saxon draw a deep breath. "Your Grace, Merina is free."

Nor did she doubt him at that moment—no matter how many mercenaries were set to Cathal's orders, how many men followed Balthasar or his son. The heart of the invasion had been Apolon, and without him it should tumble swiftly, like an ill-built wall under pressure.

It was her turn to breathe deeply. The crimson haze which had remained about the Temple was seemingly being drawn back into its walls. Before her yawned the broken door evil had forced open. She had no desire to climb those steps again, or walk to that altar. She did not doubt the Heart restored to its full glory shown there, and with it would be the Reverend Ones, all the orders which served the Great One.

She had no place among them; she looked over her shoulder toward the body-littered square. Just as they had no place in cleansing this part of Merina. Her city—for now—her duty— But no one stood entirely alone. Adele had the Talent, Shelyra had her own followers (Lydana had no doubt that the girl had had a hand in this final conflict, even if it had not been here—and that she had found others whose spirit matched her own).

No, no one stands alone—or if one does, then one becomes the not-one such as Apolon. She had been Lydana, a queen and craftswoman, a Tiger seeking lawful prey; she had been Matild, a humble dealer in beads and gauds (though always the workmanship was good). It would seem she was once more Lydana—yet a different Lydana than before.

"Lady," Skita looked up at her. "Do you go to—them?" She nodded at the temple.

Slowly Lydana shook her head. "Not now, not ever, little one. I would set sail for a different voyage." She found herself fumbling for words, yet she knew she must find them—and at this very moment, before some chance could change the future. "For a voyage one needs a captain. Is that not so, Lord Saxon?"

His sword clattered out of his hands as he reached toward her. In this moment she knew that rank and heritage meant nothing. They were battle comrades, but more, far more. Nor did she care that the river rats saw her lips meet those of their champion, nor did she even hear them cheer—she had found her Talent and none would take it from her, nor could she set it aside.

Only one thing could have broken into her thoughts at that moment: a threat to her city.

And such a threat came, causing her to end the embrace to meet the new peril.

"Fire!" cried an hysterical voice. "Fire in the city!" And rising above the rooftops, in the direction of the guild halls, real flames shot skyward as she and Saxon and all their followers ran to meet the new peril.

ॐ 67 ॐ

SHELYRA

Shelyra sat on the cold, hard stone of the Temple floor with Leopold's head cradled carefully in her lap. Others had been hurt far worse than he, and she had made no objections when the healers tended to them first. There were far too many quiet forms discreetly enshrouded beneath blankets for her to feel any resentment that the prince had to wait for treatment, but now, finally, it was Leopold's turn. She looked up anxiously into the face of Gemen Cosima. At least Leopold was getting the best healer, with the most experience.

"He'll be all right, won't he?" she asked as Cosima completed her examination of the prince's head wound. Wearily, the Gemen nodded.

"He has a concussion, dear, and he's as exhausted as any of the Reverend Ones who aided Verit in mage-battle. That's a bad combination; but for a young man, not a fatal one." Cosima bowed her head for a moment and a tear escaped—Shelyra felt instant guilt. So many of the Gemen who had fallen would not rise again—fear and stress had stopped a score of weary old hearts, and the drain on their bodies had been fatal to another half dozen, including Gemen Fidelis. Shelyra reached out a tentative hand, then pulled it back, unsure of what comfort, if any, she could offer.

But Cosima looked up again as if she sensed that tentative offer, and dredged up a faint smile for her. "We owe the two of you greatly, dear. If you had not come to face Apolon, he would have killed us all, and the way would have been clear for him to do—to do things that would make Iktcar look like a petty criminal. Don't feel guilty and don't worry about our resources; there are plenty of healers still in the houses in the city, and we'll take good care of him for you. Just give us a little time to get everything organized."

She finished bandaging Leopold's head, then moved on to the next victim of the fight, leaving Shelyra alone again with the Prince.

Concussion. What do I know about concussion? Only that it is a good thing that Apolon had a staff and not a sword, or his skull would have been split wide open. She searched her pouch for medicinals that might help, but found only a vial of liquid that was known to clear headaches and refresh exhausted minds.

Well—it might not help, but it can't hurt. She took the stopper out and wet her finger with it carefully, then traced a wet line across his forehead, cheekbones, and down his temples. A sharp scent, recalling pine forests and high meadows in bloom, cut through the heavy aroma of incense. A few breaths, and *she* felt her energy rejuvenated and a renewed optimism. After a moment, his eyelids fluttered, then opened.

He looked up at her, and to her vast relief, his gaze was sharp and full of intelligence. He coughed, winced at the pain it caused him, then carefully cleared his throat.

"I take it we are not among the angels," he said, "or my head would not hurt so much. We won, then." He took a deep breath. "I will not ask the cost; I do not think anyone here would find it too high after seeing what that vile creature had in store for us."

"I didn't see much," she confessed. *Only Light and Darkness fighting above us, and flashes of fire and something greenish yellow.* "All I really paid attention to was that you were down and *he* was gloating over you."

He managed a faint smile. "And the she-tiger leapt to the rescue once again? That is more good fortune than I deserve, my lady, and merits more thanks than—"

"Oh, hush," she said fondly. "*You* talk too much, and appreciate yourself too little. You need to find a wife who appreciates you enough to poison you for your own good."

He raised the eyebrow on the uninjured side of his head, carefully. "Like you, perhaps? I know why I would like this above all things, but what have you to gain?"

She tried to shrug casually, but had the feeling she had failed to hide her real feelings. "Well, you see angels, and Grandmother needs someone to take the position of secular head of the Temple who can see angels. It would be convenient, since I can't. You're certainly trained to rule, and you aren't the kind to have any trouble with joint rulership. That's convenient, too, since I won't give up *my* power."

His smile grew broader. "Oh, very convenient, I agree," he replied amiably. "Provided that Apolon's staff hasn't knocked that ability to see the Messengers completely out of me."

She snorted delicately. "I doubt that. And if it has—well, I'll take the Gideon Sword and use the pommel to knock it back *into* you. And besides," she added softly, "I like you. I think you are possibly the most amazing and remarkable man I have ever met. I—would also like this above all things. Agreed?"

"Agreed." He closed his eyes for a moment, and she thought he had drifted away into sleep, as people with concussions were likely to do—and she started to try to wake him. But then he opened them again, just as Adele came limping up beside them. "I had better make this official, then—Lady Shelyra, would you do me the very great favor of granting me your hand?"

"Of course," she replied matter-of-factly, while her heart leapt and capered with glee. "There, Grandmother, you're the witness."

"Well, if you haven't acquired good sense and caution yourself after all this," Adele said calmly, "at least you have the intelligence to marry it. I approve, I agree to the match, and if I have to, I'll overrule your aunt. Assuming, of course, that she's still queen by the time the wedding takes place."

Still queen? But— Before Shelyra could ask any questions, Adele signaled to a pair of men, who she recognized as having been palace servants, carrying a stretcher. "Take him to the king's suite, and be careful of him, he has a head wound," she ordered. "Put him to bed, dredge up some ice from the palace ice-cellar for him, and see if you can't somehow find his pages to attend him—failing that, leave one of Shelyra's old maids with him. He shouldn't be left unattended, so Cosima tells me."

The men picked Leopold up carefully and set him on the stretcher while Shelyra watched them, prepared to give them the sharp end of her tongue if they hurt him. But they managed quite well and carried him off without any sort of mishap to one of the side entrances that gave on the gardens.

She turned toward her grandmother, now edgy with curiosity. "What did you mean, 'if she's still queen?' " she asked. "What's been going on? What's Aunt Lydana done?"

Adele gestured for her to follow, and led her toward the smoking ruins of the main doors. "I'll start with the last question, since it has bearing on the first two," she replied. "Your aunt decided to make use of certain gemstones with some very potent curses on them. One went to Balthasar, one to the chancellor, and one to General Cathal. So far, we have only found one of them: the cursed seal-stone she sent to Balthasar in her own ring. Verit *thinks*, now that Apolon is no longer about to interfere with scrying, that she knows where the other two are."

"Where?" Shelyra asked, and bit her lip as she remembered that strange, thick voice coming from General Cathal's wrist—and what had happened to him.

"There—" Adele gestured as they came out into the open, and Shelyra's eyes went to a plume of thick, black smoke in the quarter of the guild halls. "She tried to scry both gems, and came up with flames. There—you see flames. I believe that is, or was, the House of the Boar, which Apolon had appropriated for his own use. *Why* the stones are there, I don't know, since we found what was left of Cathal and he didn't have his on him. And we haven't yet found the chancellor."

"He took an armguard from Cathal," she blurted. "He was acting like Thom did, and he took Cathal's armguard and started off somewhere."

"He was acting like Thom, one of the dead-alive?" Adele pursed her lips. "Now that is interesting. I wonder if he was acting under a basic order to bring anything interesting to his master. He couldn't know that Apolon was at the Temple and not at the House of the Boar—"

Both of them looked out over the city, eyes drawn to that pillar of oily, black smoke. "Verit gave orders to let it burn," she said finally. "We've sent people to make sure the buildings around it are safe, but she gave orders to let that house burn. I wouldn't entirely be certain that flames will cleanse that place, but it is a start. We may be exorcising and cleansing it for months before the site is fit to build on again."

"If ever." Shelyra shuddered. "But what has that to do with Aunt Lydana?"

"Verit intends to order her to expiate some of the harm she did by finding all the gems she set loose, retrieving them with her own hands, and sinking them so deeply into the sea that they can never return to plague men again." Adele's eyes looked beyond the plume of smoke into some far distance only she could see. "That will take time, and also require the kind of sea voyage Lydana always preferred over sitting on a throne. It was never her choice to rule, and I am given to understand by one of the witnesses here at the Temple that she seemed—very fond of Harbormaster Captain Saxon." Her smile widened a little. "She has always liked him; I certainly have no more objection to such an alliance than I have to yours."

Shelyra nodded, putting together the rest from what Adele didn't say. *Aunt Lydana and Captain Saxon? Well, well! I wouldn't have guessed there was anything in that quarter! She must be deeper than I thought!* "She couldn't abdicate in *my* favor—and I certainly wouldn't blame her, since I'm not really old enough—but Leopold was trained to rule."

"And he is older than you," Adele finished. "I think perhaps that we might be able to solve any number of problems this way—thanks to the convenient way in which you fell in love with the young man."

Again, Shelyra shrugged. "I don't know about love—" she replied, knowing very well that she was lying through her teeth, but determined that her grandmother would have no inkling of *that*, "but I certainly respect, admire and like him. He told me that at one time there actually was a plan to betroth the two of us. And—well, Grandmother, we both know that eventually I would have to marry *someone*, so I would much rather that it was a friend."

"Hmm," Adele said noncommittally, but with a faint hint of a knowing smile. "Perhaps good sense *is* contagious."

The rest of the day was spent in more work than Shelyra ever thought she would be able to do without falling over from exhaustion. Adele shed her persona of "Gemen Elfrida" temporarily and once again donned the gown and jewels of the dowager queen in order to help with the restoration of order to the city. In all the confusion of the past day, if anyone was bewildered by Adele's sudden "resurrection," no one said anything about it. Perhaps they attributed it to the intervention of the Heart.

The best that Shelyra could manage was her hunting garb, but between that and the fine horse she took from the stables, she found that the people accepted her—with visible relief—for what she claimed to be. She spent all of the hours of daylight and most of the night riding around the city at Adele's orders, finding out what was happening and issuing temporary decrees. In most quarters, *some* loyal citizen of Merina had taken charge; she just had to find out who it was, confirm him (or her) in the position, issue tentative orders, and quell rumors.

The mercenaries, for the most part, had already fled. With the citizens armed and looking for them to avenge themselves, Merina was no longer a healthy place for them to be. In fact, in the quarter where Cathal had established imperial houses of—dubious recreation—Shelyra rode in to discover that the girls incarcerated there had taken their own grisly revenge on every mercenary and black coat they could get their hands on. One look at the first corpse had convinced her to let the hard-bitten woman who had established order there deal with it all on her own terms.

The black coats who had been dead-alive had dropped where they were standing when Apolon himself died. The rest had not made it past the city gates. They had made themselves more hated even than Cathal's mercenaries, if that was possible, and their faces were known only too well to their victims. Shelyra was making no effort to find out if the wounds on the black coats being burned in pyres on every corner were fresh or old. There were some things it was better to ignore.

As for the imperial soldiers—those who had not slipped away, presumably trying to head for home, had wisely barricaded themselves either in the camp outside the walls or in the barracks at the palace. There, in positions where they were too firmly dug in to be easily routed, the townsfolk made no attempt to dislodge them. A cautious envoy from the camp reported to Adele that they were waiting to hear what had become of the emperor.

But one from the palace barracks said bluntly, "We don't give a hang what became of the emperor. We want our prince."

This had come as no surprise to Adele, apparently. The prince's two pages—or "squires," as the prince referred to them—had been located, stationed with these men, and protected by them assiduously. When the boys were told that Leopold was still alive—and in the Great Palace—they had to be restrained from running to his side.

With their word establishing Leopold's allegiance, relative health, and location, the entire company declared for him and would have shed their imperial uniforms on the spot had they anything else to wear.

That lack was in the process of being rectified, by dint of removing all insignia and replacing the arms of the empire with the Tiger of Merina. By morning, the new troops would be in the street, each one partnered with men of the city guard, helping to get things back to normal.

And as for Lydana—Shelyra found her at the House of the Boar, waiting for the flames to die, fiercely determined to go in and retrieve those terrible gems without ever hearing of Verit's decree. And it was there that Shelyra heard the last, and perhaps the most curious, tale of all.

It was from a servant, a wholly terrified servant, who had witnessed the last moments of Chancellor Adelphus' unlife.

The chancellor had wandered into the House of the Boar shortly before, as the servant said, "all them lights in the sky started." He simply stood there for a very long time, during which all of the still-living servants, taking advantage of the fact that the black coats were off with their master, ran away.

All but this old servant, who decided to do a bit of looting before he left.

It was while he was helping himself, completely ignored by the chancellor, when—

"Somethin' happened," the fellow said. "A kind'a howl went up, comin' from th' room th' master said niver t' go into." He began to shake. "Can't rightly say—what it sounded like—"

"Never mind," Shelyra said soothingly. "I can imagine." And so she could; there were probably dozens of evil spirits imprisoned down there, not to mention tortured and imprisoned souls of entirely ordinary folk. And when Apollon's death released them—

"Well," the man said, after swallowing audibly, "th' chancellor, he went all blue, an' started to fall over—but all on a sudden, he got hisself righted, an' th' most peculiar look come over him—"

"Like what?" she asked.

He shook his head. "Strange. Like—he was fightin' som'thin'. He holds up his hand, like this—" He held up his right hand—

That was the hand Adelphus put the armguard on! she thought, the image of Adelphus taking the guard from the withered body of Cathal flashing into her mind.

"An'—an' he sounds like he wants t' holler, but all he c'n do is whisper. Like, he couldn't get no breath. Like this—" The man gave the most uncanny impression of someone struggling to speak with a broken larynx, and the hair rose on the back of Shelyra's neck.

"*No. By the Powers, no!*" the man rasped in imitation of what he had witnessed. "*I'll—see—you—in—Hell—first!*"

He stood there with his arm upraised just long enough for Shelyra to get chills—

Then he dropped it and shrugged. "Then—he grabs a lantern; he starts to throw it at somethin', an' just—goes t' pieces. But the lantern smacks inta the curtains, an' oil goes ever'where, an—*poof*. Place's goin' up like tinder. Got me outa there, an' about got m' bum scorched doin' it."

Lydana questioned the man closely to determine precisely where the chancellor had been when he collapsed. Shelyra left her to it—for it was obvious what she was going to do.

Finally, when she really was at the end of her strength, Shelyra rode her equally exhausted horse back to the palace and collapsed into the arms of comfortingly familiar servants, who carried her off to bed.

But she didn't remain there long; come the dawn, she was up and about again, hard at work. Lydana returned to the Temple later in the day, although she didn't stay long. She looked haggard and haunted, and Shelyra guessed that she had gone into the ruins of the House of the Boar and had seen more than she ever cared to see again.

The emperor proved to be absolutely mindless, with no more ability to walk, talk, or care for himself than a baby. It was Verit's thought that his mind had probably been wiped clean by the conflict between what had possessed him and the power of the Gideon Sword.

The officers of his army were brought in to see his condition for themselves and returned to their camp immediately. Not long after, the camp broke up, each commander taking his own men with him—and all of them heading in different directions.

Leopold laughed oddly when Shelyra told him that. "You know what that means, don't you?" he asked.

She shook her head.

"They're off to carve themselves little kingdoms out of the empire, before word spreads that Balthasar is mindless," he explained. "I'd guess they had a conference and agreed not to interfere with each other for the next year or so. After that?" He shrugged. "All-out warfare. Perhaps."

"Perhaps?" she asked, and again he shrugged.

"They are soldiers who have been at war for a very long time," he said quietly, but with a depth of feeling that made her understand that this was something he, too, held within his soul. "They have a chance for peace. They may prefer it."

She chewed on her lip a moment, then offered him an idea of her own. "What if they got something that induced them to prefer it?"

He raised that eyebrow. "Such as?"

And at that, she had to laugh just a little. "What is it that always induces people to want peace? A taste of luxury—luxury you can have without needing to fight for it."

He lowered the eyebrow. "Trade?"

She nodded. "Trade."

It would be a good start.

❧ 68 ❧

ADELE

"A dele" had vanished again, as soon as the crisis was over, and Lydana and Saxon had gone off on a short voyage—pausing only long enough for a hasty marriage ceremony, and an even hastier abdication in favor of Shelyra and an unnamed husband. There were rumors even now that she had been a Messenger herself, come back long enough to put Merina in order.

That husband had been named as soon as Leopold was recovered enough to undergo the day-long ceremonies of a royal wedding. He and Shelyra proved to be very popular, lavishly using the royal treasury and the resources of the Tiger to mend what had been ruined in the city, and make what recompense they could to those whose losses were not strictly material. They themselves lived simply and frugally, refusing to make any great show of wealth until Merina itself was prospering again. Verit had made certain that the tale had been spread of their battle against Apolon in the Temple, and that had certainly helped with their popularity. After all, who *wouldn't* want warriors for the Light as rulers—especially ones who were as sensible and as sensitive to the needs of their people as these two were?

Gemen Elfrida had quietly rejoined the ranks of her fellow Grey Robes, as the two new rulers of Merina settled into their roles. And even when she was tempted by something they said or did to step forward again, she restrained herself. They needed to make their own mistakes—and perhaps things she saw as mistakes were only differences of generation and opinion.

The emperor gradually wasted away over the course of six months, despite devoted care by Cosima and the other healers. When he died, Leopold had mourned him sincerely, but without tears. As he had once told Gemen Elfrida, his father's soul had died long ago, at the hands of Apolon; this was only the long-delayed death of the body. Those sections of the empire that had not acquired new rulers from the emperor's army then revolted, when word filtered back of his death.

Leopold showed no signs of wanting to return to take the empire back, which relieved Elfrida no end. That had worried her, ever since the marriage—Leopold might have initially felt he did not want the crown of empire, but she feared what might happen once he had rested and recuperated.

But the birth of their first child was the event that convinced her that Leopold was happy ruling nothing more than a minor city-state. One look at his face as he gazed down at mother and child told her that *this* father would never put conquest and power ahead of home and family. And one thing told her that "home" for him was now Merina—for Leopold and Shelyra jointly chose the name "Fidelia Adele" for their lovely daughter.

Lydana and Saxon had returned from their second voyage with word that things were stabilizing in the former empire, and that many of the players in the game were looking for trade alliances rather than ways to open new conflicts. That was good news, and before they left again, carrying documents offering some cautious alliances, they stayed for the ceremony of the new heir's Naming.

The Temple was packed full, with the crowds spilling out into the square beyond. The royal coffers had been squeezed once more to provide food and drink enough for the entire city, and every entertainer Merina held had volunteered his or her services to aid in the celebrations. Gemen Elfrida held a position of honor next to Verit at the high altar, while Lydana and Saxon stood sponsor to the tiny, but glowingly healthy, girl child.

The Temple itself had been completely refurbished since the terrible battle. The Heart sparkled and shone above the high altar, but only with reflected sun- and candlelight, and not with any supernatural power. The spears that had been used to defend the Gemen a year ago now held tapestries as they had been intended to do. But encased in the front of the high altar, in a somber case with a transparent front, was a new addition—the Sword of Gideon—as a reminder that those who would hold to the Light must sometimes be called upon to defend it with their lives.

As the Gemen chanted joyfully, Shelyra and Leopold, dressed simply, but in matching costumes, brought the baby to the archpriestess. Verit held the child up to the Heart for her first look at the center of all faith in Merina, and Elfrida held her breath lest the child, being a child, accidentally did *something* that could be considered ill-omened.

But all she did was coo and reach for the pretty, shining object above her, and as Verit lowered her and placed her in the special cradle on the altar, Elfrida let out her breath again.

The ceremony itself now turned to the child's parents, as Verit advised them of their duties and obligations to their little one, and they responded with oaths to provide her with all the instruction, care, and love she could ask for. Elfrida ignored it all; she had heard the ceremony often enough, and she had no doubt that this little one would get everything her parents promised her. Little Fidelia—they were already calling her Delia—would lack for nothing that human minds, hands, and hearts could give her.

Verit raised her hands to bless the parents—and it was at that moment, when every eye except Elfrida's was riveted on the trio in front of the altar, that the angel appeared, bending over the baby atop it.

It was the first angel Elfrida had seen since the dreadful battle, and for a moment her heart stopped. What horrible mission brought this Messenger here today?

But the face of the angel held nothing but softness and love, and it bent over the baby and held out a finger to it.

Delia looked up into the angel's face, burbled with laughter, and reached up to grasp the proffered finger firmly.

She can see the angel! Adele realized, going limp with relief. *She can see it! The Talent is back in the Tiger!* She almost laughed aloud, so great was her joy. Finally, after three generations, *someone* in the House of the Tiger could see Them again!

"Be happy, bright, and bonny, Fidelia," the angel whispered, in a voice heard only by the baby and the great-grandmother, *"and grow in the Light."*

Then the angel vanished, leaving the child grasping only a lovely, white flower.

And Gemen Elfrida joined her voice to the rest as they raised a chant of joy.

AVONOVA PRESENTS
MASTERS OF FANTASY AND ADVENTURE

BLACK THORN, WHITE ROSE 77129-8/$5.99 US/$7.99 CAN
edited by Ellen Datlow and Terri Windling

SNOW WHITE, BLOOD RED 71875-8/$5.99 US/$7.99 CAN
edited by Ellen Datlow and Terri Windling

A SUDDEN WILD MAGIC 71851-0/$4.99 US/$5.99 CAN
by Diana Wynne Jones

THE WEALDWIFE'S TALE 71880-4/$4.99 US/$5.99 CAN
by Paul Hazel

FLYING TO VALHALLA 71881-2/$4.99 US/$5.99 CAN
by Charles Pellegrino

THE GATES OF NOON 71781-2/$4.99 US/$5.99 CAN
by Michael Scott Rohan

**THE IRON DRAGON'S
DAUGHTER** 72098-1/$5.99 US/$7.99 CAN
by Michael Swanwick

**THE DRAGONS OF
THE RHINE** 76527-6/$5.99 US/$7.99 CAN
by Diana L. Paxson

ABOVE THE LOWER SKY 77483-6/$5.99 US/$7.99 CAN
by Tom Deitz

To learn more about all the titles
from Avon Books,
visit our Website at
http://AvonBooks.com

Mystery from the Source: It's no mystery where great authors come from . . . Avon Books is *the source* for bestselling mystery fiction.

SF & Fantasy News: Devoted followers of SF and Fantasy can plug into Avon Books' web dominion for big books and favorite authors.

Books for Young Readers: Our on-line Books for Young Readers site is a treasure trove of student activities, teacher guides and author biographies.

Romance: Avon Books is one of the leading publishers of romantic fiction featuring *New York Times* bestselling authors like Johanna Lindsey and Elizabeth Lowell.

And don't forget to click on our other monthly features, including **Centerstage** and **Avon-on-Campus**.

AVN 0996